"You're the kind of guy who plays by the rules."

"Normally, yes." He moved closer. "But this isn't normal."

Becca agreed with him. She fought the urge to step back. "Being here?"

Caleb stopped in front of her, only inches away. "Being here with you. I'm tired of playing by the rules."

Her heart slammed against her ribs. She should step back. Way back. Put distance between them. For her own good.

But her feet wouldn't move. She remained rooted to the spot, waiting, hoping, anticipating.

He lowered his mouth to hers and kissed her. Hard.

Becca had never known what it was like to be possessed, but she felt possessed by Caleb's kiss. She didn't mind one bit.

Dear Reader,

In 2008 we adopted a two-year-old Norwegian elkhound named Chaos. She was a retired champion show dog who had recently had a litter of puppies.

Her pedigree didn't matter to us. We didn't even bother changing the ownership on her AKC papers. All we knew was that we'd found the perfect dog for us. It was love at first sight!

My oldest daughter decided to join our county's 4-H dog program. Soon she was doing obedience and showmanship fun matches with Chaos and loving every minute of it. She decided she wanted to try AKC Junior Handler. I knew nothing about dog-showing except what I'd seen in the movie *Best in Show*. Turns out that's not too far from the truth!

Many of our weekends are now spent at dog shows. Two of my children now compete in the Juniors' ring, as well as in the Breed ring. I always take my laptop so I can write in between events. I happened to be at a dog show when I came up with the idea for this book.

I wanted to explore the idea of a heroine from the wrong side of the tracks with the ultimate good-guy hero and toss in a few dogs—both purebreds and rescues—for fun! This book was the result.

I hope you enjoy reading about Becca and Caleb and all of the pups!

Melissa

MELISSA McCLONE

The Man Behind the Pinstripes

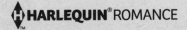

Recycling programs
for this product may
not exist in your area.

ISBN-13: 978-0-373-74246-2

THE MAN BEHIND THE PINSTRIPES

First North American Publication 2013

Copyright © 2013 by Melissa Martinez McClone

Printed in U.S.A.

HARLEQUIN®
www.Harlequin.com

With a degree in mechanical engineering from Stanford University, the last thing **Melissa McClone** ever thought she would be doing was write romance novels. But analyzing engines for a major U.S. airline just couldn't compete with her "happily-ever-afters." When she isn't writing, caring for her three young children or doing laundry, Melissa loves to curl up on the couch with a cup of tea, her cats and a good book. She enjoys watching home decorating shows to get ideas for her house—a 1939 cottage that is *slowly* being renovated. Melissa lives in Lake Oswego, Oregon, with her own real-life hero husband, two daughters, a son, two lovable but oh-so-spoiled indoor cats and a no-longer-stray outdoor kitty that has decided to call the garage home.

Melissa loves to hear from her readers. You can write to her at P.O. Box 63, Lake Oswego, OR 97034, U.S.A., or contact her via her website, www.melissamcclone.com.

Recent books by Melissa McClone:

WINNING BACK HIS WIFE
HIS LARKVILLE CINDERELLA*
IT STARTED WITH A CRUSH…
FIREFIGHTER UNDER THE MISTLETOE
NOT-SO-PERFECT PRINCESS
EXPECTING ROYAL TWINS!

*Part of *The Larkville Legacy* series

Other titles by this author available in ebook format.

To Jan Herinckx for introducing us to
Chaos and the world of dog-showing!

Special thanks to: Terri Reed, Jennifer Shirk,
Jennifer Short.

And the Immersion Crew: Margie Lawson,
Elizabeth Cockle and Lori Freeland.

CHAPTER ONE

THE INCESSANT BARKING from the backyard of his family's palatial estate confirmed Caleb Fairchild's fear. His grandmother had gone to the dogs.

Cursing under his breath, he pressed the doorbell.

A symphony of chimes filled the air, drowning out the irritating barks. Forget Mozart. Forget Bach. Only a commissioned piece from a respected New York composer would do for Gertrude Fairchild, his grandmother who had founded a billion-dollar skin care company with his late grandfather in Boise, Idaho.

Caleb was here to put an end to her frivolous infatuation with man's best friend. It was the only way to keep Fair Face, the family company, successful and profitable.

The front door opened, greeting him with a blast of cold air and a whiff of his grandmother's floral scent perfume.

Grams.

Short white curls bounced every which way. She looked fifty-seven not seventy-seven, thanks to decades of using her own skin care products.

"Caleb! I saw your car on the security camera so

told Mrs. Harrison I would answer the door." The words rushed from Grams's mouth faster than lobster tails disappeared from the buffet table at the country club. "What are you doing here? Your assistant said you didn't have any free time this week. That's why I mailed you the dog care prototypes."

He hadn't expected Grams to be so excited by his visit. He kissed her cheek. "I'm never too busy for you."

Her cornflower blue eyes danced with laughter. "This is such a lovely surprise."

Sweat trickled down his back. Too bad he couldn't blame the perspiration on the warm June day.

He adjusted his yellow tie then smoothed his suit jacket. But no matter how professional he looked, she wasn't going to like what he had to say. "I'm not here as your grandson. I need to speak with you as Fair Face's CEO."

"Oh, sweetheart." The warmth in her voice added to his discomfort. "I raised you. You'll always be my grandson first."

Her words hit him like a sucker-punch. He owed Grams…everything.

She opened the door wider. "Come in."

"Nice sari," he said.

Grams struck a pose. "Just something I had in my closet."

He entered the foyer. "Better add Bollywood to your bucket list."

"Already have." She closed the door. "Let's go out on the patio and chat."

Chat, not speak or discuss or talk. Not good.

Caleb glanced around. Something was…off.

Museum-worthy works of art hung in the same places. The squeaky dog toys and ravaged stuffed animals on the shiny hardwood floor were new. But the one display he expected to see, what he wanted to see, what he longed to see was missing from its usual spot.

His throat tightened. "Where are the—"

"In the living room."

Caleb walked around the corner and saw the three-foot U.S. Navy aircraft carrier replicas showcased on a brand-new wooden display case. He touched the deck of the USS *Ronald Reagan*.

Familiar. Soothing. Home.

"I've been making some changes around here," Grams said from behind him. "I thought they deserved a nicer place than the foyer."

He faced her. "Gramps would like this."

"That's what I thought, too. Have you eaten lunch?"

"I grabbed something on my way over."

"Then you need dessert. I have cake. Made it myself." She touched Caleb's arm with her thin, vein-covered hand. "Carrot, not chocolate, but still tasty."

Grams always felt the urge to feed him. He knew she wouldn't give up until he agreed to have a bite to eat. "I'll have something before I leave."

A satisfied smile graced her glossed lips.

At least one of them was happy.

Back in the foyer, he kicked a tennis ball with his

foot. "It's a miracle you don't break a hip with all these dog toys laying around."

"I might be old, but I'm still spry." His grandmother's gaze softened. She placed her hand over her heart. "Heavens. Every time I see you, you remind me more and more of your father. God rest his soul."

Caleb's stomach churned as if he'd eaten one too many spicy Buffalo wings. He strived hard to be nothing like his feckless father. A man who'd wanted nothing to do with Fair Face. A man who'd blown through money like a hedge fund manager's mistress. A man who'd died in a fiery speedboat crash off the Cote d'Azur with his girlfriend du jour.

Grams' gaze ran the length of Caleb. She clucked her tongue. "But you've got to stop dressing like a high-class mortician."

"Not this again." Caleb raised his chin, undaunted, and followed her out of the foyer. "You'd have me dress like a rugged, action-adventure movie star. A shirtless one, given the pictures you share on Facebook."

They walked by the dining room where two elaborate chandeliers hung above a hand-carved mahogany table that sat twenty.

"You're a handsome man," Grams said. "Show off your assets."

"I'm the CEO. I have a professional image to maintain."

"There's no corporate policy that says your hair can't touch your collar."

"The cut suits my position."

"Your *suits* are a whole other matter." She pointed at his chest. "Your tie is too understated. Red screams power. We'll go shopping. Girls these days are looking for the whole package. That includes having stylish hair and being a snazzy dresser."

And not taking your grandmother's fashion advice.

They walked into the kitchen. A basket of fruit and a covered cake stand sat on the marble counter. Something simmered on the stove. The scent of basil filled the air. Normal, everyday things, but this visit home felt anything but normal.

"Women only care about the balance in my bank account," he said.

"Some. Not all." She stopped, squeezed his hand, the way she'd done for as long as Caleb remembered. Her tender touch and her warm hugs had seen him through death, heartbreak and everyday life. "You'll find a woman who cares only about you."

Difficult to do when he wasn't looking, but he wasn't telling Grams that today. One piece of bad news a day met her quota. "I like being single."

"You must have one-night stands or friends with benefits."

He flinched. "You're spending too much time on Facebook."

A disturbing realization formed in his mind. Discussing sex might be easier than talking to Grams about her dog skin care products.

She placed her hands on her hips. "I would like great grandchildren one of these years while I can still get on the floor and play with them. Why do you think I created that line of organic baby products?"

"Everyone at the company knows you want great grandchildren."

"What's a woman to do?" She put her palms up. Gold bracelets clinked against each other. "You and your sister are in no rush to give me grandbabies while I'm still breathing."

"Can you imagine Courtney as a mom?"

"She has some growing up to do," Grams admitted, but without any accusation or disappointment. She walked into the family room with its leather couches, huge television and enough books on the floor-to-ceiling bookshelves to start a library. "Though I give you credit for at least proposing to that money-grubbing floozy, Cash-andra."

Unwelcome memories flooded him. His heart cried foul. Cheat. Sucker. "Cassandra."

The woman had introduced herself to him at a benefit dinner. Smart and sexy as hell, Cassandra knew what buttons to push to become the center of his universe. She'd made him feel more like a warrior than a businessman. Marriage hadn't been on his radar screen, but when she gave him an ultimatum, he'd played right into her hand with a romantic proposal and a stunning three-carat engagement ring only to find out everything about her and their relationship had been a scam, a ruse, a lie.

"Cash-andra fits." Grams held up three fingers. "Refusing to sign the agreed-upon prenup. Two-timing you. Hiring a divorce attorney before saying I do. No wonder you're afraid to date."

He squared his shoulders. "I'm not afraid."

Not afraid of Cassandra.

Not afraid of any woman.

But he was…cautious.

After Cassandra wouldn't sign the prenup, he'd called off the wedding and broken up with her. She'd begged him for a second chance, and he'd been tempted to reconcile, until a private investigator proved the woman was a gold digger in the same league as his own mother.

Grams waved a hand in the air, as if she could brush aside bad things in the world. Light reflected off her three diamond rings, anniversary presents from his grandfather. "I shouldn't have mentioned the Jezebel."

At least Caleb had gotten away relatively unscathed except for a bruised ego and broken heart. Unlike his father who'd wound up with two kids he'd never wanted.

She exited the house through the family room's French doors.

Caleb followed her outside to see new furniture—a large gleaming, teak table surrounded matching wood chairs, a hammock and padded loungers.

The sun beat down. He pulled out a chair for his grandmother, who sat. "It's hot. Let me put up the umbrella."

Grams picked up a black rectangular remote from the table. "I've got it."

She pressed a button.

A cantilevered umbrella opened, covering them in shade.

He joined her at the table.

"What do you think about the dog products?" Gertie asked.

No birds chirped. Even the crickets seemed to be napping. The only thing he heard was an occasional bark and his grandfather's voice.

Do what must be done. For Fair Face. For your grandmother.

Caleb would rather be back in his office dealing with end-of-quarter results. Who was he kidding? He'd rather be anywhere else right now.

"Interesting prototypes," he said. "Appealing fragrance and texture."

Gertie whistled. "Wait until you see them in action."

Dogs ran full speed from around the corner. A blur of gray, brown and black. The three animals stopped at Grams's feet, mouths panting and tails wagging.

"Feel how soft they are." Pride filled her voice as if the dogs were as much a part of her gene pool as Caleb was.

He rested his hands on the table, not about to touch one of her animals. "Most fur is soft if a dog is clean."

"Not Dozer's." She scooped up the little brown dog, whose right eye had been sewn shut. Not one of her expensive show dogs. A rescue or foster. "His hair was bristly and dry with flakes."

"Doggy dandruff?"

"Allergies. Animals have sensitivities like humans. That's why companies need to use natural and organic ingredients. No nasty chemicals or additives. Look at Dozer now." She stared at the dog with the same love and acceptance she'd always given Courtney and him. Even before their father had dumped them here after their mother ran off with her personal trainer. "That's why I developed Fair Face's new line of animal products."

Ignoring the gray dog brushing against his leg, Caleb held up his hands to stop her. "Fair Face doesn't manufacture animal products."

Grams's grin didn't falter. "Not yet, but you will. I've tested the formulas on my consultant and myself. We've used them on my dogs."

"I didn't know you hired a consultant."

"Her name is Becca. You'll love her."

Caleb doubted that. Most consultants were only looking for a big payday. He'd have to check this Becca's qualifications. "You realize Fair Face is a skin care company. Human skin."

"Skin or fur. Two legs or four. Change…expansion is important if a company wants to remain relevant."

"Not in this case." He needed to be careful not to hurt Grams's feelings. "Our resources are tied up with the launch of the organic baby care line. This isn't the time to expose ourselves to more risk."

Lines tightened around her mouth. "Your grandfather built Fair Face by taking risks. Sometimes you have to put yourself out on a limb."

"Limbs break. I have one thousand one hundred

thirty-three employees who count on me to make sure they receive paychecks."

"What I'm asking you to do is not risky. The formulas are ready to go into production. Put together a pilot sales program and we're all set."

"It's not that simple, Grams. Fair Face is a multinational company. We have extra product testing and research to ensure ourselves against liability issues." The words came out slowly, full of intent and purpose and zero emotion. His grandmother was the smartest woman he knew, used to getting her way. If he wasn't careful, he would find himself not only manufacturing her products, but also taking one of her damn dogs home. Likely the one-eyed mutt with soft fur. "I won't expose Fair Face to the additional expense of trying to break into an unknown market."

Grams sighed, a long drawn out sigh he hadn't heard since Courtney lost her passport in Prague when she was supposed to be in Milan.

"Sometimes I wish you had a little more of your father in you instead of being so buttoned-down and by-the-book."

The aggravation in her voice matched the tension cording in Caleb's neck. The tightness seeped to his shoulders, spilled down his spine. "This isn't personal. I can't afford to make a mistake, and you should be enjoying your retirement, not working in your lab."

"I'm a chemist. That's what I do. You didn't have this problem with the organic baby line." Frustration tinged each of her words, matching the I-wish-you'd-drop-it look in her eyes. "I see what's going on. You don't like the dog care products."

"I never said that."

"But it's the truth." She studied him as if she were trying to prove a hypothesis. "You've got that look. The one you got when you said it didn't matter if your father came home for Christmas."

"I never needed him here. I had you and Gramps." Caleb would try a new tactic. He scooted his chair closer. "Remember Gramps's marketing tagline."

"The fairest face of all..."

"His words still define the company today. Fifty years later." Caleb leaned toward her, as if his nearness would soften the blow. "I'm sorry to say it, but dog products, no matter how natural or organic or aromatherapeutic, have no place at Fair Face."

"It's still my company." She enunciated each word with a firm voice punctuated by her ramrod posture.

Disappointing his grandmother was something his father did, not Caleb. He felt like a jerk. One with a silk noose around his neck choking him.

"I know that, but it's not just my decision." A plane flew overhead. A dog barked. The silence at the table deepened. He prepared himself to say what he'd come here to say. "I met with the department heads before coming over here. Showed them your prototypes. Ran the numbers. Calculated margins."

"And…"

"Everyone has high expectations for your baby skin care line," he said. "But they agree—moving into animal products will affect Fair Face's reputation, not enhance our brand and lead to loss of revenue, anywhere from 2.3 to 5.7 percent."

Caleb expected to see a reaction, hear a retort. But Grams remained silent, her face still, nuzzling the dog against her neck. "Everyone thinks this?"

He nodded once.

Disbelief flickered across her face. She'd looked the same way when she learned his grandfather had been diagnosed with Alzheimer's. But then something sparked. A spark of resignation. No, a spark of resolve.

"Well, that settles it. I trust you know what's best for Fair Face." She sounded doting and grandmotherly, not disappointed and hurt. "Becca and I will figure out another way."

"Another way for what?"

Grams's eyes darkened to a steely blue. "To manufacture the products. You and those suits at Fair Face are wrong. There's a market for my dog skin care line. A big one."

The sun's rays warmed Becca Taylor's cheeks. The sweet scent of roses floated on the air. She walked across the manicured lawn in Gertie's backyard with two dogs—Maurice, a Norwegian elkhound, and Snowy, a bichon frise.

The two show dogs sniffed the ground, looking for any dropped treats or a place to do their business.

She tucked her cellphone into her shorts pocket. "Don't get sidetracked, boys. Gertie is waiting for us on the patio."

Becca had no idea what her boss wanted. She didn't care.

Gertie had rescued Becca the same way she'd rescued the foster dogs living at the estate. This was only a temporary place, but being here gave them hope of finding a forever home.

Maurice's ears perked.

"Do you hear Gertie?"

The two dogs ran in the direction of the patio.

Becca quickened her pace. She rounded a corner.

Gertie and a man sat at the teak table underneath the shade of the umbrella. Five dogs vied for attention, paws pounding on the pavement. Gertie waved.

The man next to her turned around.

Whoa. Hello, Mr. Gorgeous.

Tingles skittered from Becca's stomach to her fingertips.

None of the dogs growled or barked at the guy. Points in his favor. Dogs were the best judges of character, much better than hers.

She walked onto the patio.

The man stood.

Another wave of tingles made the rounds.

Most guys she knew didn't stand. Didn't open doors. Didn't leave the toilet seat down. This man had been raised right.

He was handsome with classical features—high cheekbones, straight nose, strong jawline. The kind of handsome women showed off to girlfriends.

The man stepped away from the table, angling his body toward her. His navy pinstriped suit was tailored, accentuating wide shoulders and tapering nicely at the hips. He moved with the grace of an athlete, making her wonder if he had sexy abdominal muscles underneath.

Very nice packaging.

Well, except for his hair.

His short, cookie-cutter, corporate hairstyle could be seen walking out of every high rise in downtown Boise. With such a gorgeous face, the man's light brown hair should be longer, a little mussed, sexy and carefree, instead of something so…businesslike.

Not that his hair mattered to Becca. Or anything about him.

His top-of-the-line suit shouted one thing—Best in Show.

She might be a dog handler, but she didn't handle his type.

They didn't belong in the same ring. He was a champion with an endless pedigree. She was a mutt without a collar.

She'd tried playing with the top dogs, the wealthy dogs, once before and landed in the doghouse, aka jail.

Never again.

But looking never hurt anybody.

Gertie looked up from the dogs at her feet. "Becca. There's someone I want you to meet."

He was tall, over six feet. The top of her head came to the tip of his nose.

Becca took two steps closer. "Hello."

His green eyes reminded her of jade, a bit cool for her taste, but hey, no one was perfect. His eyelashes more than made up for whatever reserve she saw reflected in his gaze. If she had thick, dark lashes like his she would never need to buy mascara again.

She wiped her hand on her shorts then extended her arm. "I'm Becca Taylor."

His grip was strong, his skin warm.

A burst of heat shot up her arm and pulsed through her veins.

"Caleb Fairchild." His rich voice reminded her of melted dark chocolate, rich and smooth and tasty.

Wait a minute. Fairchild. That meant he was…

"My grandson," Gertie said.

The man who could make Becca's dream of working as a full-time dog handler come true. If the dog products sold as well as Gertie expected, Becca would have the means to travel the dog show circuit without needing to work extra part-time jobs to cover living expenses.

Caleb Fairchild. She couldn't believe he was here. That had to mean good news about the dog products.

Uh-oh. Ogling him was the last thing she should be doing. He was the CEO of Fair Face and wealthy. Wealthy, as in she could win the lottery twice and not come close to his net worth.

"Nice to meet you." Becca realized she was still holding his hand. She released it. "I've heard lots about you."

Caleb's gaze slid over her as if he'd reviewed the evidence, passed judgment and sentenced her to the not-worth-his-time crowd. "I haven't heard about you until today."

His formal demeanor made Jane Austen's Mr. Darcy seem downright provincial. No doubt Mr. Fairchild thought he was too good for her.

Maybe he was.

But she wouldn't let it bother her.

Her career was not only at stake, but also in his hands.

"Tell me about yourself," he said.

His stiff tone irritated her like a flea infestation in the middle of winter. But she couldn't let her annoyance show.

She met his gaze straight on, making sure she didn't blink or show any signs of weakness. "I'm a dog person."

"I thought you were a consultant."

A what? Becca struggled for something to say, struggled and came up empty. Still she had to try. "I...I—"

"Becca is a dog consultant," Gertie said. "She's a true dog whisperer. Her veterinary knowledge has been invaluable with product development. I don't know what I'd do without her."

If Becca wasn't already indebted to Gertie Fairchild, she was now.

Gertie shot a pointed look at Caleb. "Perhaps if you dropped by more often you'd know what's going on."

Caleb directed a smile at his grandmother that redefined the word *charming*.

Not that Becca was about to be charmed. The dogs might like him, but she was…reserving judgment.

"I see you every Sunday for brunch at the club." Caleb's affection for his grandmother wrapped around Becca like a thick, warm comforter, weighing the scales in his favor. "But you never talk about yourself."

Gertie shrugged, but hurt flashed in her eyes so fast Becca doubted if Caleb noticed. "Oh, it just seems like we end up talking about you and Courtney."

"Well, I'm here now," he said.

Gertie placed her hand over her heart and closed her eyes. "To dash all my hopes and dreams."

Becca's gaze bounced between the two. "What do you mean?"

Caleb touched Gertie's arm. "My grandmother is being melodramatic."

Opening her eyes, Gertie pursed her lips. "I'm entitled to be a drama queen. You don't want our pet products."

No. No. No. If that was true, it would ruin…everything. Gertie wouldn't go forward with the dog products without her company backing them. Becca forced herself to breathe. "I don't understand."

Gertie shook her head. "My grandson, the CEO, and his closed-minded cronies at *my* company believe our dog skin care line will devalue their brand."

"That's stupid and shortsighted," Becca said.

Caleb eyed her as if she were the bounty, a half-eaten mouse or bird, left on the porch by an outdoor cat. "That's quite an opinion for a…consultant."

"Not for a dog consultant." The words came out more harshly than Becca intended, but if she couldn't change his mind she would be back to living in a singlewide behind Otto. Otto, her parents' longtime trailer park manager, wore stiletto heels with his camouflage, and skinned squirrels for fun. "Do you know how much money is spent annually on pets?"

"Billions."

"Over fifty billion dollars. Food and vet costs are the largest portion, but analysts project over four billion dollars are spent on pet services. That includes grooming. Gertie's products are amazing. Better than anything on the market."

Gertie nodded. "If only my dear husband were still around. He'd jump on this opportunity."

"Gramps would agree with me." Caleb frowned, not a sad one, more of a do-we-have-to-go-through-this-again frown. "Fair Face is not being shortsighted. We have a strategic plan."

Becca forced herself not to slump. "So change your plan."

"Where'd you get your MBA?" he asked.

Try AA degree. "I didn't study business. I'm a certified veterinary technician, but my most valuable education came from The School of Hard Knocks."

Aka the Idaho Women's Correctional Center.

"As I explained to my grandmother, the decision about manufacturing the dog skin care line is out of my hands."

Caleb's polite tone surprised Becca, but provided no comfort. Not after she'd poured her heart and soul into the dog products. "If the decision was all yours?"

His hard, cold gaze locked on hers. "I still wouldn't manufacture them."

The words slammed into Becca like a fist to her jaw. She took a step back. But she couldn't retreat. "How could you do this to your grandmother?"

Caleb opened his mouth to speak.

Gertie placed her hand on his shoulder. "I'll help Becca understand."

He muttered a thank-you.

"This decision is in the best interest of Fair Face." Gertie sounded surprisingly calm. "It's okay."

But it wasn't.

Becca had thought that things would be different this time. That she could be a part of something, something big and successful and special. That maybe, just maybe, dreams could come true.

She should have known better.

Things never worked out for girls—women—like Becca.

And never would.

CHAPTER TWO

A FEW MINUTES LATER, Becca stood where the grass met the patio, her heart in her throat and her back to Gertie and Caleb. Dogs panted with eagerness, waiting for the ball to be thrown again.

And again. And again.

Playing fetch kept Becca's shoulders from sagging. She would much rather curl up in the kennel with the dogs than be here. Dogs gave her so much. Loyalty, companionship and most importantly love. Dogs loved unconditionally. They cared, no matter what. They accepted her for who she was without any explanations.

Unlike…people.

"Come sit with us," Gertie said.

Us.

A sheen of sweat covered Becca's skin from the warm temperature, but she shivered.

Caleb had multi-millions. Gertie had hundreds of millions. Becca had $8,428.

She didn't want much—a roof over her head, a dog to call her own and the chance to prove herself as a professional handler. Not a lot to ask.

But those dreams had imploded thanks to Caleb Fairchild.

Becca didn't want to spend another minute with the man.

She glanced back at her boss.

"Please, Becca." Gertie's words were drawn out with an undertone of a plea. Gertie might be more upset about Fair Face not wanting to take on her new products than she acted.

Becca whipped around. Forced a smile. Took a step onto the patio. "Sure, I'll sit for a few minutes."

Caleb was still standing, a tall, dream-crushing force she did not want to reckon with ever again.

Walking to the table, she didn't acknowledge his presence. He didn't deserve a second look or an "excuse me" as she passed.

Gertie had to be reeling, the same as Becca, after what he'd said.

I still wouldn't manufacture them.

Becca's blood boiled. But she couldn't lose it.

She touched Gertie's thin shoulder, not knowing how else to comfort her employer, her friend. The luxurious feel of silk beneath Becca's palm would soon be a thing of the past. But it wasn't the trappings of wealth she would miss. It was this amazing woman, the one who had almost made Becca believe anything was possible. *Almost...*

"I'm so sorry." A lump burned in her throat. Her eyes stung. She blinked. "You've worked so hard and wasted so much time for nothing."

Gertie waved her hand as if her arm were an enchanted wand that could make everything better. Diamonds sparkled beneath the sun. Prisms of lights danced. If only magic did exist....

"None of this has been a waste, dear." Gertie smiled up at Becca. Not the trying-hard-to-smile-and-not-cry of someone disappointed and reeling, but a smile full of light and hope. "The products are top-notch. You said so yourself. Nothing has changed, in spite of what Caleb thinks."

He gave a barely perceptible shake of his head.

Obviously he didn't agree with his grandmother. But Gertie didn't seem deterred.

That didn't make sense to Becca. Caleb was the CEO and had final say. She sat next to Gertie. "But if Fair Face doesn't want the products..."

"You and I are starting our own company." Gertie spoke with a singsong voice. "We'll manufacture the products without Fair Face."

Our own company. It wasn't over.

Becca's breath hitched. Her vision blurred. She touched her fingers to her lips.

The dream wasn't dead. She could make this work. She wasn't sure how...

Gertie had always spoken as if working with Fair Face on the products was a done deal, but if going into business was their only option that would have to do. "O-kay."

"Your consultant doesn't sound very confident," Caleb said to Gertie. "Face it, you're a chemist, not a businesswoman." He looked at Becca. "Maybe you can talk some sense into my grandmother about this crazy idea of hers."

Becca clenched her hands. She might not know anything about business, but she didn't like Caleb's condescending attitude. The guy had some nerve discounting his grandmother.

Forget jade. The color of his eyes reminded her of cucumbers or fava beans. Not only cool, but uninspiring.

Change and *taking a risk* weren't part of his vocabulary. But they were hers. "Makes perfect sense to me. I'm in."

"Wonderful." Gertie clapped her hands together. "We'll need an advisor. Caleb?"

A horrified look distorted his face, as if he'd been asked to face the Zombie Apocalypse alone and empty-handed. He took a step back and bumped into a lounge chair. "Not me. I don't have time."

His words—dare Becca say excuse?—didn't surprise her. The guy kept glancing at his watch. She'd bet five bucks he had his life scheduled down to the minute with alarms on his smartphone set to ring, buzz or whistle reminders.

"You wouldn't leave us on our own to figure things out." Gertie fluttered her eyelashes as if she were some helpless female—about as helpless as a charging rhino. "You'll have to make the time."

His chin jutted forward. Walking across burning coals on his hands looked more appealing than helping them. "Sorry, Grams. I can't."

Good. Becca didn't want his help any more than

he wanted to give it. "We'll find someone else to advise us."

Gertie grinned, the kind of grin that scientists got when they made a discovery and were about to shout "Eureka!" "Or…"

"Or what?" Becca said at the same time as Caleb.

"We can see if another company is interested in partnering with us." Gertie listed what Becca assumed to be Fair Face's main competitors.

Caleb's lips tightened. His face reddened. His nostrils flared.

Well played, Gertie.

Becca bit back a smile. Not a scientific breakthrough, but a way to break Caleb. Gertie was not only intelligent, but also knew how to get her way. That was how Becca had ended up living at the estate. She wondered if Caleb knew he didn't stand a chance against his grandmother.

"You wouldn't," he said.

"They are my formulas. Developed with my money in my lab here at my house," Gertie said. "I can do whatever I want with them."

True. But Gertie owned the privately held Fair Face.

Becca didn't need an MBA from a hallowed ivy-covered institute to know Gertie's actions might have repercussions.

Caleb rested his hands on the back of the chair. One by one, his fingers tightened around the wood until his knuckles turned white.

Say no.

Becca didn't want him to advise them. She and Gertie needed help starting a new business. But Becca would rather not see Caleb again. She couldn't deny a physical attraction to him. Strange. She preferred going out with a rough-around-the-edges and not-so-full-of-themselves type of guy. Working-class guys like her.

Being attracted to a man who had money and power was stupid and dangerous. Men like that could ruin her plans. Her life. One had.

Of course, Caleb hadn't shown the slightest interest in her. He wouldn't. He would never lower his standards. Except maybe for one night.

No, thanks.

Becca wanted nothing to do with Caleb Fairchild.

Caleb was trapped, by the patio furniture and by his grandmother. This was not the way he'd expected the meeting to go. He was outnumbered and had no reinforcements. Time to rein in his grams before all hell broke loose.

He gave her a look, the look that said he knew exactly what she was doing. Too bad she was more interested in the tail-wagging, paw-prancing dogs at her feet. No matter, he knew how to handle Grams. Her so-called consultant was another matter.

Becca seemed pleased by his predicament. She sat with her shoulders squared and her lips pursed, as if she were looking for a fight. Not exactly the type of behavior he would have expected from a consultant, even a dog one.

He would bet Becca was the one who talked Grams into making the dog products. Nothing else would explain why his grandmother had strayed from developing products that had made her and Fair Face a fortune.

It had to be Becca behind all this nonsense.

The woman was likely a con artist looking to turn this consulting gig into a big pay off. She could be stealing when Grams wasn't paying attention. Maybe a heist of artwork and jewelry and silver was in the works. His wealthy family had always been a target of people wanting to take advantage of them. People like Cassandra. Grams could be in real danger.

Sure, Becca looked more like a college student than a scammer. Especially wearing a "No outfit is complete without dog hair" T-shirt and jean shorts that showed off long, smooth, thoroughbred legs.

She had great legs. He'd give her that.

But looks could be deceiving. He'd fallen for Cassandra and her glamorous façade.

Not that Becca was glamorous.

With her short, pixie-cut brown hair and no makeup she was pretty in a girl-next-door kind of way. If he'd ever had a next-door neighbor whose house wasn't separated by acres of land, high fences and security cameras.

But Becca wasn't all rainbows and apple pie.

Her blue eyes, tired and hardened and wary, contradicted her youthful appearance. She wasn't innocent or naïve. Definitely not one of the princess types he'd known at school or the social climbers he knew around town. There was an edge to her he couldn't quite define, and that…intrigued him.

Worried him, too.

He didn't want anyone taking advantage of Grams.

Speaking of which, he faced his grandmother. "It's not going to work."

Grams glanced up from the dogs. The five animals worshipped at her feet as if she were a demigod or a large slice of bacon dressed in pink. "What's not going to work, dear?"

A smile tugged on the corners of Becca's mouth, as if she were amused by the situation.

Caleb pressed his lips together. He didn't like her.

Any consultant with an ounce of integrity would have taken his side on this. But what did he expect from a woman who wore sports sandals with neon-orange-and-green toenail polish to work? He bet she was covered with tattoos and piercings beneath her clothing.

Sexy images of her filled his mind.

Focus.

He rocked back on his heels. "If you partner with one of Fair Face's competitors, the media will turn this into a firestorm. Imagine how the employees will react. You're the creative influence behind our products. How will you reconcile what you do for one company with the other?"

"Animal products for them. Human products for Fair Face." A sheepish grin formed on Grams's lips. "It was only a thought."

A dog tried to get his attention, first rubbing

against Caleb's leg then staring up at him. Seemed as if everyone was giving him the soulful-puppy-look today. "A ploy."

Grams tsked. "I can't believe you think I'd resort to such a tactic."

Yeah, right. Caleb remembered looking at what colleges to attend and Grams's reaction. Naval Academy, too dangerous. Harvard, too far. Cal Berkeley, too hippy. She'd steered him right where she'd wanted him—Stanford, her alma mater. "I'm sure you'd resort to worse to get your way."

That earned him a grin from Becca.

Glad someone found this entertaining. Though she had a nice smile, one that made him think of springtime and fresh flowers. An odd thought given he had little time to enjoy the outdoors these days. Maybe it was because they were outside.

"I shouldn't have to resort to anything," Grams said. "You promised your grandfather you'd take care of us."

Something Caleb would never forget.

That promise was directing the course of his life. For better or worse given his grandmother, his sister, Fair Face and the employees were now his responsibility. He grimaced. "I'm taking care of you the best way I know how."

Grams rubbed a gray dog named Blue, but she didn't say a word.

He knew this trick, using silence to make him give in, the way his grandfather had capitulated in the past. But Caleb couldn't surrender. "Grams—"

"Gertie, didn't you mention the other day how busy Fair Face keeps your grandson?" Becca interrupted. "It might be better to find someone else to help us, since Caleb is so busy."

Whoa. Becca wanted to be his ally?

That sent Caleb's hinky-meter shooting into the red zone. No one was that nice to a total stranger. She must want him out of the way so she could run her scam in peace.

"Good idea," he said, playing along. Maybe he could catch Becca in a lie or trip her up somehow. "I'm not sure I'd have a few minutes to spare until the baby product line launches, if then. You know how it is."

"Yes, I do." Grams tapped her fingers against her chin. "But I like keeping things in the family."

So much for taking her formulas to a competitor. "You wouldn't want me to ignore the company, would you?"

His grandmother's gaze narrowed as if zooming in on a target—him. "Who's trying to guilt who now?"

He raised his hands in surrender. "Fair enough."

"Maybe Caleb knows someone who can help us," Becca said.

He would rather his grandmother drop this whole thing, but once Grams saw what starting her own business entailed, she would decide retirement was a better alternative. He would get someone he trusted to advise them, someone to keep an eye on Becca, someone to steer his grandmother properly. Caleb would still be in control, by proxy. "I'm happy to give you a few names. I know one person who would be a good fit."

"I suppose it's worth a try," Gertie said.

"Definitely worth a try." Enthusiasm filled Becca's voice. "We can do this."

We? Us? Caleb straightened. Becca acted more like a partner. He needed to talk to his grandmother about what sort of contract she had with her "consultant." Something about Becca bothered him. She had to be up to no good. "I'll text you the names and numbers, Grams."

"Send Becca the list. As you said, I'm a chemist not a businesswoman."

"Will do." Caleb glanced at his watch, bent and kissed his grandmother's cheek. "Now, if you ladies will excuse me, I need to get back to the office."

Grams grabbed hold of his hand. Her thin fingers dug into his skin. "You can't leave. You haven't had any cake."

The carrot cake. Caleb had forgotten, but he couldn't forget the pile of work waiting for him on his desk. He checked his watch again.

"Gertie baked the carrot cake herself. You need to try a piece." Becca's voice sounded lighthearted, but her pointed look contained a clear warning. Caleb had better stay if he knew what was good for him.

Interesting. The consultant was being protective of his grandmother. Usually that was *his* job. Becca's concern could be genuine or a ruse—most likely the latter—but she was correct about one thing. Eating a slice of cake wouldn't take *that* long. No reason to keep disappointing Grams. He could also use the opportunity to ask his grandmother for more information about her dog consultant.

Caleb placed his arm around his grandmother. "I'd love a piece of your cake and a glass of iced tea."

Dogs raced around Becca, jumping and barking and chasing balls. She stood in the center of the lawn while Gertie went into the house to have Mrs. Harrison prepare the refreshments.

Playing with the dogs was more fun than sitting with Caleb on the patio. Becca saw no reason to make idle chitchat with a man eager to eat his cake and get out of there. At least, she couldn't think of one.

She much preferred four-footed, fur-covered company to dismissive CEOs. Dogs were her best friends, even when they were a little naughty.

"You're a mess, Blue." Becca picked strands of grass and twigs from the Kerry blue terrier's gray hair. "Let's clean you up before Gertie returns."

Dogs—no matter a purebred like Blue or a mutt like Dozer—loved to get dirty. Gertie didn't mind, but Becca tried to keep the dogs looking half decent even when playing.

Blue licked her hand.

Bending over, she kissed his head. "Such a good boy."

"You like dogs."

Becca jumped. She didn't have to turn around to know Caleb was right behind her, but she glanced over her shoulder anyway. "I love dogs. They're my life."

His cool gaze examined her as if she were a stock he was deciding to buy or sell, making her feel exposed. Naked.

Her nose itched. Her lungs didn't want to fill with air.

He stepped forward to stand next to her. "Your life as a dog consultant?"

"Gertie came up with that title," Becca said. "But I am a dog handler, groomer and certified vet tech."

"A jill of all trades."

That was one way to look at it. Desperate to make a living working with animals and to become a full-time professional dog handler was another. "When it comes to animals, particularly dogs."

Snowy and Maurice chased each other, barking. Dozer played tug-of-war with Hunter, a thirteen-inch beagle, growling. Blue sat at Becca's feet, waiting. "I need to put the dogs in the kennel."

Confusion clouded Caleb's gaze. He might as well have spoken the question on his mind aloud.

"Yes, Gertie has a kennel."

"How did you know what I was thinking?"

"Your face." Becca almost laughed. "I'm guessing you don't play a lot of poker. Unless you prefer losing money."

Caleb looked amused, not angry. That surprised her.

"Hey," he said. "I used to be quite good."

"If the other players were blind."

"Ha-ha."

"Well, you don't have much of a poker face."

At least not with his grandmother. Or with Becca.

He puffed out his chest. "We're not playing cards. But you're looking at a real card shark."

She liked his willingness to poke fun at himself. "I believe you."

"No, you don't."

Heat rushed up her neck. "Okay, I don't."

"Honest."

"I try to be." He wasn't talking about poker any longer. She picked up one of the balls. "It's important to play fair."

Caleb's eyebrow twitched. "Do you have a good poker face?"

"You realized I didn't believe you, so probably not."

"No aces up your sleeve?"

"Not my style."

"What is your style?"

"Strategy over deceit." Becca couldn't tell if he believed her, but she hoped he did. Because he was Gertie's grandson, she rationalized. "That's why I'd never sit at a poker table with you. You're too easy to read. It would be like stealing a bone from a puppy."

"A puppy, huh?"

"A manly pup. Not girly."

He grinned wryly. "Wouldn't want to be girly dog."

His gaze held hers. Becca stared mesmerized.

Something passed between them. A look. A connection.

Her pulse quickened.

He looked away.

What was going on? She didn't date guys like him. Even if she did, he was too much of a Boy Scout. And it was clear he didn't like her. "I have to go."

"I want to see the kennel."

"Uh, sure." But she felt uncertain, unsettled being near him. She pointed to the left. "It's down by the guest cottage."

Caleb fell into step next to Becca, shortening his stride to match hers. "How did you meet my grandmother?"

She called the five dogs. They followed. "At The Rose City Classic."

He gave her a blank stare.

Funny he didn't know what that was, given Gertie's interest in dog showing. "It's in Portland. One of the biggest dog shows on the West Coast. Your grandmother hired me to take Snowy into the breed ring. Ended up with a Group third. A very good day."

Blue darted off, as if he were looking for something—a toy, a ball, maybe a squirrel.

Becca whistled for him.

He trotted back with a sad expression in his brown eyes.

Caleb rubbed his chin. "I have no idea what you just said."

"Dog show speak," Becca said. "Snowy won third place in the Group ring. In his case, the Non-Sporting group."

"Third place is good?"

"Gertie was pleased with the result. She offered me a job taking care of her dogs, including the fosters and rescues, here at the estate."

"And the dog skin care line?"

"She sprang that on me after I arrived."

A look of surprise filled his eyes, but disappeared quickly. "Sounds like you're a big help to her."

"I try to be," Becca said. "Your grandmother's wonderful."

"She is." He looked at her. "I'd hate to see anyone take advantage of her kindness."

Not anyone. Becca.

The accusation in his voice made her feel like a death row inmate. Each muscle tightened in preparation for a fight. The balls of her sandals pressed harder against the grass. She fought the urge to mount a defense. If this were a test, she didn't want to fail. "I'd hate that to happen, too."

The silence stretched between them.

His assessing gaze never wavered from hers.

Disconcerted, she fiddled with a thread from the hem of her shorts.

Caleb put his hand out to Dozer, who walked next to them. Funny, considering he'd ignored the dogs before.

Dozer sniffed Caleb's fingers then nudged his hand.

With a tender smile, he patted the dog's head.

Becca's heart bumped. Nothing was more attractive than a man being sweet to animals. A good thing

Caleb's physical appearance was pretty easy to overlook given his personality and suspicions.

"You helped me with my grandmother," he said. "Trying to get me out of the way?"

At least he was direct. She wet her lips, not liking the way he raised her hackles and temperature at the same time. "It's obvious you don't want to work with us."

"I don't have time," he clarified.

"There's never enough time."

Dozer ran off, chasing a butterfly.

"It's a valuable commodity," Caleb said.

"Easy to waste when you don't spend it in the right ways."

"Experience talking?"

"Mostly an observation."

Maurice, the Norwegian elkhound, approached Caleb. The dog could never get enough attention and would go up to anyone with a free hand to pet him.

He bent over.

And then Becca remembered. "Wait!"

Caleb touched the dog. He jerked back. A cereal-bowl-sized glob of dark and light hair clung to his hand. "What the…"

Maurice brushed against Caleb's pant leg, covering the dark fabric in hair also.

Oh, no. She bit the inside of her cheek.

"This overweight husky is shedding all his fur." The frown on Caleb's face matched the frustration in his voice. "Enough to stuff a pillow."

"Maurice is a Norwegian elkhound. He's blowing

his coat." The guilty expression on the dog's face reminded her of the time he'd stolen food out of the garbage can. She motioned him over and patted his head. This wasn't the dog's fault. Unlike Caleb, she was used to the shedding, a small price to pay for his love. "They do that a couple times a year. It's a mess to clean up."

"Now you tell me."

His tone bristled, as if she were the one to blame. Becca was about to tell him if he spent any time here with his grandmother he would know about Maurice, but decided against it. If she lightened the mood, Caleb might stop acting so...upset. "Look at the bright side."

His mouth slanted. "There's a bright side?"

"You could be wearing black instead of navy."

He didn't say anything, then a smile cracked open on his face, taking her breath away. "I guess I am lucky. Though it's only dog hair, not the end of the world."

If he kept grinning it might be the end of hers.

Caleb brushed the hair away, but ended up spreading it up his sleeve and onto the front of his suit.

"Be careful." She remembered he had to return to the office. "Or you'll make it..."

"Worse." He glanced down. Half laughed. "Too late."

It was her turn to smile. "I have a lint roller. I can clean up your suit in a jiffy."

Amusement filled his eyes. "I thought you liked dog hair."

"Huh?"

"Your T-shirt."

She read the saying. "Oh, yes. Dog hair is an occupational hazard."

"Yet you keep a lint brush."

"You never know when it'll come in handy."

"Do you make a habit of cleaning men's clothing?"

His tone sounded playful, almost flirty. That made no sense. Caleb wouldn't flirt with her. She rubbed her lips together. "Not, um, usually."

Something—interest or maybe it was mischief—flared in his eyes. "I'm honored."

Nerves overwhelmed her. A guy like Caleb was nothing but trouble. He could be trying to cause trouble for her now. She took a deep breath. "Do you have other clothes with you? Getting the dog hair off your pants will be easier if you aren't wearing them."

"Easier, but not impossible."

Becca pictured herself kneeling and rolling the lint brush over his pants. Her temperature shot up ten degrees. She crossed her arms over her chest. "You can use the roller brush yourself."

He grinned wryly. "My gym bag is in the car."

An image of him in a pair of shorts and a T-shirt stretched across his muscular chest and arms rooted itself in her mind.

Wait a minute. Did he say gym bag? That meant he had time to work out, but no time to spend with Gertie.

Becca's blood pressure rose, but she knew better than to allow it to spiral out of control. Judging him wasn't right. People did that with her and usually got it wrong. Maybe his priorities had gotten mixed up. She'd give him the benefit of the doubt. For now.

"Go change," she said. "I'll put the dogs in the kennel and grab the lint brush out of guest cottage."

"Using the guest cottage as your office?"

"I live there."

His mouth dropped open. He closed it. "You live here at the estate?"

"Yes."

"Why?"

The one word dripped with so much snobbery Becca felt as if someone had dumped a bucket of ice-cold water on her head.

He waited for her to answer.

A hundred and two different answers raced through her mind. She settled on one. "Because Gertie thought it would be for the best."

"Best for you."

"Yes." But there was more to it than that. "Best for Gertie, too."

Confusion filled his gaze. "My grandmother doesn't lack anything."

He sounded so certain, not the least bit defensive. A good sign, but still…

Becca shouldn't have brought this up, but her affection for Gertie meant Becca couldn't back down now. She wanted Caleb to stop blowing off his grandmother. "Gertie thought living here would make it easier for me to do my job without having to drive back and forth all the time. But I also think she wants me here because she's lonely."

"My grandmother lonely?"

The disbelief in his words irritated Becca. She'd realized this as soon as she got to know Gertie, yet her own grandson couldn't see it. "Yes."

"That's impossible," he said without hesitation. "Gertie Fairchild has more friends than anyone I know. She's a social butterfly who turns down invitations—otherwise she'd never be home. She has the means to go out whenever she wants. She has an entire staff to take care of the house and the grounds. No way is she lonely."

What Caleb said might have been true once, but no longer. "Gertie does have a staff, but we're employees. She has lunch twice a week with friends. But she hasn't attended any parties since I moved in. She prefers to spend time in her lab."

"The lab is keeping her from her friends."

"I believe your grandmother would rather spend time with her family, not friends."

"You believe?" He grimaced. "My sister and I—"

"See her every Sunday for brunch at the club, I know. But since I arrived neither you nor your sister have stopped by. Not until you today."

"As I said—"

"You've been busy," Becca finished for him.

Caleb shot a sideways glance at the house. "All Grams has to do is call. I'll do whatever she asks."

"Gertie asked for your help with the dog care products."

"That's…"

"Different?"

A vein at his neck throbbed. "You've got a cush job living here at the estate. I'm sure my grandmother's paying you a bundle to take care of a few dogs and prance them around the ring. What's it to you anyway?"

He sounded defensive. She would, too. Realizing you'd screwed up was never easy. Boy, did she know that. "Gertie's helped me a lot. I want her to be happy."

"Trust me, she's happy. But you have some nerve sponging off my grandmother, helping her with her wild dog-product scheme and then telling me how I should act with my family."

Not defensive. Overconfident. Cocky. Clueless.

Caleb Fairchild was no different than the other people who saw her as dirt to be wiped off the bottom of their expensive designer shoes.

At least she'd tried. For Gertie's sake.

Becca reached out her hand. "Give me your jacket."

"You're going to help me after trying to make me feel like a jerk?" he asked.

Mission accomplished. If he felt like a jerk he had only himself to blame. "I said I'd help. I only told you the truth."

He didn't look as if he believed her. They were even. She didn't trust him.

"As you see it," he said.

She met his gaze straight on. "I could say the same about your truth."

They stood there locked in a stare down.

Stalemate.

"At least we know where we stand," he said.

Becca wasn't so certain, but she knew one thing. Being with Caleb was like riding a gravity-defying roller coaster. He left her feeling breathless, scared to death, and never wanting to get on again. She didn't like it. Him.

She held up his jacket. "And just so you know, I'm not doing this for you. I'm doing it for Gertie."

CHAPTER THREE

By the time Caleb changed into a pair of shorts and a T-shirt and then returned to the patio, the table had been transformed with china, crystal glasses and a glass-blown vase filled with yellow and pink roses from the garden. Very feminine. Very Grams. "You've gone all out."

"I enjoy having company." Beaming, Grams patted the seat next to her. "Sit and eat."

Caleb sat next to her. He stared across the table at Becca.

What was she doing here?

He wanted to speak to Grams alone, to talk about Becca and his concerns about the so-called dog consultant and if she was exploiting his grandmother's generosity.

Sneaky scam artist or sweet dog lover? Becca seemed to be a contradiction, one that confused him.

On their way to the kennel, he'd sensed a connection. Something he hadn't felt in over a year. Maybe two. Not since…Cassandra. But he knew better than to trust those kinds of emotions with a total stranger.

Becca wasn't his usual type—Caleb casually dated

high-powered professional women—but he'd found himself flirting and having fun with her until she'd had to ruin the moment with her ridiculous grand-mother-is-lonely spiel.

Becca was wrong. He couldn't wait to prove how wrong.

He sliced through his cake with his fork. The silver tines pinged against the porcelain plate.

As if he wanted or needed anything from Becca Taylor other than her lint roller.

"You must be hungry," Grams said.

Nodding, he took a bite.

Becca drank from her glass of ice water.

"Do the dogs usually stay in the kennel all day?" he asked.

A rivulet of condensation rolled down her glass. She placed it on the corner of the yellow floral place-mat. "No, they are out most of the time, but if they were here they'd be going crazy over the cake."

"Dogs eat cake?" he asked.

Becca refilled her water from a glass pitcher with lemons floating on the top.

A guilty expression crossed Grams's face. "I never give them a lot. Never any chocolate. But when they stare up at me as if they're starving, it's too hard not to give them a taste."

"Those dogs know exactly how to get what they want." Laughter filled Becca's eyes. "They're spoiled rotten."

"Nothing wrong with being spoiled and pampered," Grams agreed.

"Not at all." Becca sounded wistful. "I'd love to be one of your dogs."

Her words surprised Caleb. She didn't seem like the primping and pampering type. But what did he really know about her? He sipped his iced tea.

She picked up her fork and sliced off a bite of cake. Her lips parted.

Fair Face made a lipstick that plumped lips, making them fuller and, according to the marketing department, more desirable. Becca's lips were perfect the way they were.

She raised the fork.

Like a moth to a blowtorch, Caleb watched her, unable to look away. He placed his glass on the table.

She brought the fork closer to her mouth until her lips closed around the end.

The sweat at the back on his neck had caused the collar on his T-shirt to shrink two sizes in the past ten seconds.

She pulled out the empty fork. A dab of enticing frosting was stuck on the corner of her mouth.

A very lickable position.

What the hell was he thinking? Caleb wasn't into licking. At least not his grandmother's employee, one who claimed to know more about Grams's than he did.

The woman was dangerous. Caleb forced himself to look away.

If making him feel worse had been Becca's goal, she'd succeeded. Not only worse, but also aggravated. Annoyed. Attracted.

No, not attracted. Distracted. By the frosting.

His gaze strayed back to the creamy dab on Becca's face.

Yes, that was it. The icing. He placed his fork on the plate. Not the lick...

"Please don't tell me you're finished?" Grams asked, sounding distressed he hadn't eaten the whole slice.

The last thing Caleb wanted was more cake. He needed to figure out what was going on with Becca, then get out of here. "Letting the food settle before I eat more."

He sneaked a peek at Becca.

The tip of her pink tongue darted out, licking her top lip to remove the bit of frosting before disappearing back into her mouth.

Caleb stuck two fingers inside his collar and tugged. Hard. The afternoon heat was making him sweat. Maybe he should head to the gym instead of back to work. Doing today's workout at the gym might clear his head and help him focus on the right things.

He wiped his mouth with a yellow napkin. Becca should have used hers instead of her tongue to remove the icing.

Maybe Becca was trying to be provocative and flirty. Maybe Becca saw dollar signs when she looked at him as Cassandra had. Maybe Becca didn't want him to object to her involvement with Gertie. His grandmother had to be the mark here, not him.

"The cake is delicious. Moist," he said. "The frosting has the right amount of sweetness."

Eyes bright, Grams leaned forward over the table. "I'm so happy you like it. I've been working hard on the recipe."

With a sweet grin that made him think of cotton candy, Becca motioned to her plate. Only half the slice remained. "I think you've perfected it."

Grams chuckled. "Took me enough attempts."

"I've enjoyed each and every slice." Becca patted her trim waistline. "As you can tell."

"Nonsense," Grams said. "You have a lovely figure. Besides, a few slices of cake never hurt anybody. Men like curves, isn't that right, Caleb?"

He choked on the cake in his mouth. Becca's curves were the last thing he should be looking at right now. Not that he hadn't checked them out before. "Mmmm-hmmm."

"See," Grams said lightheartedly.

Warm affection filled Becca's eyes. "I'm sold."

Caleb's gaze darted between the two women. Grams treated Becca more like a friend than an employee. That was typical of his grandmother's interactions with her staff, including the dowdy Mrs. Harrison, a fortysomething widow who preferred to go by her last name.

Still, Grams and Becca's familiarity added to his suspicions given the differences in their social status, personalities and ages. His grandmother always took in strays and treated them well. Becca seemed to be playing along with her role in that scenario, but adding a twist by making sure she was becoming indispensable and irreplaceable.

Something was definitely off here. "Grams is an excellent baker."

"You should have been here on Monday," Becca said. "Gertie knocked it out of the park with her Black Forest cake. Seriously to-die-for."

"Black Forest cake?" he asked.

Grams nodded with a knowing gleam in her eyes. "Your favorite."

That had been only three days ago. Caleb stared at his plate.

Carrot cake was Courtney's favorite. Grams had made his favorite earlier in the week. Puzzle pieces fell into place like colored blocks on a Rubick's Cube. A seven-layer lead weight settled in the pit of Caleb's stomach. "How many cakes do you bake a week?"

"It depends on how long it takes us to eat one," she answered.

The question ricocheted through him, as if he were swinging wildly and hitting only air. "Us?"

"Becca. The estate staff. My lab assistants. Whoever else happens to be working here," Grams explained. "Sometimes Becca takes the leftovers to the vet clinic when she covers shifts there."

Wait a minute. He assumed his grandmother paid Becca well and allowed her to live in the guest cottage rent-free. Why would Becca work at a vet clinic, too? Especially if she was running a con?

"Sounds like a lot of cake." Caleb tried to reconcile

what he was learning about Becca as well as Grams's cake. "I didn't realize you enjoyed baking so much."

Grams raised a shoulder, but there was nothing casual or indifferent in the movement. "Can't have one of my grandchildren stop by and not have any cake to eat."

But I also think she wants me here because she's lonely.

Damn. His chest tightened. Becca was right. Grams was lonely. Regret slithered through him.

Thinking about the number of cakes being baked with anticipation and love and a big dose of hope made it hard to breathe. He figured Grams would be out and about doing whatever women of her age did to pass the time. Lunches, museums, fundraisers. He'd never thought she would go to so much trouble or imagined she would be sitting at home and waiting for her grandchildren to stop by.

His promise and his efforts blew up like a fifty-megaton bomb.

So much for taking care of Grams. He'd failed. He hadn't taken care of her. He'd let her down.

Just like his...dad.

Guilt churned in Caleb's gut. He opened his mouth to speak, but wasn't sure what to say. "I'm sorry" wasn't enough. He pressed his lips together.

"Did you have something you wanted to say?" Grams asked.

Caleb looked up. His grandmother was speaking to Becca.

Of course *that* woman would have something to

say, a smug remark or a smart-aleck comment to expose his failure aloud. Anything so she could rub a ten-pound bag of salt into the gaping hole over his heart.

"No," Becca said, but that didn't soothe him, because she had an I-told-you-so smile plastered on her face. She looked pleased, almost giddy that she'd been proven correct.

How deeply had she ingrained herself in Grams's life? He was concerned how well Becca could read his family. He needed to find his grandmother a new consultant, one with a better education, wardrobe and manners. One he trusted.

Becca's silly, sheep-eating grin made the Cheshire cat look as if he were frowning. She raised a forkful of cake to her mouth. Each movement seemed exaggerated, almost slow motion as if she knew he was waiting for her to make the next move and she wanted to make him suffer.

Good luck with that.

Caleb couldn't feel any worse than he was feeling. He had to do something to make this up to Grams.

"You can have another slice after you finish yours," Grams said.

"One is enough for today," he said. "But let me know when you bake another Black Forest cake, and I'll stop by."

A dazzling smile on his grandmother's face, the kind that could power a city for a day, reaffirmed how lonely she must be in spite of her money and friends.

That loneliness made her vulnerable to people who wanted to take advantage of her, people like Becca.

"I'll do that," Grams said.

He ground the toe of his running shoe against the tile.

In spite of his thinking he'd been a doting grandson, his phone calls, text messages and brunch on Sunday hadn't been enough. Grams wanted to spend face-to-face time with her grandchildren, to chat with them and to feed them.

Caleb's overbooked calendar flashed in his mind. His arm and shoulder muscles bunched, as if he'd done one too many Burpees at the gym.

He was so screwed.

No, that wasn't right.

This was his grandmother, not some stranger.

He'd made a promise, one he intended to honor if it killed him. And it might do that unless Caleb could figure something out. A way to spend more time with Grams. Make more time for her. Find time…

Becca's fork scraped against the plate.

Food.

That gave him an idea.

He had to eat. So did Grams.

Mealtimes would allow him to eat and appease his grandmother's need to see her grandson at the same time. The question was how often. Brunch was a standing date. Dinner once a week would be a good start.

"Let's have dinner next week on Wednesday. Invite Courtney to come," he suggested. "I'm sure your cook can whip up something tasty for us. You can make dessert."

Grams shimmied her narrow shoulders, as if she were a teenager bursting with excitement, not an elderly woman.

Maybe once a week wouldn't be enough. His chest tightened.

"That sounds wonderful," Grams said. "Do you think Courtney can make it?"

The anticipation in Grams's voice made one thing certain. His sister would be at the dinner if he had to buy her a pretty, expensive bauble or a new pair of designer shoes. Grams was worth it. "Yes. She'll be here."

Grams looked as if she might float away like a helium balloon. "Excellent, because I can't wait for Courtney to meet Becca."

Caleb rolled his shoulders, trying to loosen the knots. He didn't want Becca at dinner. The woman had overstayed her welcome as far as he was concerned. This meal was for his family, not employees.

He flashed her a practiced smile, so practiced people never saw through it. But the way Becca studied him made Caleb wonder if she was the exception to the rule. He tilted his head. "Join us for a glass of wine on Wednesday."

Becca brushed her knuckles across her lips. "I don't want to intrude on your evening."

"You aren't intruding," Grams said before Caleb could reply. "You're having dinner with us."

"No," he said at the same time as Becca.

His gaze locked on hers for an uncomfortable second before he looked away. Only ice remained in his glass, but he picked it up and sipped.

The woman was…unpredictable. One more thing not to like about her. He was more of a "load the dice ahead of time so he knew what he was going to roll" kind of guy. He didn't like surprises. He'd bet Becca thrived upon them.

Grams's lip curled. "Caleb."

Becca studied her cake as if a magic treasure were hidden inside. "It's okay, Gertie."

No, it wasn't. Caleb deserved his grandmother's sharp tone. "What I meant is Courtney is a lot to take in if you're not used to being around her. I have no doubt they'll name a Category 5 hurricane after her one of these days."

"Your sister can be…challenging at times," Grams said.

Understatement of the year. Courtney was the definition of drama princess. The rest of the earth's population was here to make his sister look good or help her out. Nothing he tried stopped her from being so selfish. Not even making her work at Fair Face in order to gain access to her trust fund. "We don't want Courtney to overwhelm Becca and make her want to hightail it out of here."

On second thought getting Becca out of the picture was exactly what he wanted to happen. No way would Grams start a business venture on her own. Caleb might have to rethink this.

"Becca won't be overwhelmed. She's made of stronger stuff than that," Gertie said.

"Thanks, but you need this time alone with your grandchildren." Becca's eyelids blinked rapidly, like the shutter on a sport photographer's camera. "I can't make it anyway. I'm covering a shift for a vet tech at the twenty-four hour animal hospital on Wednesday."

"That's too bad," he said.

She toyed with her napkin, her fingers speeding up as if someone had pressed the accelerator. A good thing the napkin was cloth or it would be shredded to bits.

"It is," Becca said. "But I'm sure you'll have a wonderful time together."

Her saccharine sweet voice sounded relieved not to be a part of the dinner. Maybe she had seen through him. That would be a first. "You'll be missed."

As much as a case of poison oak.

A dismayed expression crossed Grams's face, washing over her like a rogue wave. Her shoulders hunched. "You're working that night, Becca?"

The tremble in her voice sent Caleb's pulse accelerating like a rocket's booster engine. Unease spiraled inside him. He reached for his grandmother's hand, covering hers with his. Her skin felt surprisingly warm. Her pulse wasn't racing. Good signs, he hoped. "Grams? You okay?"

She stared at her hands. "I forgot about Becca working on Wednesday. I do have an assistant who reminds me of things, but…"

Grams shook her head slowly, as if she were moving through syrup not air.

Caleb understood her worry. His grandfather had suffered from Alzheimer's, a horrible disease for the patient as well as the family. Being forgotten by the man who'd held their lives together for so long hadn't been easy. But even at the worst of times, Grams had dealt with the stress of the disease with raw strength and never-ending grace and by making jokes. He'd never seen his grandmother act like this. Not even when she'd been stuck in bed with an upper respiratory infection over a year ago. "No worries. You've had a lot on your mind."

"That's right," Becca agreed.

Caleb wondered if she knew something about Grams's health, but hadn't told anyone. Except Becca looked genuinely concerned.

Grams gave his hand a feeble squeeze. "I should be able to remember a detail like Becca's work schedule."

"I never told you about next week's schedule." Becca's voice was soft and nurturing and oh-so-appealing. "I received the call this morning about what shifts I'll be covering. You haven't forgotten anything."

"I haven't?" Grams asked.

Hearing the unfamiliar uncertainty in her voice worried Caleb.

"Nope," Becca confirmed.

Whether his grandmother had forgotten or not, she

seemed so much older and fragile. Time to call her doctor. He patted her hand.

"I'm going to stick around this afternoon." This would cause havoc with his schedule, but he needed to be here for Grams. He could use the time to figure out what was going on with Becca. "I can finish up my work here, then we'll have dinner."

Grams straightened. All signs of weakness disappeared like a wilted flower that had found new life. Her smile took twenty years from her face. Her eyes twinkled. She pulled her hand from beneath his and rubbed her palms together. "That will be perfectly splendid."

Huh? Her transformation stunned him.

"Maura, the new cook, is making lasagna tonight. She's using my recipe for the sauce," Grams said to him. "Becca loves my sauce, don't you?"

Amusement gleamed in Becca's eyes. "I do."

Caleb didn't know what she found so funny. His grandmother's health was nothing to laugh about. "Sounds great, but let's phone your doctor first."

"Nothing is wrong with me." Grams waved off his concern, as if he'd asked if she wanted a slice of lemon in her iced tea. "I had a complete physical two months ago. Dr. Latham said I'm healthy, with a memory an elephant would envy."

That didn't explain what had happened with her only moments ago. "A call won't take long."

Grams's lips formed a perfect O. She leaned toward him. "You're worried about me."

No sense denying the obvious. He nodded.

She touched the side of his face, her touch soft and loving. "You have always been the sweetest boy."

He blew out a frustrated puff of air. "I haven't been a boy for a while."

"Very true, but I remember when you ran around the house naked." She looked at Becca while heat rose in his cheeks. "He never wanted to wear clothes unless it was a superhero costume or camouflage."

Forget the doctor. Might as well call the coroner. For him. Cause of death—embarrassment. "I was what? Three?"

"Three, four and five. It seems like yesterday," Grams said with a touch of nostalgia. She stood. "Please don't worry about me. I'm fine."

Caleb wasn't sure about that. He rose.

She motioned him to sit. "Eat the rest of your cake. I'm going to tell Mrs. Harrison you're staying for dinner."

"I'll go with you," he said.

Becca gave him the thumbs-down sign.

Caleb would have to be blind to misinterpret that signal. He sat. "Or I can finish my cake."

"Do that. Then use the study to work." The words were barely out of Grams's mouth before she bounced her way toward the house.

The French doors slammed shut.

Caleb leaned over the table toward Becca. He might not like her. He sure as hell didn't trust her, but she was the only one he could ask. "What is going on with my grandmother?"

Becca understood Caleb's concern. She'd been

worried, too, until she realized Gertie was faking her memory loss. Becca glanced at the house, biting back a smile. "I imagine your grandmother's in a mad rush to get to the pantry for the ingredients for a Black Forest cake."

Caleb's eyes darkened to an emerald-green. Make that the color of steamed broccoli. His mouth pinched at the corners. "What?"

"You know how you talked about your grandmother using ploys to get her way?"

His gaze narrowed. "Yes."

"Gertie played both of us by pretending to be a forgetful granny."

"She wouldn't."

"She did." It was all Becca could do not to bust out in a belly laugh. "You'd better work on your poker face or prepare for more of her antics, since it worked so well."

"Huh?"

"You not only stayed for cake, but you're having dinner here."

He rubbed the back of his neck. "Grams played me like a well-tuned Stradivarius, didn't she?"

"Perhaps not that well-tuned."

"Touché."

"Your grandmother is the smartest woman I know."

"You seem pretty sharp yourself."

Warmth emanated from Becca's stomach. She hoped the heat didn't spread all the way to her face. No one except Gertie had ever called Becca sharp.

"Thanks, but what she was doing wasn't hard to figure out."

"What tipped you off?" he asked.

He leaned back in his chair, looking more relaxed and comfortable. Different. More approachable. The workout clothes looked mouthwateringly good on him.

"Becca?"

Oops. She'd been staring. Her cheeks warmed. A pale pink, she hoped. "I hadn't told Gertie about my work schedule. But when she looked at your hand on hers and didn't look away, I knew something was up."

"I thought it was strange, but Grams knows how to push my buttons when she wants. She had me worried about her health."

"Desperation can drive a person to do things they normally wouldn't."

He tossed Becca one of those you've-got-to-be-kidding looks. "My grandmother is not desperate."

"I'd be desperate if someone I loved kept blowing me off."

"You don't have to keep rubbing it in. I'm going to spend more time with her."

"Glad to hear it." Becca had expected Caleb to be angry, not repentant. This softer side of him surprised her, given his obvious suspicions about her. Appealed to her, too. "You have no idea how lucky you are. Gertie is amazing. Don't take her for granted."

"You really seem to care about Grams."

Becca nodded. "I wish she was my grandmother."

"Do you have family close by?" he asked.

"Southern Idaho. I don't see them much." Becca didn't like the conversation turning toward her. She stood. "I have to go."

Caleb scooted back in his chair. "Where are you going?"

"To get your suit."

"Before you go." He stood. "One question."

"What?"

"Are Grams's dog products that good?"

"Will you believe what I say?"

"I asked your opinion."

He hadn't answered her question. Maybe he had a better poker face than she thought. "The products are so excellent, they'll sell themselves."

"You sound certain. Confident."

"I am," she said. "The line is going to make a fortune, but it's better that Fair Face isn't manufacturing the products."

His jaw tensed. "I thought that's what you and Grams wanted."

"It was, but not now."

"Trying to get rid of me?"

"Sort of."

His eyes darkened. "Why is that?"

"If Fair Face doesn't believe in the products, they won't be willing to put all their resources behind them," she said. "Fair Face will do enough, just enough, to appease Gertie. The line might not fail, but it won't succeed as well as it could with the right backing and support."

"For a dog consultant, you know a lot about business."

Becca hated that his words meant as much as they did. They shouldn't. "Not really. It's common sense."

"Not having Fair Face involved means more money for you."

She hadn't thought about that. "More money would be great."

"I'm sure it would be."

As if Caleb could understand what money would mean to her. He'd never gone hungry because there wasn't enough money for groceries. He'd never worn thrift-shop clothes and duct-taped shoes. He'd never left prison with nothing except a backpack and an appointment with a probation officer.

"Thinking about how you're going to spend all that money?" he asked.

"Thinking about our next step," she said. "I'll give you my number. Text me the names and numbers of possible advisors."

"No need."

Her heart dropped. "What do you mean?"

"I know the perfect person to help you and Grams."

She fisted her hands in anticipation. "Who?"

"Me."

No. No. No. Every nerve ending shrieked. "You said you didn't have time."

"That was before you made me realize I've been neglecting my grandmother and should spend more time her."

Oh, no. Becca had brought this upon herself. "You

should be doing something fun with Gertie, not working with her."

"You said she liked to work."

"She does. But..." Becca swallowed. "You don't want to ignore Fair Face."

"I'll work it out. This way I'll be able to help you, too." He sounded so confident, as if nothing could stop him. "I can answer any questions you have, make sure things stay on track, maybe provide angel funding. That should make you happy."

The lopsided smile on Caleb's face told Becca he expected her to be anything but happy about this. Goal achieved, because she was very unhappy at the moment. "I—"

"Trust me."

She would never trust a man with so much money and power. She chewed the inside of her cheek. "I hate to put you out like this. It really isn't necessary."

"No worries. Honest." The charming smile spreading across his face made her breath hitch. "Besides, I'm not doing this for you. I'm doing it for my grandmother."

CHAPTER FOUR

THE NEXT AFTERNOON, Caleb left his office and rode in a limousine to his grandmother's estate. He hoped the element of surprise would work in his favor today. Unlike yesterday when he'd been caught off-guard by most everything.

Spending time with Grams and being her advisor were the perfect ruses for Caleb dropping by unannounced. He could keep on eye on Becca until he figured out what she was up to.

The estate's housekeeper, Mrs. Harrison, answered the door. She told him that Grams was in the lab, which he expected, and Becca was in the study, which he hadn't.

Every nerve ending went on alert.

She shouldn't be allowed to have free rein on the estate. She shouldn't be allowed to sit in the same study where his grandfather put together Fair Face. She shouldn't be here at all.

He stood in the doorway of the study, watching Becca.

With a laptop at her left, she hunched over the desk, pencil in hand, scribbling notes on paper. She wore a green T-shirt. He assumed she had on shorts, but he saw only crossed long legs and a bare foot swinging beneath the desk.

"Working hard?" Though he imagined her brainstorming ways to con Grams out of money rather than actual work.

Becca's gaze jerked up. Her eyes widened. She set her pencil on the desk. "Caleb. I didn't know you were stopping by."

"I thought I'd see if you have any questions about the business plan we talked about last night."

"That's what I'm working on."

Convenient. Unless she was lying. He took a step toward her. "Let me see what you've done."

She frowned. "I only started this morning."

"I'm your advisor," he said in an even voice. No reason to make her aware of his suspicions. "It's my job to keep you headed in the right direction."

And make sure she didn't hurt what mattered most to him.

Becca eyed him warily. "I didn't realize CEOs micromanage their employees."

"You don't work for me." If Becca did, he would have fired her yesterday when she gave away her true intention.

Trying to get rid of me?

Sort of.

Not sort of. He had no doubt she'd wanted him gone so she could scam Grams out of as much money as possible. That was why he'd agreed to advise them, why he'd participated in a conference call on the way over here, why he'd be checking in with them daily.

To protect Grams. To protect Fair Face.

"But I'm advising you." For now. He'd hired a private investigator to do a background check, but until the man reported back Caleb was sticking close to her, even if it messed up his schedule. "I take that role seriously."

She straightened the papers and handed the stack to him. "Here."

He ran his thumb over the edges. Too many to count quickly. "A lot of pages for starting this morning."

Her mouth tightened. "I didn't plagiarize, if that's what you're suggesting."

Her defensive behavior suggested she knew Caleb was onto her. No reason to be all that subtle about his suspicions. Maybe she'd get scared and take off on her own. That would make things simpler, especially with Grams.

Tension, thick and unsettling, hung in the air.

Underneath the desk, her foot swung like a pendulum gone crazy. Back and forth, speeding up each time the blur of fluorescent-painted toenails came toward him.

"I wasn't suggesting anything." Caleb didn't trust Becca. But he couldn't deny she…intrigued him. He held the papers in the air. "Only making an observation."

"I found a business plan template online," she said to his surprise. "The website explains what to write where and gives you text boxes to fill in. You download the plan into word processing software."

"Handy."

"Yes."

Caleb read through her rough draft, making mental notes as he went. He set the plan on the desk.

"So?" she asked, her voice full of curiosity.

"Not bad." He waited for a reaction, but didn't get one. She either didn't care or had tight control of her emotions. He would go with apathy. "Hold off on working on the executive summary until the business plan is complete. That way you'll have a better idea of who and what the company is all about."

She rested her elbows on the desk and leaned forward. Her V-neck T-shirt gaped, giving him an enticing peek of ivory skin, beige satin and cleavage.

He enjoyed the view for a moment, felt his temperature rise and then looked away. This wasn't the time to be distracted by a nice, round pair of breasts.

"What else?" she asked.

Becca sounded interested, not apathetic, as if she wanted to know what was wrong and how to fix it. That was unexpected.

Caleb picked up the business plan and scanned the pages again. He'd read through enough business plans over the years with his personal venture capital/angel fund to offer some quick fixes. "This is a good start, but you need specific goals and a more concrete direction. The product descriptions are excellent, but you're missing pricing information or market comparisons. You'll need hard facts, start-up costs, projected balance sheets. 'The products will sell themselves' isn't a sales and marketing strategy."

Her shoulders slumped. "There's so much more to this than I realized."

"That's what I was trying to tell you and my grandmother yesterday." The more discouraged they got, especially Becca, the better. "There are easier ways to make money than starting your own business."

She stared at her hands. "Making money has never come easy for me or people I know."

"My grandfather told me hard work always pays off."

"I've heard your grandfather was a wonderful man, but sometimes hard work doesn't put groceries in the cupboard." Without a glance Caleb's way, she made notes on another piece of paper. "Anything else I should add?"

"Make these fixes first, then I'll review it again." He handed back her pages. "Writing something like this is an iterative process."

"That sucks, since Gertie wants the plan finished tonight."

Grams could be impatient. When she'd presented the baby products, she'd wanted them on the market in less than three months. It had taken almost a year. "I'm surprised she didn't want it done yesterday."

"Two dogs needed baths last night. Otherwise, she would have told me to get it done. In a nice way, of course."

Grams could be firm, but "in a nice way" described her perfectly. "When did you move in?"

"February."

Four months ago. Had it been that long since he'd been to the estate? He couldn't remember. "You've had plenty of time to figure out how my grandmother operates."

"She's the best boss. Ever."

So adamant. Loyal. The woman deserved an Oscar nomination for her acting abilities. "Grams likes getting her way."

Becca stared down her nose at him. "Most people do."

"You?"

"If it ever happened, I'd probably like getting my way."

If. Probably. Her words raised more questions.

"But I never get my way," she added. "Let me tell you. It sucks."

Caleb had never met a woman like Becca Taylor. She might be a scammer, but the way she spoke her mind was…entertaining. She added color and expectation into predictable life. He would miss that when she was gone. But he would survive.

The next day, Becca finished her morning run with Maurice. She walked to the kennel with the dog at her side.

Sweat covered her face and dripped from her hair. Her legs trembled from the exertion. "Let's get you put away so I can see what Gertie needs."

"My grandmother wants you up at the house."

The sound of Caleb's voice sent goosebumps prickling Becca's skin. A strange sensation, given how sticky and hot she felt at the moment.

But strange and Caleb seemed to go together. Three visits in three days. For someone claiming to be busy, he had a lot of time to check up on—make that "advise"—her. Though today was Saturday, and based on his casual attire, a pair of cargo shorts and a T-shirt, he wasn't going into the office today.

"You run," he said.

"The dogs run." She opened the kennel door. The blast of cool air refreshed her, kept her temper in check. "I hold the leashes and get dragged along."

"You're not a runner."

"Do I look like a runner?" She glanced back at him. "Don't answer that."

Caleb smiled, but whether his smile was genuine or not remained to be seen. He followed her into the kennel, the door closing behind him. "Why do you run if you don't like it?"

She not only didn't like running, she didn't like Caleb being underfoot. His wide shoulders and height made the spacious kennel feel cramped and stuffy.

"Some of the dogs prefer it to walking." Becca opened the door to Maurice's space complete with pillow bed and a doggy door that led to his own grassy dog run. She unhooked his leash and let him loose inside. The dog went straight for his stainless steel water bowl. "So we run."

"You really are a dog person."

"Muscle tone is important. Dog judges don't like to see flabby or fat dogs in the ring."

"You run the little ones, too?"

"I walk them." She checked each of the dog bowls to make sure they had enough water to get them through the next couple of hours. "How briskly depends on their legs."

"When do you walk them?" he asked.

"I already did." She wished he'd go bother someone else. Maybe he was trying turn on the charm and play nice. But he looked good today. He exuded confidence, and a part of her wanted to reach out and grab some for herself. That was bad. Becca didn't want to notice anything about Caleb Fairchild. She was thinking about him too much as it were. Maybe she was lonely. An animal control officer she'd met at the animal hospital had mentioned meeting for coffee. Going on a date with him might take her mind off Caleb. "They'll get another walk later if it's not too hot."

"Sounds like they are lucky dogs."

"Anyone who is fortunate to have Gertie on their side is a lucky dog."

"Including you?"

"I'm the luckiest." She motioned to the door. "I need to see what Gertie wants."

"I'll go with you."

Figures. "I'm sure you want to spend as much time with your grandmother as possible."

"That's right."

Liar. Becca bit her tongue to keep from saying the word aloud. Caleb spent twice as much time with her than Gertie.

Okay, his insights on the business plan had been

useful. Becca would give him that much credit. But the way Caleb watched her, as if trying to catch her doing something wrong made her so self-conscious she was having trouble sleeping. Something she hadn't had since leaving prison. She didn't like it. Didn't like him.

Maybe if she kept working hard and proved herself writing the business plan, Caleb would continue visiting his grandmother, but leave Becca alone. She hoped so because whenever he came close physical awareness shot through her like an electric shock.

She found Gertie, dressed in a lab coat and black pants, sitting on a bar stool at the kitchen's island. Mrs. Harrison washed vegetables. A young woman named Maura, who helped cook and clean, stood at the stove, stirring whatever was inside a saucepan.

"You wanted to see me," Becca said.

"Yes." Gertie clapped her hands together. "I have some news. A sort of good news/bad news kind of thing."

Becca had never known Gertie to have any bad news until today. "Start with the bad so we end on a high note."

"I can't go with you to the dog show in Oregon next weekend," Gertie announced.

Becca's chest tightened. She took a step forward. "Is anything wrong?"

"Oh, no, dear. I'm fine, but I found out an old friend is being thrown a surprise party. It's not something I can miss."

That wasn't really bad news. Not compared to

some of the bad news she'd dealt with in the past. She would miss Gertie's company, but her employer needed to get out of the lab more. "Go have fun. I'm used to doing shows on my own."

"You won't be alone." Gertie bounced from jeweled slipper to jeweled slipper and back again. "That's my good news. Caleb is going with you so he can see the products in action."

No. No. No.

Becca staggered back until she bumped into something solid and around six feet tall.

Caleb.

She jumped forward. "Sorry."

"No worries."

Maybe not for him, but this wasn't good news at all. A weekend with Caleb watching her every move, waiting and hoping she screwed up. Not to mention the strange way he made her insides quiver. She couldn't let this happen. "Have you ever been to a dog show before?"

"No, but I need to know how the products work in order to help you."

Caleb would hate wasting time at a dog show. She had work to do, but he would be standing or sitting around, bored out of his mind. She wouldn't have time to entertain him or be subjected to another of his inquisitions.

There had to be a way to convince him not to go.

On Monday, the clip of Caleb's Italian leather wingtips against the estate's hardwood floor echoed the beat of his heart. Working with Becca on the business plan, he'd learned two things about her: she was from a small town outside Twin Falls, Idaho, and her father's first name was Rob. Information his private investigator had used to perform a background check.

The jig was up. Caleb had known his instincts were right about her.

His hand tightened around the manila folder containing irrefutable proof Becca Taylor was trying to scam his grandmother. He strode into the estate's solarium with one goal in mind—get Becca away from his grandmother. "Hello, Grams."

"Caleb." She lounged on a chaise holding a glass of pink lemonade complete with a pink paper umbrella. "Thanks for letting yourself in. I was standing most of the day, and my feet hurt."

He kissed her cheek. "You shouldn't spend so much time in the lab."

"It's what I do."

Not for long. The crazy dog care line would soon be nothing but a footnote in Grams's life, a distant memory along with Becca. He crinkled the edge of the folder. "Where's your consultant?"

"At the animal hospital." Grams placed her drink on a mosaic end table she'd purchased in Turkey. "You're stuck with me."

"I came to visit you."

Grams placed her hand on her chest. "I'm touched. What did you want to talk about?

He sat in a damask covered chair next the chaise. "Becca."

Grams's eyes softened with affection. "Becca has been spending so much time writing and revising the business plan. You'll be impressed."

Caleb doubted that, but he reminded himself to be conscious of his grandmother's feelings. "I learned disturbing news today. Becca Taylor isn't who you think she is."

"I know exactly who Becca is." Grams sounded one hundred percent confident. "She's a sweet, hard-working woman and my friend."

One who takes, takes, takes before hightailing it out of there.

"Your friend Becca, aka Rebecca Taylor, is a con-victed criminal. She spent three years at the Idaho Women's Correctional Center." Caleb expected to see a reaction, but didn't. Maybe Grams was trying to take it all in. "We're not talking shoplifting, Grams. Theft, trespassing and vandalism."

Grams tapped her finger against her cheek. "How did you find out?"

"A private investigator." He raised the folder in the air, careful to keep his excitement out of his voice. "I know you consider Becca a friend and she's been helping you, but she's taking advantage of you. Fire her. Get her out of the guesthouse. Out of your life. Before she hurts you and robs you blind."

"Just because a person makes a mistake in the past doesn't mean they'll repeat it in the future."

"She is a crook." He didn't understand why his grandmother was being so understanding. She should be upset, furious. Maybe she was in shock. "I'll bet

Becca learned more ways to break the law while she was in jail."

Grams picked up her pink lemonade and stared into the glass. "Becca told me all about her time in prison."

"You knew about this?"

"She told me everything before she accepted my job offer."

Outrage choked him. "Yet you hired her anyway? Let her move in?"

"She made a youthful mistake."

He scoffed. "That mistake landed her in jail."

"She paid the price for her actions. Learned her lesson."

"We're not talking about an overdue library book." He stared at his grandmother in disbelief. "You can't have a criminal working for you. It's not safe."

"Becca would never hurt me."

"She is a convicted—"

"I respect her honesty and integrity," Grams interrupted. "I'm not going to hold the past against her. Neither should you."

"Don't make me out to be the bad guy here. I didn't rob anybody," he countered. "I'm trying to look out for you, Grams. That's what Gramps wanted me to do. You have a big heart. People have taken advantage of you in the past."

"People need the opportunity to make a fresh start."

Caleb's jaw tensed. "You gave my father plenty of fresh starts. He blew every single one."

"Becca is nothing like him."

"That's true," Caleb agreed. "My father was never in jail."

"Your father had his own issues," Grams said. "But even if he'd gone to jail, it wouldn't have changed the way I felt about him. People deserve another chance."

Everyone meaning Becca. And…his father.

A weight pressed down on Caleb's chest, squeezing the air out of his lungs and the blood out of his heart. "How many fresh starts did you give my father?"

"If your father were alive today, I'd be giving him another chance the way I'm doing with Becca. That's what you do when you love someone."

"Rebecca Taylor is a complete stranger."

"To you. Not to me. I care what happens to her," Grams said. "And I'm much more interested in the woman she is today than the girl she was at eighteen."

Caleb pressed his lips together. This wasn't how he'd imagined the conversation going. "You don't know if she's told you the truth. Read the report, then you can decide—"

"I've made my decision about Becca. Nothing is going to change my mind, but you should talk to her about this and appease your concerns."

"You're that sure about her."

"Yes," Grams said. "I want you to be sure about Becca, too. Talk to her about your concerns. Let her explain what happened."

That would be a complete waste of time.

Nothing Becca had to say would change his mind.

Absolutely nothing.

Grams's eyes implored him. "Please, Caleb. Speak with Becca. For me."

Screw Caleb Fairchild for delving into her business.

Becca balled her hands. The tenth floor of Fair Face's corporate headquarters was the last place she wanted to be tonight.

"Mr. Fairchild will see you now," a middle-aged uniformed security guard said. "Follow me."

Becca walked down an empty hallway. The fifth draft of the business plan inside her gray-and-black messenger bag bumped against her hip.

She adjusted the bag's strap. She wasn't even sure why she'd brought the plan along. Maybe to show Caleb she'd been working, not plotting a crime against his grandmother.

As if he would believe her.

She glanced at the guard. "It's quiet."

"Most folks have gone home," he said.

The carpet muted their footsteps, unlike the correction facility where sound echoed. Instead of passing walled cells with solid metal doors and slits for windows, she passed offices with mahogany wood doors and brass nameplates. No one whispered her name or called her something nasty. No one shot dagger-filled stares or tried to beat her up when the guards weren't looking.

But the memories hit her hard. The sounds. The smells. The bone-chilling cold she could never seem to shake even during the long, hot summers.

Becca crossed her arms over her chest.

She wanted to forget about all that. Not relieve the worst three years of her life to appease Caleb Fairchild's curiosity. But she would talk to him…for Gertie's sake.

At the end of the hallway, the guard pointed to an office with its door open. A light was on inside. "That's Mr. Fairchild's office."

She wondered if Mr. Fairchild had asked the guard to stick around outside his office while they spoke. After all, she was a hardened criminal. She forced a tight smile. "Thanks."

She entered the office.

Big. She hadn't expected the office to be this large, complete with a round table surrounded by six chairs, a couch and coffee table, a large desk, chairs, bookcases along her right side and floor to ceiling windows on the two far corner walls.

Then again, Caleb Fairchild was the CEO.

He sat at his desk, a portrait in concentration as he stared at his computer monitor.

Caleb looked every bit the handsome business executive—if you liked that type. Even though it was past quitting time, every strand of his hair was in place, his tie knotted tightly around his neck and his sleeves unrolled. The only thing missing was his suit jacket.

He looked clean cut, respectable and proper. But as with Whit who'd gotten her in so much trouble, Becca knew looks could be deceiving. Caleb was a shark waiting to attack and take her out. Exactly the sort she tried to avoid. But tonight she was venturing into his water without a harpoon or any way to defend herself except her word against his suspicions.

It wasn't going to be pretty.

Though he still hadn't noticed her, so maybe she had a chance of surviving. She cleared her throat.

Caleb's cool, assessing gaze met hers.

A chill shivered down her spine.

He stood. "Good evening, Becca."

She saw nothing good about it. He had some nerve hiring a P.I. As if she would have lied about her past to his grandmother. She'd dealt with enough liars and fakes growing up and while she was in jail to ever want to be one.

Becca bit the inside of her cheek.

"Close the door so we have some privacy," he said.

She hadn't seen another person in the building except the security guard. Guess he would be hanging around out in the hallway. Figured. She closed the door.

"Thanks." He motioned to one of the two black leather chairs in front of the large desk. "Have a seat."

Standing wouldn't give her that much of an advantage over sitting seeing as she was out of her element and on his home turf. She crossed his office, removed her messenger bag then sat, sinking into a chair. She ran her fingertips along the buttery soft leather. This furniture was much nicer than anything in her parents' house. "Gertie said you had questions for me."

His gaze didn't waver from Becca's. "You don't waste any time."

Her temperature increased. No doubt stress from his hawklike gaze. He saw her as a vulture circling over his grandmother. "You've made it clear you're a busy man."

He walked around the front of the desk and sat on the edge.

Needing something to do with her hands, Becca picked dog hair off her skirt.

She'd spent an hour trying to figure out what to wear, finally deciding on one of her dog-show suits—teal skirt, matching three-quarter-sleeve jacket and a lace-trimmed camisole underneath. She wasn't sure what the proper attire was for explaining one's prison record, but this was better than a pair of Daisy Duke shorts and a camisole.

"Tell me how you ended up in prison," he said matter-of-factly.

Becca took a deep breath. She glanced around the room, not really seeing anything. She took another breath, then met his gaze directly. "I was an idiot."

He drew back with confusion in his eyes. "Excuse me?"

"I did something really stupid." Becca rubbed her face. "I fell for a guy. I thought he liked me, so I trusted him. Big mistake."

One corner of Caleb's mouth rose, but she wouldn't call it a smile. Not a half-one, either. "You're not the first to be led astray by their heart."

He sounded as if he'd been there, done that, got the T-shirt. But being led astray and wearing prison garb for three years were totally different things.

Becca had been so naive to think a rich boy like Whitley would want her—a girl from the trailer park. Yet he'd made her feel so...different. Special. Glamorous. Trying to be cool had enticed her to be reckless. She raised her chin. "I should have known better. Whitley was the brother of a girl I'd gotten to know through dog showing. They were wealthy. I wasn't. But Whit didn't seem to care."

"Whit is the man."

"Boy," she clarified. "I couldn't believe when he asked me out for a smoothie. I wanted him to like me, so I tried to be the type of girl he'd want to date, even if that wasn't who I was. I fell...hard."

So hard she'd found herself thumbing through a bridal magazine at the grocery store and imagining what color dresses the bridesmaids should wear. "I'd recently graduated high school. It was summertime. We went out almost every night and then..."

Memories hit strong and fast. The flashing of red and blue lights. The accusations. The tears. The handcuffs scraping her wrists. Being read her Miranda rights.

Someone touched her shoulder.

She jumped.

Caleb held up his hands as if surrendering. His eyes were dark. Concerned. "Sorry. You looked miles away for a second."

Not miles, years. She stood, backing away from him. "Just...remembering."

"This is hard for you."

Becca nodded, not trusting her voice. A compassionate person would tell her to stop.

Not Caleb.

He didn't say a word, but remained perched on his desk as if he might attack at any minute. Not so much a shark now—more like a dangerous hawk ready to swoop down on his prey.

On her.

A thrill fissured through her. So not the reaction she should have around him.

Becca shouldn't react to him at all. Or notice all these little details about him.

She hated that she did.

CHAPTER FIVE

BECCA WALKED TO one of the bookcases, the one closest to the office's door and farthest away from Caleb. Oh, he was handsome and could turn on the charm faster than she could blink. Tonight she saw an edge to him she hadn't see before, an edge that appealed to her.

But she knew his type all too well.

Whatever she said tonight would fall on deaf ears. He'd been suspicious of her since the day they met. Nothing was going to change his mind about her.

He'd likely agreed to attend the dog show, not to see the new products in action, but to watch her because of her criminal past.

"I'm not a bad person," she said.

"I never said you were."

But he hadn't said she wasn't, either.

No one cared about the truth. "Guilty" was all that mattered to people. What happened hadn't been forgotten. And wouldn't be. It followed her everywhere.

Or had until she'd met Gertie.

Caleb wouldn't be as understanding. That was why this was so hard for Becca.

She noticed a black-framed photo of him and another man. Both men were attractive. The other guy wasn't as handsome as Caleb, but as fit with a muscular V-shaped physique. A triangle folded American flag with military ribbons sat on the shelf above the picture.

Becca realized she was procrastinating. Might as well get this over with. She looked over at Caleb.

His dark gaze met hers. "Take your time."

"I don't want to drag this out any longer." Telling him what had happened was the only thing that would loosen the tension in her neck. "Whit asked if I wanted to hang out with him and some of his friends. I said yes, thinking things must be getting serious if he wanted to introduce me to his friends."

"A reasonable assumption."

"Reasonable, but wrong," she admitted. "He was interested in me, but not as a girlfriend. I was being set up to be the patsy. The scapegoat. The one they could blame if their plans to break in to the bank president's house to steal cash to buy drugs went south."

"They don't sound like the Honor Society kids."

"Some were. Others were jocks. But they were no better than a gang of hoodlums. They just wore designer clothes and drove nice cars."

"You were part of it."

"No. I had no idea what they were planning." She forced herself not to make a face at him and read the titles of the business books on the shelf instead. A few military strategy type books were mixed in with the marketing and finance titles. "Whit said we were going to hop the fence and go hot-tubbing while the guy was on vacation. I was wearing my bikini underneath my clothing and had a towel crammed in my bag."

But not even those things, including the panties and bra she'd brought to change into, had mattered to the police.

"It wasn't until we were inside the house and not in the backyard that I realized what they were planning. But I thought Whit liked me, so I…"

Becca bit her lip. She couldn't bring herself to say the words.

"You went along," Caleb finished for her.

She nodded. Embarrassed, regretful and ashamed. "I was trying to fit into Whit's world. I was afraid to speak up, so I just followed his lead."

"I take it things didn't turn out as planned."

"No one knew about the high-tech security system in the house. The police caught us inside, and then…"

Her chest tightened with Whit's betrayal. Becca took a breath and another. It didn't help. "Everyone turned on me. Pointed their fingers at me. Blamed me. They said it had been all my idea. I had picked the lock. Stolen the money."

"But the police should have—"

"The police believed them. Why wouldn't they? My dad had spent time in the county jail for getting into a fight. I was the resident trailer trash. No one was surprised to find me involved in something like this. Not to mention my fingerprints were all over the evidence."

Caleb's eyes widened. "How did that happen?"

She understood the disbelief in his tone. Her parents and lawyer had sounded the same way. "Whit had me wrapped around his little finger. *Open the door, gorgeous. Hold this tool, beautiful. Have you ever seen this much money before? Want to hold it?*"

She hadn't, and she did.

"But the other kids were accessories to the crime," he said. "Whit, too."

"True, but they had high-priced attorneys who managed to get the charges reduced or dropped."

"That doesn't seem fair."

"It wasn't. But life has never been fair to people like me." Caleb's privileged upbringing would affect one's perspective as much as growing up in a trailer park had hers. "Luck wasn't on my side, either. I'd turned eighteen two days before, so was legally considered an adult. My parents couldn't afford a lawyer so I was assigned a public defender. Due to the evidence and witnesses..."

"Whit and his friends cut a deal."

Becca nodded. "My lawyer recommended a plea bargain."

"You took it."

"I wanted to fight the charges, but my parents thought three years in prison was better than the alternative, so I did what my lawyer wanted."

Caleb didn't say anything.

That didn't surprise her. She stared at a photograph of Caleb surrounded by bikini-clad supermodels. There was another picture of the Fairchild family—

Caleb, a young woman who must be Courtney, Gertie and her late husband. All four people looked so happy and carefree with bright smiles on their faces.

Becca wondered what it would be like to feel so happy and content. Just once she would like to know.

"You must have been scared," Caleb said.

"Terrified." She still was some days, but he didn't need to know that. "I understand if you don't believe me. But it's what happened."

"A hard lesson to learn."

She walked back to the chair, but remained standing. "I wouldn't wish the three years I spent locked up on anybody. Not even the kids who set me up me that night."

"Regrets?"

"I know people say you shouldn't have regrets, but if I could go back to change that one night I would. Being in jail…it sucked. But I learned my lesson. I'm not going to try to be someone I'm not ever again."

She waited for him to ask the inevitable questions about whether she was part of a gang or if she had a girlfriend or something else he might have seen on television.

"I'm sorry," he said finally.

Her gaze jerked up. "Excuse me."

"I'm sorry you had to go through that."

She didn't say anything. She wasn't sure what to think of his words or the sentiment behind them.

"So what happened after you got out of jail?" he asked.

"I tried to start where I left off. But it wasn't as easy as I thought that it would be."

"Why not?"

"I kept filling out applications and being turned down for job interviews. Even though I'd done my time, people still saw me as a criminal."

He shifted positions on the desk. "What did you do?"

"I'd been planning to go to college to become a vet tech before all this happened, so applied to a few programs and eventually got accepted to one. I used the scholarships I'd won through dog showing and worked every odd job I could find to cover tuition. But after I had my degree, I ran into the same problems as before. I couldn't find a veterinary clinic back home that would hire me."

"Your past."

"My past is very much my present. I fear it always will be. As our conversation tonight proves once again."

He stared at the carpet.

Feeling guilty? Becca hoped so, and she wasn't going to back down. "They say you can't be tried twice for the same crime, but that's only in a court of law. People don't forget, and they hold a grudge. I moved to Boise because I thought I'd have more opportunities here."

"Have you?"

"A few," she said. "I found a job at an animal hospital. A professional dog handler I'd known through 4-H as a kid and as a junior handler in AKC took pity on me and asked if I wanted to be her apprentice. That's how I met Gertie."

"My grandmother doesn't care about your past."

"Gertie is one in a million." Thinking about Gertie made Becca want to smile for the first tine since she'd left the estate earlier. "I wish more people were like her. But they're not."

They were more like Caleb.

That was one reason she preferred the company of dogs to people. Dogs were more loyal, understanding, loving.

"Any other questions?" she asked. "I'm happy to give you the name of my former probation officer. Though he can't guarantee I'm not trying to scam your grandmother."

A blush colored Caleb's cheeks. "She told you."

"She warned me."

"This isn't personal." He sounded defensive. "I'm only trying to protect her."

"As you should," she agreed. "If I weren't your target, I'd say your chivalry is sweet even if it's…misguided. But this isn't the first time it's happened to mc. I know it won't be the last."

"You're resigned to that."

"Annoyed by it, too. But what am I going to do?"

Nothing she'd done so far had changed people's opinion of her. But that hadn't stopped her from trying. From working the worst shifts at the animal hospital to busting her butt doing whatever Gertie asked, Becca had wanted to earn people's respect, to be…

accepted for who she was now. Not who she'd been before.

"You could move out of Idaho," he said.

"I'm far enough away from my parents as it is."

"Family is important to you."

"It's all I've got."

"Me, too," he said.

A warm look passed between them. Becca found herself getting lost in Caleb's eyes. What was going on? She never expected to have anything in common with Caleb. Well, except for liking chocolate cake and Gertie. But he was more complicated and different from what Becca expected.

"Grams told me you've been working on a revised business plan. Did you bring it with you?" he asked.

"Business plan?" She blinked at the sudden change of topic. "I have it. But I didn't think you were still going to advise us."

"Why not?"

"You only agreed because you had doubts about me."

"That's true."

Her heart fell. Spilling her guts hadn't changed anything. She shouldn't feel as disappointed as she did. "You still have doubts."

"I told my grandmother I would help her," he said. "I'm not going back on my word."

She respected Caleb for being a man of his word, especially when his agreeing had meant so much to Gertie. But he hadn't denied still having doubts about Becca.

That had happened before.

It would happen again.

But she was surprised how much it hurt now.

Caleb was wrong about Becca.

Wrong about her motives. Wrong about her past.

He loosened his tie.

Caleb had misjudged her. Completely.

What she'd said about struggling after getting out of prison jibed with the private investigator's report. She'd admitted her father had spent time in jail, too.

Her education and experience wouldn't give her the knowledge to pull off a big financial scam. Though he couldn't deny the possibility of a theft on a smaller scale.

He glanced up from Becca's business plan.

In her teal suit, standing by one of his bookcases, she looked like a consultant. Professional. Knowledgable. A world apart from the woman he'd met in his grandmother's backyard.

But whether dressed to the nines or in bright orange prison garb, she was the same woman. A woman eager to rebuild her life. A woman he found himself wanting to learn more and more about.

Her story about Whit sounded all too plausible to Caleb. He knew guys like that, his father was like that, his experience with Cassandra had been like that.

Becca was most likely exactly what she seemed to be—a hopeful dog whisperer who was caught up in one of his grandmother's schemes through no fault of her own.

Moving a foot away from him, Becca pulled out a book, read the inside flap, then placed it back on the shelf. She did the same with another.

Con artists, like his Cassandra, were good at sob stories, but Becca seemed too genuine, her behavior too natural and awkward and uncomplicated. She didn't appear to be a threat, but he'd deal with her if that changed.

For now, Caleb would go along with his grandmother's gamble. A part of him admired Becca. That was rare.

But he still had to be careful for all their sakes.

"You're welcome to borrow any of the books," he said.

"Is there one you'd recommend?"

"Strategic Marketing and Branding."

Becca touched each of the book spines with her fingertip, searching for the title. She pulled one out. "Here it is."

"You know the market and the industry, but having a thought out branding strategy can make all the difference," he explained. "The book will be a good introduction to the buzzwords and approaches being used."

She studied the front cover. "Thanks."

"You're welcome."

He thought she would walk back toward his desk. She didn't. Instead she kept looking at the items on the shelves.

"The USS *Essex*." Becca studied one of the small replicas of aircraft carriers. "Gertie has a larger version of this in her collection."

"Gramps was assigned to the USS *Essex* during the Korean War. He fell in love with aircraft carriers. Grams used to give him the models on special occasions."

"What a wonderful gift." Becca bent to take a closer look at the shelf containing the models. Her skirt rose in the back, showing off her firm thighs. "The USS *Vinson*."

His groin tightened. He tried not to stare. "Yes."

"I've seen that one, too." She straightened. "Your grandfather had large replicas at home and small models here at the office?"

"The smaller ones are mine."

She glanced his way. "Yours?"

He nodded, a part of him wishing she could be his tonight.

Whoa. Where had that come from?

He'd been working too hard if his mind was going...there.

Grams hadn't mentioned if Becca had a boyfriend, but Caleb imagined she did. A man who thought nothing of carrying lint rollers, doggy treats and poop bags wherever he went.

Someone totally opposite to Caleb.

He couldn't keep a plant alive, let alone be responsible for a pet. It wouldn't be fair to a dog or cat or fish.

Not that he wanted a girlfriend. He dated when he

had time, but kept things…light. It was easier that way, given his schedule.

He secured her pages with a binder clip. "Excellent work on the business plan."

A smile tugged at her lips. He waited for one to explode and light up her face. The right corner lifted another quarter of inch before shooting back into place as if she'd realized she was going five miles per hour over the speed limit and needed to slow down before getting pulled over.

She smiled for Grams, but not him.

That bothered Caleb. He wanted a smile.

Becca bit her lip, gnawing at it like a piece of jerky, a stale piece. "I don't think it's ever going to be ready."

"Iterative process, remember?"

She shrugged.

Ah-ha. A perfectionist. Caleb had a couple on his staff—hard workers—but their never-satisfied, not-good-enough tendencies made end-of-the-quarter more stressful. "What you've done so far is pretty impressive."

Something—pride, maybe?—flashed in her eyes. But the same wariness from before quickly took over. "You think?"

He nodded. "It's obvious you've been working hard revising the drafts."

"That's what Gertie pays me to do."

"You're doing it very well." He would have known that if he'd listened to his grandmother instead of telling her to fire her consultant. He was sure Grams wouldn't let him forget that, either.

Becca straightened, as if he'd finally gotten her attention. Or she liked what he'd said.

"There are a few areas where you'll need to do more research," he added.

"Manufacturing, for sure. And the product containers are giving me a real headache." She was one step ahead of him. "Everything is priced based on quantity. Making that initial order seems to be based on magic."

"A Magic 8 Ball, actually."

"You're…" Her gaze narrowed. "Kidding."

"Had you going for a minute," he teased.

Amusement gleamed in her eyes. "Twenty seconds tops."

"Forty at least."

Her smile burst across her face like the sun at dawn.

He couldn't breathe.

"Thirty," she said playfully. "Not a nanosecond longer."

With her eyes bright and her face glowing, she looked…gorgeous. It was his turn to speak, but Caleb didn't know what to say. All he could do was stare.

She studied him. "Have you ever consulted a Magic 8 Ball?"

"No, but my sister Courtney had one. Swore it worked."

"And you kidded her about that."

"I'm her older brother. Of course I did."

"I'm not surprised," Becca said. "You're not the kind of person who leaves things up to chance, let alone a fortune-telling game."

Interesting observation and dead-on. "Why do you say that?"

She motioned to the books on the shelf. "The business books mixed in with military ones. Strategy. War. That suggests you like to be prepared. Know what you're up against. Have a solid plan and an exit strategy. You take a tactical approach. At least you did with me."

"I may have had some bad intel."

"It happens."

She didn't sound upset. That was a relief. "You're observant."

Becca lifted one shoulder. "I keep my eyes open so I know what's going on."

A lesson learned. No doubt because of what had happened to her when she was younger. Caleb was the same way thanks to Cassandra. Interesting that he and Becca had been used in similar ways. Though hers had been much worse. "It's not good being caught off-guard."

"Nope." She motioned to the other shelf with his memorabilia. "Was the flag your grandfather's?"

"Yes. From his funeral."

She pointed to one of the photographs. "Who's this?"

Caleb crossed the office, picked up a framed photo of him with Ty Dooley. "My best friend since third grade. He's in the navy."

"The two of you look like you could be brothers."

"Ty's like a brother." He was living the dream for both of them. Right now Ty was downrange somewhere classified. Caleb couldn't wait to see him again. "We planned on being in the navy together."

A grin spread across her face. "You wanted to follow in your grandfather's footsteps."

Caleb's muscles tensed. He'd never told anyone that except Ty. Becca guessing that made Caleb feel stripped bare and vulnerable. He didn't like it. He nodded once.

She studied him, her gaze sharp and assessing. "Military service is honorable, but you're following in your grandfather's footsteps by being Fair Face's CEO."

True, but Caleb felt no satisfaction. He'd wanted to be the kind of man his grandfather had been and nothing like his father.

Becca pointed to another photograph of Caleb with itty-bitty-bikini-clad supermodels clinging to him. "Most men would kill to be in your position."

He wasn't "most men."

The decision to run Fair Face had never been his to make. His worthless father hadn't wanted anything to do with the family company. To say that everything had fallen to Caleb was an understatement. He'd had to grow up fast. "What's the saying…? The grass is always greener."

"I wouldn't have expected that kind of longing from you."

Of course she wouldn't. But this—he glanced

around the office—was never who he'd expected to be growing up. He'd dreamed about being a navy SEAL for as long as he could remember. Not the CEO of a skin-care company. "I'm sure there's something you wanted to be when you were growing up."

Becca nodded. "A vet. But I was a kid then. Very naive about how the world worked."

"Me, too," he said. "But that's what being a kid is all about. Dreaming of doing what sounds cool without understanding our places in the world."

"Too bad you couldn't trade jobs with your friend Ty for a week. Bet he'd enjoy hanging with supermodels while you swabbed decks on a ship or sub."

Caleb nearly laughed. An M4 rifle was more likely to be found in his best friend's hands, not a mop. Ty was one of the elite special ops guys, a navy SEAL, stationed in Virginia Beach on a Tier One team. Caleb would love a taste of Ty's life. "Fun idea, but I doubt I'd like swabbing decks."

"So you're more into adventure," she said. "Bet you'd like Special Forces kind of stuff. Best-of-the-best kind of thing."

Caleb didn't understand how she kept nailing him. He moved away from her. "What guy wouldn't?"

"Some might not, given the danger and risk involved, but I can see why it would appeal to you."

"Why is that?"

She tilted her chin. "The leadership skills you've honed as CEO would be useful even if the arena was different. Teamwork, too. No more profit margins, but life-or-death stakes. Kick-ass missions that would be more stressful than anything you've dealt with, but exciting due to the physical and mental challenges. You'd be surrounded by smart people. I'd assume someone who wasn't intelligent wouldn't last long, but in corporate America brainpower doesn't appear to be a prerequisite for rising to the top. At least here at Fair Face."

She might lack business experience, but she had what Grams would call gumption. "Not liking my grandmother's dog products doesn't mean employees here are stupid."

"Liking the products would prove they were smart." Becca stared at the photo of him and Ty again. "I think the real draw to your friend's lifestyle is loyalty. To the country, the service, your teammates. Heaven knows, you're loyal to your family."

Caleb couldn't move. Breathe. Blink.

How did she know this about him? A woman he'd known less than a week. One he'd underestimated.

"I suppose being in the navy would be more interesting work than sitting in meetings all day wondering what SPF of sunscreen would sell best," she added.

He found himself nodding.

"My only question is if joining the navy was so important to you, why didn't you enlist?" she asked.

"My family. Fair Face," he admitted. "They needed me."

"You wouldn't have been in the navy forever."

"No, but I was needed here. What I wanted to

do…" He glanced at the photograph of Ty and him. "It was secondary."

Her eyes softened. "You love your family."

"Everyone loves their family."

"Not everyone would sacrifice their dreams."

Caleb shrugged, but the last thing he felt was indifference. He rubbed the back of his neck. He didn't want to have this conversation. He glanced at his watch, more out of habit than anything else. "It's getting late. I'll walk you to your car."

"Thanks, but that's not necessary," she said, a hint of a tremor in her voice. "My car is at the Park & Ride lot. I rode the bus into downtown."

"You took the bus?"

"Gas is expensive."

His grandmother had to be paying her a bundle, plus providing a free place for her to stay. Not to mention her job at the animal hospital. "You can't have money trouble."

She glared at him.

Forget daggers—Becca was firing mortar in his direction.

He turned his hands palms up. "What?"

"I never said I couldn't afford it." Becca shot him a get-a-clue look. "Why should I want to waste my hard-earned cash to drive into town so you could try to get me fired?"

Stubborn. She also looked cute when she was angry. "Saving money is always good, especially when there's a motive or desire behind it. My grandfather taught me to save for a rainy day."

"Rain, thunderstorm, monsoon." Her fingers tightened around the strap of her messenger bag. "You never know what the future holds."

Caleb's life proved that was true.

"It's best to be prepared for anything." Well, almost anything. He hadn't been prepared for Becca. He should drive her home and see how deep her stubbornness ran. He shoved his laptop into his bag. "Come on, I'll walk you out."

CHAPTER SIX

WALKING ACROSS THE lobby of Fair Face's corporate headquarters, footsteps echoing on the tiled floor and questions swirling through her brain, Becca eyed the man next to her.

Caleb Fairchild looked like the perfect CEO in his gray suit—acted like one, too—but underneath the pinstripes was another man. A man who dreamed of adventure. A man who longed to serve his country. A man who sacrificed those dreams for his family.

Becca wondered if he ever let that side of himself show to anyone except his best friend. She would like to see it.

She'd been immune to pretty faces, charming smiles, killer eyes since the judge dropped the gavel in the courthouse in Twin Falls, Idaho. She went on occasional dates with working-class guys and cowboy types to have a little fun, but she always kept things casual. She was afraid of being burned again. She hadn't met anyone she'd wanted to get closer to. Getting closer to a guy made her vulnerable, a way she didn't like feeling.

Not that she wanted to get close to Caleb. But she

had to admit the guy interested her. In a way she hadn't been interested in...well, forever. That was...a problem.

Her parents had a great marriage in spite of their financial struggles. But Becca knew finding a man who could accept her and her past wasn't going to be easy. Maybe that was why she hadn't been looking too hard to find "the one."

They passed another employee who was staying late that evening. Caleb greeted him by name, the third in the past five minutes. "I hope you know how impressed we all were with those new label designs, Anthony. Great work."

The employee, an older man with gray hair and wire-rimmed glasses, walked away with a proud grin on his face and standing two inches taller.

"Do you know every single person who works here?" she asked.

"No, but everyone wears a badge," Caleb said. "That helps with the names."

Considerate of him, even though he'd accused her of trying to steal from Gertie. "The employees seem to appreciate your effort."

"They work hard." Caleb opened one of the double glass doors for her. "It's the least I can do."

"Thanks." His manners had impressed Becca the first time they'd met. She was impressed now in spite of his accusations. But she wouldn't allow herself to be taken in by him. Caleb Fairchild was no different from any other rich guy. She walked outside into bright daylight and stifling heat even though it was after seven at night. "The temperature hasn't dropped at all."

Two construction workers wearing paint splattered coveralls and carrying hard hats, walked toward them with tired smiles.

Caleb removed his suit jacket and draped it over his left arm. "Welcome to summer in Boise."

A fluorescent green food truck idled curbside with a line of customers waiting. The scent of garlic and rosemary filled the air. Becca's mouth watered. She stared at the plate of noodles and pork being dished up through the window.

"Hungry?" Caleb asked.

"A little." She hadn't eaten lunch. "Whatever they're cooking smells good."

"It does."

A siren wailed.

Goosebumps covered her skin in spite of the heat. She hated sirens. The sound brought back too many memories, memories she wanted to forget.

Hearing the handcuffs lock around her wrists. Being shoved into a police car. Feeling the heartbreak of betrayal.

Becca crossed her arms in front of her chest and forced herself to keep walking.

She wished she could forget. She wished others could forget, too. She wished people would trust her.

Not just people. A person. Caleb.

The realization disturbed her as much as the siren.

Caleb's opinion didn't matter. And if she kept telling herself that she might finally believe it.

Stop thinking about him!

The sound faded into the distance.

With a deep breath, she lowered her arms then pointed to a white sign about ten feet in front of them. "This is where I catch the bus."

Caleb looked around at the few people waiting. "Let me drive you to the Park & Ride lot. I can follow you back to Grams's place and we can have dinner."

Becca's breath caught in her throat. She opened her mouth to speak. No words came out. She tried again. "Thanks, but there's no need for you to go to so much trouble."

"I need to eat, too." He whipped out his cellphone. "I'll see if Grams has eaten or not."

Dinner with Gertie, not a date with Caleb.

Becca should be relieved, not disappointed. The guy had serious doubts about her. He was everything she didn't want in a man. He was likely asking her to make amends for making her come here tonight. Of course, she'd never said yes to either the ride or dinner.

Caleb flashed his phone, showing her a text exchange. "Mrs. Harrison was going to warm something up for Grams, but she would rather have pizza. Does salad and a pepperoni pizza with mushrooms sound good?"

"Sounds great." The words escaped before Becca could stop them. Darn, she knew better. On the bright side, Gertie would be thrilled to have her grandson there again and Becca wouldn't have to worry about making dinner tonight.

He typed on his phone. Messages pinged back and forth. "We're all set. Grams will have the pizza delivered."

Becca glanced at the bus stop, then looked at Caleb. "Back to Fair Face."

"My car is in the parking lot of the building next door," Caleb said.

"Gertie said there was parking available beneath Fair Face."

"There is."

This wasn't making sense. "Why aren't you parked there?"

"I prefer to let the employees and visitors use the closer spots."

Becca didn't want to be more impressed. She didn't want to like him, either. But she was. And she did in spite of a growing list of reasons she shouldn't. The guy took his responsibilities seriously.

She sneaked a peek at his profile. So handsome and strong and determined.

Maybe he took things too seriously.

A few minutes later, Caleb opened the door leading to a bank of elevators, blasting her with cool, refreshing air.

She stepped inside and waited for him to join her. "Please don't think you have to add me to your list."

"What list?"

"The list of people and things you have to take care of."

His eyes widened. His lips parted. Shock turned

to confusion followed by a blank expression. "What do you mean?"

Maybe he was better at poker than she thought. If Becca hadn't been paying attention, she would have missed the play of emotion across his face. "Seems like you're the one responsible for taking care of your grandmother, your sister, Fair Face and your employees. I wouldn't want you to think I need taking care of, too."

"I didn't think that," he said. "You seem capable of caring for yourself."

She nodded. "But it makes me wonder."

"What?"

"Who takes care of you?"

His eyes clouded. His posture stiffened. "I take care of myself. I also know Ty has my six."

"Your friend in the navy."

"Best friend," Caleb said.

"I wish I had a best friend like that."

"You don't?"

"I haven't had a best friend since I was in seventh grade." Cecily Parker had lived in the trailer park for six months. The best six months of Becca's childhood. She and Cecily did everything together—rode the school bus, ate lunch in the cafeteria, had sleepovers. "Her mom met some guy online and moved to Cincinnati. Never heard from my friend again."

"What stopped you from getting a new best friend?"

"No one wanted to be friends with the kid who lived in the trailer park."

"You don't live in a trailer now."

"No, but making friends is different when you're older."

"That's true."

But some things hadn't changed.

Becca hadn't spent the last few years trying to get her life back together to make the same mistake again with Caleb. He wasn't Whit, but Caleb was rich, handsome and powerful, the kind of man who could get away with anything. The kind of man who wouldn't think twice about breaking her heart.

She needed to be smart about this, about him.

She'd agreed to a ride and dinner, but that was all. He could advise them. Help them. But keeping her distance from him would be her smartest move. Even if that was the last thing she wanted to do.

After dinner, Caleb walked out onto his grandmother's patio. Becca Taylor intrigued him. He didn't need a PhD to realize she didn't want to spend one more minute in his company.

Her not saying a word on the drive to the Park & Ride lot had been his first clue. The way she'd sat at the opposite end of the table, as far away from him as possible, had been his second clue. The way she'd scarfed down her pizza and salad, as if a bomb was about to explode if she didn't eat fast enough, and excused herself without wanting dessert had been his third and fourth clues.

No other woman had been so blatant in their dislike of him.

A door opened behind him.

"I thought you were heading home," Grams said.

Him, too. But something had stopped him from leaving. Not something. Someone. "I thought I might check on Becca first."

"She seemed preoccupied over dinner," Grams said.

He felt responsible. "Telling me what happened wasn't easy for her."

"But she did."

"Becca was very open about it." More so than he would have been if he'd been the one asked to explain.

"Do you still think she's trying to fleece me?"

You still have doubts.

Earlier this evening, the hurt in Becca's voice had sliced through him, raw and jagged and deep. But she was correct. He still had doubts. Becca was a stranger, an unknown quantity.

"People have ulterior motives and hidden agendas." Both his ex-fiancée and his mother, the definition of a gold digger, had had them. "That's human nature."

"Becca wouldn't hurt me or anybody."

Caleb wished he had Grams's confidence. But that was a lesson he should have learned from his father's mistakes. Instead, it had taken Cassandra to teach him that trust was something to be earned, not given freely to a stranger. "Maybe I'll feel that way after I get to know Becca better."

Though she knew him well enough. She understood him better than his family. Better than Cassandra. Better than everybody else in his life with the exception of Ty.

That bothered Caleb. If the wrong people knew too much, they could use that to their advantage. They could hurt you.

"I'm sure you will." Grams touched his arm. "It's getting late. Check on Becca, then head home."

"Will do." He hugged his grandmother. "And before I forget, thanks for the pizza and the cake."

Grams beamed. "This is your home. You're welcome anytime."

Being here brought back good memories and feelings of contentment. "Thanks."

Caleb followed the lighted path away from the patio. Stars filled the dark sky. Satellites circled above. The moon hung low.

A beautiful night. One he would have been spending alone in his loft working if not for Becca. Sure, he could have seen the sky from the twenty-foot windows, but he much preferred being here.

A cry filled the air. Not a human. A dog. In pain.

Adrenaline surged. Caleb broke into a run.

Becca.

The moans continued. Barking from other dogs, too.

Caleb knew it was a dog hurting, but his heart pounded against his ribs.

What if he was wrong? What if she was hurt?

He quickened his pace, his breath coming hard and fast.

Only the porch light was on at the guest cottage. He continued to the kennel.

The door was open, the lights on.

He ran inside.

Dogs stood at the front of their kennels barking and agitated.

He glanced around.

Becca sat on the floor, her legs extended. A stethoscope hung around her neck. She wore an ivory-colored lace-trimmed camisole that stretched across her chest. Her suit jacket covered the dog lying across her lap. The animal was the one who'd shed all over Caleb.

What was the dog's name? Morris?

No, Maurice. The Norwegian elkhound.

Caleb kneeled at Becca's side. Touched her bare shoulder. Ignored her soft skin and warmth beneath his hand. "What's going on?"

"Maurice." She rubbed the dog. "His stomach is distended. He's gassy and in pain."

The dog looked miserable. The other dogs wouldn't stop barking. Maurice wouldn't move.

"Is it serious?" Caleb asked.

"I don't know. I'm not sure what's wrong," she said. "The staff only uses products Gertie's made or approved, so I'm not worried about chemical poisoning. But if Maurice ate too much, there's the risk of bloat. His stomach could flip. Elkhounds aren't as prone as other breeds, but his pulse is high. Heart rate, too. I gave Gertie a call, but she didn't answer."

"She was on the patio with me."

"I'm going to take Maurice to the animal hospital where I work. I'd rather not take any chances."

Becca spoke calmly and in control, but worry filmed her eyes. He wanted to kiss it away. Hell, he wanted to make the poor dog feel better, too. "I'll let my grandmother know."

About to reach for his cellphone, Caleb realized he was still touching Becca's shoulder. He hadn't noticed. The gesture felt so natural, so right. Maybe because she was so different from other women he'd known, especially Cassandra. Maybe that was why Becca felt...safe. He lowered his arm then pulled out his phone.

"Tell Gertie not to worry," Becca said. "The door to the food cabinet door was ajar. Maurice might have gotten into there and gorged himself on whatever he found."

The dog released a groan that sounded as if someone was rolling his innards through a pasta machine.

The other dogs barked. Two howled.

Becca made soothing sounds and kept rubbing Maurice. "I bet you got into the food. Is that what happened, boy?"

The dog's gaze didn't leave hers.

Caleb thought that was one smart dog. Well, except for overeating.

"It's okay," Becca said. "You're not in trouble. Not at all."

Her soft voice was like a caress against Caleb's face, even though the words were for the dog's sake, he wished they were for him.

"You're going to have to go to the vet." She kissed Maurice's head. "You won't like that, but I'll be with you."

Caleb touched the dog. "I'll drive you."

"Thanks, but I've got a crate in the backseat. I need to move my car closer to make things easier on Maurice."

"I'll stay here with him while you do that."

"He'll shed on you."

"It's only dog hair," Caleb said. "And you have a lint roller."

The corners of her mouth curved in an appreciative smile. She stood. "Thanks. Be right back."

He took her place. The dog didn't seem to mind.

"It's okay, boy." He rubbed Maurice's head. "You're in good hands. Becca's going to take care of you."

Two brown, sad eyes met Caleb's. The look of total trust and affection sent the air rushing from his lungs. It was as if the dog understood.

Maybe Maurice did.

Caleb took a breath then leaned over so he could whisper in the dog's ear. "You're one lucky dog. I wish Becca liked me half as much as she cares for you."

But she didn't and wouldn't.

For the best, he told himself.

Too bad a part of him wasn't so sure.

Becca parked outside the kennel, left the engine idling then opened the car's back door.

Maurice was going to be fine. Just fine.

Repeating the words over and over again, she ran to the kennel.

If anything, she was wasting her time, gas and Gertie's money. Becca would be happy to waste all three as long as Maurice was okay.

She entered the kennel. Froze.

Caleb sat on the floor, in his designer suit, with Maurice's head resting on his lap. He rubbed the dog, talking in a soft voice.

Her mouth went dry.

The tenderness in Caleb's eyes as he stared at the dog sent Becca's heart thudding.

Her pulse rate kicked up a notch, maybe two.

Wait a minute. This was the same man who didn't trust her, who didn't like her, who wanted her fired.

But she couldn't help herself. He'd cranked up the charm without even realizing the affect this would have on her. Best to dial that down ASAP.

She cleared her throat. "How's he doing?"

"Not feeling too well, are you, boy?"

The sweet way Caleb spoke to the dog tugged at her heartstrings. Ignore it. Him. "Thank you for sitting with him. I can put him in his crate now."

Before Becca blinked, Caleb was on his feet. He picked up the dog easily, helping out both her and Maurice. "I'll carry him."

At the car, they loaded Maurice into the crate. She double-checked the latch to make sure it was secure. All set.

Caleb opened the driver's door.

"I appreciate your help." She hadn't known what to expect from Caleb, but his assistance with Maurice hadn't been it. "Tell Gertie I'll call as soon as I know anything."

"I'll check on the other dogs, then wait with Grams until you call. She wants to go with you."

"It could be a long night."

"That's what I figured," he said. "She opened the food cupboard to get dog treats earlier. She feels awful for not double checking the door was shut."

"Tell her not to worry. We'll get Maurice fixed right up."

"If not…"

"Let's not go there."

Their gazes met. Held. The same connection she'd felt the first day they'd met. But this wasn't the time to analyze things. Not with Maurice in pain.

Caleb kissed her cheek.

More of a peck, if she wanted to be technical, a brush of his lips over her skin. But her heart pounded. Warmth rushed through her.

"For luck," he said.

Becca resisted the impulse to kiss him back, only hard on the lips. She couldn't afford the distraction. Maurice needed her. She forced herself into the driver's seat then buckled her seat belt.

This wasn't the time or the place for more kisses. Most importantly this wasn't the man she should be kissing.

Not tonight. Not tomorrow night. Not ever.

* * *

Four hours later, Becca pulled into the guest cottage's driveway. Every muscle ached from tiredness. Her eyelids wanted to close. But she wasn't going to sleep much tonight.

Not when she needed to watch Maurice.

She glanced in the rearview mirror. "We're home, handsome."

The dog didn't make a sound. He must be exhausted after all the tests and X-rays. Not to mention his stomachache.

Becca grabbed her purse, exited the car and locked the door.

"Want a hand?"

Caleb.

He walked toward her, silhouetted by the porch light. He'd removed his jacket and tie, undone two buttons at the top of his shirt and rolled up his sleeves.

Her heart stumbled. "You're still here."

"I didn't want to leave Grams alone."

Becca wished she'd been the reason. Pathetic. But she was pleased Caleb realized the difference between live-in staff and her grandson. "I hope she's not awake."

"She went to bed after you called."

"You should have gone home."

"It's fine." He spoke as if staying up half the night was no big deal. Maybe not for him, but she appreciated it. "Too bad the dog gorged himself on so many treats."

She nodded. "You should have seen the X-rays. Half his tummy was full."

"Last time he'll do that."

"Oh, no. He'll do it again if given the chance." Becca opened the crate's door. "Elkhounds will eat until they make themselves sick. They are food fiends. I knew something was wrong when he wouldn't eat his dinner."

Maurice lumbered out of the car as if each step hurt.

"Poor boy." Caleb picked up the dog. "Where do you want him?"

"On my bed," she said. "He's sleeping with me tonight."

"You really are a lucky dog."

Becca's cheeks heated. She was relieved for the darkness so Caleb couldn't see she'd blushed. "Not that lucky, considering the diet he'll be going on to get ready for the show this weekend."

Caleb was supposed to go, but he hadn't mentioned anything. Maybe he'd changed his mind.

She hoped not.

Wait a minute. That wasn't right. She didn't want him to go.

The cottage door was unlocked. She followed Caleb through the living room and into the bedroom. A sheet covered the comforter. Dogs spent so much time in here that cut down on her having to do laundry.

He gently set the dog on the bed. "Here you go, lucky dog."

"Thanks." She straightened the sheet then rubbed Maurice. "You should go. It's late."

Caleb's gaze narrowed on her. "You're exhausted."

"Long day. I'll sleep in a little while." She glanced at the dog who had curled up on her side of the bed. "I want to make sure he doesn't take a turn for the worse."

"Take a nap. I'll watch him."

A nap would be great, but she couldn't impose on Caleb. "That's nice of you to offer, but it's too late. You have to be at work in the morning."

"I'm the CEO," he said. "Grams won't complain if I show up late."

"This is *my* job."

Caleb tucked a strand of hair behind her ear.

A tremble ran through Becca. She didn't want to react to him, but couldn't help herself. He had a strange effect on her.

"It's mine tonight," he said.

A part of her wanted to let him take over, to not have to do everything herself tonight. She'd been on her own for so long with only herself to depend upon. But she couldn't...

Not when Caleb took care of so many others.

She raised her chin. "I'm not your responsibility."

"No, but how about we say you and Maurice are for the next couple of hours?"

The beat of her heart matched the quickening of her pulse. "You're making it hard for me not to like you."

His eyebrows wagged. "There's a lot to like."

His lighthearted tone made her smile. Something she hadn't thought possible at this late—make that early—hour. "Maybe, but it's hard to tell with dog hair all over you."

His mouth quirked. "You're covered in dog hair, too."

Becca didn't have to look to know it was true. "I'm always covered in dog hair."

"Grab some clothes." He kicked off his leather shoes. "Get comfortable on the couch."

"This is my bedroom."

"Not tonight." He crawled into bed with Maurice. The dog moved closer to him. "The boys have taken over."

"Are you always this bossy?" she asked.

"Yes," he said. "Get some sleep. Us boys will be fine. Won't we, Maurice?"

As if on cue, the dog licked Caleb's hand.

"See," he said.

Becca stared at him with a tingly feeling in her stomach. Funny—or maybe not so funny—but she could get used to "the boys" being here.

CHAPTER SEVEN

THLURP.

What was that? Caleb opened his eyes. Daylight filled the room. A mass of black and grey fur stood over him.

Thlurp.

A tongue licked his cheek.

He bolted upright.

Maurice's moist nose and his warm, smelly mouth were right in Caleb's face.

"Morning breath is one thing." Caleb turned away. "But yours is toxic."

The dog panted, looking pleased.

"At least you're up and about," Caleb said. "You must feel better."

Maurice stood on top of him. His paws pressed into Caleb's thighs.

"You're too big to be a lap dog."

The dog didn't listen. He plopped down, making himself at home on top of Caleb's legs.

"Okay," he relented. "You can sit here for a minute. But no longer."

"Are the boys having trouble this morning?" Becca asked.

The sound of her voice brightened his day like the first rays of sunshine through the window.

Caleb peered around the dog to see Becca standing at the foot of the bed.

She wore a pair of striped fleece pants and a tie-dyed ribbed tank top. Her hair was messy, as if she'd crawled out of bed or in her case, off the couch. Totally hot.

Waking up to Becca licking his face would have been much better. Too bad she couldn't join Caleb in bed now. He wasn't in the market for a relationship, but a fling would be fine. Fun.

Becca yawned, stretching her hands overhead.

His gaze shot to her chest, rising with her arm movement.

"You didn't wake me," she said.

He was staring. Gawking at her breasts. Not good. He looked at her face. "You were tired."

"So were you."

He'd checked on her in the middle of the night. She'd looked so peaceful with a slight smile on her face. He'd thought how appealing inviting her into bed with him would be. He'd imagined carrying her to bed. But that had bad idea written all over it. So he'd covered her with the blanket she'd kicked off and returned to bed with Maurice. "I wasn't."

"You stayed up all night."

"Not all night." Caleb's gaze kept straying to her tank top. "Once Maurice settled down, I dozed."

Becca moved closer.

The scent of her filled Caleb's nostrils. Wanting more, he breathed in deeper this time.

She touched the dog, leaning into him. Her hand brushed Caleb's thigh, sending shivery sparks up his leg.

"He looks better this morning," she said. "I'll take him outside."

"I took him outside around three."

Her lips parted, full and soft and kissable. If not for the dead weight on his lap, he would have tried to kiss her.

"I didn't hear you," she said.

"We were quiet." He glanced at the digital clock on the nightstand. "It's only five-thirty. Go back to bed."

"You're in my bed."

A sensual awareness buzzed between them.

A comfortable queen-size bed. A beautiful woman. A couple hours to kill until he was due at the office. This was looking pretty good.

"I'll scoot over. Maurice won't mind." Caleb moved closer to the far edge. It would be better if Maurice gave up his turn on the bed and went to the couch, but the dog didn't seem like the selfless type. Becca had that role locked up.

She watched him.

"The dog's on my side." Caleb kept his tone light, half-joking so he wouldn't scare her off. He patted the empty spot on the mattress. "Plenty of room for you now."

Her gaze shifted from him to the bed. "Better be careful, who you invite into bed, Mr. Fairchild."

"It's your bed."

"Then you should be even more careful. You wouldn't want to give away any corporate secrets over pillow talk."

He grinned. "Who said anything about talking?"

"You're full of surprises this morning."

He would be happy to surprise her more. All he needed was the opportunity and an invitation. "You're seeing only what you want to see."

"I'm seeing a pot and a kettle. Which one are you?" Amusement twinkled in her eyes. "I'd say the pot. But I suppose it doesn't matter, since they're both black."

Damn. Caleb shouldn't be so attracted to her. This went deeper than her looks. She challenged him, kept him on his toes. He liked that.

His ex-fiancée had always tried to suck up and sweet-talk him. Most women went along with him, rarely disagreed, as if he wanted a yes-woman instead of someone who spoke her mind and pushed his buttons.

Not that he wanted a woman. But he'd take this one for the morning. Hell, he'd stretch it to lunchtime if she were game. "That makes you the kettle."

"Works for me," she said. "I love kettle corn."

What was it about Becca Taylor that could get him turned on talking about cookware and popcorn?

Keeping his distance was the smart course of action if he wanted to avoid a complicated and messy situation. But leaving Becca's bed, especially if there was any chance of her climbing in it, didn't appeal to him in the slightest.

A fling would be fun. Easy. Safe.

And then Caleb remembered where he was....

The guest cottage at his grandmother's estate. With Grams's employee. His advisee.

A woman who made it hard to think straight when he was around her. A woman who knew too much about him. A woman who was the definition of dangerous.

Alarm bells sounded in his head. Maybe not so safe.

"It's all yours." Caleb moved the dog then slid off the bed. "I have to go."

"Okay." Becca bit her lip. "Thanks. Again. For, um, everything."

She looked as confused as he felt.

No matter. Time to get out of here before he changed his mind and did something really stupid, like trying to kiss the confusion out of her eyes.

Caleb patted the dog then slipped on his shoes. He tried to ignore how sexy Becca looked right now. "I need to put in extra hours at Fair Face with the dog show this weekend."

"You don't have to go." The words rushed out of her mouth faster than the rapids on the Snake River. "I can handle the show on my own."

She didn't want him to go. "I know, but I want to see about the products and my grandmother wants me there."

"Gertie is a worrywart when it comes to her dogs."

And when it came to Becca, too. Caleb was torn. As appealing as a weekend away from work sounded, spending more time alone with Becca wasn't smart. But he couldn't forget about his grandmother's wishes. "I'd rather not disappoint Grams."

"Gertie will understand if you're busy and have other plans." Becca's mouth tightened. "Say a date or something."

She'd baited the hook and cast the line. He didn't mind biting, if only to see her reaction and appeasing her curiosity about his going out with anyone. "No date. Work."

The lines around her mouth disappeared. "It's not a problem if you stay in Boise. Really."

"Well, since you don't mind…"

"I don't."

"I'll talk to Grams."

"Do."

She seemed too adamant about his not going. Maybe he'd misread her curiosity. Maybe she didn't want him to go to see what she'd be up to at the dog show. "I won't be around as much the next few days, possibly the entire week."

"Good. I mean…it'll be good to have time away. At Fair Face."

Becca sounded nervous. Flustered. She seemed so natural and unstudied and artless. Maybe he hadn't misread her after all.

A smile tugged at his lips. "Call me if you have any questions about the business plan."

"Will do. Thanks again for taking care of Maurice."

As if on cue, the dog jumped off the bed. He nudged Becca's hand with his nose so she'd give him attention.

Too bad that trick didn't work for Caleb. "You're welcome."

She bit her lip again. "You were on your way out?"

"Yes." Caleb grabbed his jacket and forced his feet to move in the direction of the front door. He'd better get going or he could end up staying here all morning. "Have a great day."

"Wait," she called out.

He stopped, hoping she was going to ask him to stay. A long shot, but this was as good a day as any to try being an optimist.

Becca handed him a lint roller. "Take this."

This was the last thing he expected. So much for optimism. Caleb laughed. "You need it."

"I have more than one, including two in my car."

"Always prepared."

"I never want to find myself unprepared again."

"I feel the same." He wasn't prepared for how much he wanted to stay with her now. Time to put some distance between him and the oh-so-appealing Becca Taylor "If I don't talk to you before the weekend, good luck at the dog show."

More than once after Caleb left the guest cottage, Becca picked up her cellphone to call Caleb. More than once she put away her cellphone.

That afternoon, she worked with Dozer on obedience training. The little guy needed to learn to behave and obey if he was ever going to find a forever home. Gertie would adopt him before sending him to live at the rescue shelter, but she and Becca agreed he'd do better with a family.

"Sit."

The dog sat.

"Stay."

She walked to the end of the leash, approximately six feet away, and hit the timer on her cellphone.

Dozer remained in place. Now to see if he sat for the full sixty seconds, a long sit in obedience training.

The seconds ticked off.

Becca wondered what Caleb was doing. He'd been on her mind since he'd left. She had questions about the business plan. As soon as she figured out one thing, that raised a bunch more questions. But she could find the answers herself if she searched online. The reason she wanted to call Caleb was to hear his voice.

Pathetic.

Hadn't she learned anything?

Even if Caleb was handsome, polite, hardworking, liked dogs, getting involved, at whatever level, with a man who had money was a bad idea. Like dumping water on an oil fire. Explosive. She'd been burned once. No reason to repeat that experiment.

Stop thinking about him.

Becca needed to forget about Caleb and focus on getting ready to leave for the dog show on Thursday. She'd gotten her wish. She was going alone. If she needed a hand with the dogs, she could ask one of the Junior Showmanship kids to help her. Most of them were eager to help and learn more. She'd been that way.

Dozer rose to all fours and trotted toward her, as happy as a dog could be.

She glanced at the stopwatch. Forty-five seconds. Fifteen seconds too short. She gave him a pat. "We'll have to try this again.

Her cellphone buzzed. A new text message arrived. She glanced at the screen. From Caleb. Her hands tightened around the phone with excitement.

How's Maurice?

A ball of heat ignited deep within Becca. Caleb might have some faults, but he cared about the elkhound. She typed out a quick reply.

Good as new. Hungry again.

Maybe Caleb would find some spare time to stop by to see the dog. Maurice would like that. She would, too.

Becca waited for a reply. And waited. And waited.

She didn't hear from him. No texts. No phone calls. Nothing.

Tuesday gave way to Wednesday. Becca packed her suitcase and readied the RV for the trip to Central Oregon.

She tried not to think about Caleb. Or ask Gertie if she'd heard from him. He'd told Becca he wasn't going and would be busy. No. Big. Deal.

Thursday arrived. She packed everything she needed for the next three days in the RV.

Gertie said goodbye to each dog. "Don't cause Becca any trouble."

"They'll be fine," she said.

Gertie hugged her. The woman smelled like flowers and sunshine and the color pink. "Call me when you get there."

Becca loaded the dogs into their crates. "I will."

"I'm sorry you have to go alone."

"Caleb's a busy man." That was what she kept telling herself.

Concern filled Gertie's gaze. "Too busy. He's going to wake up one day and not have anything to show for it."

Becca thought a huge checking account balance would show for a lot, but she'd never had any money so what did she know?

Having so much responsibility thrust upon him at a young age had to have taken its toll. She wasn't going to add to his burdens. "Caleb will figure things out when he's ready. He's been spending more time with you."

"Last week, yes. This week, not so much. But you're right. Any time is an improvement. I just wish…"

"What?"

"I hate to think of you being alone this weekend."

"I'm not alone. I have the dogs to keep me company," Becca said. "I'll be fine."

The worry from Gertie's eyes didn't disappear. "I know. You're quite capable, but humor an old woman."

Becca's parents loved her. But they didn't have the luxury to sit around and worry about her the way Gertie did. Becca had been on her own from a young age because they'd worked multiple jobs. Knowing Gertie cared so much gave Becca a true sense of belonging. Something she hadn't found outside the trailer park or dog shows or the animal clinic where she worked. "How about I text you each time I stop to let the dogs out? I'll let you know what's going on during the show, too."

Gertie's features relaxed. "That would make me feel better."

Now, if Becca could stop thinking about Caleb and what he would be doing while she was away, she might feel better, too.

What the hell was Caleb doing here?

He glanced around the fairgrounds in Redmond, Oregon. White fenced outdoor show rings, dogs of every color and size, bright sunshine and green grass.

He was supposed to be working today, Saturday, not at a dog show. But Grams had said between showing the dogs and passing out samples of their dog products Becca had sounded exhausted and she still had two more days to go.

Caleb was responsible for so much. Now he had to take on his grandmother's dog consultant?

He could have said no to Grams insisting he attend. He could have sent someone else. But he'd wanted to see Becca.

If only Caleb could find her among the RVs, dogs, crates, grooming tables, rings and people. He'd tried calling and texting her, but couldn't reach her. He walked along the row of show rings.

On his left, vendors sold everything from dog-imprinted tea towels to doggy massage services. One booth had a dog treadmill for owners who couldn't—didn't want to, perhaps?—take their animals for a walk. People passed out samples of food and treats. Seeing all these products first hand made one thing clear...Grams's skin care line didn't stand a chance against all the edible wares and dog-inspired tchotchkes.

He didn't see Becca anywhere.

Women and men dressed in business attire scurried around with combs, brushes, spray bottles and raced from the grooming stands to the ten show rings set up at the county fairgrounds.

Two big dogs barked at a group of smaller black-and-white papillions. Others from the show ring next to them joined in. Annoying, but they were dogs. Dogs barked and shed.

Outside the fenced area of Ring Six stood Becca. She wore a lime-green suit that showed off her curves nicely. She looked professional, as she had in his office on Monday night. But today she appeared more confident.

A puff of white stood at her side. Snowy must have spent his morning being bathed and primped to look like a cotton ball.

He walked toward her. Snowy saw him first and barked.

Becca turned. Smiled.

Her eyes widened. Twinkled.

Caleb's heart slammed against his ribs. He hadn't expected her to be so excited to see him. He'd thought she wanted him to be at the show, but her reaction told him otherwise. Maybe coming here hadn't been such a waste of time. "Hello."

"What are you doing here?" she asked, a breathless quality to her voice.

"Gertie said you sounded exhausted on the phone last night."

"What?"

"Grams said you were totally overwhelmed passing out samples and showing dogs and needed help."

Becca inhaled sharply. "So she sent you to the rescue."

He gave a mock bow. "At your service, milady."

"Thanks, but I have no idea why Gertie said what she did. I'm not overwhelmed or tired. Things are going well. I've passed out samples and feedback fliers. The interest has been high. Eighty percent of the people I've spoken with have taken the packages. I only have a few left."

"Then why am I here?" Though seeing Becca felt

good. Thoughts of her had distracted him all week. He'd forced himself not to call her each day.

Becca scrunched her nose. "Gertie must have a reason."

But what? Grams never did anything without a reason. Well, except shopping. "Did my grandmother say anything to you?"

"Just that she hated the thought of my being here alone."

Alone. Alone. Alone.

The word echoed in his mind.

She didn't want Becca alone. Grams didn't want Caleb alone. She wanted them…

Together.

That would explain everything going on recently. "My grandmother's up to her old tricks."

"That's a relief," Becca said. "For a minute I was worried Gertie didn't trust me."

"That's not the case at all."

"So what's going on?

"Matchmaking."

"Matchmaking?" Lines creased Becca's forehead. Her mouth gaped. "With us?"

"It's the only thing that makes sense."

"I really don't think—"

"Can you come up with a better reason?"

"I…Well…" The startled look in her eyes matched the way he felt. "No, I can't."

"Grams has been vocal about wanting great-grand-children, but I never thought she'd stoop to match-making." Caleb had to give Grams credit. She'd picked a woman who was the polar opposite of Cassandra. "But she created a line of baby products, so who knows how far she'd go?"

Snowy pulled away to sniff a small terrier, but Becca tugged on the leash stopping him.

"I don't think Gertie is playing matchmaker." Becca motioned to herself. "I'm not corporate trophy wife material."

Caleb took a long, hard look. "Don't sell yourself short. I like what I see."

"I'm not talking physical appearance." Her mouth slanted. "Imagine me schmoozing at a client party. Think about my past. I'm not the kind of woman you take home to meet your mother."

"My grandmother thinks you're amazing."

Becca straightened. A satisfied smile lit her face. "The feeling's mutual. But your grandmother is a special person."

"That's true." Becca's lack of pretense was far more appealing than the pretentious poise of his ex-fiancée and mother. "But you should know you're in a class so high above my mother it's not even funny."

Becca gave him a confused look. "Gertie said your mother died."

"She did, but if she were alive I would never want to introduce you to her. My mother married my father for his money. She ran off with her personal trainer. Once the divorce was finalized, we never saw or heard from her again."

Becca touched his arm. "What a horrible thing for a mother to do to her kids."

He shrugged. "Even before my mother deserted us, my grandparents were the ones raising us. It was them or a team of nannies."

"Sounds like you were better off with your grandparents."

He nodded, but this conversation was getting too personal. He'd never told anyone except Ty about his mom. Caleb wasn't sure why he'd shared the story with Becca. Maybe because she'd been so self-deprecating when she shouldn't have been. She was also easy to talk with.

Dogs continued barking. People milled about. Applause filled Ring Seven.

"When do you go?" he asked, changing the subject.

"After the Tibetan terriers."

"Snowy looks like a puffball."

"It takes time for him to be whitened, washed, volumized, combed, teased and sprayed."

"Do you do that with every dog?"

"Each breed is different," she said. "I have a schedule. I know who to work on when. Snowy's grooming is intensive, but he loves going in the ring, so he's more patient than some others. Maurice hates being on the grooming table. Blue doesn't mind it much."

A man in a suit and red striped tie approached. "Rebecca, isn't it?"

She nodded. "Hi, Dennis."

Caleb moved closer to her, unsure who this fellow was or why he seemed so interested in Becca.

Dennis smiled. "Nice job with the elkhound this morning. I thought you'd get Best of Breed."

"Thanks, but Gertie's happy with Select," Becca said. "This is Gertie's grandson, Caleb Fairchild."

"I'm Dennis Johnson." The man shook his hand, then looked right back at Becca. "Nice looking bichon. What products are you using on him?"

"Prototypes Gertie developed using all-natural, organic ingredients. I've been using them on all her dogs." Becca didn't miss a beat. "Would you like samples to try?"

The man looked as if he'd hit three sevens on a slot machine. "Yes, please."

"Find me at my RV. I have a package with the products and a form for you to give us your feedback."

"I'll be by later," the man said. "Good luck in the ring."

Caleb found the exchange interesting. The man recognized something different about the products Becca was using on her dogs. "Giving away samples with a feedback form is a good start, but maybe a little soon since you're not ready to manufacture products."

"Not on a large scale. But we can do something smaller in the interim."

"Sounds like Grams talking."

Becca nodded. "She's eager."

"More like a runaway train."

Which was why Grams playing matchmaker would mean trouble. Not only for Caleb, but Becca.

A woman in a purple apron walked past at a fast clip with an angry expression on her face. "That bitch didn't want to free stack."

Caleb waited for the woman to pass then looked at Becca. "That's…"

"Dog speak." Laughter filled her bright eyes. "I'm assuming you know that a bitch is a female dog. Stack means placing a dog in a position that shows off the breed standards. Hand stacking is when a handler manually positions the dog's paws. Free stacking is when the handler uses bait, calls or signs to get the dog to position himself."

Dog showing didn't only have it's own vocabulary. A sociologist could have a field day studying these people and their interactions with each other and their dogs. But this was the most comfortable he'd ever seen Becca. Except at the kennel.

She adjusted the chain collar around Snowy's neck. "It's our turn."

A tall, thin man with a beard and in a three-piece suit called her number. Becca entered the ring with the dog. Three other handlers and their dogs, replicas of powder puff Snowy, followed them. The judge studied each of the dogs.

The dogs all looked the same to Caleb, but he couldn't take his eyes off Becca. She ran around the ring with Snowy, then positioned him in front of the judge. Caleb assumed that was hand stacking. They ran diagonally across the ring and back. One by one the other handlers did the same until all circled the ring in a line once again.

The judge pointed. Snowy won and was awarded a ribbon.

A few minutes later, Becca and Snowy returned to

the ring and went through the same routine. Snowy was named Best of Breed, BOB for short, and Becca received a large ribbon.

Becca skipped out of the ring. "Gertie is going to be thrilled. I need to get Snowy in his crate so he can rest before Group, then I'll call…"

Caleb didn't know why her voice trailed off. "What?"

"Would you mind holding Snowy for a minute?"

He had no idea what was going on, but took Snowy's lead, a black leather leash with silver beads.

Becca walked twenty feet away to a little girl, who looked to be around seven or eight. The child sat on a folding chair. She held the leash of an Irish setter puppy with both hands and wiped tears from her face with her arm.

"Hello, I'm Becca." She knelt at the girl's side and put her hand in front of the dog nose. "What's your name?"

"Gianna."

"You have a pretty dog."

Gianna hiccupped. "Thank you."

Caleb had no idea what Becca was doing, but moved closer so he could find out.

The dog sniffed her hand. "What's your puppy's name?"

"P-Princess."

"Is Princess going to be shown today?"

"No." Gianna sniffled. "My mommy twisted her ankle, so can't show her. This would've been Princess's first time in the ring."

Becca looked around. "Where is your mommy?"

"Getting ice for her foot."

"When your mom gets back, why don't we ask if she'd let me show Princess for you."

Gianna's tears stopped flowing. Her mouth formed a perfect O. "You're a handler?"

Becca petted the dog, and Gianna scooted closer to her. "I'm a dog handler and I'd be happy to show Princess."

Caleb knew Becca had a full schedule, especially with Snowy continuing on, yet she wanted to help this little girl.

Becca's action filled him with warmth. How many people had walked past the crying child without noticing or pretending not to see her? But she'd done something about it. The woman was...special. He couldn't believe he'd doubted her motivations and accused her of being a scam artist.

A thirtysomething woman with her hair in a bun and wearing a purple suit hobbled toward them. She carried a plastic bag full of ice. "Gianna?"

The girl leaped out of her chair. She bounced from foot to foot, her ponytails flying up and down. "Mommy, Mommy, this lady can show Princess for us. She's a handler."

Becca rose and held out her hand. "My name is Becca Taylor. Your daughter told me about your ankle. I'd be happy to show your puppy for you."

"Oh, thanks." The woman's gaze flitted from Becca to her daughter and the dog. "That's nice of you to offer, but I can't afford to pay for a handler."

"No charge," Becca said without any hesitation. "I wouldn't want Princess to miss her first time in the ring."

Caleb's chest tightened, a mix of affection and respect, at her generosity. One more attribute to add to Becca's growing list. But she wasn't being a smart businesswoman, given her first priorities were Grams's dogs and the product samples. He assumed Grams wouldn't mind, given her kind heart, but even if she did, Caleb wasn't about to say a word. Becca was doing exactly the right thing.

Gianna tugged at her mother's arm. "Please, Mommy. Please, oh, please, oh please."

The woman looked stunned. Relief quickly took over. "Th-that would be great. Thank you."

Becca glanced back at Caleb. "Do you mind holding unto Snowy a little longer so I can work with Princess?"

"Happy to." He would do whatever she asked. She was so genuine he wanted to help her, not make things harder. "I'll put him into his crate."

"That would be great."

"Come on, Snowy." If Caleb hurried, he might make it back to watch her in the ring. "I don't want to miss this."

But whether Becca Taylor was in the ring or out of it, she was a very special woman. There was no other place he'd rather be this weekend than right here with her.

CHAPTER EIGHT

Becca stood outside the ring where Best in Show, aka BIS, would be held in a few minutes. She wiggled her toes inside her black flats. The dogs, including Princess, had all placed in their events and Snowy had won his group. The buzz surrounding Gertie's dog-care samples kept increasing. Gertie was beside herself with pride. Win or lose in the next few minutes, the day couldn't get much better.

"You look so calm and cool." Caleb stood next to Becca. "Not the least bit nervous."

She glanced his way. Her stomach did a somersault. She was so happy he was here.

"I'm more excited than anything else." Becca wanted to pinch herself to make sure her eyes were open and she wasn't dreaming. She adjusted Snowy's lead in her hand. "No matter how Snowy does, we've already won. People are very interested in Gertie's new line of dog products."

"It can't hurt your reputation, either."

"Or Snowy's. He's on his way to Grand Champion," she said. "But he's never won BIS."

"Today could be the day."

Caleb's words, spoken with sincerity, pierced her heart like an arrow. She double-checked Snowy to make sure he looked his best, then rerolled his lead. "I hope so."

"Good luck." The tender look in his eyes made her feel as if they were the only two people at the fairground. Her breath caught. Her temperature rose. "Not that you need luck."

Her heart melted. If only he'd wished her luck with a kiss the way he had when she took Maurice to the vet on Monday night.

Caleb's gaze lingered, tenderness turning to something resembling desire.

Her pulse skittered. He might want to kiss her again.

Please, oh, please. She realized she was acting like a little girl, like Gianna.

Becca didn't care. She parted her lips, in case he was looking for an invitation.

Then she realized…they weren't alone. Hundreds of people stood and sat ringside, many who knew Gertie. Going down this path with Caleb was fruitless and dangerous. He might have decided Becca wasn't a scam artist, but a kiss would mean nothing to him. A kiss would mean more to her. Kissing him, even if she might want that, wasn't right or smart or even sane.

She was about to go in for Best of Breed. She needed to concentrate on Snowy, not think about Caleb.

Becca pressed her lips together.

The ring steward announced the competition.

She took a deep breath and raised her chin.

"You're going to kill them," Caleb whispered, his warm breath against her ear. "No one stands a chance against you and Snowy."

His words provided an extra jolt of confidence. Not needed, but nice. Very nice, actually.

She fell in line with the six other handlers and their dogs.

With a grateful smile in his direction, Becca squared her shoulders, then stepped into the ring with Snowy.

It was show time!

Best in Show!

Snowy—registered name White Christmas in Sunny July—had been awarded Best in Show.

Pride flowed through Caleb. His chest expanded with each breath. A satisfied smile settled on his lips.

The crowd applauded and cheered.

He videotaped the award ceremony. Snowy pranced around as if he knew he was top dog, but Becca's wide smile and joy-filled eyes defined the moment for Caleb. A photographer snapped official winner pictures with the judge. Handlers shook Becca's hand. She juggled the gift basket, flowers and three feet long ribbon she'd been awarded.

Caleb stood back, away from the entrance to the ring, and waited. He wanted to watch Becca savor the win.

People congratulated her on the way out of the

ring, but she gave all the credit to Snowy, who soaked up the attention as if he knew he'd be getting extra doggy treats tonight. Little Gianna and her mom hugged Becca.

The crowd dispersed.

Becca made her way to him, her arms extended outward with the basket and flowers and Snowy's leash and ribbon in the other. "Best in Show!"

"Congratulations." Caleb wrapped his arms around her. Her breasts pressed against his chest. The feeling of rightness nearly knocked him back a step. Holding her felt good, natural. He didn't want to let go. He chalked it up to working too hard on the baby product launch and not going out on many dates. He forced himself to drop his arms. "You killed it."

She blushed, a charming shade of pink. "Thanks, but Snowy did all the work."

Becca was too modest. But that was something he liked about her. "We need to celebrate. Bend has some nice restaurants."

"Thanks, but I don't want to leave the dogs alone in the RV."

The dogs. He'd forgotten about them even though he couldn't look anywhere without seeing one dog or twelve. "We can find a place that delivers."

"I'm all set for food for the weekend. I never leave the grounds of a show once I arrive," Becca said. "I'm positive Gertie will want to celebrate when we're home. She's never had a dog win Best in Show. She'll probably throw a party."

"Sounds like Grams." But Caleb didn't want to

wait. He wanted to make tonight special for Becca. "But we can still celebrate here."

"I thought you were going to fly home tonight. Don't you have to get to the airport?"

"I was…am." But Caleb wasn't sure he wanted to leave now. "Unless you want me to stay."

"Don't waste your entire weekend here. Fly home so you and your sister can have brunch with Gertie."

Caleb did that every Sunday. He would rather have brunch with Becca. Preferably after spending the night together. The idea of having a fling with her had been floating around his head since he saw her standing next to the bed Tuesday morning.

She juggled the items in her arms.

He took the basket and flowers from her. "I've got these."

"Thanks." A smile brightened her face. She walked with a playful bounce to her step. Neither of which he had anything to do with.

He wanted to be the reason she was so happy, but only dogs got that honor. He was at a disadvantage without four legs and fur.

The light fragrance of the flowers tickled his nose, teasing him, as if the blossoms knew he wouldn't be around in the morning, but they would be.

People streamed out of the fairgrounds. Engines roared to life. Horns honked. Dogs barked. People were clearing out, returning to their hotels off-site. Others returned to their RVs parked in a special area at the fairgrounds.

Becca placed Snowy into his pen under the shade

of an awning then checked the other dogs. "Want a drink or a snack before you head to the airport?"

"What makes you think I'm leaving now?"

Her eyes widened. "I assumed you'd want to get home."

"Home is a three-thousand-square-foot loft in downtown Boise." A quiet place—a lonely place—compared to the activity and noise here. He breathed in the fresh air. "This is a nice change. No need to rush back."

"You're more than welcome to join me for dinner. I'm grilling hot dogs."

He did a double take. "Hot dogs."

"Does wiener dogs work better? Or how about Dachshund dogs?" she teased. "We're at a dog show. A themed meal makes sense."

"What else is on the menu?"

Laughter filled her eyes. "Saluki Slaw, Bloodhound Beans and Pekinese Potato Chips. Oh, and Corgi Cookies for dessert."

"Corgi cookies, huh?"

"There's also Bernese Brownies."

A quick thinker. He liked that. "Not a bad job coming up with those names on the fly."

And turning a meal into fun. He needed to have more fun.

"Not bad." A corner of her mouth slid upward. "Darn good if you ask me."

"You've convinced me to stay. I'll fly back to Boise after dinner so I can still have brunch with Grams in the morning."

Panic replaced the laughter in Becca's eyes. She shot him a what-have-I-gotten-myself-into smile. She tugged her bottom lip with her teeth. "Win-win."

She was a good sport. "Those are the games I like."

Except he wasn't sure what he was doing with Becca right at this moment. There was no reason for him to stay and every reason in the world to go. Hot dogs weren't his typical Saturday night dinner fare, but he was more interested in the company, Becca's company. And, how could he turn down a Corgi cookie?

Win-win any way he looked at it.

After dinner, Becca stood at the RV's sink. She placed the paper plates and plastic utensils from dinner in the garbage. She kept a smile on her face, but tension wreaked havoc inside her. Awareness of Caleb flowed down her spine and pooled at her feet. She slanted a glance over her shoulder. "I'm almost finished."

Caleb sat in one of the leather lounge chairs. His legs were extended and crossed at the ankles. His gaze on her. "You'd be finished if you'd let me help."

Cleaning up after dinner gave her something to do with her hands other than combing her fingers through her hair and straightening her clothes. Being around Caleb made Becca self-conscious about her appearance, about everything. It wasn't anything he did—he offered to help prepare the meal and clean up. Or anything he said—he was easy to speak with and complimentary. It was just…him.

She placed the now-dried pans in the cabinet above. "There wasn't much to do."

"Maybe not in the kitchen," he said. "What about the dogs?"

She checked the clock on the microwave. "I need to take them for walks."

Caleb rose. "I'll go with you."

"What about your flight?"

He took a step toward Becca. His tall, athletic frame made the spacious and luxurious RV feel like a pop-up trailer. "It's Grams's jet. There's no set departure time until I tell them I'm ready."

"Must be nice." Becca was still trying to get used to Gertie's top-of-the-line RV, purchased specifically for dog shows. She held out a plastic container containing the leftover cookies. "Want more?"

"If I eat another bite, I'll need a crane to get me out of here." He patted his flat stomach. "I forgot how good hot dogs tasted."

"Must be a big change from the haute cuisine you eat."

"Prime rib is about as fancy as I get," he said. "I take after my grandfather when it comes to food. Gramps was a meat-and-potatoes man. Much to the chagrin of Grams, who liked to experiment in the kitchen the way she does in the lab. We usually ended up with two dinners when I was a kid. One for Gramps that our cook made and one for the more adventurous appetites that Grams provided."

"Which did you eat?"

"Both. I took one bite of whatever Grams cooked.

Sometimes more. Only once did I spit it out. I made her promise never to tell me what it was."

"Growing up with Gertie must have been interesting."

"It was never boring. But no matter how busy my grandparents were with Fair Face, we always ate dinner together. That was our special time."

"Sounds nice." She felt a twinge of envy, even though she knew she'd been loved. "My parents worked multiple jobs so eating meals together didn't happen much."

"That had to have been rough."

"It's all I knew." She put the lid on the cookies, then set the container on the counter. "My folks worked hard to make ends meet so it was difficult for me to complain."

"You get your work ethic from your parents."

She nodded. "I wish things were easier for them. Maybe someday…"

"Invite them to visit you at Grams's house."

"Gertie suggested that, but my parents don't have the same days off," Becca said. "I emailed them pictures. They thought the estate looked like something from a TV show. The grounds impressed my dad. His dream is to have a lawn to mow."

"We've always had gardeners to take care of that, but I thought the rider mower looked fun."

"I take it your loft doesn't have a yard."

"No. There's a terrace with planters and a lap spa. Grass would be impractical."

She exited the RV. Caleb followed her out. The sun

had disappeared beneath the horizon. Street lamps along the roads that now doubled as walkways around all the RVs lit up the area.

"Well, if you ever want a lawn up there, there's always Astroturf"

He gave her a look. "You can't mow Astroturf."

"Vacuum it."

"Vacuuming doesn't sound like fun."

"Let me guess—you've never vacuumed."

"I haven't."

Their lives were so different. Too different. She couldn't forget that even if she liked talking and being with him and wondering what kissing him would feel like. "Try it sometime. Vacuuming is a good way to clear your mind."

"Maybe I will."

She locked the RV door. "Maybe means you won't."

A sheepish grin spread across his face. "Wouldn't want to offend the team that cleans my place."

Whoa. He lived in a completely different universe than her. "You have a team of cleaners?"

"Doing my part to stimulate the economy."

Okay, that was funny. She liked his sense of humor. With a smile, she shook her head. "Working for Gertie sure has given me a glimpse into how the other half lives."

"What do you think so far?"

His question didn't sound flippant, but why would he care what she thought? Few people except her parents and Gertie did.

"That bad, huh?" he asked.

"No, not at all."

"So…"

He sounded genuinely interested in knowing Becca's opinion. "Honestly, it's been nice," Becca said. "Gertie is eccentric and loves luxurious things, but she's more grounded than I imagined someone as wealthy as her to be. It'll be hard to leave behind."

His gaze narrowed. "Planning on going somewhere?"

"Not in the near future, but I want to be a full-time handler. Care for the dogs in between shows. Teach handling classes to kids and dog owners."

"You can make a living doing that?"

His disbelief didn't surprise her. "The top handlers in the country make over six figures a year."

"I had no idea people did this as a full-time job."

"A few do," she said. "Most work other jobs and handle part-time or as a hobby. Some save money so they can take time off."

"Saving for a rainy day."

She couldn't believe he remembered their conversation in his office. "Yes."

"You realize you could have a lucrative career working for Grams, especially if the dog-care products take off. You'd earn more than you'd make as a dog handler."

Becca shrugged. "I never set out to be a business person."

"You care about what you do. You're not just out to make a buck."

"No, but having a few bucks in the bank doesn't hurt."

He smiled. "You belong here. In this dog-show world."

"I think so." She hoped this was where she belonged. "I appreciate Gertie giving me the opportunity to show her dogs."

Becca attached Maurice's leash to his collar and released him from the pen. The dog ran straight to Caleb.

"You have a new friend," she said.

He rubbed the dog's head. "It's only because I have no dog hair on me. Maurice needs to mark his territory."

"As long as he's not marking it another way."

Caleb gave her a look. "Don't give Maurice any ideas."

Becca peeked in on Snowy. The dog slept soundly, his back leg jerking as if dreaming. She would take him out later.

"Come on, Blue." She removed the gray eighteen-month-old puppy from his pen. "Time for your walk, boy."

Caleb walked next to her with the dogs out in front, leading the way.

A man, a well-known handler from California, walking four beagles, greeted them with a nod and a hello.

Caleb looked back at the dogs. "Some people show the same type of dogs. Why doesn't my grandmother stick to one breed?"

"Gertie loves all dogs, not a particular breed. She also owns dogs others weren't sure about or gave up on. She could have the pick of most litters, but she'd rather choose a dog who needs a second chance."

"Why would they need a second chance? They're purebreds."

"Yes, but not every purebred meets the breed standard. Reputable breeders have those dogs neutered or spayed and placed in homes as pets." Becca pointed to Blue. "This guy was the runt of the litter. No one expected him to be show quality, but your grandmother saw something in him and took a chance. Now he's on his way to being a champion."

"I'm not surprised," Caleb said. "Grams has always been fond of strays."

"No kidding. She took me in."

"My sister and me, too."

"You weren't strays," Becca countered. "You're family."

Caleb shrugged.

"Gertie treats her rescue and foster dogs the same as her show dogs." Becca could tell he didn't want to talk about this. "Your grandmother has a big heart."

"So do you."

His words meant more than they should. Becca tried to down play the fluttery feeling in her stomach. "It's easy with dogs."

"There was that little girl Gianna today."

"Just trying to be nice."

"Is that what you're doing now? Being nice to me when you wish I'd left hours ago?"

Becca didn't know what she was doing. Feeling. But she didn't like how Caleb saw right through her, as if her every thought and emotion were on display especially for him. They were too much in sync, able to understand each other even though they were in very different places in life.

He made her feel vulnerable, a way she'd felt for three long years in prison. A way she never wanted to feel again. She tightened her grip on the leash and looked up at the sky full of twinkling dots of lights. "Lots of stars out tonight."

"You're changing the subject."

"You're supposed to pretend you don't notice and play along."

He stopped walking to allow Maurice to sniff the grass. "What if I don't want to do that?"

"You're the kind of guy who plays by the rules."

"Normally, yes." He moved closer to her until she could feel the heat of him. "But this isn't normal."

She fought the urge to step back. "Being at the dog show?"

Caleb stopped inches away from her. "Being here with you."

The light from the streetlamp cast shadows on his face. He looked dark and dangerous and oh-so-sexy. Becca swallowed. Last time she'd thought that about a guy she'd ended up in jail. That might not be what would happen to her next, but she shouldn't take any unnecessary chances and do something stupid again.

His gaze locked on hers. "Do you want to keep playing by the rules?"

Her heart slammed against her ribs. She should step back. Way back. Put distance between them. For her own good. And his.

But her feet wouldn't move. She remained rooted in place, waiting, hoping, anticipating.

Caleb tilted his head down, bringing his lips close to hers.

Becca rose up and leaned forward.

Their lips touched.

So much for rules.

He wrapped his arms around her, pulled her close and kissed her hard.

Hot, salty, raw.

His lips moved across her, skillfully. His kiss possessed, as if staking a claim and declaring she was his.

Becca had never felt that way before. She shouldn't like it, either. She was independent. She didn't need a man to give her value. But at the moment, with tingles reaching to the tips of her toes and fingers, possession seemed a small price to pay.

Pleasurable sensations pulsed through her, heating her from the inside out. He deepened the kiss. She followed willingly, arching toward him.

Ruff.

Caleb jerked backward. His arms let go of her.

Becca stumbled to the right.

Grrrrowl.

Maurice and Blue lunged toward two teeth-baring Pekingese with satin bows on their ears.

She yanked on the leash. "Heel!"

Caleb grabbed Maurice by his collar.

The other two dogs didn't back down. Their owner, a petite woman with spiky white hair, a shimmery short robe and flower-trimmed flip-flops, frowned. "Next time get a room."

Becca's cheeks burned. Her lips throbbed.

Oh, no. She'd been so wrapped up in Caleb she had forgotten about the dogs. What if they'd gotten into a fight and been hurt? Not acceptable.

The woman marched away, dragging her wannabe fighters behind her. The dogs looked back and growled.

"That didn't turn out like I expected. Maybe Grams knows something we didn't." Desire flared in his eyes. "We should try that again."

Oh, yes. Becca would love another kiss. Make that kisses. But she couldn't. She glanced at Blue, who sniffed the grass as if nothing had happened. If only she could forget…The past. Who Caleb was. Who she was. "I can't."

"Can't or won't?"

"Does it matter?

His jaw was set, tense. "If not for those bow-toting dogs—"

"If it weren't for them, I'd still be kissing you."

A sinfully charming grin lit up his face. "Then let's pick up where we left off."

Temptation flared. "Kissing you was…amazing. But I forgot everything, including the dogs. They could have been hurt. They're my responsibility. I can't be distracted."

Approval tempered the desire in his gaze. "I understand and respect that."

Respect was all she'd wanted. Until this moment. Now she wanted more of his kisses. Uh-oh.

"Thanks." She tried to remember all the reasons Caleb and more kisses weren't good for her. "I appreciate it."

"Just know when you're back in Boise and the dogs aren't around, I want to kiss you again. If that's what you want, too."

Her heart lodged in her throat. She couldn't breathe, let alone speak.

Heaven help her, but Becca couldn't wait to get back to Boise.

CHAPTER NINE

Two NIGHTS LATER, the party at Grams's place was going strong when Caleb arrived. He handed his keys to a parking valet.

A big crowd for a Monday.

But when Gertie Fairchild issued an invitation, few sent regrets.

Inside the house, Caleb greeted people he'd known his entire life and made his way toward the patio.

Leave it to Grams to pull together an impromptu gathering for two hundred of her closest friends in honor of Snowy winning Best in Show. On the patio, a DJ spun music in the backyard. Bartenders fixed drinks. Uniformed servers carried trays of delicious smelling appetizers.

Caleb searched for the two women he wanted to see most—his grandmother and Becca. He caught a glimpse of Grams, wearing pink capris and a sparkly blouse, and wove his way over through the crowd.

"Caleb!" Grams hugged him. "I've been wondering when you'd arrive."

"I had a few things to finish up at the office."

"Take off your jacket and tie," she said with a smile. "Get a drink. And relax."

He glanced around.

"Looking for Becca?" Grams asked.

"Yes."

"She's here. Courtney, too."

His sister never turned down a party invitation, even if the average age of the guest list was twice hers. "I hope Courtney's staying out of trouble."

"Probably not." Grams waved at someone who'd stepped out onto the patio. "You should find Becca and see if you can get yourself into trouble."

"Grams!"

"What?" She feigned innocence. "Thirty-one is too young to be so serious about everything. Becca would be good for you. Help you to lighten up and enjoy life."

Maybe in the short term. He'd enjoyed their time together at the dog show. Talking, laughing, kissing. Best not let Grams know or she'd be hiring a wedding planner to come up with the perfect proposal, one that would go viral on YouTube. "Becca and I figured out you've been playing matchmaker."

Grams pointed to herself. *"Moi?"*

"Oui, Grandmère."

"Speak French to Becca," Grams said. "Women like that."

Caleb shook his head, but made a mental note to give speaking French a try.

"Becca is a special woman." Grams lowered her

voice. "But it's going to take a special man to break through her hard shell."

"Becca and I are friends." Friends who had shared a passionate kiss before being rudely interrupted by a pair of Pekingese dogs. He might want more of Becca's kisses, but he wasn't that "special man." The last thing he needed was a girlfriend. He didn't want to be responsible for one more person. "Nothing more."

"Your loss is another man's gain."

The thought of Becca kissing another man made Caleb's shoes feel too tight. He stretched his toes. "I'm going to see if I can find Courtney."

"Have fun." Grams flitted toward the house, taking on her role as Boise's most gracious hostess.

Caleb grabbed a bottle of beer from the bar. He took a long swig. Just what he needed after a long day at the office. Now, if he could find Becca.

"Hey, bro." The scent of his sister's perfume surrounded him. Her ruffled miniskirt barely hid her underwear. Her two tanks showed as much skin as a string bikini top. Her blonde hair was clipped on top of her head with tendrils artfully placed around her face. Her make up was magazine layout perfect. Typical Courtney. Somewhat disturbing for a brother who worried about his younger sister. "I met your new girlfriend."

He nearly spit out his beer. He forced himself to swallow. "I don't have a girlfriend."

"Becca."

"She's not…What has Grams been telling you?"

"Only that she found the perfect woman for you."

Courtney took a flute of champagne from the tray of a passing waiter. "Becca is cute. With a wardrobe makeover, some highlights and makeup she could be totally hot. I'm happy to assist—"

"Becca is fine the way she is."

"You like her."

"I don't…" He lowered his voice. "Becca is sweet. She doesn't need to be pulled into Grams's match-making scheme."

"Better her than me." Courtney sipped her champagne. "The alarm on Grams's great-grandbaby clock is ringing louder and louder."

"Don't look at me. I do enough as it is."

"Well, I'm not ready to be a mom. I've never dated a guy longer than a month."

Caleb stared at her over the top of his beer bottle. "Considering your choice in men, that's a good thing. Maybe you should have Grams fix you up. Bet she'd pick a winner for you."

"Yeah, right. Someone totally respectable, proper and boring like you." Courtney shook her head. "Don't forget I lose everything. Imagine if I misplaced a kid. That would be bad."

"Very bad," he agreed. "No worries. Grams will get over the idea of great-grandchildren eventually."

"I hope so, but I think we should be proactive about this," Courtney said. "Let's buy Grams a kitten."

"Grams is a dog person."

"That doesn't mean she can't be a crazy cat lady, too. Kittens are cute and cuddly. Kind of like a baby, but you don't have to deal with diapers, only litter boxes."

Caleb wasn't in the mood to try to understand his sister's twisted logic, especially after she'd called him boring. He downed what remained of his beer. "Hold off on the kitten for a while. And stay out of trouble tonight."

Courtney stuck her tongue out at him. "You're no fun."

Walking away, he realized Courtney was correct. He used to be fun. When he was younger, he and Ty had had nothing but fun. After Caleb took over Fair Face for his grandfather, life revolved around the company and family. Nothing else.

He followed the path past the guest cottage—only the porch light was on—to the kennel.

A dog barked from inside.

Caleb couldn't see which one, but he recognized the sound.

Maurice.

Caleb entered the kennel. More barks erupted, drowning out the pop music playing from an iPod docking station.

"Quiet." Becca faced Dozer's door. Her floral skirt fell two inches above her knees. The green sleeveless shirt showed off toned arms. Her white sandals accentuated thin ankles. "We don't want Gertie's guests to hear you."

The dogs stopped barking. Maurice stood with his front paws on his door.

"What's gotten into you?" Becca asked the dog.

Caleb stopped two feet behind her. "So this is where you've been hiding."

She gasped and whirled around.

The hem of her skirt flared, giving him a glimpse of her lower thighs. Much more enticing than a super short skirt that left nothing to the imagination.

Her eyes were wide, her cheeks pink. She placed her hand over her heart. "Caleb."

"I didn't mean to startle you."

She peered around him, as if to see if anyone else was behind him. "What are you doing here?"

"I was going to ask you the same question." Seeing her felt good. He couldn't believe they'd only been apart two days. It seemed longer. "The party's up on the patio. But you're down here. Alone."

She motioned to the dogs, watching them intently from their individual stalls. "I'm not alone."

"You know what I mean."

She nodded. "It's a bit…overwhelming."

"The party?"

"And all the people. Guests, servers, bartenders, DJ, parking valets," she said. "Gertie introduced me to about a hundred people tonight. No way can I keep the faces and names straight."

"So you escaped here."

Another nod. "This is my favorite place at the estate. It's where I'm…"

"Comfortable," he finished for her.

"Yes. It's where I fit."

The way he knew her, understood her was…unsettling to him.

He cut the distance between them in half with one step. "You love the kennel and the dogs, but you also fit in up at the house with everybody else."

She ground the toe of her sandal against the floor. "I don't know about that."

"I do." Caleb used his finger to raise her chin. "You're smart, beautiful, kind."

The pink on her cheeks darkened. "You don't have to stop."

"I don't plan on stopping unless you want me to stop." He didn't want to frighten her off "I'd like to pick up right where we left off."

Her lips parted.

He grinned. "I'm going to take that as an invitation."

"Please."

Caleb kissed her. Something he'd been thinking about doing since he drove away from the fairgrounds on Saturday night. But he never expected her to melt into his arms as if she'd been looking forward to this moment as much as him.

He pressed his lips against hers, soaking up the feel and taste of her.

So sweet. Warm. His.

He wrapped his arms around her, pulling her close. She went eagerly. Her soft curves molded against him.

So right.

His temperature shot up, fueled by the heat pulsing through him.

Her hands were on his back, in his hair, all over.

His tongue explored her mouth, tangled with her tongue. He couldn't get enough of her.

Caleb's hand dropped to her skirt. He lifted the hem and touched her thigh, the skin as soft and smoothed as he imagined. His hand inched up, with anticipation, with desire.

"Well, I'll be damned."

Grams.

He jerked his hand from underneath Becca's skirt. He jumped back totally turned on, his breathing ragged. Becca's flushed face and swollen lips were sexy as hell and exactly the last thing he wanted his grandmother to see.

Too late now. He faced the woman who had raised him. Courtney stood next to his grandmother.

Grams had her hands clasped together. She looked giddy, as if she'd been granted three wishes from a magic lamp. She needed only one, because the silly grin on her face told him exactly what she was thinking—great-grandbabies.

Her eyes twinkled. "Nothing more than friends, huh?"

"So this is how it feels not to be the one in trouble." Courtney smirked. "I kind of like it."

Caleb positioned himself between his family and Becca. "It's not what you think."

"Yes, it is." Grams rubbed her palms together. "And I couldn't be more delighted."

Becca's heart pounded in her chest, a mixture of embarrassment, passion and pride. The way Caleb shielded her from his family like a knight in gray pinstripes made her feel special.

He might be everything she didn't want in a guy, but at this moment she wouldn't want to be with anyone else.

Her lips throbbed. Her breathing wouldn't settle. Her insides ached for more kisses.

She'd experienced those same reactions in Redmond. But something felt different, awakened, as if she'd finally met a man who saw beyond her past and could accept her for who she was today. No guy had ever made her feel like that.

Becca longed to reach forward and lace her fingers with Caleb's in support and solidarity. But that would only fuel Gertie's speculations.

It's not what you think.

But it could be. And the possibility gave Becca hope. Strength. She stepped forward and took her place next to Caleb.

Gertie rose up on her tiptoes, acting more like an excited child than the creative genius of a skin-care empire.

Courtney's snicker turned into a smile, transforming the beautiful young woman from a life-size cardboard cutout of the latest fashion trends to someone more real and genuine.

"People want to see Snowy," Grams said.

Becca glanced back at the dog that stood at his door all fluffed and ready to go. "He's ready."

"We'll bring Snowy up there in a few minutes," Caleb added.

Gertie winked. "Don't take too long."

Her suggestive tone sent heat rushing up Becca's neck.

A vein twitched at Caleb's jaw. "We won't."

Gertie and Courtney, looking as if they were about to burst out laughing, exited the kennel.

As soon as the door shut, Caleb looked down at the ground, shaking his head.

Becca touched his shoulder. "I'm sorry."

His gaze met hers. Softened. "You have nothing to be sorry about."

"But Gertie's going to think—"

Caleb kissed Becca, a gentle whisper of a kiss. The tender brush of his lips made her feel even more cherished, as if she was meant to be treasured. Her chest swelled with affection for this man. He backed away from her slowly, as if he didn't want to end the kiss.

Becca swallowed a sigh. She wished he could keep on kissing her…forever.

"Don't worry about my grandmother or my sister." He touched her face again, lightly tracing her jawline with his thumb. "It doesn't matter what they think is going on between us."

Becca nodded, but she was worried. All they'd done was kiss. But something was happening between her and Caleb, something big. At least, it felt that way to her. If he didn't feel the same…

"I'm happy I finally got to kiss you from beginning to end—even if we were interrupted again. Now that we've finished that, we can go from here."

His words swirled around her and squeezed tight,

like a vise grip around her heart. Her breath hitched. Her throat burned.

Caleb wasn't talking about kisses. He wanted more. A hookup. A one-night stand. That was why he'd said what he had to Gertie. The kisses hadn't meant the same thing to him.

Becca's shoulders sagged. At least she'd found out before any real damage had been done. She straightened and raised her chin. "I need to get Snowy."

Caleb's eyes darkened. "What's wrong?"

A "nothing" sat on the tip of her tongue. But "nothing" wouldn't keep her stomach from knotting a thousand different ways. "Nothing" wouldn't keep her from staying up all night analyzing the situation until exhaustion took over.

She'd been there before. She wasn't eager for a return trip.

With a deep breath, she mustered her courage. "So now that we've finished—"

"We—" he twirled a short strand of her hair with his fingertip "—are going on a date."

Hope exploded inside her—short-lived, as caution shouted a warning. "A date?"

"Dinner at Pacifica."

Pacifica was a new restaurant in town. "I've heard Pacifica's incredible, but impossible to get a reservation."

"I'll get us a table."

His confidence attracted her as much as it repelled. Less than a minute ago she was ready to write his kiss and him off. Now she was going on a date with him. The tennis-match-worthy back and forth was enough to make her light-headed.

Becca wasn't interested in his money or power. She liked the way he cared about people and took care of them. But she was pleased he was trying to do something special to make her feel important. She found it endearingly silly because she would be happy going out for hot dogs. "Sounds great."

"Are you free Wednesday?" he asked.

That was only two days away. No worries. He'd never get a table. "I am."

He typed on his smartphone. "This shouldn't take long."

"What are you doing?"

"Making a reservation." His phone buzzed. He stared at the screen. "Wednesday at eight. It's a date."

"How did you manage that?"

"I grew up here." He looked so pleased with himself. "I have a few connections."

And now she had a date with Caleb Fairchild.

The realization of what she'd agreed to hit her like a two-hundred-pound Newfoundland dog wanting a hug. Hope turned to an impending sense of dread. Her sandals felt more like cement blocks. Becca trudged to Snowy.

A date with Caleb Fairchild.

She opened the door and attached Snowy's leash to his collar. She would need something nice to wear, nicer than one of her dog-show suits.

Snowy trotted out.

She would need to know what utensils to use when.

Was the saying from the outside in or was it the inside out? She would need to look up rules of etiquette and table manners on the Internet.

She would need to figure out what to say or not say to Gertie about going out with Caleb.

"Snowy looks like a champion," Caleb said.

Becca nodded, but she couldn't relax.

Her muscles bunched. Her stomach clenched.

A date with Caleb Fairchild.

A man who could get a table at the hottest restaurant in town with a simple text was the last guy she should ever want to date. Or kiss. Or…

No falling for him. A date was one thing. A kiss another. Anything more could be…disastrous.

On the patio, Caleb stood back while Gertie, Becca and Snowy took the spotlight. Becca's confidence blossomed around the dog. He wished she exuded the same confidence when she wasn't with one of the dogs.

Courtney sidled up next to him. "Not what you think. Really?"

"Drop it."

"No." She leaned closer, sending a whiff of expensive perfume up his nostrils. "I saw the direction of your hand. Becca didn't seem to mind one bit. You like her."

"I enjoy spending time with her."

"You like her."

Becca stacked Snowy, the way she had in the ring.

The dog ate up applause and attention as if it were beef jerky.

"How long have you been dating?" Courtney asked.

"You're not going to let this go."

"You dating someone takes pressure off me."

She flipped her hair behind her shoulder with a practice move rumored to have cut men to their knees. Not any man Caleb would want to know.

"So spill," she said.

"We're not dating, but I'm taking Becca to Pacifica on Wednesday."

"Fancy-schmancy." Courtney used her favorite saying since childhood. The words described his sister's lifestyle perfectly. "You're out to impress Becca."

"I want her to enjoy the evening." But Caleb realized he did want to impress Becca. "I want her to feel comfortable, not intimidated."

Courtney grinned as if she'd been handed a platinum Visa card with no spending limit. "Leave it to me, bro."

Two women couldn't have been more different. He eyed his sister warily. "What do you have in mind?"

Wednesday morning, Becca released the dogs into their run. She cleaned the kennel from top to bottom—sweeping, scrubbing, disinfecting. The entire time she thought about Caleb. Tonight was their date.

She ran through all the things she'd been learning online about eating at an expensive fancy restaurant. Use flatware from the outside in. Napkins are for dabbing, never wiping. Bread should be torn, not cut with a knife. Her parents had taught her a few of the rules like no elbows on the table, don't take a bite until everyone had been served and don't slurp soup or drinks. Maybe she would be able to pull this off.

If not, it was only one date. No big deal.

Yeah, right.

This was the biggest deal since Gertie had hired her.

Mopping the floor outside the dog stalls, Becca pictured the outfit she was going to wear. She'd gone through every piece of clothing she owned and settled on a slim black skirt, white blouse and a pair of black pumps. A scarf would add a burst of color. Silver hoop earrings and a bracelet would be her jewelry.

She wanted to look elegant. Most likely she would be dressed too plainly for a place as trendy and hip as Pacifica.

Maybe she should cancel.

Becca rested against the mop.

You could take a mutt into the show ring, but no matter what she wore or how she acted, the maître d' would know she was a mixed breed, not a purebred. No sense pretending otherwise.

Her cellphone rang. "Hello."

"Please come to the house right now."

The urgency in Gertie's voice made Becca drop the mop. "On my way."

She ran to the house. The family room was empty. The kitchen, too. "Gertie?"

"Upstairs."

Becca climbed the stairs two at a time, her heart racing, worried about Gertie. She entered Gertie's bedroom, her gaze scanning the room. Unique antiques. Luxurious textiles. Exotic treasures.

On the bed was something new. A pile of clothing. Shoes, too.

Gertie stood with a beaming smile on her face and a familiar twinkle in her eyes. Courtney was next to Gertie. Mrs. Harris and Maura were there, too.

"What's going on?" Becca asked.

Courtney motioned to the bed with a pile of clothing and shoes on top. "I have a bunch of stuff that isn't the right color or style. We're about the same size. Maura, too. I thought the two of you might want to see if there's anything you like."

Becca imagined her not unsuitable but not perfect outfit for tonight. She couldn't believe her luck or Courtney's generosity. A lump of gratitude clogged Becca's throat. Tears stung her eyes. She covered her face with her hands.

Gertie put her arm around Becca. "What's wrong, dear?"

"This is so nice. The timing is perfect," Becca sniffled. "I have a date tonight, but I don't have anything nice enough to wear, so I've been thinking about canceling."

"Don't fret," Gertie said in a voice that made it seem as if the world could end and everything would still be okay.

"And please don't cancel," Courtney said. "We'll

find you a knockout outfit to wear. Some of the clothes still have the tags on them."

Becca rubbed her eyes. She didn't understand rich people.

"Courtney is a shopaholic. Something she may have inherited from me," Gertie said to Maura and Becca. "It's about time others benefited from my granddaughter's addiction."

Maura stepped forward. "I'd love some new clothes. Tags or not."

Most of Becca's clothes came from thrift stores or consignment shops. She had no issue with hand-me-downs. "Me, too."

"Where are you going tonight?" Gertie asked.

As soon as Becca told them where, they would know she was going with Caleb. But she couldn't lie. "Pacifica."

Both Mrs. Harris and Maura gasped.

A snug smile formed on Courtney's lips.

"A lovely restaurant." Beaming, Gertie led Becca toward the bed. "Let's find something that'll make Caleb's eyes bug out and want to go straight to dessert."

CHAPTER TEN

DINNER AT PACIFICA was a hundred times better than Caleb had expected. It wasn't the mouthwatering Northwest cuisine from the award-winning chef. It wasn't the all-star service from the waiter dressed in black. It wasn't the romantic atmosphere with flickering votive candles and fresh flowers atop a linen-covered table for two. It was the woman sitting across from him who made the night memorable.

Caleb squeezed Becca's hand. "Have I told you how stunning you look tonight?"

Her smile meant only for him made Caleb feel seven feet tall. "About ten times. But I don't mind."

"Then I'll keep saying it." She wore a one-shoulder floral dress with a tantalizing asymmetrical hem. The heels of her strappy sandals accentuated her long legs. She'd glossed her lips and wore makeup. "You're the most beautiful women in Boise."

Her cheeks flushed, a pale pink that made her more attractive. "Only because I had your sister to help me."

"You don't need makeup and clothes to be beautiful." He pointed to her heart. "It's all right there. The rest are optional accessories."

Gratitude shone in the depths of her eyes. "Thank you."

"You're welcome." Caleb didn't have room in his life for a girlfriend. But he liked being with Becca. Maybe she'd be up for a casual relationship. Time permitting. He kissed the top of her hand. "But even though your dress is spectacular, I kind of miss seeing you covered in dog hair."

Her laughter, as melodic as a song, caressed his heart.

"I doubt they would have let me in with a speck of hair or lint on me." She glanced around, then lowered her voice. "I'm so relieved I made it through dinner. I kept thinking if I made a mistake, used the wrong fork or something, they'd kick me out."

"You didn't make any mistakes."

She kissed his hand. "It wasn't as hard as I thought it would be."

Their waiter, dressed in a black tuxedo with a gleaming bald head and an equally bright smile, dropped off the leather case containing Caleb's credit card and the bill.

Becca rubbed his hand with her thumb. "Thank you for tonight. I'll never forget this evening."

He wouldn't, either. "We'll have to do it again."

"I'd like that, but…"

"What?"

Mischief filled her eyes. "You've given me a peek

into your world. If we do this again, I want to show you mine."

"Not if, when. That sounds like fun."

She shimmied her shoulders, as if excited.

Caleb wanted to lean across the table and kiss her bare shoulder, then trail more kisses up her neck until he reached her lips.

"How does Friday sound?" he asked.

"This Friday?"

He might not want a girlfriend, but a few dates didn't mean anything. He liked hanging out with Becca. No big deal. He could walk away any time. But for now he would enjoy her. "Yes."

On Thursday, Becca printed out a stack of emails for Gertie. "These are product orders. Too bad we don't have any products to sell."

Gertie's smile kept widening as she thumbed through the pages. "We can make up some batches in the lab. Sell those."

"Is that legal?"

"We're using natural, known ingredients, so we shouldn't have a problem." Gertie looked at Becca. "But double-check with Caleb to be on the safe side."

Becca would love to hear his voice. His good-night kiss in the parking lot had tempted her, but common sense won out over raging hormones. She was growing fonder of him each time she saw him. Still no sense taking a swan dive into an empty pool. "I'll text him."

She didn't really need to hear his voice.

Gertie tapped her chin. "We should pick a show, set up a booth and debut the products."

"Stumptown is in July, but that's too soon. The Enumclaw show is a couple weeks later in August. That one draws people from all over and has lots of breed specialties going on, too."

"Sounds good. Mark your calendar."

August wasn't that far way. "It's going to be a busy summer with all the dog shows we've entered."

"Have Caleb go with you."

Thinking about spending the summer at dog shows with Caleb made her pulse race faster than a Greyhound chasing a rabbit. But Becca could never ask him to do that. She couldn't lower her guard that much and open herself up to more heartache. "We're not…"

"Friends? I've seen the way he looks at you." Gertie raised a white eyebrow. "He's never looked at another woman like that. Not even his ex-fiancée."

Becca had heard about his ex from Courtney the other night doing Becca's makeup for her date. Becca realized how much Caleb and she had in common with their past romances. No wonder he hadn't trusted her when he first met her. It would be hard to trust anyone after almost being scammed by someone who claimed to love you. At least they were past that now.

"That makes you happy." Gertie said.

Yes, very much so. But Becca didn't dare admit that aloud.

A little voice inside her head whispered a warning. The caution reverberated through her. Getting her hopes up too high could mean a long, hurtful drop. The last thing she wanted—needed—was for her heart to go splat. But there was something she could say. "Caleb is a nice guy."

"Yes, but my grandson is still a man," Gertie said. "They'll take whatever you offer and try to keep the status quo as long as possible."

"I don't understand."

"Don't sleep with Caleb until there's a wedding band on your finger."

Becca's cheeks burned. "We've only kissed a few times."

"Some pretty hot kisses from what I saw."

She covered her mouth with her hand, unable to believe Gertie talked so openly about kissing and…sex.

"Don't be embarrassed. I might be old, but I was young once," Gertie said. "Remember the adage about the cow and getting milk for free is as true today as it was when I was your age."

Becca knew her boss had only her best interest at heart, but this was awkward. "I'll remember."

Not that she and Caleb were even close to…that. Taking things to the next level would be a game changer.

What had Caleb said?

Win-win.

She'd always come out on the losing side before. She didn't see that changing, even if a part of her wished it would.

But Becca knew one thing. She wasn't sure she was ready to trust her heart again. Or if she ever could.

Friday evening, Caleb arrived at what looked to be an Old West saloon for his date with Becca. He hadn't seen her in two days, two of the longest days of his life.

If he wasn't thinking about her, he was texting her. If he wasn't texting her, he was figuring out the best time to call her. If he wasn't calling her, he was back to thinking about her. A vicious cycle. One that left him distracted and behind at work. One he wasn't used to and wanted to stop.

No matter. This wasn't some serious relationship. They shared a few interests and sizzling chemistry. That was what drew him to her, nothing more.

Becca stood outside the restaurant, waiting for him. She wore jean shorts, a red lace-trimmed camisole with a red gingham button-down shirt over it.

His heart tripped over itself at the sight of her. His temperature skyrocketed at the tan, toned skin showing.

"You came straight from the office," she said.

"I got stuck in a meeting." He kissed her cheek. She smelled sweet like strawberries. "I'm overdressed."

"Take off your jacket and tie."

"It's fine."

She tugged on his tie. "I'm serious. You need to take this off now."

"Don't worry."

"You're going to regret not—"

He touched his finger to his lips. "Shhh."

"Your loss."

Caleb had no idea what she was talking about. "How was your day?"

"Good. I reviewed our new website and made a list of changes for the web designer."

"Text me the URL. I can't wait to see it."

"Courtney came up with the name. Gertie's Top Dog Products."

He opened the door to the restaurant. "I'm surprised Grams dragged my sister into this."

Becca entered. "Courtney wanted to help."

"She must have an ulterior motive."

"Being nice isn't enough?"

"Not for my sister." Inside, he took a step. Something crunched beneath his shoe. He looked down. Peanut shells. "Interesting floor covering."

The entire place was interesting. The hole-in-the-wall grill was a far cry from Pacifica. The smell of hops and grease filled the air. The din of customer's conversations and cussing rose above the honky-tonk music playing from speakers.

Becca pointed to a No Ties sign. "You should take yours off."

"No one cares what I wear here."

She dragged two fingers over her mouth, zipping her lips. "Won't mention it again."

The hostess wore supertight, short jean shorts, a spaghetti-strap top and a ponytail. She led them to a table.

Caleb sat across from Becca. A tin pail full of

shelled peanuts sat in the center of the table next to a roll of paper towels.

The hostess handed them menus. "Your server will be right with you."

He looked around. Customers had engraved their names on the wood planks covering the walls. He doubted they used a butter knife. That told him a lot about the clientele. He would have to bring Ty here the next time his friend was home. "Come here often?"

"No, but it's one of my favorite places in town."

"I've never heard of it."

"It's time you discovered one of Boise's hidden gems."

Hidden, yes. A gem? Becca would have to convince Caleb. But he had no doubt Ty would love this place.

Caleb read the menu. Lots of red meat and potatoes. Fried, French, mashed, baked. Okay, maybe this place was okay.

"Howdy, partners. I'm Jackie, your server." A perky, voluptuous woman with equally puffy big hair stood at their table. She wore tight jean shorts and a T-shirt two sizes too small. "I see we have a new visitor to our fine establishment. Welcome, fine sir. I take it you did not see the sign."

"What sign?"

Becca shook her head.

"The No Ties sign," Jackie said.

"I saw it," he admitted.

"Then there's only one thing left for me to do." She

pulled out a pair of scissors from her back pocket, leaned toward him giving him a bird's-eye view of her breasts and cut off his tie right above one side of the knot.

"What the…" He stared at where his tie used to hang. The spot was empty. "That was a silk tie."

An expensive one.

"I told you," Becca said. "More than once, if you remember."

"You never said they'd vandalize my tie."

Jackie shrugged. "You saw the sign. You disobeyed the sign. You pay the price."

This was unbelievable. "What happens to the tie now?"

"It becomes part of our decor," Jackie said. "Look up."

Caleb did. Hundreds of colorful ties hung from the ceiling.

"You should have listened to me," Becca said. "But I didn't try that hard to convince you. I've never been all that fond of your yellow tie. No big loss, if you want my opinion."

"Red is a power color." Jackie tucked the tie into her bra. A good thing they had a use for it, because he wasn't going to want it back now. "Yellow is too…"

"Understated," Becca said.

Unbelievable. His grandmother had said the same things. He half laughed.

"You've got your peanuts and menus and sense of humor," Jackie said. "I'll be back in a jiff to take your drink orders."

With that, the server walked away.

"I hope you're not too upset about your tie?" Becca asked.

"Not upset," he admitted. "It's my fault. You warned me. I chose not to listen to you. Lesson learned."

With a smile, Becca grabbed a handful of peanuts. "Dig in."

He took one from the pail. "You just toss the shells on the floor?"

"You've led a sheltered life. Watch." She illustrated what to do. "Your turn."

Caleb took another peanut. Opened it. Removed the peanut. Tossed the shell on the ground.

"Easy-peasy." She dumped a handful of peanuts in front of him, then pointed to a target painted on the aisle between the tables. "Now we can get serious. High point wins."

That sounded fun. "What's the prize?"

She shrugged. "What do you want it to be?"

You. In the horizontal position. But he didn't think she was up for that. At least not yet. Maybe later tonight. "I don't care."

"Then I'll have to think of something—until then… go for it."

With each peanut shell he tossed, the stress of his day spent working at Fair Face and attending meetings slipped away. Nothing mattered, not Grams or Courtney. There was only here and now. And Becca.

He threw another peanut. "This is more fun than I thought it would be."

"Fun is the name of the game here."

Caleb saw that. He liked it, too. "I like having fun."

Becca had brought fun back into his life. The kind of fun Grams said he needed. And Caleb knew one thing.

He didn't want it to end.

At least not anytime soon.

Becca didn't want the night to end. Delicious food. Interesting conversation. A handsome date who made her think of slow, hot kisses.

Charmed by Caleb, yes. Totally enchanted by him—she was on her way.

Time to pull back. Though that was hard to do when he held her hand in the restaurant's parking lot.

"I had a great time tonight," Caleb said. "Want to get together tomorrow and go tie shopping?"

Her heart leaped. Common sense frowned. She laughed, not knowing if he were serious or not.

"I mean it."

Okay, he was serious. She bit her lip.

The list of reasons she shouldn't want to see him again was long. But those things were easy to forget when Caleb's gaze made her feel like the only woman in the world. His world, at least. That could be oh-so-dangerous. "You should ask your sister to go. I know nothing about ties."

He brushed his lips over Becca's hair, making her knees want to melt. "Courtney might know fashion, but you know me."

Her heart bumped. The thought of spending more

time with Caleb made her want to cancel her plans. But she couldn't. "I would love to go tie shopping, but I'm driving down to see my parents tomorrow."

"Overnight?"

"A day trip," she said. "I need to be back for the dogs."

"Ah, yes, the dogs."

He sounded funny. "What do you mean by the dogs?"

"I never thought I'd be jealous of some pups."

"Jealous, huh?"

"You're at their beck and call."

"It's my job."

"Admit it," he said lightheartedly. "You like the dogs better than you like me."

He was teasing, but there was some truth to his words. Becca liked dogs better than most people. But better than Caleb?

"It's a different kind of like," she said. "Dogs are loyal, protective and think I'm the center of their universe. That's pretty appealing."

"True, but a dog can't do this."

Caleb dipped his head, touching his mouth to Becca's. Electric. His lips moved over hers, sending pleasurable tingles shooting through her. She savored the feel and the taste of him. Forget the dinner they'd eaten, this was all she needed for nourishment. He drew the kiss to an end much to soon.

"You're right." She rubbed her throbbing lips together. "A dog can't to that."

His chest expanded. "Damn straight they can't."

She laughed. "Thanks for dinner. It's been a lovely evening."

"We don't have to call it a night."

Oh, Becca was tempted. But keeping her heart under lock and key was becoming more difficult each time they were together.

Thanks to Caleb, she felt more confident, competent, sexy.

She liked it. Liked him. And felt herself growing closer to him. But she wasn't sure she could trust her feelings. Or his. He didn't seem eager to get into a relationship. She had avoided them herself. "There's no reason to rush into anything, right?"

"No," he said. "But I would like to see you tomorrow. How about I go with you to your parents' house?"

She stared at him in disbelief. "Seriously?"

He nodded. "You know Grams. Seems fair I should meet your parents."

"Sure." Becca wiggled her toes. "That would be great."

On Saturday afternoon, Caleb drove into the trailer park outside Twin Falls. He wasn't sure what to expect, but so far seemed stereotypical. Singlewides, doublewides and RVs filled the various lots. Cars and trucks were parked haphazardly on the narrow streets. Cats lounged in the sun. Dogs barked at his car.

"Turn left at the Statue of Liberty. You can't miss it," Becca said.

"I'm looking forward to meeting your parents."

"They can't wait to meet you."

A six-foot replica of the Statue of Liberty stood like a sentry at an intersection. Nearby, two men with handlebar mustaches and tattooed arms eyed his sports car. An elderly woman sat in a rocking chair with a Chihuahua on her lap on the porch of another trailer.

Becca pointed out the windshield. "My parents live in the trailer with the chicken wire fencing and the Jolly Roger flag."

O-kay. Caleb gripped his steering wheel and parked. Not only was there chicken fencing, but also live chickens. Was that even legal in the city limits? He turned off the ignition.

"My parents are normal folks, so don't be nervous," she said.

A couple thoughts ran through his mind. One, this was going to be interesting, if not enlightening. Two, he doubted he'd ever see the hubcaps on his car again. At least he had insurance. "I'm not nervous."

Not much anyway.

"Good, because I am."

Caleb fought the urge to kiss her nerves away. He squeezed her hand. "No reason to be nervous. They're your parents."

"Exactly." She rewarded him with a grin. "If my father wants to show you his gun and knife collection, say no. Otherwise, he'll try to intimidate you."

Caleb knew from what Becca had told him as well as the private investigator's report that her father had been arrested and jailed for fighting, so this didn't surprise him. "Good to know."

"If my mom mentions UFOs and government conspiracies, smile and nod. Whatever you do, don't mention Roswell or Flight 800."

"Maybe I should have brought a tinfoil hat."

"If you had, you would endear yourself to her forever." Becca moistened her lips. "I'm not kidding."

Her serious tone told him she wasn't.

If Becca considered this "normal folks," he wondered what her version of not-so-normal would be like. Given the Taylors' daughter had grown up to be such a lovely, caring and hardworking woman, he shouldn't rush to judgment. He'd made that mistake with Becca. "Let's go meet your folks."

A man and a woman in their early forties stood on the porch and waved.

"That's my mom and dad, Debbie and Rob," Becca said.

The woman had the same brown hair as Becca, only longer, and a similar smile. The man had lighter brown hair and the same blue eyes as his daughter. "They look so young."

More like an older brother and sister, not her parents.

"My mom was seventeen and my dad eighteen when they got married. I arrived a week before her eighteenth birthday."

"Kids having kids."

"They thought they were grown up enough at the

time, but both told me I should wait until I was older, maybe even in my thirties, to get married."

He opened the gate for Becca. "Good advice."

"Make sure none of the chickens escape."

Caleb closed the gate behind him and double-checked the latch was secure.

Introductions were made. Becca's parents were friendly. He received a handshake from Rob and a hug from Debbie. The four of them entered the house. Their trailer was small, tidy and welcoming. Pictures hung on the walls. Knick-knacks covered shelves. But no pets. Not a dog or a cat in sight. That surprised him given Becca's love of animals.

Caleb studied the photographs of a young Becca riding a tricycle and one of her winning a ribbon at a 4-H dog show.

He motioned to her high school graduation picture. "You used to have long hair like your mom's."

She nodded. "I'm not that same person anymore. I like my hair shorter."

"I like it, too," Caleb said, noticing her parents watching the exchange with interest.

"Why don't you help your mother with dinner," Rob said to Becca. "I'll keep Caleb company."

Becca followed Debbie into the kitchen.

Rob slapped him on the back. "So Caleb, you into guns and hunting?"

He remembered what Becca had told him, but he wasn't about to be intimidated. "My grandfather used to take my best friend and me elk hunting. Cross-bows, not guns."

"Bag anything?"

"A buck." Caleb remembered his surprise when he'd hit the animal. He'd felt a burst of excitement at making the shot and a rush of sadness at seeing the elk fall. "He was so much bigger than me. Had a helluva time getting him back to camp."

Bob looked toward the kitchen. "I've done some bear hunting."

Caleb expected to be invited to see the gun collection next.

Bob leaned closer. "Never could bring anything I shot home or Becca would cry. You might not want to mention that elk. She's fond of animals. Might hold it against you."

So much for being intimidated. "Thanks for the advice."

"You're welcome." Bob's gaze drifted to the kitchen again. He lowered his voice. "My daughter's caught some bad breaks."

"Becca told me."

"She works hard. Sends us money, even when she doesn't have much herself." Rob's gaze met Caleb's in understanding. "I don't want to see my little girl hurt."

"Me, either. She's a special woman."

"Good to hear you say that," Rob said. "Becca's never brought a man, or a boy for that matter, home before."

Caleb straightened. That surprised him. But she hadn't asked him home to meet her parents. He'd invited himself. She must be taking her parents' advice about waiting to get married until she was older. She had goals and dreams. The last thing she needed was a boyfriend to get in the way. The same way he didn't need a girlfriend. This would make life easier for both of them.

They wouldn't have to worry about things getting serious and complicated. They could keep having fun together and enjoying each other's company.

Yes, this was going to work out well.

In the kitchen, Becca put the tray of biscuits into the preheated oven. She set the timer. "Dinner smells good."

"Meatloaf with mashed potatoes and pie for dessert," her mother said. "Caleb's handsome."

"He's got the prettiest eyes and the nicest smile."

"You really like him."

"We haven't been seeing each other long."

"That doesn't mean you can't have feelings for him." Her mother stirred the gravy simmering on the stove. "I knew your father was the one a week after we met."

Becca had heard the story of how they met at a local burger joint over chocolate milk shakes and French fries many times. "How did you know?"

"It was a feeling." Her mother tilted her head. "We fit from that very first day. When we were apart it wasn't awful like the world was ending or someone had died, but when we were together things were better. We were a team. We complemented each other. If that makes sense."

That was how Becca felt with Caleb. "It does."

"Do you think you and Caleb might turn into something serious?"

Yes! She was afraid to voice her desire aloud. Afraid to believe in a happily ever after with him. "Maybe."

Her mother removed a bottle of salad dressing from the refrigerator. "How does he make you feel?"

"Special. Important. Like I can do anything." Her breath caught. "I think I'm falling for him."

"You think?"

Becca laughed. "Okay, I'm falling. I may have already fallen. It feels scary."

"Falling for someone is very scary. That's a normal feeling. But good, too." Her mother touched her shoulder. "You can't live stuck in the past. Afraid. Caleb isn't Whitley. If you like Caleb, give him a chance."

"I always thought all I needed in my life were dogs, but after meeting Caleb…"

Kissing him…

"You want more," her mom said.

"Yes." Becca not only wanted more, she needed more. That terrified her. The last time she wanted more, she'd ended up heartbroken and in jail. She hated to think that could happen with Caleb, too. "But we're so different. I'm not sure it can work. Do you think I can really fit into Caleb's world?"

"Yes. Just be yourself. If who you are doesn't fit, then he's not the right man for you."

"Mom."

"I'm serious." Her mother wrapped her arms around Becca. "You are a sweet, generous, smart woman with so much love to give the right man."

"I think Caleb might be the right man for me."

"Only time will tell."

Caleb wouldn't waste hours to drive to her parents' house if she didn't mean something to him. He acted as if he accepted her and her past. He called, texted and wanted to spend time with her. He had feelings for her. The only question was what kind of feelings. "I hope it doesn't take long."

"Patience is a virtue," her mother said.

Becca checked the biscuits. "I spent three years being patient. You'd think I'd get a break this time."

"Sorry to say, baby, but there aren't many breaks when it comes to love."

Love.

Becca liked the sound of that, liked it a lot.

She only hoped Caleb would, too.

And this time wouldn't turn out to be another big mistake.

CHAPTER ELEVEN

FOUR HOURS LATER, the headlights of Caleb's car cut through the darkness. Becca sat in the passenger seat, cocooned in the comfy, leather seats. Looking at his handsome profile, warmth flowed through her. "I thought the visit went well."

He glanced her way. "I had fun. Your parents are great."

"They like you."

"I like them." Caleb maneuvered the car around an orange semi-truck. "Your dad didn't pull out any guns or knives."

"Lucky," she teased. "He'd threatened to do that if you turned out to be a bozo or an idiot."

"Good to know I'm neither of those things." He re-adjusted his hands on the steering wheel. "Your mom is a kick. She should have been a lawyer. She had me almost convinced we never landed on the moon."

Becca laughed. "My mom can argue with the best of them."

"But I'm glad she had you instead of going on to college."

The pitter-patter of her heart tripled. "Me, too."

"What's your week like?" he asked.

"Busy. There's a local dog show on Saturday and Sunday. I'm going to be driving back and forth each day. We're too busy producing products in the lab for me to be away."

"It's going to be a busy week for me, too."

Bummer, but she wasn't about to complain after spending today with him. "Maybe we can see each other online."

"We'll figure something out."

The perfect end to a perfect day. Well that, and Caleb's toe-curling good-night kiss.

After he left, Becca brought the dogs to the guest cottage. "I'm in such a good mood you guys can sleep with me tonight."

She changed into a pair of flannel shorts and T-shirt and closed the blinds.

With two dogs on the bed with her, another three on the floor and a laptop in front of her, she answered emails about the products, a result of the samples she'd been handing out at dog shows and word of mouth. The lab had been turned into a mini-manufacturing plant, but Gertie's research assistants were taking the temporary change in job responsibilities in stride.

Becca's cellphone rang.

She glanced at the clock on the nightstand—11:28 p.m. Late for a call. Unless it was Caleb.

Adrenaline surged. She grabbed the phone. The name on the screen read Courtney Fairchild.

Becca hit answer. "Courtney?"

"Sorry to call so late." Courtney sniffled. "I'm in a bit of a jam."

The words came out stilted. Something was wrong. "What's going on?"

"My, um, car's in the Boise River."

Concern ricocheted through Becca. "Are you hurt?"

Her sharp voice woke the dogs. Maurice tried to climb on her lap. Hunter jumped off the bed.

"I'm…I think I'm okay." Courtney's voice quivered. "My car is ruined. Caleb's going to kill me. That's why I called you and not him or Grams. You won't be mad at me."

"Of course I'm not mad." Becca changed out of her pajamas and into clothes. "Where are you?"

Courtney gave her the crossroads. "Just follow the flashing lights. I'm going to need a ride home. If I don't end up going to the hospital. There's a cute firefighter who thinks I should go."

"Listen to him."

"Okay. I'll do whatever he says." Courtney sounded strange, mixed up, in shock. "I can't believe I ruined another car. Caleb's going to…"

"Don't worry about your brother." Becca slipped on her sandals. "I'm going to put the dogs in the kennel, then drive over. If you're not at the river, I'll drive to the nearest hospital, okay?"

"Thanks. I appreciate this."

Becca hoped Caleb wouldn't be upset for not calling him immediately. But she'd been in a similar spot. Calling anyone was difficult. She was happy to be there for Courtney, and as soon as Becca knew more she'd contact Caleb. "See you soon."

Hours later, Becca dozed in the waiting room of the hospital. She'd been sitting with Courtney until they took her for more tests due to the nasty bump on her head.

"What are you doing here?"

She opened her eyes to see a not-so-happy-looking Caleb standing in front of her. His gaze was narrowed. His mouth set in a firm, thin line. No wonder Courtney didn't want to call him.

"Courtney called me. She was hurting," Becca said. "Scared."

"My sister should be terrified." He shifted his weight from foot to foot. "Texting while driving. She could have been killed or killed somebody else."

"Thankfully, she wasn't, and she didn't."

"Her car is ruined."

"The airbag saved her life."

Caleb looked tense like a spring ready to pop open. His jaw was as rigid as a steel girder.

Becca touched his arm. His muscles bunched beneath her palm. "Courtney's going to be okay."

"This time. Like the last time." He exhaled slowly. "One of these times she won't be. That will kill Grams."

And him.

Becca could tell this was tearing Caleb up inside. She put her arm around him.

His body stiffened tightly—she might as well be

hugging a tree. He backed out of her embrace. "You shouldn't butt into my family's business."

Where had that come from? He was upset. She realized that, but his words were like a slap to her cheek. She took a breath. And another. "I'm not butting in. I told you Courtney called me."

Suspicion filled his gaze. Something she hadn't seen since they first met. "Why didn't you call me?"

"Courtney wasn't ready to see you."

"And you didn't think I should know what happened to my sister."

Becca tried not to take his anger personal. "It was late. If her injuries had been more serious—"

"The police thought it was serious enough to call me."

"The police?"

"I'm co-owner of the car. But that's the last time I do that." He brushed his hand through his hair. "Courtney needs to deal with the consequences of her actions. Clean up her messes. Not have others do it for her."

"She's still young."

"Only a year younger than you."

That surprised Becca. "She seems younger."

"That's because Courtney still acts like a spoiled little girl. She's too much like our father. My grandmother bailed him out of so many jams he never learned from his mistakes. Courtney's the same way."

"Learning from mistakes isn't always easy," Becca said. "Sometimes the lessons are so in your face it's hard to miss them. But other times it's not as clear."

He studied her for a moment, the anger clearing from his eyes. "You learned."

"I had three years to think about what I did."

But right now she wondered if she'd learned anything during that time. One thing was clear tonight. Caleb didn't want her here. He wanted to keep family stuff private. She ignored the sting in her heart. She needed to focus on Courtney right now.

Becca took a deep breath. "The point is everyone makes mistakes."

Including Caleb.

"Courtney makes more mistakes than most."

"You're her big brother." Becca softened her tone. If only he could see that he was making a big mistake with his younger sister. "Help Courtney figure out what she should be doing instead of getting into so much trouble."

"I've tried."

The anguish in his voice hurt Becca's heart. She touched his back. This time he didn't tense. "Try harder. You have a lot on your plate, but Courtney is your sister. I just met her, but it's clear she's bored out of her mind. She hates her job at Fair Face."

"She's never in the office."

"Why not?"

"She's off shopping or sleeping in late."

"So Gertie isn't the only one who lets Courtney get away with stuff."

"My sister is a handful."

"Yes, but threatening to kill her or cut her off from her trust fund if she messes up isn't helping matters."

"I don't want her to end up like our dad."

"No one does, but she's not happy. You can't force her to work at a job she doesn't want. She might be better off working in a different department or even another company," Becca said. "Getting Courtney pointed in the right direction isn't enabling her. It's supporting her. Helping her. That's what family does for one another."

"I'm being a jerk."

"Courtney will understand."

"I meant with you." He touched Becca's face. His gaze softened. "I wasn't expecting to see you here. It caught me off-guard."

"I understand."

And Becca did. She might want to let Caleb into her life and heart, but he wasn't there yet. For all she knew, he might never be there.

And that realization sucked.

The week dragged for Caleb. He hadn't seen Becca since the night at the hospital. He'd been a jerk to her. But he couldn't help himself.

Grams adored Becca. Courtney turned to Becca in her time of need. Caleb wanted to spend all his free time with Becca.

She'd become a pivotal person in his family. Something no one, not even Cassandra, had managed to do.

That bothered him. Immensely.

She'd gotten under his skin, but he couldn't allow her into his heart. He wasn't ready to get into something too deep. Not that she was pushing him into a relationship. Or had mentioned the word.

Maybe all he needed was distance.

So he didn't call her the rest of the week. Didn't text her.

But that didn't stop him from thinking about her.

He'd tried focusing on work, but thinking about her interfered with him accomplishing much. Sitting through one boring meeting after another hadn't taken his mind off her.

And here he was again in another meeting on a Friday afternoon.

To make matters worse, there was a weird vibe in the conference room. He looked around the table, pen between his fingers.

Glen, the vice president of Sales and Marketing, checked his watch for the twelfth time in the past fifteen minutes. Ed, the usually messy director of advertising, played housekeeper—wiping off the table, pushing in unused chairs and straightening papers. Julie, the new head of PR, kept sneaking peeks at the door as if HGTV were about to burst in and award her a dream house.

People were ready to kick off their weekends, but that didn't explain why the three of them were acting so strange.

Caleb tapped his pen against the table. "Anything else we need to discuss?"

Glances passed between them. Glen to Ed. Ed to Julie. Julie to Glen. All over Caleb's head. They might as well have been tossing a ball back and forth for their lack of subtlety.

"What's going on?" Caleb asked.

"Nothing."

"Nada."

"Not a thing."

The three spoke at the same time, their words falling on top of each other.

Something was definitely going on. He might be the CEO, the closest thing to a puppet master Fair Face had, but right now he felt as if someone else was manipulating the strings. He didn't like it.

"Talk to me," he said, using his hard-as-nails-don't-mess-with-me CEO voice he'd perfected for use in conference calls with suppliers.

Another shared glance passed among the three.

Glen cleared his throat. "Just a little anxious."

Caleb understood wanting to go home. He hadn't made plans to see Becca tonight, but maybe it wasn't too late. "Let's call it, then."

Julie jumped to her feet, her brown eyes widening and her gaze darting to the door. "Wait!"

Both Glen and Ed nodded furiously like Buster Bronco—the Boise State mascot— bobble-head dolls.

"I thought you wanted to get out of here," Caleb said.

"There's one more thing." Julie practically skipped away from the table, her shoulder-length red hair swinging behind her. She opened the door.

A bright light shone into the conference room.

Caleb dropped his pen. "What's—"

An attractive woman dressed in a maroon suit burst into the room. She held a microphone in one hand and a bottle of champagne in the other. Her straight, bleached teeth were as blinding as the camera light behind her.

"I'm Savannah Martin with *Good Day Boise*." The woman pronounced each word with precision. "Congratulations, Caleb Fairchild, you've been named Boise's Bachelor of the Year."

What the...

With lightning-quick moves that would make a ninja in high heels proud, Savannah thrust the champagne into his hands and shoved the microphone into his face. "Exciting news, isn't it?"

Caleb's gut churned, as if the gyro he'd eaten for lunch was waging war on his internal organs. He had no idea what being Bachelor of the Year entailed, but he doubted any of the hoopla would include Becca.

A predatory gleam filled the reporter's eyes, making him think she'd eat her young to get a story.

Not having a clue what to say, he stood. After all, that was the polite thing to do. Sweat dampened the back of his neck under his lightly starched collar. "Thank you."

The words rushed out faster than he'd intended. But he hadn't planned on being ambushed by the media and his own people.

Where was Ty when Caleb needed him? No one had his six here.

He glanced at the champagne and composed himself with a breath. "This is quite...an honor."

"Indeed." Savannah batted her eyelashes. Predator or flirt? "You had several nominations."

Who would have nominated him for Bachelor of the Year?

Not Grams's style, but Caleb wouldn't put it past Courtney with her odd sense of humor.

Caleb now knew why his coworkers had been acting so strangely during the meeting. The three stood together grinning like fools, as if year-end bonuses were going to arrive five months early. No doubt they'd had a hand in a few of the nominations. But… why?

"This is unexpected." He wished they had picked some other bachelor in town, someone who cared about this sort of thing. "I'm…stunned."

"I'm not." Savannah gave him a look that would make Jack Frost blush. "Trust me, ladies, this is one bachelor you most definitely want to get to know better. He's a hot one."

Hot, yes. Because of the damn light in his face.

Caleb didn't know how to respond, so he kept smiling instead, a tight smile that hurt the muscles all the way to his toes.

The reporter failed to sense his discomfort or his plastic smile. She seemed more interested in the camera than in him. "This is Savannah Martin with Fair Face CEO, Caleb Fairchild, Boise's Bachelor of the Year."

The light went off. The camera lowered.

He could see again. And breathe. But that didn't

loosen the bunched muscles in his shoulders or the fist-sized knot in his stomach.

A twentysomething man with a goatee and wearing faded jeans with a green T-shirt walked out of the meeting room carrying the camera.

Savannah's smile dimmed, as if her on switch connected to the camera's power button. "See you on Tuesday."

"Tuesday?" Caleb asked. Did he look as dazed as he felt?

"At the studio." The reporter's gaze ran the length of him—slow, methodical, appreciative.

She needed to stop looking at him like that. Becca wouldn't like it.

Whoa. Shock reverberated through him. He'd never worried about other women sizing him up when he was engaged to Cassandra. He shouldn't care now. Becca didn't own him. They weren't serious or exclusive. Had he gotten in deeper than he realized?

Julie skipped forward still looking as if she was in a hazy, dreamy mode. "You're being interviewed by *Good Day Boise*. I have all the details."

This was totally insane. There'd better be a good reason for the insanity, or three people would be looking for new jobs come Monday.

"See you on Tuesday, then." Caleb tried to keep his voice pleasant. Savannah left the room, closing the door behind her. "Sit."

His three employees took their places. Caleb sat, placed the champagne bottle on the table and let his smile drop. "What the hell was that all about?"

Ed and Julie looked at Glen, who twirled his pen like a baton. The pen rotated faster and faster.

Caleb's annoyance increased at the same rate of spin. He shot his vice president a tell-me-now-if-you-know-what's-good-for-you look. "Glen."

"My wife told me about the contest," he said. "I thought it would be good publicity for Fair Face."

"I agreed," Ed said.

"Me, too," Julie added. "It's a fantastic opportunity."

"Boise's Bachelor of the Year?" The words tasted bitter in Caleb's mouth. He picked up his pen and tapped it against the table. "Sure about this?"

Because he wasn't.

Two months ago, he would have popped open the champagne to celebrate. Two months ago, he would have phoned his grandmother to share the news. Two months ago, he would have texted Ty to rub it in.

Two months ago, Caleb hadn't known Becca Taylor.

He couldn't stop thinking about her melodic laughter and her hot kisses and when he could see her.

Even if seeing her again didn't make sense.

He didn't know what to think. Do. Say.

"This is a no brainer," Ed said. "Rave reviews about the baby line products are pouring in. Mothers are calling asking for samples. This is perfect timing."

"You can't buy this kind of PR," Glen said. "That's why we nominated you."

"The three of you?" Caleb asked.

"Our staffs," Glen admitted.

"And a few other employees." Ed made it sound like no big deal, but for all Caleb knew the entire company had nominated him. "This is a win-win situation for everyone involved."

It was lose-lose for him. Someone—okay, Becca—would be upset. That would make him unhappy.

Ed rested his elbows on the table. "We need you to play this right to maximize our exposure."

It sounded so calculated. Business often was, especially with advertising, and Caleb's job was to be the perfect CEO and present the correct image to the public. His grandfather had instilled that into him. "Tell me the slant."

Julie opened a manila folder. "Play up being single, but how you're looking to settle down."

Caleb drew back. "Whoa. Settle down?"

"And have a family," Julie said.

His empty hand slapped the table. The harsh sound echoed in the room. "What?"

"Mentioning you want a family will be the perfect segue to Fair Face's new baby products. The whole reason Gertie created the line is because she wants great-grandchildren, right?"

Caleb shifted in his chair. "Ri-i-i-ight."

"But you don't want to mention Gertie. This is about you, not your grandmother." The strategic glint in Glen's eye made him look more like a shark wearing a tie than a business executive. "Say you can't wait to use the new organic, all-natural baby products on your kids."

Caleb imagined Becca, her stomach round with their child. What the hell? He shook the image from his head. "I'm not married. Having kids is years off."

Julie's excited eyes and flushed face made her look as if she were about to bounce out of her chair. "That's where the contest comes in."

Ed nodded. "*Good Day Boise* wants to run a contest on their website."

"What's the prize?" Caleb asked.

Glen smiled. "A date with you."

Caleb stared in disbelief. "Please tell me you're kidding."

"This isn't any old date," Julie said, as if he hadn't said a word. "A dream date. Limousine. Romantic dinner for two at Pacifica. A dance club."

That was where he'd taken Becca on their first date. He couldn't take another woman—make that the contest winner—there.

"You can also do whatever else you want once the official date is over," Glen said with a wink-wink, nudge-nudge to his voice.

Caleb slunk in his chair. Becca was not going to like this.

Not that she had a claim on him, but just the fact he was putting her feeling first was out of character for him. He didn't understand it. He wanted it to stop.

"We'll do a billboard to promote the contest somewhere visible where most of Boise can see," Ed said. "We'll put it on the Facebook page. Take it national if we can. Offer a plane ticket and hotel accommodations if the winner isn't from Boise."

"Who picks the winner?" Caleb asked.

Julie rubbed her palms together as if she were trying to spark a fire. "A modern-day matchmaker."

Dream dates. Matchmaker. "This has to be a joke."

"Do I look like I'm joking?" Glen looked ultra-serious, as if the fate of the company were riding on this. "Your qualities for the perfect woman will be listed on *Good Day Boise*'s website. Viewers who believe they qualify can fill out a profile and see if they're a match."

He tossed his pen. It skidded across the table. "That's…"

"Marketing genius," Ed said. "If you end up dating the winner—"

"Imagine if you marry her," Julie said, her voice rising with each word as if Caleb was such a grand prize.

His stomach roiled. He was going to be sick. And it had nothing to do with what he'd eaten for lunch.

He needed to speak up, put an end to the craziness. "I'm seeing someone."

"Seeing?" Glen asked. "Or dating?"

Caleb hesitated. "It's not that serious."

It wasn't. So why was Becca branded on his brain? Affecting his working life? His family? Why was he putting her feelings ahead of what was best for Fair Face?

"Then it shouldn't be a problem," Glen said.

Caleb wished he had that much confidence. He didn't want to hurt Becca's feelings. They might not be that serious, but he didn't want to do anything to push her away. At least not that far away. "Put yourself in my shoes."

"A pair or two of new shoes might soothe any hurt feelings," Julie suggested.

Becca couldn't care less about fancy shoes. But she might like a new pair of grooming scissors. So not enough to smooth out this fiasco.

"This isn't personal. It's a business decision," Ed said. "Remember when we featured Gertie and Courtney in that series of ads for the moisturizing lotion. Sales shot through the roof."

How could Caleb forget? That campaign's success had floored everyone, including himself, and driven the company's brand recognition to new highs. Profits, too. "One in five women in the United States has tried a Fair Face product. You think we can achieve the same results here?"

"I do," Ed said. "As Bachelor of the Year you'll be the Grand Marshal of parades, do interviews and cut ribbons at grand openings. By the time we milk the last drop out of your title, two in five moms will be using our new products on their babies."

"Those numbers would make you happy," Glen said.

"I'd be thrilled." And Caleb would be.

He thought about the numbers. The exposure. The profits.

Face it. The website contest wasn't that big a deal in the grand scheme of things. One date. With a stranger. No big commitment.

Except for Becca.

Becca.

What was he worried about?

He liked her. They weren't exactly dating. They had fun together. Getting seriously involved with her would be too complicated and only add to his list of responsibilities. Becca. Her parents, Debbie and Rob. All the dogs.

That would be too much with everything else on Caleb's plate.

This Bachelor of the Year award would be the perfect reason for him to refocus on work and get Becca out of his heart—make that head. He was blowing a few dates—uh, get-togethers—out of proportion. He wasn't about to fall in love with her.

No worries at all.

Besides, Becca was one of the most practical women he knew. She would understand that he was doing this for Fair Face. She wouldn't care.

At least she shouldn't.

They weren't boyfriend and girlfriend. They hadn't made any type of commitment to one another. He wasn't going down that path again any time soon. If ever.

"Okay," Caleb said. "Let's make this work."

CHAPTER TWELVE

AT AN ITALIAN café in downtown Boise, Becca sat across from Caleb. "Thanks for inviting me out to dinner tonight. I didn't expect this at all."

"I'm glad you didn't have other plans."

She couldn't think of a better way to spend a Friday evening. "Well, I must admit it was a tough choice. Going out to dinner with you or getting ready for the dog show tomorrow."

He glanced up from his menu. "I'm honored you picked me."

Her heartstrings played a romantic tune that matched the violin music playing in the restaurant.

Romantic, indeed, with a lit candle stuck into a wax covered bottle of Chianti. A single red rosebud sat in a small glass vase, looking so perfect she'd wondered if the flower were real. One sniff of the sweet fragrance answered that question.

Real.

Just like tonight.

Becca looked over her menu at Caleb. He wore a navy suit, white button-down collared shirt and a colorful red tie with swirly patterns.

Proper CEO, definitely.

Handsome, oh yes. Swoonworthy, no doubt.

Becca swallowed a sigh. She liked spending time with him. It didn't matter what they did, either. His company and his kisses were more than enough. A good thing he seemed to agree.

She'd worried what happened at the hospital with Courtney had changed things between them. He hadn't called or texted. But Becca knew he had to be busy like her. "I wanted you to know Courtney is working on the labels for the dog products. She has an eye for design."

"Wait until you see the finished product."

"Caleb…"

"Okay, that wasn't nice of me." He looked over the top of his menu. "You'll be happy to know Courtney's going to be doing four-week rotations through various departments to see what type of jobs are available at Fair Face."

"That's wonderful."

"We'll see how it goes."

"Have faith."

"You haven't been through this with Courtney before."

"No, but I've been through it," Becca said. "Imagine if Gertie hadn't taken a chance on me. We wouldn't be here tonight."

The thought sent a chill down her spine. Becca expected Caleb to say something funny or sincere. She wanted him to smile or laugh. Instead he returned to reading his menu.

That was…odd. Maybe he'd had a rough day at the office. "Good day at work?"

"Typical."

His one-word answer was atypical. Usually he told her about something he'd done, a story from a meeting or an office anecdote. She wondered if something had happened that he didn't want to talk about.

"Know what you're going to order?" she asked.

He perused the menu. "The salmon looks good. You?"

"The halibut special sounds tasty."

"It does."

Standard dinner conversation, except it wasn't standard for them. Each word made her want to squirm in her seat. Maybe she was being paranoid. Overly analytical. Or maybe something was really going on.

She crinkled the edges of the menu. The words blurred. She couldn't stand it. "Is something wrong?"

"I wouldn't say wrong."

Okay, she wasn't paranoid. But that didn't make the churning of her stomach any better.

"What's going on?" Becca tried to sound nonchalant. She wasn't sure if she succeeded. She took a sip of water, hoping to wash away the lump in her throat.

"I was named Boise's Bachelor of the Year today."

Becca choked on the water in her mouth, coughed, but managed not to spit the liquid out. She swallowed instead.

"Wow." She tried to think of something to say other than *But aren't you going out with me?* "You must be…excited."

"I wouldn't say excited."

That made her feel a little better. She bit the inside of her cheek. "So this isn't that big a deal?"

He set his menu on the table. "Everyone at Fair Face is calling it a PR coup."

"A coup?"

"I'm being interviewed on *Good Day Boise* next week."

"Wow." Oops. She'd already said that. But her mind was reeling. "A TV interview is huge."

"I've done interviews before."

Caleb was downplaying this. Maybe Bachelor of Year was like the Sexiest Man Alive award, more of an honorary title than anything else. No reason for her to freak out. They might be dating, but technically he was still a bachelor.

Becca needed to be supportive, not act like a shrew. She raised her glass in the air. "Congrats."

He studied her with an odd expression. "You don't…mind."

"Why would I mind?" She asked the question as much for her benefit as his. "I don't see a ring on your finger."

Or one on hers.

But even though she knew better, even though his harsh words at the hospital had stung, she could imagine a tuxedo-clad Caleb sliding a shiny gold wedding band on her finger.

Her insides twisted. She took another sip of water. It didn't help.

He picked up his menu. "Thanks for being so understanding about this."

"Why wouldn't I be understanding?" She asked herself aloud. "It's an honor."

"You're really great, you know that."

So that was what being understanding got her. She would take it. "Thanks. Though I have no doubt women are going to be throwing themselves at you wanting to capture the Bachelor of the Year's heart."

His smile returned, reaching all the way to his eyes. "They can try, but they won't succeed."

Caleb's words put her at ease. His heart wasn't up for grabs because it was spoken for…by her. Even Becca's fingernails felt as if they were smiling. "Good to know."

"Don't worry about any of this," he said. "It'll be a big infomercial for Fair Face's new organic baby product line."

"Bachelor and babies. Not the usual combination."

"It's how things are done these days."

Business, she reminded herself. Nothing personal. How many times had she heard that since meeting Caleb?

More times than she could remember. Except…

Something niggled at her. Something she couldn't quite explain.

The feeling was familiar, like a little voice of caution whispering inside her head. The voice she should have listened to before going out with Whit and his friends that fateful night.

224 THE MAN BEHIND THE PINSTRIPES

Crazy. She was thinking crazy thoughts now. Going overboard with the paranoia.

Caleb Fairchild was nothing like those rich kids back in high school. He might wear designer labels, drive an expensive car and have a ton of money, but he cared about her.

Everything he'd done, everything he was doing, proved that.

Maybe he hadn't fallen for her as she'd fallen for him. But he liked her. She should enjoy this time with Caleb, not borrow trouble. Things would only get better between them. A satisfied smile settled on her lips.

"You look happy," he said.

"I am."

"You've put me in a much better mood."

That pleased her. "Being with you makes me happy."

"I want you to be happy."

Becca's heart sang with joy. He did care. She knew it.

Ever since Caleb had entered her life, things had gotten better, not worse. The words *I love you* sat on the tip of her tongue. They would be so easy to say.

But she wanted the timing to be right. She wanted the place to be perfect. She wanted him to say the words back to her.

Becca needed to wait. Just a little while. Let this bachelor thing blow over. Give them more time to make memories together.

But soon. Very, very soon.

* * *

Tuesday morning at the television studio, the lights beat down on Caleb. Sweat streamed down his back, a mix of heat and nerves.

The red light on the two cameras reminded him the show was being shown live. He needed to at least act like he'd rather be here than at the dentist for a root canal.

But sitting on the couch with Savannah and Thad, the hosts of *Good Day Boise*, was the height of awkwardness. The two looked like pictures from a plastic surgeon's office with their bleached smiles, pouty fish lips and straight, proportioned noses. They droned on about this year's bachelor candidates and why Caleb had been chosen number one.

He kept a smile super-glued on his face and nodded when he thought appropriate.

Savannah leaned toward him with a coquettish grin. The V-neckline of her dress gaped, showing her cleavage. Caleb looked away.

Thad laughed, though Caleb had no idea at what. "The big questions our female viewers want to know—"

"Single female viewers," Savannah interrupted. "Though there may be a couple married ones, too."

Thad guffawed. Or maybe it was another of his fake laughs. "Is there a special woman in your life, Caleb?"

Becca. An image of her appeared front and center in his mind. Her sweet smile made his day. Her beautiful eyes lit up each time she saw him. Her hot kisses turned him on. She was special, more special than any other woman he'd dated.

Saying Becca's name would be easy. Saying Becca's name felt right. Saying Becca's name wasn't part of the script he was supposed to follow.

It didn't matter anyway. She understood. She'd said so herself on Friday night. She wouldn't care or be upset. They weren't serious.

Caleb took a deep breath. "No one special. Which is too bad."

"Why is that?" Thad asked.

The hosts gobbled the bait, exactly the way Ed had said they would. Time to reel them in with the money shot. Or in this case the perfect sound bite. Caleb straightened. "Because I want to start a family."

Savannah and Thad exchanged glances. Excitement danced in their eyes. "Boise's Bachelor of the Year wants a family?"

They spoke in unison, in a creepy kind of sing-song voice.

The image of Becca remained front and center in mind, calling to Caleb.

Speak up, his heart cried.

Why the hell was his heart involved in this? It shouldn't be. No woman could touch his heart. Not even...

Get with the program, Fairchild.

Caleb swallowed around the lump in his throat. He pushed the image of Becca from his mind. He needed to follow the script. "Yes, I want a family. Having one is important to me."

Savannah touched his sleeve with her bright red painted nails, making him think of a spider, the kind who eats their mates. "What is a handsome, rich industrialist looking for in his perfect woman?"

Perfect woman.

The two words made his stomach turn.

Caleb knew what he wanted. Who he wanted. But the PR department had dreamed up a list for him. A list that technically fit his position and roughly reflected his interests for a woman who Caleb would have, up to this point, considered an ideal spouse. "Educated, a keen sense of humor, stylish, fit, well-traveled, social, a little sophisticated, a foodie, a discriminating ear when it comes to music and plays tennis."

Each word rang hollow.

Such a woman was safe, dull, orderly.

Like his life.

Becca was so much more than the sum of all those items on the list. Fun, energetic, nurturing.

He wanted to tell the hosts and the audience about Becca, about her amazing qualities. But Fair Face was counting on him. It didn't matter what he thought. It didn't matter what he wanted.

Ty was downrange fighting bad guys to keep their country safe. Caleb was stuck on a couch lying his ass off because safe and dull had made his family company successful.

"Sounds like there might be a woman or two in Boise who share some of those characteristics," Savannah said.

Yes, but he wanted only one woman.

No, he didn't.

Caleb was getting in too deep. The fact that Becca kept coming up told him that. He'd lowered his guard too much and let her into his heart. Bad move. He couldn't trust romantic relationships. Being involved in a serious relationship was too difficult. Too much work and responsibility. He'd had enough of that already. "I hope so."

Except being with Becca hadn't been work, his heart countered. She made him happy.

He wanted his heart to shut up.

He'd tried getting married. That relationship had been a disaster. Becca wasn't trying to scam him. As special as she was, as much as she hadn't been a burden, he didn't want to fall in love with her. He couldn't do that to himself. Or her.

Caleb had gotten too close to her, too fast. He needed to pull back, stop seeing her, focus on Fair Face.

The expectations of the marketing and PR departments were riding on Caleb's every word, weighing him down and making him sweat. He always did what was expected of him. This was no different.

Stick with the script.

"I'd hate to think I'd never be able to use Fair Face's new line of organic baby products on my own children."

Savannah sighed along with the audience full of smiling women. "Baby products."

He'd elicited the right response from her and the audience. Good, except his victory felt empty.

"My grandmother's ready to be a great-grand-mother. She created the products as a not-so-subtle hint to me. All I'm missing is…"

"A wife," Savannah said with glee.

"Perhaps we can help you find her," Thad said.

Savannah nodded enthusiastically. "We're going to hold a contest on our website to find Boise's Bach-elor of the Year's perfect woman."

"She could be sitting in our studio audience. Or maybe she's watching at home," Thad said. "Go to our website and find out if you have the qualities to be Caleb's perfect woman. The prize is a dream date with Boise's Bachelor of the Year. Who knows? The date could turn into something more!"

"Thanks." The word felt as if Caleb was eating tar. "I could use all the help I can get finding her!"

One thought ran through Caleb's head. Too bad he couldn't have been voted the second most eligible bachelor in Boise this year.

At least this would be over soon. He would go on the stupid date, then get on with his life. Alone, the way he liked it.

Win-win, right?

Becca stared at the television set in the guest cottage. She held on to two dogs, Dozer and Hunter, one on each side of her. Each breath took concerted effort. Her throat burned. Tears filled her eyes.

Don't cry. Don't cry. Do not cry.

She blinked back the tears.

She'd set the DVR to record the interview. She never wanted to watch it again. Not ever.

Her heart ached, a painful, squeezing kind of hurt. Disappointment. Betrayal.

Caleb had made her think this bachelor-of-the-year thing was no big deal. That it was business.

PR opportunity or not, his words on this morning's interview stung. More than she ever thought possible.

So much for protecting her heart.

Becca hadn't. It had splintered into a million razor sharp shards. And now…

Women all over Boise, likely northern Idaho and eastern Oregon, were going to be vying to be Caleb's perfect woman and go on a dream date with him in hopes of being his wife.

Thank goodness she hadn't told him she loved him.

She wanted to throw up.

It was clear she wasn't his perfect woman.

Tears continued to sting her eyes.

Judging by the list of qualities, he was looking for a woman with a similar background and upbringing. She might be able to write a business report, but an AA degree didn't count as educated. Preferring hot dogs to fancy food meant she couldn't call herself a foodie. She'd never travelled outside the Pacific Northwest.

Hurt sliced through her stomach. All her insecurities rushed to the surface.

The dogs squirmed out of her arms. She let them go.

Why had Gertie played matchmaker when Becca was so wrong for Caleb?

Becca wrapped her arms around her stomach.

Gertie should never have chosen some fish out of water to put in the rich, corporate aquarium for her grandson. Dating might not influence Fair Face's bottom line, but there was intrinsic value to the woman Caleb...married.

Becca rocked back and forth.

Caleb had shown his practical side during the interview. He didn't need someone who preferred the company of dogs, not dressing up and eating hot dogs. He needed a corporate wife. Someone who could entertain, dress the part and play hostess. A trophy wife.

The vise tightened around Becca's heart, pressing and squeezing out the blood. She sniffled.

How had she completely misread the man? Maybe she'd ignored signs because she enjoyed being with him. The same way she'd ignored the signs with Whit.

It hadn't felt the same, but she could have been fooling herself. She had to have been fooling herself.

Caleb hadn't told her about the dream date contest, only being named Bachelor of the Year and doing an interview. He'd lied by omission, making her wonder if he'd lied about other things. Lied or...been practical?

She'd told him she wouldn't pretend to be someone she wasn't after what happened with Whit. If she wasn't what Caleb wanted, was this his way of breaking up with her?

Becca couldn't answer that question herself, but she intended to find out the answer.

If not for the time of day, champagne would have been flowing at Fair Face. Interest in the new baby line had skyrocketed following Caleb's interview. Whatever issues he'd had about saying he wanted to settle down had disappeared.

Genius. Brilliant. Smart move.

The words described how wonderfully they'd pulled off the PR coup on *Good Day Boise*. There was only one loose end to tie up, and he could relax.

Becca.

His assistant buzzed him. "Ms. Taylor is here to see you."

Okay, that was weird. He hadn't expected her to come to him. But he might as well get this over quickly so he could attend the celebration in the company's cafeteria in honor of his award and interview. "Send her in."

Becca entered his office. She was dressed casually in a pair of plain khakis, a blue blouse and canvas tennis shoes. She looked neat, fit and very pretty. But she wasn't smiling

He didn't blame her.

As she walked in, the others in his office walked out.

"See you in the cafeteria," Ed said.

Caleb nodded. "Be down shortly."

The door closed. He walked around to the front of his desk and leaned against it. "You saw the interview."

"I did." She raised her chin. "I'm sure the show's servers are going to overload with all the women wanting to win a dream date with you."

Her sarcastic tone matched the expression on her face. "It's a contest. A promotion."

She pursed her lips. "Then why didn't you tell me about it?"

"I didn't think it mattered. It's just business."

"Business?" Disbelief filled her voice. "You listed all the qualities you're looking for in the perfect woman. None of which I have."

"The PR department provided the list. It was a publicity stunt. Nothing more."

"It hurt hearing you say all those things you were looking for and imagining the perfect corporate trophy wife who fits the list. A woman who wasn't me."

"I told you it wasn't my list," he said. "But it's not like we're seriously dating."

"Ouch." She stared at him as if he'd grown a third eye and horns. "At least I have bruises on both cheeks now."

"I never wanted to hurt you." But Caleb had, and he couldn't take it back.

Her bottom lip quivered.

It was all he could do not to take her in his arms so she would feel better. But he couldn't.

This was the best. For Becca and for him.

"So what happens next?" she asked. "And I don't mean your dream date. I'm talking about you and me."

You and me. Not us. That had to be a good sign. "I'm not in a place to have a serious relationship."

"I figured that much."

"You have a lot going on with the dog products and developing a handling career."

Her gaze narrowed. "Don't put any of this on me."

Guilt coated his throat. Okay, bad move. "It's me."

"Yes, it is." She wet her lips. "I want to know why you went out with me."

"Being with you was fun."

"Fun," she repeated twice. "I thought things were more serious than that."

"No. I can't. I'm sorry. I've been distracted. I need to get back to work."

"So this is about Fair Face?"

"After my father died, my grandparents' hopes and dreams for him were transferred onto me. I've spent my life trying to do everything my father didn't do. For my family and for Fair Face. I can't take anything else on."

"You mean me."

"Yes."

"I don't want to be your responsibility. I'm doing fine on my own."

Becca was. And she was cutting through his reasons like a skilled surgeon. He would try again.

"I'm not ready to make an emotional commitment." The last time he did that it blew up in his face. Desire had a way of turning him inside out. He couldn't screw up again. "I can't risk the indulgence of a relationship right now."

Flames ignited in Becca's eyes. Her jaw tensed. "Indulgence of a relationship?"

"Perhaps that's the wrong word." He was bungling this up. He wasn't usually so clumsy and the hurt in Becca's eyes was killing him. He couldn't think straight. Not when she was around him. Even more proof he needed her out of his life. "I need to focus my attention on Fair Face. Nothing else. Not even the dog care products."

His words slammed into him, as if he'd punched himself in the gut. But he'd had no other choice than to say them. He couldn't keep seeing her.

Becca swallowed, but said nothing. Hurt dulled her eyes.

He reached for her, then drew his arm back. If he touched her, he might not want to let go. "Look, I could have gone about this differently. But I didn't. We had some good times together. Let's not have this blow up into something awful."

"That's the first thing you've said that I agree with." She met his gaze. "Thanks for opening my eyes to the truth."

"The truth?"

"You don't deserve me."

"Becca—"

"You act responsible and practical, but you're not." Her voice rose. "I'm guessing you went out with me to appease Gertie and keep her happy. You could make sure I wasn't trying to scam your grandmother and you could have a little fun at the same time."

"No." Her words hit him like a dagger to the heart. "I went out with you because I wanted to be with you. No other reason."

"But once things turned into something real, where you would have to take risk, you decided it was over between us. You could have spoken up, but that would have been too scary, so you followed someone else's script, the way you've done your entire life."

"That's not true." But his words didn't have a strong conviction behind them. He would try again. "Not true at all."

"It is true, because I was once there myself. But I'm over the wariness of my past. In part, thanks to you. But you're not because of your mother, your father and Cassandra. I'm not sure you ever will be, either." Squaring her shoulders, Becca met his gaze. "I never thought I'd say this, but I feel sorry for you, Caleb Fairchild."

She turned and walked to the door.

He stood, his heart pounding in his chest. "You have no idea what you're talking about."

Becca didn't glance back. She kept walking out of his office and out of his life.

Which was exactly what he'd wanted to happen.

So why did it hurt so badly?

CHAPTER THIRTEEN

BECCA FOUGHT THE urge to run out of Caleb's office. She made a conscious effort not to slam the door to his office behind her. She wasn't going to make a scene.

Or cry.

Her anger spiraled.

She knew her worth. She wasn't going to forget that or become someone else to make Caleb love her.

Screw him.

Becca should have seen through his BS, through the sweet words and tender smiles and hot kisses. Caleb couldn't accept her for who she was. He wanted someone more suited to his world. He wasn't willing to take a risk on her.

On them.

She marched to the elevator.

Caleb could blame his job at Fair Face or his family or a hundred other things, but bottom line…he wasn't capable of loving her as she was.

That was what Becca deserved.

What she wanted.

The elevator dinged. The doors opened.

Becca stepped inside. She poked the button for the lobby, nearly breaking one of her already short fingernails.

How could she have been so stupid again?

She'd been trying to fit in and prove herself in order to gain Caleb's acceptance. But the people who truly loved her and knew her accepted her fully, the way the dogs did. People like Gertie and her parents. Anything Becca accomplished was the proverbial icing on the cake.

She hadn't needed to earn their love.

Love was unconditional. And if it wasn't, she wasn't interested. Period.

The weeks ran into each other. Caleb tried to focus on work, but thinking about Becca distracted him as much as when she was a part of his life. He kept telling himself things had worked out for the best. Breaking it off now had saved them both from suffering any real hurt. It was time to move on.

But tonight, on his dream date at Pacifica, he had to wonder if moving on had been for the best.

Sweat dripped down the back of Caleb's neck due to the heat of the camera light and nerves.

A cameraman stood next to the table for two, filming every moment Caleb spent with a beautiful blonde thirty-year-old woman named Madeline Stevens. He had to give the matchmaker credit. Madeline met all the PR department's qualifications and then some. She'd graduated from Yale, studied in Paris and owned an art gallery. She sat on the board of two local nonprofits. She had a centerfold-worthy body and wore a sexy little black cocktail dress that showed off her curves. She was everything a man in his position should want in a girlfriend, a wife even.

Except she wasn't…Becca.

Madeline glanced at the camera. "I had no idea tonight would be a threesome."

Sense of humor, check. He'd been crossing off the qualities she met from his mental list. "No one mentioned we'd have a chaperone and everything would be on camera."

He would never have agreed to this if he'd known a follow-up story, complete with film footage, would be shown on *Good Day Boise*.

"Well, I guess we're getting a taste of what being on a reality TV show would be like," she said.

"I'll pass."

"Me, too." She stared up through her mascara-covered eyelashes at him and lowered her voice. "Maybe we can ditch him and find some place private where we can…talk."

The suggestive tone of her voice told him talking wasn't what she had in mind. But strangely, Caleb wasn't the least bit interested in doing anything other than calling it a night.

He didn't want Madeline to feel uncomfortable, though he sure did. He hated being here. Hated having to pretend to be interested in such a lovely woman when he'd rather be eating hot dogs at home by himself or peanuts with Becca.

The cameraman moved in closer, then adjusted the microphone.

Caleb needed to keep the conversation flowing, something he'd struggled to do with Madeline. Unlike with Becca. If she were here, the discussion would flow, uninterrupted, from topic to topic.

He didn't understand why he was out with a stunningly attractive woman and thinking about Becca, especially after what she'd said to him. But he couldn't get her out of his head. "So, do you have any pets?"

"No," Madeline said. "I work long hours. I don't think it would be fair to a dog or cat to leave them alone."

Good answer. One that Becca—make that Grams—would approve of. "I don't have any pets or plants for the same reason."

She leaned forward. Her face puckered in distaste. "There are silk plants. But at least live plants don't shed dog hair."

Caleb remembered Maurice and Becca's lint roller. "My grandmother has a couple of dogs that leave hair everywhere. It's not that bad. Unless you're wearing black."

Madeline's eyes narrowed. She wet her lips. "Oh, no. I never meant that it was bad. I'm an animal lover. Dogs are the sweetest things. One of these days, I'll adopt one from a rescue group."

Her backtracking reminded him of Cassandra, who'd said whatever she thought he wanted to hear.

The total opposite of Becca, who spoke her mind, whether he wanted to hear it or not.

He remembered being at the dog show with her. "Dogs are a lot of work."

"That's why people use doggy day cares."

The words made him cringe. Becca would never take a dog to a place like that. She would rather care for them herself.

The way she'd taken care of Grams's dogs and Grams and Courtney and...

Him.

His mouth went dry. He picked up his water glass and drank. It didn't help. He took another sip. The funny feeling in the pit of his stomach only worsened.

What had he done?

He'd been so worried about taking on one more responsibility, but he shouldn't have been. Becca had been taking care of all of them, especially him, from the day he met her.

He'd been wrong about her past.

He was wrong about her.

But he couldn't see that until sitting here with a woman who on paper should have been perfect for him, but wasn't.

Not Madeline's fault. She was too much like Cassandra and totally different from...

Becca.

Tomorrow he would go to her. Apologize. Ask for a second chance.

All he had to do was survive the camera and the

rest of his dream date. He hoped that the rest of the evening didn't turn into a nightmare.

The next morning Caleb arrived at the estate and rang the doorbell.

Mrs. Harrison opened the door. "Your grandmother is in her bedroom."

"What about Becca?"

"I believe she's on her way to a dog show."

Damn. That would complicate talking with her. He entered Grams's room to find her packing. "Where are you going?"

"Enumclaw, Washington." She folded a pink T-shirt. "Big dog show. We have a vendor booth for our products."

"Is Becca going to be there?"

"She left yesterday in the RV with the dogs and her parents. I'm meeting her there later today." Grams stopped packing. "How was your dream date last night? Did you find your perfect woman?"

The sarcasm in Grams's voice was clear. Caleb took a deep breath. "I won't be asking the winner out again, if that's what you're asking."

"At least you haven't lost all your brain cells." Grams returned to packing. "Before I forget, I need you to schedule a week's vacation. I'll give a range of dates to your assistant before I head out."

"Why?"

"Your birthday present."

"My birthday isn't until January."

"With your schedule, I need to plan ahead."

"Where am I going?"

"A navy SEAL training camp."

His heart skipped two beats. He could barely breathe. He'd always wanted to attend one. He had the money, but not the time. He'd also never told anyone he wanted to go, not even Ty. "How did you…?"

"I buy your gift in the summer, since your birthday is close to Christmas. That way I make sure it's different. Special."

"But SEAL training?" he forced the question from his dry throat.

"Becca. It was her idea, " Grams said. "I wasn't sure about it."

"It's the perfect gift."

"That's what Becca said."

Becca.

Of course she would be the one to suggest the gift. She knew him, really and truly knew him.

And she was exactly the woman he needed.

He'd been such a fool. An idiot.

I learned my lesson. I'm not going to try to be someone I'm not ever again.

No wonder hearing that list had hurt Becca so much. Caleb had known what she'd gone through with Whit, but he'd been thinking only about Fair Face and himself. Not how hearing the list of his perfect qualifications would affect and hurt Becca. She was correct, he didn't deserve her.

But he loved her. He wanted her back.

His chest tightened with regret.

Becca was the one for him.

He should have screamed her name during his interview, not gone along with someone else's script for his life and taken another woman on a dream date. He should have held on to Becca with both hands, not let her walk out of his office and out of his life. He should have told her she was his perfect woman, not let her think she wasn't.

"Grams…"

She walked to his side and touched his face. "You're pale as a ghost."

He was so used to taking care of everyone, but he hadn't taken care of Becca. Not the way she'd taken care of him. "I've made a big mistake. The biggest mistake of my life."

"With Becca?"

Caleb nodded. He had always done what was expected of him. He'd put his own dreams aside. He'd put his life on hold. He'd hurt someone he cared about because that was what everyone expected him to do.

No longer.

Becca had been right. He'd been following a script. That was easier than risking his heart only to be hurt again.

He was in the doghouse, but he was willing to beg, to perform tricks, to do whatever was needed to be a part of her life. She didn't need him. But he needed her. Her smile, her sense of humor, her love.

Grams smiled. "So how do you intend on fixing it?"

Becca walked out of Ring Five with Hunter's leash in one hand and a Best of Winners—the prize for a dog still working on his championship ribbon—in the other. The sun beat down, but the beagle didn't seem to mind. She couldn't wait to remove her suit jacket.

Gertie stood, her hands clasped together and a bright smile on her face.

Becca handed off the ribbon. "He needs one more major and he's a champion."

"So proud of both of you."

"Thanks." The word sounded flat. Becca couldn't help it. Normally she would be thrilled with the win, bouncing on her toes and tingling with excitement, but it was all she could do to keep her feet moving and not retreat to the RV to nap.

Maybe some caffeine would help. She'd been living off coffee lately.

Heaven knew she needed something to get her out of this funk. She couldn't quite shake her sadness. She'd tried pushing Caleb out of her thoughts. She'd succeeded somewhat, but she couldn't get him out of her heart.

At least not yet.

The feeling would pass. Someday. Someday soon she hoped.

But she was better off having met Caleb. He'd shown her what she wanted and didn't want.

"Let's go see how your parents are doing at the booth." Gertie had hired Becca's parents to sell the products at dog shows and fill online orders. "I also want to show off Hunter's ribbon."

They walked along the row of vendor booths, tables and displays set up under pop-up canopies that provided shade.

"Your parents have company at the booth," Gertie said.

Becca was pleased by how much her parents enjoyed talking to dog owners about the products. Gertie called them "natural salespeople." Maybe so, but Becca also knew they were friendly hard workers who didn't want to disappoint Gertie or their daughter. "Customers are a good thing."

"I don't think this one is interested in dog products."

Becca looked over and froze.

Caleb.

Her heart tumbled. She couldn't breathe.

"What's he doing here?" she asked, her voice shaking as much as her insides.

"Let's find out."

"No." Becca's feet were rooted to the pavement. She couldn't have moved. Even if she were being chased by vampires or brain-eating zombies or ax-wielding murderers, she would be eaten or slain where she stood. "You go."

She stared at him in his khakis and polo shirt. She could only see his backside, but every nerve ending tingled as if she'd touched a live wire and sent a jolt of electricity through her.

Gertie pulled on Becca's arm. "Come on. You're no coward."

"Yes, I am."

Gertie gave a not-so-gentle shove. "Chin up and move those feet, girlie."

Becca moved. It was either that or fall over. With each step, an imaginary boom, like a timpani, echoed through her. "I can't—"

"Yes, you can," Gertie encouraged. "One step in front of the other."

Becca crossed the aisle toward their booth. Light-headed and stomach churning, she thought passing out was a distinct possibility. At least in that case, she wouldn't have to face him.

"Caleb," Gertie said.

He turned. Smiled.

Becca went numb.

"Hello," he said, as if his being at a dog show in a different state was to be expected.

She opened her mouth to speak, but no words came out.

He looked at Becca with warm, clear eyes. "I missed you."

Her heart slammed against her ribs. Anger surged. "Is this some kind of joke?"

"No joke." Caleb motioned to the booth. "Looks like the products are selling thanks to your top-notch sales force."

Becca's parents smiled at her.

She stared at Caleb, her temper spiraling out of control. "You discard me like garbage. Hurt my feelings worse than anyone, which is saying a lot. Then show up here as if nothing had happened. Unbelievable."

Tension sizzled in the air. People glanced her way, but kept walking. Two dogs barked at each other.

"You're right." He sounded contrite, but that didn't make her feel any better. "You've always been right."

Okay, she hadn't been expecting that.

"I am here. I don't blame you if you don't want to talk to me, but I hope you'll hear me out."

A beat passed. And another. "Five minutes."

He pulled her to one side and glanced at his watch. "I was getting too attached to you. I was distracted at work. I was happier with you than my own family. That scared me. You scared me. I was too afraid to take a risk. Too afraid you might be the one to break me. So I played it safe. Too safe. And I lost the one person I need most in my life. The one person who understands me. The one person who makes me stronger. You took care of me in a way no one else had. I miss that. I miss you."

The air rushed from her lungs. A lump burned in her throat. Tears stung her eyes. She couldn't think. She couldn't speak.

"You're amazing, unique and everything I didn't realize I wanted until you came into my life, and then I stupidly let you go," he continued. "I'm sorry for the crappy way I treated you. I was no better than that idiot Whit. But I apologize. For doing the asinine interview and agreeing to the contest. For not telling you and then breaking up the way that I did. I don't blame you for not loving me after all I've done, but I love you. And if there's any way you could find it in your heart to forgive me, I'll make it up to you. I want to spend the rest of my life making it up to you."

She forced herself to breathe. "That's why you came here?"

He nodded. "I was going to go crazy if I had to spend another day without seeing you."

Her heart melted. She knew better, but it didn't matter.

"I think I have at least another two minutes. Maybe three." His eyes were earnest, his voice sincere. "Do I stand a chance?"

She wanted to say no. She wanted to tell him to go. She wanted to move on without him.

His smile practically caressed her.

But her heart wanted something different. Wanted him.

"For as long as I can remember I've been trying to prove myself. If I did that, then I thought I could be accepted." Becca took a deep breath. "But Gertie encouraged me. Then you. I realized I didn't have to do anything special. I had to accept who I was and the rest would happen."

"It's happening."

Becca could feel it. Acceptance. Joy. Love.

"I forgive you." The way she'd finally forgiven herself for her past mistakes. "I'm ready to try a relationship, but I want the man beneath the pinstripes. The guy who grew up wanting to be a navy SEAL."

"He's yours." Caleb kissed her forehead. "But I don't want to try anything. I know the right woman, the perfect woman, for me."

He dropped down on one knee.

Becca gasped.

Caleb held her hand. "Will you marry me, Becca? Be my wife and partner and dog whisperer?"

Maurice trotted toward Becca. Her father held one end of the long leash. The dog came closer. A white ribbon was tied to his collar. Hanging from the ribbon was a...ring.

Her throat tightened. "You're serious."

Caleb nodded. "I asked your dad's permission."

Based on her parents' beaming faces, Caleb had no doubt received approval and been offered help with the proposal.

"So what do you say?" he said.

"I come with baggage."

"You also come with lint brushes," he said. "A fair trade-off in my book."

That was all she needed to hear. Know.

"Yes." Happiness flowed through her. "Yes, I'll marry you."

He removed the ring from Maurice's collar. The entire gold band was inlaid with tiny diamonds. In the center were bigger diamonds in the shape of a dog's paw. "I thought a large diamond would get in the way of all the things you have to do with the dogs. If you'd rather have—"

"This is perfect. I can't tell you how perfect."

He slid the ring onto her finger. "I love you."

"I love you."

He kissed her gently on the lips.

Maurice barked.

"Think he's jealous?" Caleb asked.

She glanced at the sparkling ring, then back at him. "No, that's his bark of approval."

"Let's give him more to approve of."

Caleb lowered his mouth to hers and kissed her. Hard.

Joy flowed through Becca, from the top of her head to the tip of her toes. The Boise Bachelor of the Year was off the market and would be ineligible to win ever again. But his kiss definitely deserved the prize for Best in Show. The first of many.

* * * * *

COMING NEXT MONTH from Harlequin® Romance
AVAILABLE JULY 1, 2013

#4383 A COWBOY TO COME HOME TO
Cadence Creek Cowboys
Donna Alward
Cooper Ford will do anything to regain his best friend Melissa Stone's trust. But can he convince her that he's ready to start a family?

#4384 HOW TO MELT A FROZEN HEART
Cara Colter
Brendan Grant's heart has been in the deep freeze since his wife's death. Can Nora and her orphaned nephew defrost his defenses?

#4385 THE CATTLEMAN'S READY-MADE FAMILY
Bellaroo Creek!
Michelle Douglas
Tess Laing moves to the Outback with her niece and nephew to start a new life. Are they the key to cattleman Cameron Manning's happiness?

#4386 RANCHER TO THE RESCUE
Jennifer Faye
Meghan Finnegan flees her wedding...and runs straight into the muscled torso of ex-rodeo champion Cash Sullivan. Is he the answer to her prayers?

You can find more information on upcoming Harlequin® titles, free excerpts and more at www.Harlequin.com.

HRLPCNM0613

LARGER-PRINT BOOKS!

GET 2 FREE LARGER-PRINT NOVELS PLUS
2 FREE GIFTS!

♥ HARLEQUIN®

Romance

From the Heart, For the Heart

YES! Please send me 2 FREE LARGER-PRINT Harlequin® Romance novels and my 2 FREE gifts (gifts are worth about $10). After receiving them, if I don't wish to receive any more books, I can return the shipping statement marked "cancel." If I don't cancel, I will receive 4 brand-new novels every month and be billed just $4.84 per book in the U.S. or $5.24 per book in Canada. That's a savings of at least 19% off the cover price! It's quite a bargain! Shipping and handling is just 50¢ per book in the U.S. and 75¢ per book in Canada.* I understand that accepting the 2 free books and gifts places me under no obligation to buy anything. I can always return a shipment and cancel at any time. Even if I never buy another book, the two free books and gifts are mine to keep forever.

119/319 HDN F43Y

Name	(PLEASE PRINT)

Address		Apt. #

City	State/Prov.	Zip/Postal Code

Signature (if under 18, a parent or guardian must sign)

Mail to the **Harlequin® Reader Service:**
IN U.S.A.: P.O. Box 1867, Buffalo, NY 14240-1867
IN CANADA: P.O. Box 609, Fort Erie, Ontario L2A 5X3
Want to try two free books from another line?
Call 1-800-873-8635 or visit www.ReaderService.com.

* Terms and prices subject to change without notice. Prices do not include applicable taxes. Sales tax applicable in N.Y. Canadian residents will be charged applicable taxes. Offer not valid in Quebec. This offer is limited to one order per household. Not valid for current subscribers to Harlequin Romance Larger-Print books. All orders subject to credit approval. Credit or debit balances in a customer's account(s) may be offset by any other outstanding balance owed by or to the customer. Please allow 4 to 6 weeks for delivery. Offer available while quantities last.

Your Privacy—The Harlequin® Reader Service is committed to protecting your privacy. Our Privacy Policy is available online at www.ReaderService.com or upon request from the Harlequin Reader Service.

We make a portion of our mailing list available to reputable third parties that offer products we believe may interest you. If you prefer that we not exchange your name with third parties, or if you wish to clarify or modify your communication preferences, please visit us at www.ReaderService.com/consumerschoice or write to us at Harlequin Reader Service Preference Service, P.O. Box 9062, Buffalo, NY 14269. Include your complete name and address.

HARLEQUIN® *Romance*

Grab your Stetson and put on your cowboy boots because July at Harlequin Romance is all about gorgeous cowboys and everything Western!

Travel with us from the Rocky Mountains to New Mexico, from Western Canada to the Australian Outback and watch as our four plucky heroines lasso their very own hero.

Find out in…

Donna Alward—*A Cowboy To Come Home To*

Cara Colter—*How to Melt a Frozen Heart*

Michelle Douglas—*The Cattleman's Ready-Made Family*

And introducing **Jennifer Faye** with *Rancher to the Rescue!*

An unforgettable collection!

Available wherever books and ebooks are sold.

HRWEST0613

綺色佳

小說

媽媽

Water.1.96

綺色佳 • 亦　舒

出版：天地圖書有限公司

香港皇后大道東109～115號智群商業中心十三字樓

電話：2528 3671　　圖文傳真：2865 2609

香港灣仔莊士敦道三十號地庫（門市部）

電話：2528 3605　2865 0708　　圖文傳真：2861 1541

承印：亨泰印刷有限公司

香港柴灣利眾街27號德景工業大廈十字樓

電話：2896 3687　　圖文傳真：2558 1902

發行：利通圖書有限公司（港澳）

九龍紅磡民裕街41號凱旋工商中心8樓C

電話：2303 1010（13線）　　圖文傳真：2764 1310

故事，是否都應當從頭說起呢？

抑或，挑中間比較有趣的情節先讓讀者看了，然後才把劇情往前推？

那是需要很大的技巧的吧。

還是從頭做比較好，條理也清楚些。

況且，陳綺羅與甄嗇色這對母女的關係，大抵是要從頭細說的。

母第一次看到女，是在十二年前。

那時嗇色約十二歲，長得高且瘦，膚色欠佳，似營養不良，戴着一副近視眼鏡，有蛀牙，怎麼看都不算一個標致的小孩。

可是嗇色有一個好處，她性格十分沉靜，而且，即使乏人督促，功課一流，霸定第一。

綺羅已與甄文彬約定，由她先開口。

於是，在甄家，她先自我介紹：「我叫陳綺羅，你可以叫我羅姨。」

甄文彬點點頭，不出聲，穿着新裙子的她拘謹地在一邊坐下。

甄文彬的神色略見焦急。

1

綺羅不慌不忙，「我叫你什麼？」

甄文彬已搶答：「在家，我們就叫她嗇色。」

綺羅嗯嗯地一聲，「嗇色，我與你父親，打算下個月結婚。」

嗇色低聲說：「父親已與我說過。」

綺羅問：「你願意來參加我們的婚禮嗎？」

嗇色努力地點點頭。

她不是要討好未來繼母，那是非常吃力的一件事，她只是不想得罪任何人。

只聽得陳綺羅說：「那好極了，婚後，你會自祖父母處搬回來住。」

嗇色一聽，放下一半心。

祖父母並不特別喜歡她，他們討厭她生母，故此也不看她，尤其是祖母，多年來眼皮也不大抬起，嗯、哼、呵幾乎是全部字彙。

三四歲幼兒都知道自己不是受歡迎人物，何況是嗇色。

故此，知道能回到自己家來，真是有點高興。

陳綺羅樣貌娟秀，衣着時髦，據說是留學生，又有事業，看情形會是個合理的人。

可以和平共處嗎？嗇色的心忐忑。

「屆時，我們會搬到一個比較寬敞的地方，你會住得比較舒服。」

嗇色點點頭。

那天，她統共說了不到十個字。

可是人們喜歡嗇色的身體語言，她沉靜安寧。

那天晚上，嗇色仍然回到祖父母家。

她聽得祖母說：「文彬這下可走運了，那位陳小姐頗有粧奩，並且願意取出與文彬共組家庭。」

「嗇色呢？」

「一併帶過去住。」

「這就很偉大了。」

「真是，才貌雙全，又有愛心，文彬轉運了。」

一直到很久之後，嗇色都認為，才貌雙全，又有愛心這八個字，用以形容陳綺羅，至貼切不過。

3

「文彬以前那個人……文彬眞倒楣。」

「算了，過去事一筆勾銷。」

「可是你看，她還生了這個孩子，長得又同她一模一樣，又扔不理，造成別人負擔。」

薔色一直躲在一角不出聲。

兩老聲音並不低，居所狹小，薔色又無私人書房臥室，可是，爲什麼要避忌？爲什麼要尊重這小孩？

在客廳一角借張書桌做功課的薔色只得默默忍受。

不過，吃晚飯之際，喉頭特別乾，古人說的食不下咽，大概就是這個意思。

過兩日，父親帶她參觀新居。

薔色不相信天下會有那樣好的地方。

牆壁地板潔具全是新的，三間房間，她佔一間，有張小小單人床、書桌茶几五斗櫃全齊，全室光線明亮，浴室就在對門。

父親微笑，「你看怎麼樣？」

4

嗇色緊抱着父親的腰身。

父親輕輕說：「綺羅走進我生命，給我一切，對我來說，她是一個非常重要的人，

嗇色，我希望你可以好好與她相處。」

嗇色肯定地點頭。

她有一個這樣好的房間可以躲藏，她不會騷擾任何人。

十二歲的她長手長腳，十分尷尬。

最令她煩惱的是衣服時時不夠大，常常需要買新的，要花大人的錢，她不敢出聲。

老師說：「嗇色，鞋子太小，鞋跟已經擠爆，要買雙新的了，同家長說，穿小鞋有

礙足部健康。」

襪子也穿洞。

可是祖母永遠佯裝看不見，為什麼要看見？衣服洗好了，冷冷說：「一套校服起碼

可穿三五天，何用時時洗。」

現在，新家裏有家務助理，天天幫嗇色做洗熨。

嗇色感覺如小奴婢進化為小公主。

5

可是她沉默猶勝往時，吃完飯便進房做功課，可是體重漸漸增加，面色紅潤，笑容漸多。

她父親也一樣。

綺羅陪她去添置衣服鞋襪，有熟悉的店，售貨員一見到她，立刻過來叫陳小姐。

綺羅替嗇色全身內外都添了合身的衣服，她是那樣慷慨，無論什麼都一打半打那樣選購。

只有很會賺錢的人才會如此出手吧。

嗇色忽然之間富庶起來。

她擁有兒童專用的牙膏，整罐潤面霜，水果香的肥皂，甚至消毒膏布上都印着米奇老鼠。

她從不知道生活上除卻衣食住行還有如此多的奢侈細節。

可是她還有恐懼，童話中都說後母的眞性情會在若干日子後才暴露出來。

會不會是眞的呢？

在綺羅帶她去箍牙之際，她幾乎相信傳說全是眞的。

6

要過一段日子，才知道眞爲她設想。

物質歸物質，最重要的是綺羅關心她。

每晚必坐下看她功課，並且毫不掩飾、眞誠、熱情地讚揚她。

「嘩，英文作文都一百分，世上有這樣高的分數嗎，小時候吃何種奶粉，是它的功勞嗎？」

言語幽默、風趣、大膽。

時時叫嗇色感激莫名。

她不似後母，她似一個朋友。

可是少年時的甄嗇色不擅詞令，不懂表達。

一日，到晚飯時間，她尚未在飯桌出現。

綺羅問：「這孩子怎麼了？」

「隨她去，」甄文彬說：「她鬧情緒。」

「什麼事？」

「在學校，高材生普遍受到尊重，可是，永遠有存心挑釁之人。」

7

「怎麼了？」

「今日下午，有兩個同學，言語間諷刺嗇色沒有母親。」

綺羅不語，可以看得出雙目中有怒意隱現。

她放下筷子，到嗇色房去。

「今日有你愛吃的蛋餃呢。」

嗇色立刻換上笑容，可是鼻子紅紅，是哭過了。

「你爸難得在家吃頓飯，快去陪他。」

嗇色識趣，「我馬上來。」

綺羅把手按在嗇色肩膀上，嗇色感覺有股力量傳遍全身。

她握住繼母的手。

第二天，陳綺羅約見校長。

校長出來，見到陳女士那身打扮，知道她是在社會佔一席位之人，俗云，先敬羅衣

後敬人，校長也不能免俗。

陳綺羅滿面笑容，講清前因後果。

8

然後很誠懇地作出結論：「即使沒有母親，也是悲劇，不是錯誤，貴校若干同學似乎沒有教養與同情心，況且，甄嗇色怎麼沒有母親？我就是她的母親。」

校長心服口服。

結果那兩個同學被校務處口頭警告，再不改，就得受處分，記小過。

甄文彬有點意外，「我真沒想到可以那樣據理力爭。」

綺羅說：「我至討厭人欺人。」

嗇色流下淚來。

從來無人為她出頭。

無母之女事無大小均得強忍，否則只有更惹人厭。

甄文彬靜靜問女兒：「同學說你母親什麼？」

同學說：「聽說你母親與男人私奔走掉了。」

嗇色不願作答。

這名同學的表姨與甄文彬的舅母有點親戚關係，可見這件事在親友間廣泛流傳。

而這的確是事實。

9

九歲那年某一日，嗇色放學後回來，已不見母親。

房間裏所有屬於她的東西都不翼而飛，空空如也。

她甚至沒有向孩子告別。

陳綺羅曾說：「對一個小女孩來說，這必定是天下最可怕的事。」

還不止，接着嗇色發覺父親開始拚命工作，每晚深夜才返，有時醉醺醺，有時索性不回家，人們似乎已忘記這小女孩。

一次生病進急症室後，甄文彬才把女兒送到父母處。

然後，天無絕人之路，陳綺羅在甄文彬生命中出現。

中國人命理中，有救星一詞，陳綺羅便是甄文彬的救星。

當下甄文彬再問：「同學說你母親什麼？」

綺羅勸說：「嗇色，你願意談一談嗎？」

嗇色輕輕說：「他們說我沒有母親，如此而已。」

綺羅示意甄文彬別再追究。

嗇色忽然笑了，「不要緊，他們的功課都不如我。」

10

好像已經決定出人頭地。

嗇色回房做功課。

隔半晌，甄文彬問綺羅：「你想不想知道她為何離家出走？」

綺羅不慌不忙微笑地說：「我一點好奇心也無，你呢，你想知道嗎。」

甄文彬頓解愁眉，他由衷佩服綺羅，她從來沒問過，她是真做到不管過去的事，魍

魍魎魎都埋葬在腦後，永不提起。

甄文彬舒出一口氣。

那樣，一家人才可以真正從頭開始。

那幾年，日子過得真適意。

陳綺羅有組織天才，無論對外對內，經她整理過，萬事均井井有條。

廚房永遠有熱茶，抽屜有乾淨內衣，賬單全部付清，家居整潔，全家雜物小至郵票

藥丸牙籤她全知道放在何處，立刻可以拿出來。

別以為這些都是輕而易舉之事，陳綺羅每週上班超過五十小時，同時她得維持個人

容貌整齊，她並非全職主婦，這樣算來，身兼數職，照顧週全難得之至。

11

嗇色覺得繼母似那種自圖畫裏走出來打救落難書生的仙女。

從她出現之後，父可專心工作，女可專心讀書。

奇是奇在連祖父母見了嗇色，也比較從前客氣。

可是，嗇色在心中喊：我一直是甄家的女兒呀。

現在，她由繼母親自開車送上學。

為此，綺羅需早起半小時，故嗇色從來不敢叫她等，延伸出去，她也不會叫任何人

等，她從不遲到。

同學還是那班同學，見她鞋襪光鮮，又有一位漂亮的女士管接管送，嘴臉頓時不一

樣。

都主動起來：「嗇色二字是什麼意思」，「這名字挺別致，可以一說來源嗎」，

「有空請為我們補習」……

全世界不知什麼地方來那麼多勢利的人，全堆在甄嗇色身邊。

開頭，嗇色以為這世界理應如此，後來才明白，那純粹是她少年時的不幸，不不

不，世間好人比壞人多。

她更加沉默，一天上課六小時，可以不與同學說一句話，獨來獨往。

這其實是不正常的，可是老師們欣賞得不得了，「你們要向甄嗇色同學學習。」

作文課有條題目叫「我最要好的朋友」。

甄嗇色這樣寫：我最要好的朋友，是我的母親。

其餘的同學，半數在懷念童年時的小鄰居，另外半數，選同座的同學。

只有嗇色作文有新意。

老師批了一個甲，對她說：「你有那麼一個好母親，真是幸運。」

嗇色答：「我知道。」

現在，她穿的鞋子永遠合腳，上學上街各一雙，還有運動球鞋，冬天尚有爬山靴，

不奢侈，可是豐足。

按着時候上理髮店修理頭髮，統統由繼母付賬。

綺羅常常摟着女兒肩膊進進出出，一日說：「噯，長這麼高了。」

然後，在十五歲那年，她已高過繼母。

生日並無特別慶祝，買一隻蛋糕，做一窩麵大家吃，一家三口私底下高興。

13

這次甄文彬夫婦給女兒一件禮物，他們把薔色送到歐洲旅行。

綺羅說：「你要是不放心一個人去⋯⋯」

「不，我喜歡極了！」

這是她第一次乘搭飛機。

祖父母深深納罕。

「薔色這是什麼命？倒也奇怪，有不相干的人來這樣疼她。」

「只恐怕好景不長，待有了親生兒，繼母便原形畢露。」

「特別是添了兒子之後。」

「可不是。」

語氣是那樣幸災樂禍：看你好到幾時去！

有什麼理由他們特別不希望薔色過好日子？

老人不喜歡她生母，故遷怒於孫女，深覺那女人生的孩子永遠不配有美滿生活。

那個時候，薔色幾乎已經忘記母親外貌。

一日，在早餐桌子上，薔色不小心碰跌牛奶杯子潑濕校服裙子，一臉懊惱慚愧，又

14

嫌更換衣服麻煩，一副哭笑不得模樣。

然後，發覺父親呆呆看着她。

接着，甄文彬衝口而出：「你同你媽一個印子印出來似。」

那日，放了學，嗇色呆呆對牢鏡子細看自己的五官，一個印子，她母親就是這個樣子？

這肯定是個壞模子，嗇色忽然伸手出來掌摑自己，出盡力，左右開弓，直至雙頰激辣辣腫起來。

然後，她流下眼淚。

冰涼淚水流經紅痛熱的面孔，永誌不忘。

嗇色厭憎生母，比誰都更甚。

她有生母照片，只是不想取出看。

倒底年輕，歐洲之行已使她將所有煩惱丟在腦後。

回來她說：「行萬里路有時真比讀萬卷書更勝一籌。」

其實不過是忽忽忙忙走馬看花。

15

甄文彬循例問：「最喜歡哪個城市？」

「倫敦。」

「考試成績好，送你往倫敦讀書。」

「那需要花費很多。」

甄文彬笑着問：「什麼，你不打算考獎學金？」

「聽師兄們說，生活費比學費更貴。」

「不怕不怕，只得你一個孩子，總負擔得起。」

嗇色遲疑，「也許……會添弟弟……」

綺羅忽然說：「沒有這回事。」

嗇色訝異。

綺羅補充：「我不會是一個好母親。」

嗇色忍不住說：「可是你對我那麼好！」

綺羅坦誠地說：「但我一向只把你當朋友。」

甄文彬笑起來。

16

陳綺羅說：「我是職業女性，從學堂出來做事至今，我不耐煩整日在家陪伴幼兒同他們唱兒歌拍手掌，我知道自己的短處，我不願做母親。」

甄文彬說：「這件事可從詳計議。」

陳綺羅雙手亂搖，「太吃苦了，不幹不幹，做得好，老應該，做不好，萬人踐踏，天下最無報酬的是母親一職，吃力不討好。」

這想法倒很新奇。

「可以聘請保母呀。」

「我天性多疑，不信任任何人帶我的孩子。」

甄文彬揚手，「過幾年了，到了三十五六，你自然會天性發作。」

綺羅忽然說：「大都會裏找生活的人，日子久了，哪裏還有天性，都不過是水門汀縫子裏長出來的草。」

嗇色一愣，綺羅一向樂觀，這話，不像是她說的。

傍晚，她坐在書桌前核數。

「嗇色，我寫給你的支票有三張尚未兌現。」

17

「是，我上次的零用還未用完。」

這是一個節省的好孩子。

一切都選最樸素的款式：外套、書包、鞋子……齋色不希望引起任何人注意，免得又有人指出她的母與男人私奔。

能把自己收藏得緊緊就好，況且，像她那樣一個孩子，也不配穿玫瑰紅的夾克、粉紫色的裙子。

跟是繼母過生活，是有分別的，她怎麼不知道。

十全十美的繼母也不是生母。

她見過同學李潔卿同母親發脾氣。

一日放學時間忽然下大雨，李母帶了傘來接她，心急，在課室門口張望，被老師發覺，輕輕掩上課室房門。

鈴聲一響，眾學生魚貫而出，李潔卿便發起脾氣來，當眾把書包扔在地下踩兩下，叫母親以後，一生一世、永遠不要再來接放學。

李太太一直訕訕站一邊，不出聲，也不生氣。

18

那是生母。

至於繼母，再好，似一個朋友，你不會為小故得罪朋友，因為朋友會掉頭而去。

可是嗇色已知道自己夠幸運。

她得到的，肯定是最好的繼母。

隔數日，李潔卿向她請教功課，她輕輕說：「你不該向母親大聲吆喝。」

李潔卿略覺慚愧，「是，我一時覺得她失禮，沉不住氣。」

嗇色的聲音更低，「她們會比我們略早離開這個世界，我們遲早會成為沒有母親的孤兒。」

李潔卿吃驚了，用手掩住嘴巴。

「伯母那樣愛你……」

李潔卿再也忍不住，哭了起來。

她丟下功課，趕回家去。

片刻，綺羅駕車來接，嗇色笑嘻嘻上車。

嗇色一見有人，總是笑臉迎之。

19

然後，關入房門，死做功課。

功課是挽回她自尊的起死回生靈藥。

她在班上地位出神入化，老師有事走開去聽電話，會叫她坐在教師席上暫代一陣。

可是甄嗇色不驕矜，不多話。

因父親把整個家交給繼母，而親父毋需故意討好，識趣的嗇色有意無意與父親也分

出一個距離。

一家人都像朋友。

生活一平靜，祖父母的話更多。

「文彬說什麼也是個專業人士，怎麼老賺不到大錢。」

「他妻子倒是夠精明，會做生意。」

「日子長了，會被人說他靠老婆。」

「這年頭，無所謂吧。」

口角冷淡，也像朋友，不過不是那麼好的朋友。

嗇色想像中的一家人不是這樣的，但或者，她想像得太好了，也許一般人的家，就

20

是這樣。

十六歲生日那天，繼母把她約到山頂吃下午茶。

明敏的嗇色知道有事。

茶廳很漂亮，茶具雪白，綑一道金邊，格雷伯爵茶香氣撲鼻。

陳綺羅一向不是吞吞吐吐的人，她很坦白地說：「嗇色，我同你父親共同生活了四年。」

一開頭，就完結了，一句話只說了一半，文法上不對。

嗇色靜靜等待下文。

「我發覺，我倆緣份已盡。」

嗇色耳畔嗡地一聲，呵，好景不長。

「我已決定同他分手。」

嗇色十分艱澀地問：「他知道了嗎？」

綺羅歎口氣，「嗇色，你真聰明，不，他還不知道。」

「他受得了這個打擊嗎？」嗇色好不沉重。

21

「成年人，應當承受生活中不如意事。」

綺羅一愣。

嗇色忍不住問：「為什麼你們終於都離開他？」

嗇色點頭，「我知道，你累了。」

綺羅忽然笑了，「可是我本人生活目標卻不是成為他人的得力助手。」

「你是他生活中至寶。」

綺羅答：「我不知道別人為什麼離開他，至於我，我不想說他壞話。」

嗇色問：「你知道我母親為什麼要走？」

「我一頭霧水，不過即使知道，我也不會說。」

「你與父親似相處得那麼好。」

「真可惜，感情像兄弟姐妹一樣，可是，今年我已年近三十，我希望男女關係之中還有激情，像見到一名男子，整圈臉龐會得不由自主地發熨⋯⋯唉，你太年輕，你也許要隔些時候才會明白。」

綺羅總是替她留有餘地，不說她不懂，而是今日不懂，將來會懂。

22

這幾年來，她是她生活中唯一的錨，嗇色神色露出對未來的恐懼。

綺羅按住她的手，「你放心嗇色，我會安排你的生活。」

「為什麼，為什麼對我那麼好？」

「因為路見不平，因為我能力做得到。」

嗇色落下淚來。

一個陌生女子，願意照顧她的生活。

她羞愧地低下頭。

「你放心，你仍是我的女兒。」

嗇色只覺心酸。

「你父，他是好人，只是稍欠組織能力，我會替你到英國找寄宿學校，尋監護人，

「對不起。」綺羅內疚了。

嗇色迅速抹乾眼淚，「你對我們父女已經夠好。」

「我稍後會親口告訴你父親。」

「為什麼反而倒先告訴我？」

23

「唉，你好似更有智慧接受此事。」

茶涼了，綺羅叫侍者過來換新茶。

嗇色問：「你找到了新的伴侶？」

「可遇不可求。」綺羅略爲含蓄。

「這次父親可能永遠站不起來了。」

「別把事情想得太壞。」

嗇色頹喪地低頭。

「看看你的生日禮物。」

是一條珍珠鑲鑽墜子⋯項鍊

「太美麗了。」

「我幫你戴上。」

嗇色擁抱繼母，「至少我也過過四年好日子。」

母女二人哭得四目紅紅。

回到家，嗇色忽然對父親不耐煩起來。

她冷眼看他。

她要找出爲什麼女人都不得不離開他的原因。

他下班回來，一言不發，先做他要做的事、淋浴、更衣，每隔些時候問：「牙膏放在何處，白色毛巾都用光了嗎，」並不關心其他的事。

完全忘卻獨生女兒的生日。

日子久了，前來報恩的仙女也不過如一個普通家庭主婦，他倚賴性重，並且願意躲懶。

嗇色所不知道的是，在公司裏，甄文彬可以三個鐘頭會議不表示一點意見，這樣，他至少可以達到不做不錯的目標，而且，上頭一問起什麼，他第一個反應便是推卸，永不承擔任何責任。

上司同事都有點怕他，有事都不與他商量。

是這樣，永遠升不上去。

但他仍然是個好好先生，從來不會陷害人，許多沒與他交過手的人都不介意他，況且他十分勤工，日以繼夜，時時埋頭苦幹，慢工出細貨，公司也需要這樣的人。

嗇色忽然像祖父母一樣，有點厭憎父親，因爲他的無能，她吃了多少苦。

她討厭他。

晚餐桌子上，他把菜盛在大碗裏去看電視上的足球賽，一邊說：「嗇色，替我拿條濕毛巾來。」

他一天工作已經完畢，儘管妻女不由他養活，可是妻女總還得服侍他。

可是，甄文彬仍不是壞人。

是這樣，陳綺羅累壞了吧。

嗇色一聲不響轉回房中。

她聽得父親說：「這孩子又怎麼了？」

這之後，她又不知會被送到何處去。

現在，她身軀與思想都完全似一個大人，不是那麼容易安置，不比從前，像一隻小貓，隨便丟在哪個角落，給點吃的，就可解決問題。

她爲前途問題深深煩惱。

隔了個多月，甄文彬依然故我，絲毫沒有異樣，嗇色知道綺羅尚未向他攤牌。

26

嗇色這時發覺，什麼都是不知道的好，不知不痛，反而她倒像囚籠裏待判決的犯人，坐立不安。

「你還沒同他說？」

「真不知怎麼開口。」

每次叫他，他總是很愉快地問：「什麼事？」一點也不懷疑對方會得變心，驟然把這件事告訴他，彷彿等於在談笑間拿一把利刀插進他的心房。

似乎應該安排一點預兆，像下班後故意拖延着不回家，或是對他們父女冷淡之類。

可是陳綺羅實在做不出來。

即使分手，也可以做得好看一點，不必踐踏對方自尊，況且，她得顧住嗇色這孩子的顏面。

嗇色道：「如果你心意已決，不要躊躇了。」

綺羅忽然說：「我沒有把我的身世告訴過你。」

嗇色看着她。

27

綺羅聲音很輕，「我父母並無正式結婚，我自幼跟外婆生活。」

這完全出乎意料之外，嗇色呵地一聲。

「外婆對我很好，可是老人家對生活另有一套準則，日子過得相當刻苦，」綺羅微笑，「我像個小小清教徒，衛生紙及肥皂用多了都受外婆警告。」

嗇色聳然動容。

綺羅的遭遇與她有太多相同之處。

「然後，我十七歲那年，家父去世，遺囑中，撥給我一筆金錢。」

怪不得。

嗇色聽得入神。

「那只是他財產小得不能再小的一部份，以致他其餘的正式子女認為微不足道，任由那野孩子吃點掃在地上的餅屑也是應該的，可是，對我來說，已是筆豐盛的粧奩。」

「我立刻啓程到英國讀書，天天穿新衣串舞會觀劇，整個夏季在歐陸旅遊，戀愛、失戀、再戀愛……」

嗇色衝口而出：「我也要那樣！」

綺羅笑了，「沒想到我是壞榜樣。」

這時，上課鈴響了。

綺羅說：「進課室去吧。」

「你把事情講完了再說。」

「後來，也終於畢業了，回來之後，買了房子，找到工作，忽然渴望安頓下來，被

愛、愛人，我從來沒有一個家，於是——」

上課鈴第二次響。

「於是我結婚了，很幸運，你父親是個好人，去上課吧，明天再說。」

那一整天，薔色都想，在一段感情中，她才不要扮演好人的角色。

寧缺毋好。

情願飾一個歹角，壞人往往最能叫人思念一輩子。

隔了二十年，對方說起她的時候，仍然咬牙切齒：「這個人呀……」恨恨不已，情

不自禁。

老師看見甄薔色一手托腮，雙目漫無焦點地望着窗外，對黑板上筆記視若無睹，不

29

禁暗暗好笑，這樣的好學生也會有遊魂的時候，可見少年始終是少年。

老師故意刁難，叫她答問題。

天資聰穎的嗇色卻又即時可以流利地把答案詳盡列出。

那天晚上，甄文彬叫她：「嗇色，過來，有話同你說。」

呵，攤牌了。

待嗇色坐下來，發覺又不是那回事。

「嗇色，公司派我出差到倫敦一個月，順便可以替你找學校。」

原來如此。

甄文彬笑道：「你們母女儘量自己過日子，別太掛念我，我轉頭就會回來。」

嗇色聽了這話，受了刺激，忽然歇斯底里地笑出來，他竟一點蛛絲馬跡都看不出來。

他還以爲她們沒有他不行。

甄文彬愣住，問：「我說的話有什麼可笑？」

嗇色抹去眼角眼淚，「沒什麼沒什麼。」

他壓低聲音：「輪到你照顧綺羅。」

嗇色一怔。

「這一陣子，她早出晚歸，回來雖嚷倦，在書房又做到半夜，你看着她些，勸她休息。」

「是。」嗇色低下頭。

「綺羅眞是不可多得的好女子，做了四年夫妻，我心滿意足。」

嗇色一怔，「怎麼說這話。」

難怪綺羅開不了口。

他卻岔開話題，「公司一直怪我沒表現，這次是我的機會，我決定好好做出成績來。」

替他收拾行李的，自然又是綺羅。

連小小救傷藥袋也替他準備好：眼藥水、消炎藥、止痛丸、消毒膏布、棉花捲……

綺羅說：「待他回來，一定同他說。」

也不能再拖了。

31

因為，已經有人送花上來。

白色的，栽在盤裏的，謝了還會再生的蘭花。

清晨起來，走過書房門，可以聞得到清香。

真奇怪，他們完全不介意她是有夫之婦。

不一直傳說女性離婚後很難再找到理想對象嗎，可見不能一概而論。

嗇色這樣分析：陳綺羅長得漂亮，性格獨立，最重要的是，她經濟寬裕，為人慷慨，不會造成異性負擔。

她不會追着人要房子要車要珠寶。

這一點已經夠吸引，故略表心意，追求者便明目張膽上門來。

你看，嗇色不無感慨，做人是不是要自己爭氣，屆時，愛同什麼人在一起都可以，拋棄人或被拋棄亦全不是問題，得意與失意時均可大灌香檳酒。

十六歲的嗇色有頓悟。

甄文彬走了，母女十分輕鬆。

二人都覺得時間鬆動許多。

32

綺羅說：「我陪你去配隱型眼鏡，過兩年，用激光徹底治好這對近視眼。」

嗇色感慨：「第一次同祖母說看不到黑板上的字，她還不信，笑嘻嘻反問：『你是騙我要副眼鏡玩可是』，又趁我不在意，指向遠處：『哪是什麼？』」

綺羅問：「你常騙她？」

「你看我這八百多度的近視。」

「這就比較怪了，怎麼老認為孩子會騙她。」

漸漸把童年時的委屈傾訴出來。

「從來沒有，我根本很少與他們說話。」

「便宜呀。」

綺羅頷首：「這是真的，老人總想省。」

「是眼鏡沒配好，驗光師說你那些眼鏡全在後巷眼鏡店馬馬虎虎購得。」

「父親給的生活費已經不多，老人還想從中獲利，生活豈有不艱難的。」

綺羅不語。

嗇色低下頭。

33

「嗇色，說些高興之事。」

嗇色抖擻精神，「是，我已經找到暑期工。」

綺羅說：：「我介紹一個人給你認識。」

嗇色低聲問：「是送花的人吧。」

嗇色靜下來。

「是。」

嗇色很想見一見這個人，可是潛意識覺得不對，綺羅是她的繼母呀，她現在另外有男朋友，亦即是出賣她的父親，她怎麼可以與她朋比為奸？

可是，在這世界上，她只有這個毫無血緣關係的親人，她不得作出取捨。

這大抵是一個人吃人的社會，況且，像她父親那樣遲鈍的人，被人賣了，也許還幫那人數錢，他不會介意。

嗇色抬起頭來，「好呀，我每天放學都有空。」

綺羅很高興，「我去安排。」

父親不常打電話回來，只偶然寄回一兩張明信片，那些明信片，由傭人開信箱取到

34

屋內，放客廳一張長型茶几上。

陳綺羅下班回來，一邊脫鞋子一邊順手看信，重要的取返書房細閱、次要的一撇，順手扔回長几上。

那些由丈夫自遙遠的地方寄返的明信片，便遭受此等待遇。

隔了好幾日，仍然扔在那裏，嗇色過去，輕輕把它們收起，夾在書本中，作爲書籤。

人微、力薄、言輕，寫的信也無人要看。

嗇色十分困惑，這真是一個勢利的社會。

她要把這一切細節好好記住，將來，倘若遭遇到同樣的事，可作心理預防。

明信片不見了，綺羅也不問起，可見早已丟在腦後。

這段時間內，嗇色發覺綺羅置了許多平時不會買的新衣，式樣華麗、誘人，顏色出乎意表。

她並沒有試穿給嗇色看，可是掛在房內，嗇色走過，自然看到。

嗇色盡量低頭疾走，這是規矩，寄人籬下者必學，人家要你看，你要高高興興的

35

看，人家不想你看，你最好做一個亮眼瞎子。

一天早上起來，嗇色看到一件小小上衣搭在沙發上，淡湖水綠，裁成Ｔ恤模樣，可是釘滿薄透明膠片。

她伸手輕輕摸一下，上學去。

她是為那個人所穿的吧。

女為悅己者容。

那天下午，父親的電話來了。

嗇色正在做功課，傭人進來說是找她。

「嗇色，綺羅在何處？」

「這是她辦公時間。」

「請同她說，我一時無法聯絡到她，我將延遲返來。」

「是嗎，一個月已經過去了嗎，他該回來了嗎？」

「公司叫我在倫敦再做一個月，你請綺羅撥個電話給我，或許，她可以告假來與我

36

一聚。」

嗇色唯唯諾諾。

「你好嗎?」

「很好,勿掛念我。」

「此間一級寄宿學校尚有空位,可是學費寄宿費之貴,無出其右,原來,世上並無有教無類一事,看來不但富者愈富,再愈有學養教養。」

嗇色不語。

「此事回來再作商量。」

嗇色忽然問:「你好嗎?」

「連續下雨已近兩個星期,我發覺自己原來有風濕痛。」

「吃用還過得去嗎?」

「有一樣相當恐怖的東西,叫牧羊人餡餅,不幸將來你會有機會領教。」

嗇色驚疑不定,「我還以為是約克布甸。」

「不要去說它了,早餐有種貓魚,腥臭撲鼻⋯⋯唉。」

37

嗇色安慰他：「到唐人街去吃。」

「在所難免，記住叫綺羅撥電話來。」

可是那一整天，嗇色都不會見到她。

嗇色用英文寫了張字條，放在綺羅的書桌上，英語措辭比較大方。

她那小小書房有股幽香，一枚水晶紙鎮壓着是月需要應付厚厚一叠賬單。

將來，她也要學陳綺羅，憑雙手付清一切賬單。

第二天清早，綺羅在喝黑咖啡。

「我看到你的字條了。」

她對嗇色，始終是那麼尊重親暱。

「我立刻撥電話給他，可是沒找到，不過留了言。」

嗇色一直點頭。

「他在那邊好似如魚得水。」

嗇色不語。

綺羅放下日報，「又得出門了。」

嗇色連忙拾起書包。

「嗇色，今日無暇送你，你乘計程車吧。」

「呵好。」

「還有，星期六有空嗎，我們一起去喝下午茶。」

她朝嗇色眨眨眼。

「啊，有空有空。」

雨天的計程車都有一股霉臭味，眾人公用的東西都有點齷齪。

呀由侈入儉難，這話真沒錯。

從前，陳綺羅沒出現的時候，小小的嗇色是電車常客，慢是慢一點，可是一定會到達目的地，她喜歡坐樓下，上落快捷一點。

沒想到今日她已嫌計程車髒，寵壞了。

一整個早上她都有被遺棄的感覺，身上那股沾自破爛車廂的氣味揮之不去。

繼母要離開他們父女了，他們即將要打回原形。

嗇色恐懼地用手遮住面孔。

39

放學，看不到綺羅那輛香檳色的跑車，嗇色內心忐忑。

她等了十分鐘，決定去乘電車。

忽然看到車子在轉角出現，高興得淚盈於睫。

嗇色的笑臉是眞的。

她衝口而出：「我以爲你不來了。」

綺羅笑：「怎麼，我會永遠照顧你。」

「永遠是一個很長的日子。」

綺羅又笑，「不見得，人無百歲壽。」

她總是這樣，在最出乎意表的時候，表示她對人生的一絲悲哀。

嗇色上車去，舒出一口氣。

「你父親叫我到倫敦會他。」

嗇色只呵地一聲。

「你願意代表我去嗎？」

怎麼可能，「我不能曠課。」嗇色想也不想。

回來之際，進不了家門，那可怎麼辦。

綺羅答：「我也告不到假。」

「那麼，據實告訴他。」利害關頭，她遺棄了他。人在人情在，他根本不應在這種敏感時刻離開這個家。

「他一回來，我就同他說。」

過一刻嗇色問：「會叫他搬出去嗎？」

綺羅想一想：「假如他不方便，我搬走好了。」

「可是，房子是你的產業。」

「沒關係，我還有別的公寓可住。」

這樣子，實在已經仁盡義至。

分手之後，她還願意照顧他的生活。

嗇色有點羞愧。

「是我不好，我沒有一輩子同他在一起。」

嗇色說：「一輩子是段很長的時間。」

41

綺羅又笑，「不，並不是真如想像那麼長。」

嗇色不出聲。

星期六，她們剛預備出門去，不湊巧甄文彬電話來了。

「你們母女都不來看我？」

嗇色只是支吾。

綺羅在旁打手勢，叫她快點。

雖然遲到無所謂，可是她喜歡那個人，就不想叫他等。

嗇色真尷尬，只得胡亂說：「有人等我，下次再說。」

掛上電話之前還聽得父親喂喂喂之聲。

她儘量壓抑懊惱之情，面孔漲得通紅。

可是綺羅一點也不察覺，不是粗心，而是不經意。

她穿一件貼身黑色西服，更顯得膚光如雪。

嗇色只穿白襯衫及牛仔褲。

那男人遲到。

42

嗇色不由得生氣，內心一聲冷笑。

早知可與父親多說幾句。

叫了冰茶，他還沒有出現。

嗇色暗暗注視綺羅，她神色卻悠然，看樣子好像已經等慣了他。

嗇色內心已開始排斥這個人。

然後，她看到一名男子大踏步走近，他一臉陽光，穿白襯衫卡其褲，揮着汗，動作卻輕俏敏捷，如一隻豹子般潛到綺羅背後，站定，不顧嗇色訝異的目光，伸出一隻手，放在綺羅的肩膀上。

綺羅立刻知道這是誰，她把臉傾向他的手背，神色陶醉，垂着眼，一時也不轉過頭去。

嗇色雖然年輕，看到這種情形，也知道什麼叫做戀愛。

綺羅笑了，「嗇色，我跟你介紹，這個人，叫利佳上。」

他伸出大手，「嗇色，你好。」

嗇色被他握着手，熱情地搖兩搖，知道他把她當孩子。

43

這樣更好，人們對小孩沒有防範之心。

「我剛自郊外趕回來，遲了一點，對不起。」

看到嗇色眼中有點詢問神色，他又解釋：「每週末我做義工，敎障殘孩子們游泳。」

嗇色在心中呵地一聲。

他叫的礦泉水來了，豪爽地鯨飲。

然後，靜下來，什麼也不做，只是看着女友，微微笑。

嗇色要到這時才看清楚了他，這人有一雙會笑的眼睛，身型好到極點，寬肩膀穿白襯衫已經夠漂亮。

最吸引是他渾身上下散發的一股活力，這是都會男性少見的魅力。

嗇色這樣想：城市太多大腹賈，太多權勢、太多名利，可是人人如行屍走肉，營營役役。

這利佳上是完全不一樣的一個人。

可是，他何以為生？

44

他已經開口了：「讓我介紹自己，我在大學裏教數學，你對數學有興趣嗎？」

嗇色忍不住微笑，他把她當十一歲。

綺羅一直不出聲，任由他們自由對答。

「不，」嗇色回說：「我對數學興趣不大，可是分數卻還不錯。」

「綺羅說你是好學生。」

嗇色客氣地答：「一個人，總得做些什麼。」

她注意到他頭髮近額角處有點鬈曲，這個人，一切外型上的優點都讓他佔齊了。

只坐了一會兒，他便看看錶，「我得回去更衣，有學生稍後來找我。」

他再與嗇色握手，「很高興認識你。」

然後走到綺羅身後，雙手搭在她肩上，他不知為什麼那樣喜歡站到她背後。

只見綺羅的上身稍微往後仰，靠在他胸上，他俯下身來，吻她額角一下，轉身離去。

嗇色這時才領會什麼叫做如膠如漆。

母女靜了好一會兒。

45

過一刻，綺羅才問：「你覺得他怎麼樣？」

嗇色猶疑半晌，才老氣橫秋地說：「好像很危險。」

綺羅一聽笑得翻倒，「不不不，他至文明不過，今日他知道要來見你，有點緊張，表現失常。」

「他為什麼要緊張？」

「我同他說，你是我的女兒。」

嗇色有點尷尬，「這不妨礙你嗎？」

綺羅訝異，「又毋需他操心，何妨礙之有。」

是，只有人在簷下討生活的才叫油瓶，否則，各歸各。

嗇色點點頭。

綺羅按住她的手，「來，走吧。」

她們二人都喜歡用身體語言，又那樣爽朗活潑，真是配對。

嗇色黯然，父親已永遠失去陳綺羅。

「他不介意你結過婚嗎？」

綺羅大吃一驚，「他應該介意嗎？」

「我不知道，她好像，呃，社會，對離婚婦女——」

綺羅強忍住笑，「你聽你祖母說太多的天方夜譚了。」

一定是，嗇色氣餒。

「可是，」綺羅說：「離婚仍然是十分痛苦的一件事，切勿誤會我將之當家常便飯。」

嗇色不再言語。

那天晚上，她做夢，老有人握住她的手，她並無掙扎，也不想放鬆，那是一隻溫暖的大手，伸開五指足夠遮住她整張小臉。

半夜，電話鈴響了，嗇色在床上翻個身。

一定是父親不甘心，再次打來。

可憐的父親，這裏已經沒有他的位置。

嗇色在睡夢中歎息數聲。

天亮，鬧鐘把她叫醒。

她如常梳洗完畢，走到客廳，看到繼母坐在沙發上，手裏拿着一杯拔蘭地。

嗇色立刻走過去：「什麼事？」

綺羅抬起頭來，淚盈於睫：「倫敦打電話來，車禍，你父親——」

「我們馬上去看他——」

「他已經辭世。」

嗇色張大嘴，一時間無法適應，全身僵硬，剎時還不知悲傷，只是突兀。

「一個年輕人醉酒駕駛，衝過紅燈，與他迎頭相撞。」

嗇色緩緩坐下。

綺羅沒有即時叫她，好讓她睡到天亮。

「我得即時趕去辦事，你要不要一起來？」

嗇色麻木地頷首。

「現在，我要知會甄氏兩老。」

那天大抵是天下最痛苦的任務。

天全亮了。

傭人如常捧出咖啡，綺羅伸手去接，杯子碰到碟子，嗒嗒作響，她才發覺手在顫抖。

她撥電話到公司，找到私人助手，請他們過來幫忙，那一男一女年輕人在半小時內就趕到了。

一進門就與綺羅擁抱一下，然後馬上開始辦事，不消片刻，已訂好飛機票及酒店房間。

那叫甘婉兒的助手說：「我跟你去，我對倫敦熟如手掌。」

「那好，李智強，你留下在這邊接應。」

那小李回說：「甄家已經知道消息，我會留下安撫他們。」

在他們來說，好似沒有難事。

一小時後，母女已抬着行李由小李送往飛機場。

甘婉兒折返家中，十分鐘後提着一隻手提包下來。

看樣子她這件隨身行李是一早收拾妥當隨時準備出門用。

「我已訂好黑色禮服，屆時有人會送往酒店。」

嗇色在飛機場又看到了利佳上。

他一見嗇色便上前擁抱她。

嗇色聞到他身上藥水肥皂香味，像是剛淋過浴，果然，他頭髮還是濕的。

他送她們上飛機。

綺羅一直垂頭不出聲。

一路上她十分緘默，由得甘婉兒張羅一切。

到了酒店，原來三個人分房住。

甘小姐叮囑嗇色：「即使走開一步，也請通知我。」

黑色衣物送上來，連深色絲襪都在內，可見考慮週詳。

嗇色去看過花束，全部都是雪白的百合花，只有她署名那一隻小小花籃，是粉紅色的玫瑰花：愛女嗇色。

嗇色知道這是事實，急痛攻心，落下淚來。

綺羅過來，擁住她，二人哀哀痛哭。

接着是火化儀式。

50

綺羅一直沒除下素服。

她很倚賴拔蘭地酒。

嗇色聽見甘婉兒勸道：「今天喝到此為止，再繼續，便成酗酒。」

綺羅不住飲泣，雙目紅腫，寢食不安。

自酒店窗口看下去，街上有淡淡陽光，可是誰也提不起興趣去逛一下。

然後，利佳上來了。

他並沒有通知誰，一日早上，有人敲門，甘婉兒去開門，進來的是他。

他同綺羅說了幾句，然後向嗇色道：「我們到海德公園門口走走。」

嗇色站起來，他這才真正看清楚這個皮膚白皙的女孩子，她原來長得那麼高，身型同大人完全一樣，可是面孔十分稚嫩，一如小孩。

她心情十分差，並無好好梳洗，長髮束在腦後，沒梳好，碎碎鬢髮全在臉邊冒了出來，一個個都是小圈圈，襯着濃眉大眼，像拉斐爾前派畫家筆下的主角。

他替她搭上一件大衣，拉着她的手出門去。

嗇色身型其實十分高大，可是站在利佳上身邊，猶如一根小羽毛。

51

走近公園，嗇色凝望天空，眼淚似斷線珠子般落下來。

利佳上不是沒有見過人哭，可是這次才發覺大顆淚水原來那麼動人，嗇色扭曲的面孔不但不難看，反而表露了真情。

他輕輕把手帕遞給她。

他倆在公園一張長櫈上坐下。

「我與綺羅會在明年結婚。」

嗇色垂着頭，知道那是必然之事。

「之後，你會與我們共同生活。」

嗇色有點意外。

「綺羅的女兒，即是我的女兒。」

嗇色這時不得不抬起頭來，「可是，我並非陳綺羅的孩子。」

利君微笑地擁着她的肩膀，「當然你是，她是你合法繼母，法律上她是你未成年前的監護人。」

但，嗇色蒼白地想，實際上她是一個孤兒。

52

「你會適應新生活，我們會替你安排。」

薔色又忍不住流淚。

利君輕輕說：「我至怕人無情，幸虧你與綺羅都不是那樣的人。」

他們在公園一定逗留了頗長一段時候。

一位街頭畫家朝他們走來，手裏拿着一張速寫，笑嘻嘻說：「三十鎊。」

利佳上一看，見是他與薔色坐在長橙上的素描，薔色一雙淒惶的大眼睛十分傳神，

他喜歡得不得了，立刻掏出鈔票買下來。

那畫家千謝萬謝地離去。

「我們回去吧。」

他仍然緊緊握着她的手。

回到酒店，綺羅已換下黑衣改穿淺色套裝，正與助手甘小姐談論細節。

「——款項全數付清了吧。」

「總數幾近四萬鎊。」

綺羅呼出一口氣，「不妨，還負擔得起。」

53

抬頭，看見他們回來了，有點高興，努力振作，「去了什麼地方那麼久」，可是眼睛又紅起來。

利君說得對，陳綺羅是個多情的人，嗇色緊緊與她擁抱。

那晚，大家在綺羅的套房內吃了點簡單食物。

不要說是他們母女，連甘小姐都明顯消瘦。

當天深夜，利佳上趕着要走，他只能逗留十多小時。

他吻別她們母女，「回去再見。」

傍晚已經再刮過鬍髭，可是稍後又長了出來，刺着嗇色的臉。

有人搬了一隻紙箱來，裏邊裝了甄文彬的遺物，都是一些零星雜物，像筆記本子雜誌袋裝書口香糖等。

嗇色憔悴地坐在盒子前，手上拈着屬於父親的一副眼鏡。

她聽見繼母在一旁輕輕的說：「幸虧一直沒有告訴他。」

嗇色同意：「是。」

綺羅苦澀地自嘲：「我很少做對事，這還是第一次。」她神情疲乏。

54

嗇色說：「在他生命最後幾年，他沒有遺憾，他生活得很好。」

綺羅點點頭，這是事實。

助手這時過來請她聽長途電話。

回來的時候，她發覺嗇色已在長沙發上睡着。

甘小姐問：「要不要叫醒她？」

「這幾天她還是第一次睡着，隨她去吧。」

甘小姐輕輕問：「一個女孩子，怎麼會叫嗇色？」

「據說是信佛教的外公所改，佛家云色即是空，故應嗇色。」

「外公人呢？」

「她與母系一支親戚已無來往。」

「那真是可惜，照說娘舅阿姨是至親中至親，還有，搖搖搖搖到外婆橋，外婆叫我好寶寶。」

「祖父母呢？」

「人生總無十全十美。」

「這次回去，想必也將疏遠，他們一直不喜歡她。現在更可賴她不祥。」

甘婉兒跟着陳綺羅日子久了，說話百無禁忌：「咦，不祥人不是你嗎？」

綺羅沉默一會兒，「我財宏勢厚，誰敢給我戴帽子。」

真是，柿子揀軟的捏，甘婉兒吐出一口氣，「都會找孤苦的人來踐踏。」

「是，弱的、小的。」綺羅忽然笑了，「無力反抗，就像我年輕時候，親戚中有哪個孩子頑劣無比，就被大人指着罵：『這副德性，同綺羅一模一樣』，我這個人竟成了反面教材典範，直至承繼了遺產。」

「他們不再揶揄你了嗎？」

「我已經聽不見了。」

甘婉兒笑片刻，「明天下午，我們也該動身回去了。」

整件事因為辦理得非常迅速，嗇色覺得像一個夢似。

回到家中，更加詫異，一個星期不到，家居已改了樣子，客廳與休息室換了傢具，她的睡房沒變，可是父親原有的起坐間已經拆掉。

甄文彬這個人已在屋中消失，所有痕跡經已抹淨。

嗇色無言。

房子不屬於她，她沒有資格爲他留下什麼作爲紀念。

嗇色滿以爲新人會接着搬進來。

可是沒有。

利君總是在午夜十二時之前離去。

回到學校，同學紛紛表示同情。

老師把筆記補發給她，她又回到書桌前苦讀，如今她的身份比從前更加尷尬百倍，正好埋頭讀書，佯裝什麼都不知。

每月繼母簽支票給她交學費，她都鬆一口氣，又過了一關，她對生活仍然缺乏信心。

然後一日放學，發覺客廳裏坐着一位客人。

本來不關她事，可是不知怎地，她悄悄問傭人：「那是誰？」

「一位姓方的小姐，一定要進來等太太。」

「陌生人怎麼可以放進門。」

57

「兩對一，不怕她。」

嗇色抱怨：「我不會打架，你請她走吧，太太不知幾時回來。」

「她一直按鈴按個不休，我又不好意思叫司閽上來干涉。」

下人確是難做。

「不如你去打發她。」

嗇色走到客廳，那女客察覺，滿面笑容抬起頭來。

嗇色與她一照臉，感覺就如照鏡子一般，對方容顏與她似乎一模一樣。

嗇色立刻知道她是誰，呆在當地動彈不得。

女客熟絡地說：「你放學了。」

嗇色要隔一會兒才說：「你好。」

「大家好，陳綺羅什麼時候回來？」

「你們約好幾時？」

「五時半。」

「也許交通擠。」

58

「那，應該早些出門呀。」

嗇色坐下來，看着她，「你，有點不耐煩。

「不，我已移民澳洲悉尼。」

嗇色點點頭，「這些年來，一點消息都沒有。」

她笑道：「也不會有人想念我吧。」

嗇色張開嘴，想說什麼，又閉上嘴。

輪到她反問：「你一直住這裏？」

嗇色點頭。

「生活不錯呀，比跟着我強多了。」

嗇色提醒她：「父親已經去世。」

「我知道。」

嗇色提起勇氣，「你可是來帶我走？」

方女士一愕，「呵，不，走，走到哪裏去？」

嗇色本來還抱着一絲希望，聽到她如此反問她，心中一涼，連忙低下頭。

她鼻子發酸，說不出話來。

接着，方女士說：「我聽見他不在了，前來接收遺產。」

嗇色退後三步，這才眞正看清楚來人。

像，像得不能再像，連鬍髮都遺傳自她，面形，身型，都大小同異，可是，她的雙

目含一股精悍之氣，把嗇色擋在一個距離之外。

並且隱隱帶着納罕，什麼，你想什麼，帶你走？

「你在這裏生活得很好呀。」

嗇色鼓起勇氣再說一遍，「可是，我父親已經去世。」

對方似不能領會她的意思，「看你的衣着就知道了。」她像恭唯陌生人，「多合身

多舒適。」

嗇色完全靜下來，她從未想過與生母重逢會是這個情況，她以爲雙方至少會沉默地

流下眼淚，可是她居然絮絮閒話家常，不讓嗇色有開口機會。

正在這個時候，大門打開，嗇色抬頭一看，鬆口氣，是陳綺羅回來了。

她身邊還跟着一位穿西服拎公事包的男士。

60

綺羅一臉笑容，一進門便向嗇色招手，嗇色走到她身邊，她輕輕問：「你還不去做功課？」

把嗇色撥到身後，似保護一隻小動物那樣。

然後，她才過去與客人握手，「是方國寶女士吧，我來介紹，這位是石志威律師，對不起我回來遲了，叫你久候，下次大駕光臨，請早些通知我。」

看一看茶，吩咐傭人：「換熱的龍井上來。」

兩位女士面對面坐下。

——「我來接收甄文彬的遺產。」

這時，嗇色已退回自己臥室，可是客廳外頭的聲音可以聽得到。

「甄文彬沒有遺產。」

「陳小姐你開什麼玩笑！」

「所以我請了石律師來，他可以給你看文件，他願意向你擔保，甄文彬沒有遺產。」

「這幢房子呢？」對方驚呼。

61

「這幢公寓是我五年前所置，那時我還沒認識甄文彬其人，石律師會清楚向你交待。」

石律師站起來，「方女士，請隨我到書房，我會解答你的疑難。」

方氏霍一聲站起來，一臉不忿，咚咚咚跟律師進書房去。

嗇色坐在書桌前，垂頭緊緊握住雙手。

綺羅端着蛋糕與牛奶進來。

「怎麼了？」

嗇色的頭垂得更低。

綺羅歎口氣，輕輕說：「她把你當陌生人，也只有好，互不相干。」

嗇色仍不出聲。

頭垂得那樣低，綺羅把手擱在她後頸上，「她來看看有什麼遺產，也不過是人之常情。」

甄文彬唯一遺產便是甄嗇色，為什麼她不要她？

「石律師會向她解釋一切，她還是特地乘飛機前來的呢，個人環境並非富裕，在悉

62

尼一間中國菜館裏做掌櫃。

嗇色呆呆地聽着。

「不相愛有不相愛的好處，像我，從來沒有思念過那班親戚，不知多輕鬆。」

可是，嗇色覺得羞愧。

綺羅勸道：「她是她，你是你，你不必為她行為負責。」

書房門打開，方國寶女士大聲而急躁地說：「這些年來，甄文彬一毛錢也沒剩下？」

律師聲音很清晰：「我已交待得一清二楚。」

方女士頓足，她似鬥敗公雞似跌坐在沙發裏。

綺羅站在門口看着她。

過片刻，她抬起頭，「你是否一早已把一切產業轉到自己名下。」

「你知道沒有這樣的事。」

方女士很頹喪，「我問同事借了錢買飛機票來。」

綺羅立刻對石律師說：「把那筆款子算給方女士。」

63

嗇色不相信她會接受。

可是親眼看着方女士把支票唰一聲收入手袋。

嗇色忽然微笑，她終於心死了。

她相信人窮志短，財大聲粗這兩句話，可是問人借飛機票趕來爭前夫的遺產，純屬貪念，與貧瘠無關。

人窮了，志不能窮。

她大口吃蛋糕，毫無忌憚，統共沒有自尊，擦過嘴，沮喪地說：「白走一趟。」

石律師是一個沉着的中年人，這時，雙目不能控制地露出厭惡的神色來。

嗇色覺得這種目光就似射到她身上一樣，無地自容。

然後，方女士沉醉在失望中，看也不看嗇色，就自顧自走到大門口。

綺羅同石律師說：「勞駕你送她一程。」

石律師斷然拒絕：「我還有事。」

傭人開門，讓方女士出去。

石律師鬆口氣，「幸虧帶齊文件。」

64

「我們告訴她的，都是實話。」

石律師聲音低下去，「我替嗇色難過……」

「不必，嗇色有的是前途，她的生活還沒開始，我替方女士難過才真，她前來領取遺產，一進門就看到完全屬於她的瑰寶，可是她視若無睹，竟是個亮眼瞎子。」

嗇色知道繼母口中的寶物是她，不由得流下淚來。

石律師說：「本來，你囑我向她提出正式領養手續──」

「不必了，免她拿腔作勢，嗇色很快到廿一歲有自主權，你看，現在由我白白得到世上最有價值的產業。」

「綺羅，你真的那樣想？」

「是，我自幼同嗇色一樣，是個在家族中被踢打的角色，我在她身上看到太多自身的影子，我想為她一盡綿力。」

「這是很難得的一件事。」

「加雙筷子而已。」

「仍打算送她往英國寄宿？」

65

「我會與她商量。」

石律師笑，「希望她喜歡打曲棍球。」

「讓她學好詠春拳才去，有洋童難爲她，可以還擊。」

石律師吃驚，「以暴易暴？」

「保護自己而已。」

片刻，石律師離去。

綺羅見嗇色仍然躲在臥室之中，不禁詫異，「倒底還小，這樣一點事就抬不起頭來？將來你才知道，世上不知還有幾許尷尬之事。」

「可是，那是我的生母。」

「咄，我的牛兄牛姐，坐在一起何嘗沒有足足一桌。」

「但生母——」

「再計較與你何益？」

「她竟把我丟在陌生人家中。」

綺羅靜下來，

「我是陌生人？」綺羅的聲音大起來，「我是陌生人？」

66

「不不不——」

「這下子你得罪了我，後患無窮。」

嗇色雙手亂搖，忽然放棄，放聲大哭。

像極小極小之際，在百貨公司裏迷路，不見了大人，徬徨恐懼淒涼到極點，除了哀

哀痛哭，一點辦法也無。

門鈴一響，利佳上來了。

「都走了嗎？」

綺羅笑，「你叫什麼絆住？遲到個把鐘頭，幸虧札平解決，毋需勞駕你出力。」

「她有無帶走嗇色？」

嗇色一怔，沒想到他第一句問這個話。

「沒有，嗇色同我們在一起。」

「送出去寄宿。」

「她要找她，你也不能不讓她見她。」

嗇色低聲說：「我願意出去寄宿。」

67

綺羅頷首：「那也好。」

這一句話叫嗇色在約克郡一間私立女校逗留了三年。

她學到的東西之多，非筆墨可以形容。

像華裔叫清人，像約克布甸是一堆麵粉，像用詠春打女同學要記一次大過，像打人之後誰也不敢惹她，像一整個秋季日日下雨人的身體似要長出青苔來。

而功課實在太容易了。

嗇色喜歡用一種黃色的藥水肥皂洗澡，洗完之後整天渾身都有一股清香的味道。

天天都是霏霏細雨，有時霧同雨結在一起，一片白濛濛。

第一年冬假綺羅與利佳上來看她。

那便不是一個假日。

清晨，她與同學正自公園練打曲棍球回校，雨勢已十分急，可是無人介意濕身，你要是真正無法忍受雨，你就無法在那裏住。

利佳上一眼就看到了嗇色。

她已除下近視眼鏡，人又長高了，穿着格子校服，那體育褲極短，露出少女修長纖細的腿，泥漬斑斑，寒天，她口中呼出白霧，長髮鬈曲地在雨中飛舞。

粉白的臉如阿拉巴斯特美玉，大眼睛忽然閃出興奮光芒，她也看到了他們。

她高興地揮舞着手，奔過馬路另一邊。

「你們來了，怎麼不通知我。」

穿着凱斯咪長大衣打着傘的陳綺羅直笑說：「你不冷嗎？」

嗇色答：「今天不算冷。」

「已替你請了假。」

「我得換衣服。」

「上車來再說。」

鑽進車廂，他自小水壺中倒出熱可可給她。

利佳上取出手帕，替嗇色抹去臉上泥巴。

嗇色喝一口，道謝。

「生活如何？」

「很好。」

「食物很差是不是，據說閉上眼睛，一切都像吃地布。」

「萬幸，我不是來吃的。」

「能這樣想就好。」

然後，利佳上微笑地說：「嗇色，我同綺羅打算在明年初夏結婚。」

「那多好！」

「屆時我們到歐洲蜜月，你與我們一起。」

「可是，」嗇色說：「歐洲太繁忙，不是蜜月好地方，」好似很有見地。

「正適合我們，」綺羅笑，「太靜了，思前想後，說不定會後悔。」

那幾天她陪他們住在旅館裏。

半夜，嗇色發覺綺羅坐在窗前喝酒。

「睡不着？」

綺羅有點歉意，「吵醒了你。」

「是否做夢？」

「是，夢見文彬，他正在寫字枱前忙得不可開交。」

70

嗇色沉默一會兒，「你是愛他的吧。」

綺羅意外，「那當然。」

「為什麼？」

「因為他十分倚賴我，我覺得我需要照顧他。」

嗇色不出聲。

「你有無夢見過父親？」

「沒有。」

綺羅納罕，「這倒奇怪。」

嗇色在半夜意旨力薄弱，心不由主，說出實話，「我並不想念他，也不愛他，他不是一個好父親。」

綺羅十分震驚，靜了下來，等到再要說些什麼，發覺嗇色已經睡着。

三天後他們轉程往劍橋。

嗇色不知這是否屬蜜月演習。

通常在路上，她一個人咚咚咚走在前面，走遠了，回頭看，他們總在偷偷接吻。

71

嗇色每次都忍不住笑，佯裝看不見，繼續往前走。

有時也故意墮後，看他倆拖手。

他喜歡把她的手握在大衣口袋保暖。

他總是穿着長大衣，像他那樣身段，穿起大衣，真是要多好看，就有多好看。

待他們結了婚，他就是甄嗇色的繼父。

嗇色是少數把父母全部更換的成功例子。

她苦笑地在日記本子上揶揄地寫：「誰說一個人不可以選擇父母。」

可是想深一層，綺羅並非由她挑選，而利佳上，更與她眼光無關。

甄嗇色一切處被動。

一次，趁利佳上不在身邊，嗇色問：「你在何處認識他？」

綺羅笑，不願作答。

嗇色這次十分不識向，「告訴我。」

「好好好，某次出差，在紐約五街一間書報攤前。」

「什麼？」

「我去買報紙，他也在選雜誌，他看到我，走过來說：『小姐你看上去氣色好極了，願意一起喝杯咖啡嗎』。」

嗇色接着道：「於是你立刻跟他走。」

「不不不，」綺羅神情如少女一般腼腆，我怎麽會接受那種吊膀子技倆，我覺得尷尬，轉頭就走。」

「噫，人海茫茫，那可怎麽辦？」

「就是呀，回酒店想了一天，第二天，身不由主在同樣時間踱回那個書報攤。」

「他在那裏！」

「可不是，他也正在那裏等我，雙手挿口袋裏，看見我，微微笑，我走到他跟前，

『咖啡?』我說。

啊。

嗇色覺得這件事盪氣迴腸。

「其實那時我還是有夫之婦。」

「你有無告訴他？」

73

「那是我的私事，與人無尤。」

嗇色也認為真確。

「真奇怪，再次看到他的時候，時間彷彿停頓，其他人漸漸淡出，耳畔聲音嗡嗡，一切都不像真的。」

「似一齣電影。」

「對。」

「那可算一見鍾情？」

「大概是。」

「那不是很危險嗎？」

「我們都是成年人，大約知道自己要的是什麼，不會很錯，你，你還小，你就得小心。」

「那次，可也是冬天，他是否也穿着長大衣？」

「不不不，那是一個瘋狂的炎夏，大家的白襯衫都被汗水浸得差不多發黃，佔盡了天時地利人和。」

74

「回到家……以後的事你知道了。」

「他是否富有？」

綺羅微笑，「那重要嗎？」

「呵十分要緊。」

「是，他是長子，他承繼了身家。」

「他的父母可喜歡你？」

「那將來去到天堂才能問他們。」

嗇色說：「我看他不是壞人。」

嗇色真替綺羅高興。

忽然又想起來，「他以前可有愛人？」

綺羅笑，「那可真是他家的事，我管不着。」

「你又怎麼辨認？」綺羅笑嘻嘻。

嗇色感喟：「他對孩子好，有許多正經人都不介意賤視兒童，因他們無力反抗，任

由擺佈。」

嗇色是有感而發。

夏天，他們在倫敦碰頭。

新婚夫妻的膚色如在蜜糖裏浸過那樣顏色，穿着細麻布，一個上午就團得不能再

皺。

他們出發到歐陸去。

在梵帝崗西西庭教堂內，他們被教士勸止，「不准親吻、不准攝影」，拍照的是嗇

色。

到了碧藍海岸，他們在酒店泳池暢泳。

嗇色年輕的目光灼灼，看着她新任繼父。

利君有點尷尬，「有什麼不對？」

嗇色連忙別轉頭去。

她第一次發現他胸膛毛茸茸，而且看上去似嬰兒頭髮，稠密柔韌。

嗇色納罕觸覺如何。

而且，洗完澡，可需要吹乾。

忽爾她笑了，也一定很麻煩吧。

利佳上就坐在她對面，看到她笑，不知怎地，別轉頭去，不敢再看。

那是什麼樣的笑？他曾於清晨見過在露珠下綻放的玫瑰花蕾，是，那笑容就是那個樣子。

嗇色整張臉粉藕色，一雙漆黑大眼睛，長鬈髮，仍然手長腳長，但已與身軀配合得十分得宜。

綺羅輕輕在利君耳畔說：「嗇色多出色。」

他聽見他自己這樣答：「小孩子耳。」

那真是個愉快的假期。

否極泰來，嗇色趁機盡情享樂。

她吃了很多意大利冰淇淋，買了數不清的時裝皮鞋。拍了大疊照片，然後才回宿舍去。

臨別之際依依不捨。

綺羅應允，「我們會再來。」

77

同學艷羨地說：「你是歐陸常客。」

「不，這次主要在南部玩。」

「你父母看上去似你大哥大姐。」

「許多人都那樣說。」

「你家很富有？」

嗇色學着繼母的語氣笑問：「錢多很重要嗎？」

「當然，可以到歐陸旅遊。」

「可是，本校一般學生環境都不差。」

「我們只到湖區而已。」

「湖區可是個極美之處！」

「你真認為如此？」

「我希望可以在那處住上一個春季。」

那些漂亮的衣服都沒有機會穿，幸虧她身量已經長足，不會再高，只要不怕式樣過

時，年年可穿。

同學們都來借雲裳。

在這方面，嗇色慷慨，一如繼母，任由同學借穿，她們本地人總有舞會可去。

撕破了或是染了漬子，均不予計較，嗇色因此成了最受歡迎人物。

待她自己要穿之際，發覺紐子裙扣統統不齊，笑置之，仍穿毛衣牛仔褲。

秋季某個週末，她在宿舍寫功課，有人找她。

取起走廊裏電話，她聽到利君的聲音。

「三十分鐘後我來接你。」

「太好了。」

她準備妥當，站在宿舍門口等。

利君準時來到。

車子一停，嗇色探頭進車廂，用英語說：「咦，我媽媽呢？」

「她沒有來，她要同客戶開會，我也只停這半日。」

嗇色上車，「我好想念她。」

利佳上笑，「我何嘗不是。」

嗇色說：「昨晚午夜夢迴，想到如果沒有我媽媽，日子不知怎麼過。」

說這話的時候，她雙臂枕在腦後，神情悠然，可是聲音中卻無限淒酸。

利佳上聽在耳中，不覺惻然。

他這次行程中本無此行，可是千辛萬苦，他卻想擠出半天時間來見一見她。

「你沒穿足衣服。」

「天氣並不冷，我們還淋冷水浴。」

利佳上搖頭。

他們到一間酒店附設的茶廳喝下午茶。

嗇色笑，「這裏一三五舉行茶舞，甚受老先生老太太歡迎。」

「你會跳舞？」

「不會，沒人教過我。」

「你想不想學探戈？」

「探戈？」嗇色大笑起來，「不不不，我想學的只是森巴。」

「森巴！」輪到利君驚歡。

「是，半裸紗衣，一隻搖鼓，不住顫抖，發出沙沙節奏，即可起舞，跳至大汗淋

漓，我愛煞森巴。」

「四步呢。」

「我不介意四步。」

「來，讓我們跳這隻四步。」

他們笑着下舞池。

嗇色抱怨：「你長得太高了，不是好舞伴。」

利佳上忍不住笑。

他握着她小小短指甲的手，「生活如何？」

「絕對是我生命中最好的數年。」

「要不要回家來？」

「不，一到家，寄人籬下之感油然而生，在宿舍，避得一時是一時。」

她試着把下巴擱利君肩膀上，可是不夠高，放棄，利佳上的下巴反而扣在她頭頂。

「喂喂喂，」她笑着說：「我不跳了。」

81

嗇色把碟上的三文治及司空餅一掃而清。

「真能吃，真羨慕。」

「晚上到何處請客？」

利佳上溫柔的說：「我五點半就得離開此地。」

嗇色的小面孔收縮一下，寂寥地低下頭。

「不如回家來。」

「不，」她斷然拒絕，「我情願寄宿。」

回程中，她問他：「婚姻生活可好？」

「好得不得了。」

「幾時生孩子？」

利佳上意外，「我們從來沒考慮過這件事。」

他們真是一對。

「一日，在百貨公司看到一對孿生兒，才三個月大，可愛得緊。」

利佳上只是笑。

「是加以詳細考慮的時候了。」

「我倆年事已長，已經太遲，為人父母，要趁年輕，廿五歲之前養三四名，那樣才有精力同他們廝混。」

「我希望看到小弟小妹。」

嗇色接着說：「我知道我永遠不會結婚生子，所以希望有弟妹。」

這倒好，那麼小經歷那麼多，可是對生命仍具希望。

「你這些預言未免說得太早了一點。」

「不，我知道我的事。」

「老氣橫秋，你的生命還沒有開始。」

距離近了，他看到她的濃眉長睫與粉紅色的小腫嘴，似畫中人一樣。

她也轉過頭來看他。

利君的早上刮淨的鬍髭此刻已經長出一層青色陰影。

嗇色想：他有那麼多毛髮，天天打理它們，也真夠麻煩。

嗇色隨即不好意思地別過頭去。

「升了大學，搬離宿舍，可以自由請朋友到家玩。」

「我會努力爭取獎學金。」

「我們到了。」

「謝謝你來看我。」

他捉着她的頭，在她額頭響亮地吻一下。

他給她一大袋陳皮梅帶返宿舍。

同學前來敲門，「星期六你要出去嗎？」

「同誰？」

「我可替你找一盲約。」

嗇色想一想，「也好。」

同學沒想到她會欣然應允，有點意外。

那臉上長着疱疱的男生一見她就把手臂搭在她肩膀上，她幾次三番摔甩那隻毛手。

同學暗示她毋需如此拘謹。

那隻手又搭上來。

嗇色拉下臉，「管住你的手，否則我用刀剁掉它！」

那男孩神經質地笑。

結果還由嗇色付賬。

三人吃了牛排，那真是難得的大菜，宿舍中經年累月極少得到吃肉，有也只是薄薄一片，下邊用椰菜墊底。

收那樣貴的食宿費尚且那般虐待顧客，真正不可思議。

那男生飽餐一頓，尚感滿意。

嗇色喚侍者替她叫了一部計程車獨自返回宿舍。

當然也有比這個略爲好一點的經驗。

像在中央圖書館裏認識的呂德提君。

他相貌端正得多，人品亦佳。

她幫他做功課，他拾了母親做的巧克力屑餅乾來招待她。

他想借的書，她全知道放在什麼地方，在他心目中，她宛如神奇女俠。

他在家說起她，家人都不相信有那樣漂亮以及功課優秀的女孩，他姐姐特地跟了來看。

在圖書館正門對面，敏感的嗇色發覺有人看着她，一轉頭，見是另外一個女孩子，不由得笑了。

呂德提介紹她們認識，他姐姐笑笑滿意地離去。

「姐姐在家幫忙做生意。」

「輟學在家幫忙做生意。」

「姐姐在哪一間大學？」

「你家做哪一行？」

「開餐館。」

「她不愛讀書？」

「嗇色，世上像你那樣喜歡讀書的人實在是很少的。」

嗇色腼腆地笑。

「聽說你代表國家去歐洲參加純數比賽。」

「是，我是十一名隊員中其中一個。」

「功課那樣好，一定很開心。」

嗇色忽然語氣寂寥，「你知道我這個人，不比人特別漂亮，或是富有，或是聰明，或是好運，能在功課上特別用功，也是一項成績。」

呂德提訝異得張開了嘴，品貌俱優的她一點自信都沒有，這真是天底下至奇怪的一件事。

週末她到他店裏去吃點心。

餐館一早知道有那樣一個貴客來臨，準備了年輕人愛吃的麵食小點招待她。

嗇色特別愛吃棗泥鍋餅以及高力豆沙，吃完了，替東家把菜單譯為英文。

這可能是唐人餐館唯一沒有文法拼字錯誤的英譯菜單。

「你呢，」她問呂德提：「你打算讀到幾時？」

「我不知道，中學畢業再算吧。」

嗇色說：「美國已有兩千多間學校取銷暑假制度，節省時間兼盡量利用校舍，我們不知幾時效法，漫長暑假多討厭，浪費生命！」

呂德提聽了黯然，他知道她不是他的對象，這個女孩怎麼會甘心躭在小鎮裏守住一間餐館。

姐姐白來相看。

他囁嚅答：「可是暑假用來休養生息……」

「是嗎，」嗇色大惑不解，「讀書很辛苦嗎，你我為功課傷了元氣嗎？」

呂德提不知道如何回答。

即使如此，他還是約她到鎮上看電影，每次都請她吃一客覆盤子冰淇淋。

呂德提輕輕說：「將來，很久之後，你會不會記得在戲院裏看戲的情境？」

嗇色詫異，「當然，我記性一向甚佳。」

翌年暑假，她被繼母叫了回家。

九月開學之後，一連三個月都沒在圖書館見到呂德提。

她掛住他，到唐人餐館去找他。

見店門大開，還在營業，不禁歡喜。

可是掌櫃另有其人，不是他那個小姐姐。

那位陌生太太說：「呂家舉家搬到倫敦去了，你不知道嗎，這店頂了給我們，現在做粵菜。」

哎，他沒有告別。

就這樣消失在人羣中。

這叫嗇色恍然若失。

本來她想把暑假發生的事一五一十告訴他。

呵是，那個暑假。

「嗇色，我需要你陪着我，回來如何？」

「遵命。」

那是無論如何一定要答應的，又不是苦差，即使是，也得咬緊牙關上。

家裏又裝修過了。

她的房間仍在那裏，兩年來都沒動過，單人床顯得非常小，可是躺上去賓至如歸。

傭人見到她喜極而泣。

夏天，即使有空氣調節還是覺得熱，嗇色穿着短褲背心倒處跑。

感覺特別自由，因為繼父並不與她們同住。

是，沒有人說正式結婚的夫婦不能分居。

陳綺羅笑說：「蓬頭垢面打呵欠口氣欠佳之時就無謂見面破壞印象你說可是。」

但夫妻不是要坦誠相見嗎？

「你倒試試看，那些不信邪的人婚姻全部泡湯。」

「應該分開住嗎？」

當然。

去看過利君的住所，便知道省不得，絕對不能同住。

他的家沒有間隔，全部打通，一張乒乓球桌上擺着書本筆記電腦報紙雜誌資料等物。

四壁全是參考書，一塊大黑板，上面寫滿功課。

床放在不顯眼地方，只如一張長沙發，衞生間倒是設備先進，光潔明亮。

開放式廚房用具應有盡有，煮起湯米，近三千平方呎大的空間香氣溢然。

全屋並無一件女性用品。

綺羅連一盒胭脂也不留下。

完全各歸各。

90

嗇色只不過略坐一會兒，已有學生陸續上來。

「教授不在？」

「不要緊，我們會得招呼自己。」

可是目光被嗇色鈎住，再也脫不了鈎。

綺羅笑，「這地方是臨時教室。」

嗇色問：「這些學生都唸幾年級？」

「都在做博士論文了。」

其中一人咳嗽一聲，搭腔道：「師母這位是小師妹吧。」

綺羅答：「你們全是大師兄，要多多照顧她。」

可是說完話就把嗇色帶走。

「都廿五六七歲了，仍然靠家裏，博士生全體遲發育遲成熟，不是好對象。」

嗇色駭笑。

片刻問：「教授人呢？」

「我不知道，我沒問。」

「可以不理他行蹤嗎？」

「嗇色，我有更重要的事要做，彼此偵查，實在浪費時間。」

嗇色十分興奮，「將來我一定要向你學習。」

「你功課進展如何？」

「美國有大學收我。」

「哪幾家？」

「我不想計較校名，只要有獎學金即可。」

「學費我全替你準備好了。」

「不，我會自己想辦法。」

「私校比較矜貴，不如申請史蒙夫或布朗。」

「不。」

「一直以來，聽得至多的是這個不字。」

嗇色情急，淚盈於睫，急急低頭。

晚上，到工人間與老傭人聊天。

92

傭人請她喝沙示汽水。

一隻小小飛蛾闖進來停在日光燈旁邊。

嗇色看半晌，欲揮手趕。

被老傭人阻止，「隨牠去，牠不礙事。」

嗇色過一會兒問：「傳說，飛蛾是一個什麼人的靈魂？」

「嗯。」

嗇色凝視那隻灰棕色小小昆蟲。

你是誰。

爲何來探望我們。

你是父親嗎。

你還認得路。

她呆呆地看着飛蛾良久。

老傭人點着一枝煙，吸一口，緩緩噴出：「我今秋便告老還鄉了。」

嗇色一驚，「什麼？」

93

「六十五了，該退休了。」她直笑。

「不，不讓你走！」

真是好人，一點也不勢利，從來沒慫恿過主人說「又不是親生何必如此勞心勞力」，待嗇色一直不亢不卑。

如今竟也要走了。

工人間小小收音機裏恰巧播放着粵曲，一把蒼老的聲音唱：「一葉輕舟去，人隔萬重山——」

嗇色忽然張大了嘴，大聲號哭起來。

老傭人嚇一跳，按熄了煙頭，前來安慰嗇色。

她那雙勞工手的指節已經彎頭，指甲厚且灰，歲月如流，出來做工人時幾乎是最後一批志願者，熬到每年有法定假期，真不容易。

「東家給我很豐厚的退休金。」

她是第一代經濟獨立女性。

「想想還是有工作好，一班姐妹都能得到東家善待，反而是期望伴侶兒孫施捨的那撮人，終於失望了。」

她為嗇色抹乾眼淚。

嗇色靜靜聽着。

「陳小姐真是好人。」

嗇色點點頭。

「可惜——」

嗇色抬起頭來。

「我磨了新鮮豆漿，給你喝一口。」

嗇色追問：「可惜什麼？」

老傭人笑，「陳小姐淨喜吃外國食品，她愛喝牛奶，不喜豆漿。」

「我來幫你推銷。」

可惜什麼，老人看到什麼？

深夜，綺羅返來，見嗇色站露台上，便說：「來，聊聊天。」

嗇色笑着回過頭來。

襯着露台外一天一地的燈色，嗇色的臉到深夜仍然晶瑩如新。

綺羅喝聲采，「你真漂亮。」

「我？」嗇色不置信，「也許，在一個母親眼中，女兒永遠最完美。」

綺羅脫下鞋子。

「我幫你按摩。」

綺羅把腳擱在嗇色膝上，嗇色替她揉捏。

「看，」綺羅感慨地說：「終於什麼都有了。」

嗇色靜靜聽她說話。

「小時候生活多清貧，我現在是巴不得可以穿過時光隧道，回到過去，好好照顧那個小孤女。」

嗇色微笑，「這真是名副其實自己照顧自己。」

「可惜已不能夠，時光逝去，永不回頭。」

「你現在照顧我也是一樣。」

「是呀，總算償了心願。」

嗇色看着天空，都市的夜空被霓虹燈照耀得一片橘紅色，看不到星宿。

嗇色忽然想回到約克郡去，站操場上，一抬頭，可以看到一天星光燦爛。

「讀完書，出來幫我做生意。」

自始至終，嗇色不知道繼母做的是何種生意。

「我做出入口，轉手賺錢，將來我會敎你。」

老傭人斟茶出來。

「以後不再會有這種事了，只有老派家務助理才會如此盡忠職守，新的一代工人到了時間關上門，外頭天塌下來也不理。」綺羅惆悵。

嗇色笑，「我會替你倒茶。」

「屆時到什麼地方去找你這個人。」

「我一定在家。」

「那些追求者會放過你嗎？」

「誰會喜歡我。」

「這就不對了，為什麼不喜歡你？」

嗇色微微笑。

綺羅歎口氣，「也難怪你，我的自信心也在很後期才培養起來，這就得多謝你父親了，他事事讚美我、信任我，把一個家交在我手中，使我堅強起來。」

這是眞的。

「少年時眞是一點自尊自信也無，在老人家寄住，可是不准我叫外婆，『婆婆，把我叫老了』，只能低着頭聽訓示。」

「那何故收留你？」

「因爲收了一筆膳宿費，他們需要每月那微薄的金錢。」綺羅深深太息，「你看，咱們母女倆同病相憐。」

嗇色微笑說：：「不，我比你好多了。」

「你眞那麼想？」

「差天共地，我有你人力物力支撐，而且，我們是眞正朋友。」

「聽到你那麼說眞高興。」

這時候，電話來了。

98

沒有鈴聲，只有一盞小小紅燈，在話筒上不住閃爍。

是利佳上打來的。

綺羅在黑暗中接聽，一臉陶醉。

嗇色會心微笑。

這麼些日子了，仍然男歡女愛，如膠如漆，真是難得。

怕是因為不一起住的緣故，依依不捨，每夜話別。均留下一點新鮮感覺。

清早各管各洗刷打扮，稍後，在最佳狀態下見面。

當然，他們開頭必需是相愛的。

怎麼樣他會自心中發出無盡愛戀憐惜，內心深處又帶着一絲蕩意，希望與他有肌膚之親……嗇色十分憧憬。

一看他會自心中發出無盡愛戀憐惜，內心深處又帶着一絲蕩意，希望與他有肌膚之親……嗇色十分憧憬。

怎麼樣他會自心中找到這個人呢。

第二天大早，嗇色一出客廳，便看到利佳上與繼母已在喝咖啡看報紙。

兩人都白衣白褲，好一對俊男美女，看到嗇色，向她招手。

嗇色訝異，「這麼早？」

利君說：「我是清晨五時來的。」

嗇色駭笑，「這麼早，做什麼？」

一出口，便知造次，立刻噤聲，燒紅耳朵。

可幸綺羅給她接上去：「做賊。」

利君立刻說：「別在孩子跟前說這些。」

嗇色笑，「誰，誰是孩子？」

利君說：「我來送你們飛機。」

嗇色問：「誰乘飛機？」

「嗇色，你陪我到台北去一趟。」

嗇色一怔，「那我馬上去收拾行李。」

「才兩天，十套八套衣裳夠了。」

利佳上駭笑，「兩天需換十套衣裳？」

綺羅給他白眼，「所以不同你住！」

嗇色見他們打情罵俏，非常欣賞。

100

綺羅真幸運，在甄氏之後又找到新生活，這同她的性格有關吧，她對身邊總是盡心盡意，不過，也得到極佳回報。

「幹嗎收拾了六七條長褲？」

嗇色猛地抬起頭來，見綺羅已站在她身邊，「呵，我弄錯了。」

她們乘中午飛機出發。

綺羅如帶着一個私人秘書。

嗇色也樂意替她打點一切瑣事：接聽電話特別用心，外出衣裳均吩咐酒店熨好掛起、聯絡好車子接送⋯⋯

綺羅暗暗說：「長大了。」

同父母溺愛的子女不同，那票幸運兒永遠不會成長，到三十歲仍住家中茶來伸手飯來開口。

每次自外開會回來，嗇色替她準備的茶點已在房間裏：一壺格雷伯爵紅茶，兩塊乾吐司。

她撫摸嗇色頭髮，「初見你，如一隻小貓。」

101

嗇色說：「至今我不敢伸懶腰，十分瑟縮，最怕誇張。」

「姿勢是含蓄點好。」

嗇色跟綺羅跑遍台北。

意外地她十分喜歡這個地方，它是一個充滿色相的城市，大千世界，曼陀羅般奇幻冶艷，天氣激烈多變，艷陽天忽然下大雷雨，寂靜午夜隨時地震，婦女們在晴天也習慣打傘防曬。

最新的最舊的、最美的最醜的都有，對比強烈，無比新奇。

可惜三兩天內就要離開。

嗇色依依不捨，她剛發現美味的台菜，還有，金舖叫銀樓，牙醫叫齒科，交通混亂，一如羅馬。

「下次再來。」

綺羅這樣應允，她洽談生意成功，心情大佳。

對方商業代表是一個姓林的中年人，對陳綺羅有着明顯的仰慕。

可惜西服領帶皮鞋的款式都過份時髦，顏色全不配，而且頭髮過長。

102

綺羅對他很客氣，介紹嗇色是「我女兒。」

對方無比訝異，「無論如何沒有可能！」

這時，嗇色覺得美貌女子跑江湖說什麼方便些，兇險歸兇險，可是成功率高得多。

綺羅並無故意賣弄色相，可是相貌與生俱來，扔也扔不掉。

晚上，綺羅說：「做完這一宗生意，以後我就不再親自出馬。」

「是累了嗎？」

綺羅笑，「不。」

嗇色訝異，「這是退至幕後的原因嗎？」

回來全沾上煙味，多腌臢，有時醺得耳根敏感發癢。

「一則要讓小孩子上來，二則你看看，這正是所謂拋頭露面，好好的套裝穿一日，

「真實原因是什麼？」

嗇色希望聽到「我已懷孕」。

可是不，綺羅只是笑笑答：「我已賺夠。」

103

嗇色有點失望，不過，亦對答案感到滿意。

上一次你聽到有人說賺夠是幾時？抑或，從來沒有人表示已經賺夠？

綺羅說：「你看我，根本不是那種沉溺於縱容自身的人，我又只得一個女兒，開銷有限，我對生活極端滿意，毋需更多物質填充心靈，況且，應有也都有齊，還那麼辛苦鑽營幹嗎。」

聽到這樣的話真高興。

「唯一的遺憾是童年及青少年時的不足，可是，時間既然已經過去，也無可奈何。」

嗇色不住點頭。

「一般人認為肯熬窮至偉大清高不過，其實賺錢更需忍辱負重，辛苦得不得了。」

綺羅訕笑一會子，稍後與嗇色出去吃晚飯。

林先生一定要作東，叫了十個人吃的菜，其中有甲魚及兔肉，嗇色不敢吃。

第二天就要走了，綺羅陪他說些風土人情，以及在歐美接生意需要注意些什麼。

林先生忽然說：「我在溫哥華西岸有幢房子……」

104

嗇色豎起耳朵，聽綺羅如何應付。

綺羅微笑答：「那多巧，我在西溫也有物業，房子在高原路，府上呢？」

嗇色覺得答案太精彩，不禁咧開嘴笑。

那位林先生有點氣餒，「原本我的意思是，假使你到了那邊，可以不用住酒店。」

可是今日的陳綺羅已毋需任何人照顧。

她很得體地道謝，「我大部份假期在倫敦度過，我女兒在英國唸書。」

林先生忍不住，「她無論如何不是你的女兒。」

第二天她們就走了。

「林先生有家眷嗎？」

「有時假裝獨身是一種樂趣。」

「那，不太好吧。」

綺羅為這天真的說法笑出來。

她們回到家，利佳上卻飛往北歐開會去了。

綺羅說：「我知道這種事遲早會發生，待我退下來之際，該他神龍見首不見尾了，

105

我結果變成空守閨房的怨婦。」

嗇色渴望回到宿舍去。

那裏才是她的世界。冷冷的窗戶，雨水如一個人的眼淚在玻璃上掛下，呵氣成霧，

一到九月便能穿上厚大衣帽子，脾氣可以名正言順跟着天氣壞。

她不喜歡這個沒有四季的都會。

誰要是坐在這繁華功利城市豪華住宅的窗台上看雨，會被人誤會是十三點。

那一日早上，嗇色在閱報，忽然聽得綺羅叫她。

嗇色放下報紙立刻趕去寢室。

綺羅披着白色毛巾浴袍，頭髮濕漉漉，有點心急，「嗇色，你來替我看看。」

嗇色馬上用毛巾替繼母擦頭髮，「什麼事，哪裏不對？」

綺羅脫下一邊浴袍，指着左胸，「這裏，這裏有點不妥。」

她舉起手，胸前硬塊不明顯，可是腋下囊腫，肉眼可見。

嗇色心情沉重，可是臉上微微笑，「緊張什麼，讓我看看。」

106

她輕輕去砸那地方。

然後，替綺羅穿好衣服。

半晌她說：「我替你約醫生。」

綺羅呆一會兒，才說：「快去。」

來到客廳，接到利佳上的電話。

她很簡單地問：「你在何處？」

「赫爾辛基。」

「快點回來。」

利佳上並沒有多問，「我下午可以走。」

嗇色把電話接給綺羅。

醫生至快待下午才有空。

到了診所，例牌人山人海，她們已算特權份子，拔號搶先見到醫生。

醫生態度倒是很好，嗯嗯連聲，並非太緊張，「這裏是脂肪瘤，可以拿掉，也可以任它存在……可是結論是『你儘快入院，我幫你在腋下抽樣檢查。』」

107

嗇色一聽，懊惱到極點，胸口鬱塞，想跑到街上去大叫洩憤。

可是面子上一點也不做出來，只是輕輕說：「我們即時去辦入院手續。」

綺羅忽然轉過頭來凝視她，眼神明澄得像個幼兒，嗇色一言不發，與她緊緊擁抱。

利佳上趕回來，先與嗇色碰頭。

看到她神色無異，本想放心。

但是且慢，這女孩子一向喜怒不形於色，況且又到英國去了那麼久，想必又學到了英國人的深沉。

單看表面，實無從辨別真偽。

他問：「事情怎麼樣？」

「開頭以為是乳癌。」

「結果呢？」

「淋巴腺出了事，已有五處佈滿壞細胞。」

「那可算嚴重？」

「醫生說只是初發。」

利佳上用手掩着臉，「現在我開始明白為什麼大部份家長都希望子女肯做醫生，你看，學數學有什麼用。」

嗇色勸道：「自有許多好醫生為我們服務。」

「她心情如何？」

「還不錯。」

「有無哭泣？」

「我從未見過她流淚，相信將來這種可能性也極低。」

「你可有應付家人患病的經驗？」

嗇色搖頭。

「我也沒有。」

嗇色忽然說：「我們都需堅強。」

「是。」

她伸手過去，他握住她的手。

嗇色神情鎮定，外人看去，只覺平常，絲毫不見淒惶失措，也許還會想：這女孩怎

109

地沒感情。

可是利君認識她較深，短短數日，她已瘦了一圈，消瘦是耗神的表示。

嗇色的心情像走入一間緊閉密室，無門無窗，叫天不應，叫地不靈，只能伏在牆壁上拚命搥撻，希望有人聽見聲響前來打救。

過兩天，她接陳綺羅出院。

綺羅吩咐：「你回約克郡去吧。」

「我無論如何不走。」

綺羅怒道：「你這個孩子好不討厭，有事自然會叫你回來，你就在身邊，我百忙中邊治病邊還得照顧你心情，那還不累壞我。」

這是事實。

利佳上勸她：「未來一年會是很可怕的一段日子，你避開一點也是好的，有我在這裏也已經足夠，她治病過程難免吃苦，心情煩躁無好言語，彼此得罪反而不美，你回去考大學試吧。」

嗇色只得走開。

110

一下飛機，迎接她的是苦風淒雨。

她放下行李，跑到圖書館去找呂德提不獲。

得到消息是呂家已搬往倫敦。

她本想借他的肩膀靠着好好哭一場。

可惜睎借一向不易。

嗇色失望淒苦到絕點，獨自走向公園，一邊走一邊大聲哭，反正不會有人聽見，即使有，管它呢。

半晌，有人與她迎面而過，那人已經走過了頭，忽然之間，又打回頭，叫住她。

「嗨你，」他說：「爲什麼哭，可以幫忙嗎？」

嗇色睜大淚眼，答陌生人曰：「家母重病。」

「啊，怪不得，你願意聊一聊嗎？」

嗇色點頭。

那年輕人挑一張長橙，清一清落葉，「坐吧。」

他同她說的是粵語。

111

嗇色看清楚了他，他是一個華人學生，身上穿的黑色醫學院制服袍尚未除下。

「你叫什麼名字？」

他笑嘻嘻答：「叫我耳朵，因為，我有一雙好耳朵。」

嗇色苦笑。

「你呢，你是誰？」

「你給我一個名字吧。」

「叫你花不語。」

「什麼意思？」

「淚眼問花花不語，亂紅已隨千秋過。」

嗇色約莫知道他在吟詩，她那古文詩詞根基極差，完全搭不上嘴，慚愧之至。

「令堂如何？」

嗇色又嗚嗚地哭起來。

那叫耳朵的年輕人歎口氣，「家母在三年前去世，我至今不敢一人站在空曠地方，

我悲苦地思念亡母，並且覺得天下至大慘事，是知道餘生都要做一個孤兒。」

112

他說得那樣眞摯動人，嗇色用手帕掩着臉哭得更厲害，不消一會兒，自覺整張臉腫了起來。

太陽落得早，寒氣襲人。

「公園快關門，我送你回宿舍，如何？」

嗇色點點頭。

「哪個學院？」

「我是高中生。」

「啊，那更應快快回去。」

「謝謝你。」

「什麼事？」

「耳朵──」

「四海之內，皆兄弟也。」

他是一個性格詼諧，富同情心，能言善辯的男生。

嗇色想再見他，可是又假設耳朵不會對中學生有興趣，故只得作罷。

每天下午七時，她均接到利佳上的電話。

「綺羅治療過程良好。」

「頭髮如何？」

「那是我至不關心的一件事。」

「誰說你呢，她感覺怎樣？」

「無奈。」

「說我愛她。」

「她知道。」

嗇色自圖書館借來許多有關資料閱讀。

她一連幾次都沒有交功課。

老師並沒有責怪她，只是說：「至影響學生心情的是父母的健康，以及戀愛。」

嗇色答：「我是前者。」淚盈於睫。

一日，實在過意不去，坐在書桌前寫功課，有人敲她房門：「有客來訪。」

她只得走到會客室去。

一個個子小小，其貌不揚的男生滿面笑容地站起來。

他說：「花不語，你今日好看得多了。」

「耳朵！」

「可不就是我。」他笑嘻嘻。

嗇色腼腆，「什麼風把你吹來。」

「倒處找你呢，原來貴校華人學生極多，女生共有三十七名。」

嗇色頗為感動。

「你母親怎樣？」

「還好。」

「我看是吉人天相。」

這小子就是會討人歡喜。

他語氣忽然轉得溫柔，「花不語，即是各嗇色相，你說是不是。」

嗇色很詫異，咦，可以這樣說。

「讓我們出去吃頓飽飯？」

席間，嗇色把她的事告訴他。

耳朵靜靜聽着，啊，花終於說話了。

嗇色沮喪，「所有倒楣之事，已全部發生在我身上。」

耳朵給她續上去：「所以以後不會再有不幸之事。」

「眞的？」

「已經滿額。」

「超額！」

「對，將來，會一天好似一天。」

「耳朵，你眞是好人。」

「你眞姓名是什麼？」

他笑，希望這漂亮的女孩子別只是認定他是好人。

「耳朵。」

嗇色被他逗笑。

她也可以去查他。

不過，既然他愛自稱耳朵，她又何必去拆穿他。

結賬之際，她搶先付鈔。

他抗議：「喂，怎麼可以？」

嗇色大膽地說：「你是個苦學生吧。」

「你怎麼看出來？」他驚訝。

嗇色但笑不語。

他的皮鞋。

收拾得很乾淨，可是鞋底前後都打過掌，由此可知，環境馬馬虎虎，這一頓飯足夠

他買雙新鞋，怎可叫他付鈔。

會不會傷他的自尊心？不會啦，這年頭，誰不樂得省一點。

可是，嗇色的估計錯誤，那耳朵漲紅了臉，壓低聲音對她說：「對於我的消費，我

自有分寸，下次，下次你要是再嫌我窮，我與你絕交。」

嗇色愕住，「不，我需要你的耳朵。」

「剛才吃了多少？」

「連小費三十鎊。」

他把錢還她。

「一人一半。」

「瞎說！」

嗇色臉色稍霽。

嗇色不敢再與他爭。

耳朵臉色稍霽。

嗇色一直沒有到醫學院去查探他真姓名。

寒假，她忙不迭訂飛機票回家。

順帶問耳朵：「你可要回去？」

耳朵苦笑：「何不食肉糜。」

嗇色溫言說：「你又何用處處諷刺我。」

耳朵攤攤手，「我籌不到盤川。」

嗇色伸出手去扭他臉頰，「回來見。」

她對他竟這樣親暱，叫嗇色對別人動手動腳那是不可思議之事，可是對他又不同，耳朵有否因此竊喜？

不，他是一個聰明絕頂的人，他知道這種親暱動作只不過視他如一隻可愛的小動物，殆矣。

嗇色笑着點頭。

「記住，我等着你回來。」

忽然，他不甘心，又問：「我的真名叫什麼？」

「耳朵。」

「天下哪有叫耳朵的人。」他鬧情緒。

「也是你自己說的。」嗇色詫異。

耳朵平靜下來，女孩的母親患病，她哪裏還有心情去調查他的真名。

他極之溫柔地說：「記住，耳朵在等你。」

嗇色回到家，發覺利佳上已搬來與綺羅同住。

一開門她先見到綺羅。

她氣色比嗇色想中好得多。

119

她與嗇色彼此在陽光下凝視。

二人都說對方：「瘦多了。」

利佳上的聲音傳出來，「嗇色回來了嗎？」

他一出現，嚇嗇色一跳。

他胖許多，滿面於思，頭髮長得要在後腦用一條橡筋紮住，只穿一件舊T恤，看得到手臂、腰身的肌肉鬆弛，完全不修邊幅。

外型像那種半生潦倒的藝術家。

真是黑色幽默，綺羅的頭髮經過電療，掉光了重生，只有三兩公分長，看上去不知多奇突。

綺羅歎口氣，「你看你們，一胖一瘦，多難看。」

利佳上哈哈大笑，「聽聽是誰在嫌我們。」

一家人天殘地缺似相視而笑，歇斯底里，直至眼淚流下來。

由此可知皮相是何等靠不住。

嗇色輕輕地吟莎士比亞十四行詩：「（美色）被意外或自然轉變方面剝奪。」

120

嗇色終於面對面問出她要問的問題：「你病情如何？」

「壞部份已用手術切除，接着用藥物及化學治療，嗇色，我已痊癒。」

嗇色聽得綺羅親口說出好消息，彷彿被人移去心頭一塊大石，又頭上一鬆，除去了緊箍。

她一時說不出話來，在客廳中央團團轉，「好了，好了。」

綺羅說：「拜託拜託，你們倆可否理個髮？」

嗇色慷慨地說：「當是送給你的禮物。」

立刻打電話請相熟的理髮師傅上門來。

那是一個金髮碧眼的年輕女子，看見他倆的頭髮大吃一驚。

「嘩，起碼一年沒修剪過。」

嗇色辯曰：「才六個月罷了。」

綺羅相當感動，「是為着我的緣故嗎？」

嗇色搔着頭，她不便說出來，那段日子，想到繼母病重，真是萬念俱灰，心如刀割，誰還會去理整儀容。

今日她興奮地同理髮師說：「什麼髮式最流行？」

師傅微笑，「你別後悔才好。」

大剪一揮，剪到齊耳朵，然後洗濕，繼續颼颼颼地剪。

利佳上在一旁看着，連忙害怕地站起來取外套，「我不剪了。」

理髮師轉過身子來，厲聲喝道：「坐下！」

笑得嗇色彎下腰來。

嗇色摸一摸被剪成小男生那樣的頭，「像剃羊毛一樣。」

綺羅知道她不過想陪她短髮，微笑着頷首。

接着，利佳上理了一個陸軍裝。

嗇色溫柔地問他：「剃渡的感覺如何？」

利佳上平靜地答：「一片澄明。」

嗇色說：「接着，我要增重，你要減磅，其中牽涉二十公斤脂肪。」

「這可不那麼容易做得到。」

這時，有電話找綺羅，她轉到起坐間去。

嗇色送走理髮師，見利佳上站在露台上，他的背影似一個小型胖子。

嗇色忽然放下警惕之心，站他身後笑着說：「總共胖多少？」

「不知道，只曉得吃得飽，可解憂慮。」

嗇色歎口氣。

嗇色說：「她是對的。」

利佳上輕輕說：「她又不讓我告假，堅持我照常教課。」

「這時想起來也是，不過當時吵得很厲害。」

「吵鬧也是抵銷恐懼的一種方法。」

「你好像懂得很多。」

「我找了許多資料來讀，這也可以解憂。」

「那麼，你怎麼看她的病情？」

「她若認為經已痊癒，醫生又再找不到壞細胞，那即表示健康。」

「可是——」

嗇色聽到一點聲響，即向利佳上使一個眼色，轉過頭去，發覺是女傭收拾地方。

123

她說下去：「不要露出任何疑心。」

若不是為着綺羅，她無論如何不敢出言教訓利君。

那麼，還有，他忽然胖了，醜了，把二人之間距離拉近，嗇色覺得有話不妨直說。

嗇色把所有時間用來陪繼母。

穿着家常便服，不拘小節，自早到夜，幫繼母做茶、讀報紙給她聽、陪她散步、看電影、喝下午茶，形影不離。

利佳上沒有課就躭家裏，高談闊論，嗇色時時駁斥他，氣氛熱鬧，她要到這個時候，才真正與他熟稔，發覺他學識淵博，談吐幽默，無論什麼題目，自無線電到原子彈，從史蒐夫松尼恩博物館到各種賭博方式，都知道得十分詳盡。

他又是各種球類好手，對於美術雕塑，又甚有研究，更是旅遊專家。

一日，綺羅對他說：「即使你瘦不下來，永遠胖下去，我也一樣愛你。」

利佳上大樂，問嗇色：「聽到沒有？承恩不在貌。」

嗇色只是笑。

他沒有瘦，她倒是胖回來了。

124

年輕人比較容易控制體重，但利君假使要減磅，也並非難事，可是下意識他拿身體洩憤減壓。

食量真是驚人，他邀請嗇色與他一起採購食物，親自下廚，調味下手甚重，然後一家子大快朵頤。

連新來的傭人都抿着嘴說：「我也胖了。」

雖然高興非凡，但心頭倒底有疾病陰影，努力不去想它，苦中作樂。

經過觀察，嗇色發覺綺羅健康情況穩定，最壞的似乎已經過去。

她利用假期與繼母盡情相聚。

一日，綺羅同她說：「你都十八歲了，身邊一點首飾也無也不好，你來看看這幾件。」

「我不要。」

綺羅大奇，「為什麼？」

「老女人才戴珠寶。」

綺羅氣結，「神經病。」

125

「真的，越老寶石越大，俗氣到極點。」

「那是因為人俗。」

傭人過來說：「嗇色電話。」

「我現在沒空。」

傭人笑，「那人說，他叫耳朵。」

綺羅奇問：「還有沒有人叫眼睛、鼻子？」一定是男朋友。

一看嗇色躊躇，便說：「去聽電話吧。」

順手把一隻絲絨袋放在嗇色手中。

嗇色取起聽筒：「耳朵，別來無恙乎。」

知道他經費不足，不能常撥長途電話，無論科技多麼方便，還需金錢支持。

「聽你聲音愉快，便知令堂安好。」

「一點不錯。」

「那麼，新年過後，當可見面。」

「應無問題。」

126

「耳朵聽不到你的聲音，十分寂寥。」

「這裏少一對聽我傾訴的耳朵，也恍然若失。」

他只是笑。

「天氣很冷了吧。」

「下雪雨。」

「多穿件衣裳。」

「知道。」

「不多講了。」

綺羅問：「耳朵是男朋友？」

嗇色側着頭，「算是吧。」

「不肯定？」

嗇色坐下來，「還不是他。」

「這樣模棱兩可，肯定不是。」

掛斷電話，打開絲絨袋，先看到一串晶瑩的珠子，順手戴在脖子上。

這句話說到嗇色心坎裏去，「對！」

綺羅說：：「真喜歡一個人的時候，絕對沒有誤會。」

「是。」

嗇色雖然經驗不足，也明白感覺第一。

「還有，喜歡就是喜歡，絕非同情、感激、憐憫或是友好其他因素。」

綺羅講得再正確沒有了。

由此可知，耳朵仍然不是那個人。

她甚至不會去查探他的真姓名。

也許他姓爾、也許他姓李，待他自己說出來吧。

再轉過頭來，綺羅已經睡着。

她服藥後時常累得不得了，睡着時倉猝，雙眼有一點點沒閉上，嗇色怕她眼球乾涸，輕輕替她拂下眼皮。

綺羅嘴角笑嘻嘻，像是在做一個好夢。

但願每個人都有好夢。

128

利佳上自廚房出來，看一看，「你可要陪我吃啤酒蟹？」

薔色找到一塊披肩，輕輕搭在綺羅身上。

然後走進廚房，坐下來，取起蟹蓋，就用調羹挖出膏吃。

利君看着她微笑。

薔色笑道：「吃死算了。」

利佳上答：「我也是那麼想。」不約而同。

「這些日子幸虧有你。」

「人生本無恒久順景。」

「有些人比較幸運，一生無太大上落。」

「那種人生活多數十分沉悶，你不會喜歡。」

薔色忽然說：「讓時光永遠停留在綺羅未曾患病之時豈不是好。」落下淚來。

「可是，彼時你只得十五歲，你願意永不長大嗎？」

可見他眞是十分堅強。

薔色洗乾淨手，托着頭，「我開始覺得一切都是我的錯。」

利佳上說：「很小的孩子才會那樣責怪自己，父母離異、親人死亡，傷痛之餘，他們都覺得是自己不好，你已成年，你應當明白一切與你無關。」

嗇色不語。

片刻綺羅醒了。

她向嗇色要水喝。

嗇色笑，「我一服傷風藥也是這樣睡個不已。」

「我錯過了什麼，怎麼無緣無故睡着了？」

「我做了夢。」

「說來聽聽。」

嗇色微笑，「這話也只得我一個人才聽得懂。」

「在夢中看到了少年的自身，我知道那是我，但是那個我卻不知我是誰。」

「我陪我說了很多話，還買了糖果新衣送給我。」

「那多好，人是應該自愛。」

綺羅也微笑，「只有你明白。」

130

利佳上在一旁道：「胡說，我何嘗不明。」

綺羅輕輕說：「我少年時眞正寂寞。」

嗇色勸道：「每個少年都那樣想。」

綺羅感喟：「日子過得眞快。」

嗇色訝異，「是嗎，我眞不覺得，考試時期，度日如年。」

綺羅笑，撫摸她短髮，「那自然，孩子們都那樣想。」

三人一起訕笑起來。

「還夢見什麼？」

綺羅笑答：「醒來，一鍋黃粱剛剛煮熟。」

嗇色有點淒惶，伏在繼母胸前。

有人按鈴，利佳上去開門。

綺羅輕輕說：「我還夢見你父親。」

嗇色愕住。

「他氣色很好，像是剛從地盤回來，與我閒話家常，問我有無去探訪他的父母。」

131

嗇色專心聆聽。

「然後我醒了。」

嗇色一點表示也無。

嗇色答：「不。」

「嗇色，或者，你可以代表我去探訪那兩位老人。」

「奇怪，你這固執遺傳自什麼人呢。」

「我們彼此不相愛亦不相熟，我不想再見到他們。」

綺羅微笑，「他日在黃泉總要相見。」

嗇色也笑，「不見得，黃泉不過是華人對冥界一個統稱，像世界那麼大，不一定碰得上頭。」

綺羅吁出一口氣，「難為你，那樣有科學頭腦。」

利佳上回來說：「石志威律師派人送燕窩來。」

綺羅說：「我一向不吃這種東西。」

嗇色問：「怎麼弄，直接扔到湯裏去？」

利佳上笑，「過年的時候再送回去。」

綺羅仍然企圖游說：「他們是你唯一真正親人。」

「恕不從命。」

「我的話你也不聽？」

「沒有意思就不聽。」

利佳上詫異，「好端端吵什麼？」

綺羅反而笑起來。

她很高興，倘若嗇色凡事唯唯喏喏，覺得應當感恩圖報，反而不是真心。

嗇色說：「去按鈴，不一定開門給我呢，一向假裝耳聾，只挑愛聽的話來聽，後來真的聾了，名正言順什麼都聽不到。」

「我以為你一早就原諒了他們。」

「不牽涉到原諒，毫無感情，不必虛偽。」

利佳上問：「吵完沒有，大家出去看電影如何。」

那是一部極之喧嘩的動作片，十五分鐘後綺羅便說要走。

133

他們陪她離場，嗇色說：「吵得人神經衰弱。」

「療程告一段落時我會偕綺羅到湖區小住。」

「太好了，」嗇色拍手，「那麼，我不去美國上大學了。」

回到家，看到耳朵寄來的卡片。

嗇色不是不感激，可惜絕不心跳，那還是不足夠的。

「告訴我他是怎麼樣的一個男孩子。」

嗇色答：「可親。」

「還有呢？」

「熱心。」

「唷，眼睛會笑嗎？」

「不，他不是那樣的人。」

「嗯，外型比較老實。」

嗇色見綺羅講得那樣客氣，不禁笑出來。

「他貌不驚人。」

「是醫學院學生？」

「是，讀得很累，錄音機上錄了功課放在枕頭底徹夜不停播放，連覺也睡不好。」

「唔，很想出人頭地。」

「是呀，那多累。」

綺羅承認：「我也有點怕那種非成功不可的人。」

「是家庭給的壓力吧。」

「可能，背景怎麼樣呢？」

「從沒問過他，我只知道他叫耳朵。」

「將來，你會遇到靈魂。」

嗇色微笑。

屆時，會否渾身顫抖？

假期告終，最後一晚，她睡不着，走到客廳，看到利佳上在吃宵夜。

「來嚐嚐我做的橘皮布甸加吉士汁。」

嗇色站得遠遠，笑咪咪，「閣下體重有多少？」

135

「一百公斤而已。」

嗇色仍然沒有過去，「給我裝一片在塑膠盒裏帶上飛機吃。」

「沒問題。」

「真捨不得你們。」

「你應該去探望祖父母。」

「你知道了。」

「他們看到我也不會認得我。」

「你那樣明目張膽拒絕，我很難不聽到。」

「但求心安而已。」

「我心並無不安。」

「年輕真好。」

兩人離得相當遠，卻聊起來。

「復活節再見面。」

「祝我考到好學堂。」

「一塊蛋糕。」

嗇色很高興，「你真的那麼想？」

「那還不易如反掌。」

「謝謝你，利敎授。」

她很想走近去，但是沒有，雙腿有點不聽使喚，靠著牆不想動。

他吃完了用濕毛巾擦擦嘴，抬起頭。

她這次回來，他還沒看清楚過她。

她彷彿又長高了一點，瘦許多，雙眼更大、鼻子更高，藉故剪短了頭髮，輪廓更加

分明。

他每次見她，她都變得更可愛。

她穿一件舊T恤一條牛仔褲懶洋洋靠在牆上。

利佳上歎口氣，「時間已經很晚了。」

嗇色答：「我不是每個晚上都睡覺。」

什麼？

「三天睡兩次已經足夠，睡得太多很煩。」

利佳上忍不住問：「每次休息多久？」

「也需要六七個小時。」

利佳上笑，年輕人都有無比精力。

「睡不着幹什麼？」

「溫習、寫功課。」

「看樣子今夜也不打算睡？」

「那又不是，我累了。」

嗇色挪動雙腿，笑着走進寢室。

她先去看繼母。

綺羅的臉壓在枕頭上，她輕輕幫她轉過身子來。她沒有醒，這是她一天之內唯一忘我輕鬆的時刻，幸虧上帝賜給人類睡眠，無論如何，假死一刻，從頭再來。

嗇色握着她的手。

她記得很清楚，第一次看到綺羅，她伸手過來，手指潔白，指甲修理得十分整齊，

138

無名指上戴着一枚不大不小的鑽戒，端的好看。

嗇色把那隻手放在臉頰旁邊。

這是她唯一知道的親人。

嗇色悄悄落下淚來。

一個人喜歡另一人不是偶然的事，彼此都需要有所付出。

時常流淚的眼睛容易虧損，而且，不應逗留太久，怕吵醒她。

第二天，綺羅比她早起，正指揮傭人幫嗇色收拾行李。

嗇色問：「這是幹什麼？」

「你看你的內衣睡衣與襪子都破舊不堪，我給你買了新的替換。」

綺羅笑問：「人呢？」

「唉，衣不如舊。」

「都是舊的好。」

「看樣子你一輩子才嫁一個人。」

「希望有這種福氣，否則實在太煩了。」

綺羅笑，「萬中無一呢。」

「這些內衣太漂亮了，配T恤破褲好似過份。」

利佳上本想進房來，一眼看到行李上那麼多褻衣，感覺非常震盪，連忙退出去，定定神，才說：「都起來了？」可是猶自像看到了不應看的東西似。

嗇色笑着拉上皮箱拉鍊，「時間充裕，別擔心。」

依依不捨之情，洋溢室內。

嗇色說：「不如轉回來考試。」

「折騰什麼？只得三個月時間罷了。」

綺羅說：「放心，我一定還在。」

「一百多個日子呢。」

嗇色生氣，「這是什麼話。」

嗇色幫她更衣。

綺羅說：「你看我膚色大不如前。」

「色相至靠不住。」

140

綺羅無奈地扣好紐扣。

嗇色幫她梳埋那短短頭髮。

綺羅握住嗇色的手，「機能經過化學治療破壞，我已不能懷孕生子。」

啊，嗇色蹲下來，感覺悲哀。

「我其實不一定決定生育，可是自願不生孩子是一回事，由醫生告訴你不能生孩子，又是另外一回事。」

嗇色表面上若無其事，「你不是已經領養了我。」

「其實你比任何人都像我。」

「品德像你，是我的願望。」

綺羅說：「哪有你講得那樣好。」

嗇色答：「我絲毫沒有誇張。」

「但是倒底，孕育一個由本身細胞繁衍的小生命……是一種享受吧。」

嗇色勸道：「我從沒聽任何女性那樣形容過懷孕過程。」

綺羅嗒然：「我永遠不會知道其中感受。」

141

嗇色無言。

「也許，你將來可以把經驗告訴我。」

「不不不，」嗇色厲聲拒絕：「我已決定永不生育。」

綺羅駭笑，「這是怎麼一回事？」

嗇色厭惡地說：「生命是至大一種浪費，我再多七倍時間，也決不將之用在撫養一團肉上！」

「奇怪，」綺羅笑，「我小時候也那樣想，這與我們童年時不愉快生活有很大的關係吧。」

「撫育幼兒何等費時失事，結果又有幾人能夠不負父母期望。」

「那看你期望什麼，要求不宜太高。」

「單是健康快樂，做得到嗎？」

嗇色聲音中充滿悲怨。

利佳上進來說：「嗇色你怎麼天天吵架似。」

「對不起。」

142

利佳上已看不到那堆粉紅色的褻衣，他鬆了一口氣。

「該去飛機場了。」

綺羅道：「我還有話要說。」

利佳上溫柔的說：「女人的話永遠說不完。」

那一天早上，嗇色發覺繼母的神色有點呆滯，眼珠大而無神，如蒙着一層灰樸樸的薄膜。

她需要很堅強才能頭也不回的走上飛機。

到了學校放下行李立刻去找耳朵。

她到醫學院門口去等，自知成數渺茫，因完全不知耳朵什麼時候有課，可是嗇色覺得有運氣。

果然，等不多久，演講廳門一開，頭一個出來的便是耳朵。

嗇色笑嘻嘻迎上去。

耳朵呆住，他的同學也愕住，什麼地方跑來這樣標致的女生，他們狗一般苦學生涯裏眼睛最渴望吃冰淇淋。

143

他高興過度，鼻子發酸，一時說不出話來，用手搭住嗇色肩膀，一路走出去。

嗇色頭上戴着一頂鴨舌帽。

他半晌才輕輕說：「破帽遮顏過鬧市。」

嗇色哪裏聽得懂，「嗄？」

他凝視她，「你這笨女孩。」

嗇色很愉快地答：「是，我是笨得不得了？」

他用手臂勒着嗇色脖子，嗇色嗆咳起來。

「回來了。」

「可不是。」

「媽媽還好嗎？」

「大家都知道那顆定時炸彈尚未熄滅。」

「且苦中作樂吧。」

「也只得如此。」

「我苦澀地思念你。」

144

嗇色只是笑，他說話一向傳神。

「最低限度，你可以說『我也是』。」

嗇色仍然不語。

耳朵生氣，「你來幹什麼？」

嗇色仍然笑。

「你的眞名叫什麼？」

「不告訴你。」

嗇色仍然笑。

他漸漸被那笑容融化，五臟六腑都黏貼在一起，膩嗒嗒，討厭得不得了，一點氣概都沒有，他無比訝異，這，以後還怎麼做人？

他的頭垂得低低，已知道受到災劫。

「請到我陋室來坐一下。」

眞是陋室，總共得一床一几一桌一椅，還有一隻書架子。

就那樣，寒窗數載。

你說慘不慘，若不願咬緊牙關熬過此劫，餘生以後日子更加不好過。

嗇色笑，「吃得苦中苦，方為人上人。」

有一位同學十分存疑，他問：「什麼叫做人上人，是騎在人家肩膊上嗎，人家一動，我是否要摔下來，然則，做人上人是否更加辛苦？」

是的，做了人上人，成為衆目睽睽之人物，也十分吃苦。

站在窗前，嗇色說：「你有空也這樣站着看窗外的足球場？」

「我很少抬起頭來，我需伏着身子做功課。」

嗇色看到筆記本子面上寫着蓋伯利爾張。

「你叫蓋伯利爾？」

「不，那是我師兄，他把筆記借我用。」

「耳朵，全間宿舍都不見你的名字。」

「你渴知我姓甚名誰？」

嗇色答：「不至於想得睡不着。」

耳朵凝視她。

今日她穿着一件深藍色大衣，懶佬鞋上沾滿泥漿，臉色有點蒼白，看上去特別稚嫩

146

可愛。

「你神情憂鬱之極，有什麼問題嗎？」

嗇色的面孔轉向窗外，「耳朵，我繼母不行了。」

他嚇一跳，「胡說，不是已經治癒了嗎？」

「她有事瞞着我，我知道。」

她垂着頭抽噎。

耳朵將她的臉撥過來，只見嗇色淚流滿面，他將她輕輕擁在懷中。

嗇色嗚咽，「那麼多年，她都沒有讓我覺得我是負累，到了今日，還堅持叫我回來完成學業。」

耳朵一字不漏地聆聽，可是心中想的卻完全是另外一些事。

嗇色有用香水嗎，彷彿是玫瑰花香，聞仔細一點，又不是了，會不會是天然體嗅，真令人意亂神迷，傷心的她楚楚可憐，必需讓她盡情傾訴，他是耳朵，耳朵不聽主人申訴，還要來何用。

她雙臂摟住他的腰身，他受寵若驚。

147

運氣真好，遇上她家有突變，她情緒不安，他才有機可乘，不不不，心腸太壞了，不該這樣想，該死，幸災樂禍是會有報應的。

正胡思亂想，聽得嗇色又說：「我真徬徨。」

接着，她痛哭起來。

她伏在他結實的胸膛之前，好好哭了一場，眼淚把恐懼、哀傷，以及其他毒素一起衝走。

耳朵一直摟着她，替她拭去眼淚。

然後她說：「讓我們去大吃一頓，我餓極了。」

耳朵撫着她頭髮，「你說什麼就什麼。」

「謝謝你，耳朵，我需要聽這種捧場話。」

在走廊裏，同學向他打招呼，「你好，耳朵。」

嗇色訝異，「你真的叫耳朵？」

耳朵猙獰地說：「你這輕佻的女子，連對方姓甚名誰都不知道，就跟他上樓。」

嗇色咭咭咭地笑。

148

他們到西菜館去飽餐一頓，由嗇色付賬。

耳朵看着她，「這樣漂亮又願意出錢，我真正幸運。」

他送她返宿舍。

舍監一見嗇色便說：「你母親來看你，在會客室等了好久了。」

嗇色怔住。

她的母親？

她何來母親？

嗇色輕輕推開會客室門。

一位華裔女士坐在沙發上讀泰晤士日報。

抬起頭，看到她，像是老朋友一般說：「中午抵達的飛機，怎麼到現在才回來？」

嗇色目定口呆，口角真像一位母親，她也的確是她的生母方國寶女士。

不知多久沒見，可是方女士佯裝當中那些日子不存在，她像老朋友般，再度出現在嗇色面前。

「坐下來。」

149

嗇色脫下外套，坐在她對面。

「坐過來。」

這次嗇色並沒有照做。

「我有話要說。」

「請講。」

「我最近才知道陳綺羅病重。」

嗇色看着她。

「我去打聽過，她將不久於人世。」

嗇色的目光變得凌厲，可是方女士沒有察覺。

她自管自說下去：「你是她的合法養女，你可別那麼笨，你得設法取得遺產承繼權。」

嗇色一動不動地坐着。

方女士並沒有老，她仍然秀麗苗條，衣着時髦，事實上，任何外人一進會客室來，看到她們，就自然會知道她們是母女，因二人長得十分相像。

150

可是，嗇色欽佩生母那副獨特的心腸，連寒暄都沒有，你快要畢業了吧、生活還過

得去嗎、一個人可覺寂寞……全部與她無關。

她只一心一意關心嗇色的遺產承繼權。

方女士壓低聲線說下去，「你還做夢呢，那些錢本來就是你的，她由你父處奪得，

現在她一撒手，眼看一切就白白流到陌生人名下，你甘心嗎？」

方女士咬牙切齒，她不甘心。

「將來你住何處吃什麼？嗄，你還吊兒郎當就來不及了。」

嗇色緩緩站起來，「你說完沒有？」

「那利佳上是什麼東西，她的錢到了他手裏，還會有剩？你別胡塗。」

嗇色長長呼出一口氣，拉開會客室門，「出去。」

「什麼，你說什麼？」

「滾出去。」

「你這樣同母親說話？」

「我沒有母親。」

151

方女士不願走，她提高聲線，「我好心來提醒你，你倒恩將仇報？」

嗇色沒料到自己如此孔武有力，可叫把方女士推着塞出門去。

她哇哇大叫，一失足，跌在地上。

嗇色猶自不放過她，把她自地上拉起，拖着她走過走廊，再大力推她出宿舍大門。

方女士繼續尖叫，這時，已有好奇的同學前來圍觀，也有人去通知舍監。

可是嗇色已將生母推出大門。

回到樓上，她雙臂酸頓無力，頹然倒在床上。

第二天，受到舍監嚴厲責備，嗇色自知理虧，只是低頭不語。

她一向是品學兼優的好學生，偶一犯錯，也可過關。

每晚，半明半滅，即將入睡之際，嗇色都會聽見一把女聲對她說：「你將來吃什麼穿什麼？」

醒來，一身冷汗。

那樣，也終於捱到畢業。

利佳上特地來接她回家。

這真是他最最胖碩的時刻，外型似足北極熊。

嗇色很懷疑他以後是否還會瘦回去。

他說：「我來給你一個心理準備。」

「我明白。」

「綺羅的病是不會好的了。」

其實嗇色早已猜到，可是真確地聽見佳上這樣說出真相，也彷彿鼻子上中了一拳。

「她精神尚可，你回到家，請隱藏傷心之態。」

「是，我省得。」

「她心願是一起坐船到地中海，請你押後升大學。」

「一定，不成問題。」

「你需要與同學話別嗎？」

「已經說過。」

「那麼，我們走吧。」

153

嗇色只得隨身兩件行李，跟着利佳上到飛機場。

她忘記告訴耳朵幾時走。

等耳朵來找她之際，只看到人去樓空。

有人告訴他：「嗇色今早已經走了。」

空房間還未有人來收拾，角落有她丟棄的玩具熊及上課時間表。

耳朵珍重地拾起，藏到懷中。

他忽然哭了。

這真真確確，是他的初戀。

可是她只把他當作一雙耳朵。

幸虧沒把真姓名告訴她，那樣，反而可以使她對他留有印象。

——那讀醫科的男孩是誰？他叫耳朵，真姓名是什麼？不知道。

畢竟已經超過廿一歲，知道世上還有許多其他重要之事，稍後，耳朵沒精打彩的走了。

他還是低估了嗇色。

她幾乎一離開就忘記當地所有事情，包括耳朵與眼睛在內。

利佳上在飛機上不停喝酒，並且咕嚕：「人類花的飛行時間實在太長。」

嗇色想一想，「應當說，人類該慶幸終於可以飛行。」

「可見你還是樂觀。」

嗇色溫柔地看着他：「你何嘗不是。」

甚至綺羅也一絲不見頹廢。

他們略為收拾行李便上船去。

在遊輪上，嗇色遇見幾個年紀相若的年輕人，成大來找她一起玩。

綺羅說：「嗇色人緣好。」

嗇色笑說：「在船上打困籠，沒有選擇。」

她總是匍伏在繼母身邊，侍候她。

綺羅反而胖了，面孔有點虛腫，雙目畏光，通常坐在陰涼之處。

一日，船經過愛琴海，眾皆為那蔚藍驚艷，綺羅忽然輕輕對嗇色道：「我夢見死亡。」

嗇色一驚，可是不動聲色，「是否似傳說中身披長袍手執鐮刀的骷髏？」

「不，是一個好看的小女孩，與我討價還價。」

嗇色納罕，「有這種事？」

「是，我同她說，我有一事不放心。」

「何事？」

「我擔心你的歸宿。」

「我會得照顧自己。」

「沒有人做得比你更好。」

「你父親將你托付給我，嗇色。」

「我同死亡說：要我跟你走亦可，但是你要讓我瞑目。」

嗇色企圖顧左右而言他，「一般是一片海水，爲何愛琴海特別蔚藍？眞無道理。」

綺羅不爲所動，自顧自說下去：「她道：『你不必擔心，我同你說兩句話：遠在天邊，近在眼前』。」

嗇色鼻子都酸了，無暇細聽，她自問自答：「傳說這藍是因爲伊卡勒斯掉到愛琴海裏溺斃的緣故，他穿上蠟與羽毛製成的翅膀，飛上天空，可是太過接近太陽神阿波羅，翅膀融掉了，這個故事告訴我們——」

這時利佳上走過來，「兩位女士，甲板這個角落風大，請移玉步。」

她們跟他進艙。

嗇色答：「愛琴海。」

綺羅說：「死亡。」

「兩位談些什麼？」

利君接上去：「這真是個優美的譯名。」

嗇色用手托着腮，「不知是誰的傑作。」

綺羅說：「其實甚至太平洋、大西洋、北冰洋，又何嘗不好聽。」

「似乎無人願意拾起我的話題。」

利佳上看着妻子，「你能夠怪我們嗎？」

綺羅索性說：「地中海一名才最美。」

嗇色笑：「波羅的海最奇怪，可惜沒有香蕉的海或是橘子的海。」

可是說到這裏，嗇色不由得緊緊摟住繼母。

這時幸虧那班年輕人來找嗇色。

「咦，嗇色，你怎麼哭了？」

嗇色霍一聲站起來大聲喝罵：「誰哭了？你才哭！」

他們見她心情不好，一哄而散。

其中一名留了下來。

他叫鍾藉良，一看便知是個混血兒，高大英俊，年輕稚氣面孔充滿對嗇色的仰慕。

當下嗇色對他說：「你也是，去去去。」

他笑着說：「我去看看網球場有無空。」

他走了，利佳上說：「嗇色，這男孩不錯。」

嗇色是由衷納罕，「同別人沒有什麼不同呀。」

利佳上倒抽一口冷氣，由此可知，她身邊不知幾許裙下之臣。

綺羅喃喃說：「奇怪，不知什麼樣女子嫁外國人。」

嗇色完全同意：「與他們越熟，越覺得是完全另外一種人，喝杯茶跳隻舞不要緊，

158

可是天長地久那樣生活，還要養孩子，如何適應？」

「而且，有無必要作出那樣大的犧牲？」

利佳上見她們公然談外國男人，也就放下心來，總比討論死亡的好。

嗇色說：「不過，他們的身段真正好。」

利佳上豎起耳朵。

嗇色讚道：「那眞胳臂是胳臂，腰是腰，高大壯健，無論多粗線條的女子站在他們身邊，都變成依人小鳥。」

綺羅微笑，「是，那是不同的。」

利佳上駭笑，沒想到男性的身段也會被她們評頭品足。

嗇色接着說：「也許就是爲着那一身男子氣概吧。」

利佳上輕輕咳嗽一聲。

她們母女倆看着他笑了。

利佳上雙目不敢與嗇色接觸，轉到別處去，接着說：「我去打幾個電話。」

綺羅看着丈夫背影，「這些日子眞冷落了他。」

159

「那是他長胖的原因嗎？」

「是，快接近一百公斤了。」

可憐的男人。

綺羅說：「或許，他不忍看我一人日漸憔悴，立心陪我。」

「他愛你。」

綺羅語氣溫柔，「是，在這方面，我真幸運，我確實享受過男歡女愛。」

「那一定極之難得。」

「都說是可遇不可求之事。」

「我真代你慶幸。」

「嗇色，你與利佳上其實毫無血緣關係。」

嗇色一怔，「那我自然知道。」

綺羅微笑，「你們若是相愛的話，我真可完全放心。」

嗇色心中驚疑不已，面子上卻十分平靜，「你想得太多了。」

綺羅抬起頭來，「你認為我妙想天開可是？」

160

「你不過是想你所愛的兩個人永遠在一起。」

「不，我只是勸你莫錯失良機，要是喜歡一個人，就莫理世俗目光。」

嗇色看往別處。

繼母的法眼洞悉一切。

沒有事瞞得過她。

「你是聰明人，話說到此為止。」

嗇色有點抬不起頭來的感覺。

「我已立定遺囑。」

「這個話題至討厭不過。」

綺羅微笑，「許多子女巴不得父母明確提到此事。」

「因為我並非你親生女兒，故我不愛聽。」

「我們關係豈非更加難能可貴，嗇色，將來，你不虞生活。」

嗇色把臉伏在綺羅背上。

她流下熱淚。

161

「你可以繼續升學，做你喜歡做的事。」

「我欠你實在太多。」

「這些年來，你帶給我的歡笑及友誼，何止此數。」

嗇色無言。

「去跳舞吧，他們在等着你呢，請把利佳上叫進來，我有話同他說。」

嗇色不得不退出去找利君。

她在泳池畔看到他，雖然塊頭那麼大，可是泳術毫不遜色，事實上他在水中靈敏一

如北極熊。

他躍出泳池。

「綺羅找你。」

他用毛巾擦乾身子，頷首道：「可是有吩咐？」

嗇色卻不及邊際地說：「無論是棕熊白熊，吃起魚來，單吃魚頭，不吃魚肉。」

「為什麼？」

「魚頭至營養。」

162

「熊有那麼聰明？」

「是，撲殺海豹亦如此，肉只留給狐狸等享用。」

「自然界生存律例十分殘酷。」

「是，我從來不明人類爲何一生中要歷劫多次生離死別。」

他把手按在嗇色肩上一會兒，然後進艙房去見綺羅。

一進門便輕輕說：「船傍晚停蒙地卡羅，你我去玩幾手廿一點如何？」

綺羅坐在沙發上微笑。

「爲何如太后般把我等一個個召進來傳話？」

「因爲我自知不久於人世。」

「胡說八道。」

「我有話要說。」

他蹲下來，「我在聽。」

「看得出你喜歡嗇色。」

「她是個可愛的孩子。」

163

「我所認識，最不似孩子的孩子，便是嗇色。」

「我不覺得，像所有少年人一般，她的眼淚尚未流到臉頰，已經乾掉。」

「也許轉流到心底去變成暗流。」

「是嗎，我沒發覺。」

「她並非我親女。」

「這我一早知道。」

綺羅微微笑。

利君輕輕問：「你想到什麼地方去了。」

「我想你知道，對於你們，我永遠祝福。」

利君深深吻她的手。

「也許，」綺羅溫柔的說：「我的出現，就是爲着要把你倆拉在一起。」

「不，你的出現，是要給我一段至美好的感情。」

綺羅緊緊擁抱他。

那一邊，嗇色走進酒吧，坐到酒保跟前。

164

酒保看她一眼，「未滿十八歲人士不得飲用含酒精飲品。」

嗇色給他看護照上出生年月日。

酒保笑了，「失敬失敬，這位小姐，想喝什麼？」

嗇色毫不猶疑，「容易入口容易醉，醉死了猶自心甘情願的是何種酒？」

酒保即時答：「香檳。」

「給我開一瓶。」

「小姐，你知道你在做什麼吧。」

「咄，我心如明鏡。」

酒保連冰桶帶瓶子遞給嗇色，「別掉到海裏去。」

嗇色坐在酒吧一角自斟自飲。

半晌，一個人找進來，看到她，連忙問：「你沒喝醉吧。」

嗇色停睛一看，「沒有。」

「那麼，告訴我，我是誰。」

「鍾藉良。」

165

「好好好，來，放下酒杯，告訴我，你爲何淚流滿面。」

「我預備喝完了去找你。」

「爲什麼？」

「酒可壯膽。」

這個年輕人一怔。

嗇色說：「帶我去你房間。」

「我哥哥在艙中。」

「那麼，到我房間來。」

一個美少女作出這樣的要求，婉拒簡直是無禮，鍾藉良硬着頭皮扶起她。

「回房去洗把冷水面就好。」

他與她走向房間。

說也奇怪，嗇色的腳步相當穩，臉上帶甜美笑意，一絲不覺異樣。

進了房，她緊緊擁抱小鍾，把嘴唇送上去。

鍾藉良明知這是飛來艷福，感覺一如親吻柔軟花瓣，可是來得太過突然，手足無

166

措。

嗇色放開手，責怪地問：「你沒有經驗？」

他獸瓜似答：「我沒有，你呢？」

嗇色頹然，「我也沒有。」

二人啼笑皆非坐下。

然後嗇色歇斯底里笑出來。

小鍾解嘲地說：「也許，我們需要更多酒精。」

「不，可否聽其自然？」

「我是都市人，不知什麼是自然。」

嗇色笑得前仰後合，翻倒在床上。

等到笑聲停止，小鍾搔着頭皮，想再與她說幾句話，一看，她已經睡着，正微微打

鼾。

他也笑了。

他知道這美麗的女孩子心情不好，可是沒料到她這次會如此失態。

167

他替她蓋上一層薄被，悄悄離開艙房。

稍後他問兄長：「倘若有女投懷送抱，應該如何？」

他兄長已經廿一歲，頭也不抬地說：「我勸你有便宜莫貪。」

他說：「謝謝你。」

第二天，嗇色來敲他門。

他笑說：「早，睡得好嗎？」

嗇色與他走到甲板上，「昨夜真對不起。」

「你尚記得隔宵之事？」

「沒齒難忘。」

嗇色咧着嘴向他笑，色若春曉，一朵芙蓉花般容貌，要待她沒了牙齒，不知尚需幾

許年。

鍾藉良想，出了洋相也值得，能叫她沒齒難忘是難得的。

他握着她的手。

她滿不好意思地掙脫。

168

「爲何如此不安？」

「家裏有事，令我煩躁不已。」

「先把陸上地址告訴我，以便日後可以聯絡。」

他似有預感。

當天中午，陳綺羅昏睡未醒，經過船上醫生檢查，決定把她用直升飛機送上岸診治。

他們走得十分忽忙。

在尼斯逗留一天，便乘飛機返家。

嗇色沒有向鍾藉良話別。

晚上，他與船長吃飯時才得知這個消息。

因此他份外珍惜手上的地址。

可是鍾家住紐約長島，千里迢迢，如何再發展這段友情？

「到家了。」綺羅疲乏地說。

嗇色這才知道，電影或小說中，病人垂危還不住說話眞是藝術誇張。

原來講話需要那樣大的力氣，而陳綺羅已經氣息微弱。

斷斷續續，她也道出心中意思。

「有一位友人，」她說：「母親逝世後始終不能釋然，一夜，被犬吠吵醒，她啟門，淚流滿面，大聲問：『媽媽，是你嗎，是你嗎』。」

嗇色很小心地伏在她身邊聆聽。

停了很久，陳綺羅說下去：「我不會回來，你不用開門喚我。」

她辭世那天，差數日才到三十八歲。

嗇色傷痛，精神恍惚，握住綺羅的手良久不放，兩隻手都瘦骨嶙峋，一時不知是誰的手。

接着一段日子，她整晚起床。

她聽見聲響，繼母房中有人。

她推開房門，看到綺羅與父親正坐在床沿聊天，看到她，拍拍床褥，「嗇色過來。」

嗇色進房去，看到父親頭髮烏黑，十分年輕，再低頭看自己雙腳，發覺穿着雙小小黑色漆皮鞋，原來她還是小孩。

就在這個時候，夢醒了。

一時不知身在何處，睜大眼睛半晌，前塵往事，才咎沓回轉。

天濛濛亮起來，在這個時分，嗇色決定去美國東岸升學。

利佳上已搬回他自己的家去住，綺羅患病好似已有十年，其實不，頭尾只得十九個月。

有事他才約嗇色會談。

他迅速消瘦，不到一個月，已去掉一半多餘脂肪。

神情鎮定，只在他眼睛裏可以找到一絲哀傷。

他們談論綺羅，如說及一個遠方的朋友。

「她對錢財視作身外物。」

「是，從來不是擁物狂，這點值得學習。」

「她有一個奇怪的心願，她同我說，她希望可以走回時間隧道，去同少年時的自己做朋友。」

嗇色微笑，「那自然是沒有可能的事，稍後，她找到了我，她說我像她，所以深愛我。」

大家都笑了。

「她有無入夢？」

「沒有，你呢？」

「也沒有。」

「她一早說明不會來看我們。」

「綺羅不似這般無情之人。」

「已去到另外一個更好的地方，還回來幹什麼。」

「不想念我們嗎？」

「將來總會見面。」

嗇色親自辦理入學手續。

一百日過後，她才去理髮，接着除下素服，不過，她最常穿的衣物是白與深藍，無甚分別。

她把頭髮剪成小男孩那樣，省時省力，不用花時間打理。

利佳上外型變化比她更大，他已恢復到從前模樣，嗇色知道他也在康復中。

利君自嘲：「看，身體如氣球，一收一放，相差三十公斤。」

「醫生怎麼說？」

「要小心飲食，不能再有第二次暴漲。」

嗇色笑得彎下了腰。

利佳上看着她如花一般的笑靨，怔住半晌。

年輕的生命又漸漸恢復生機。

「學校方面怎麼說？」

「歡迎我加入大家庭。」

「你那成績真無往不利。」

「是，學校看分不看人，社會看錢不看人。」

利佳上十分困惑，「什麼人看人？」

嗇色答：「戀人。」

173

利佳上說：「可是戀人往往看錯人。」

「所以你說慘不慘。」

半晌嗇色站起來，「我去問媽媽可要外出吃飯。」

談得忘形，一時忘卻繼母已經去世，話一出口，立刻察覺，不禁惻然。

過兩日，嗇色剛起床，在盤點升學行李，聽見有人按鈴。

她似有預感，連忙摔下紙筆跑出去阻止傭人開門，已經來不及。

方國寶女士已經站在她面前。

方女士若無其事坐下，吩咐女傭：「給我一杯黑咖啡。」

嗇色一時不知是厭惡還是悲傷。

方女士說：「聽說你承繼了八位數字，做得很好呀，若不是我提點你，你也不會知道怎麼做，服侍她那麼多年，都是你應得的。」

嗇色握着拳頭。

真諷刺，方女士倒似回魂一般，時時出現。

她說下去：「你好歹得分些給我。」

174

什麼？

「朋友尚有通財之義，你發了這一注，不能忘了我。」

嗇色凝視她。

「以前發生過什麼事，我不與你計較，」她厲聲說：「錢可不能少了我。」

嗇色仍不出聲。

「你生活既無問題，就應該照顧我！」

嗇色忍無可忍走過去打開大門。

「你撥十份一出來，百來萬，我馬上走。」

嗇色聲音十分平靜，「你不走，我即時報派出所。」

「你竟這樣對我？」

「走。」

方女士聲音變得歇斯底里，「一百萬對你來講不是大數目，你輕而易舉可以拿出來。」

這時門口忽然出現兩個人，一個是利佳上，另一個是石志威律師。

175

石律師認得方女士，他呵哈一聲，「真巧，方小姐，我們又見面了，快隨我來把話說清楚。」

他真有辦法，一手拉起方女士，一陣風似刮走。

嗇色嗤一聲笑出來。

利佳上詫異問：「是怎麼一回事？」

「討錢。」

利佳上莫名其妙，「你何來的錢？」

「她硬派我承繼了千萬財產。」

「沒有的事，不過由石律師按月發放生活費給你。」

「那真得由別人的嘴巴說出來她才會相信。」

「要待你廿五歲後才可動用部份財產。」

「即使我手上有現金，也不會給她分毫。」

利佳上不再加挿意見。

嗇色深深呼出一口氣。

「你們找我何事？」

「石律師打算把學費及生活費交給你。」

嗇色點頭，「我真幸運。」

希望永遠可以擺脫生母，開始新生活。

利佳上忽然輕輕問：「你不是要故意避開我吧。」

嗇色一怔，輕輕別轉頭去。

隔很久才說：「明知何必故問。」

「綺羅所說，不必當真。」

嗇色微微笑，「她洞悉一切，她知道我愛你。」

利佳上十分意外，整個人僵住。

「那時才得十二歲罷了，就知道除出你，不可能有他人。」

利佳上像一尊石像，動也不敢動，屏息。

「可是，你是繼母的丈夫，一度是，終身是，我還是遠走高飛的好。」

要過了很久很久，利佳上才回過頭來，「你自幼無父，渴望寄托。」

嗇色失笑，「我是那樣幼稚的人嗎。」

利佳上無言。

過片刻她站起來，「我還要出去辦一些事。」

她側身而過，沒有再與利君的目光接觸。

吐了眞言，心裏舒服得多。

可是這並非說眞話的時候，二人的心因綺羅離世受傷又腫又痛，已無能負荷更多。

才到仲夏，嗇色已動身到紐約。

石律師替她租的公寓靠近中央公園，是條內街，好地段，可是看不到園景，故房租不算頂貴。

嗇色選購了一輛二手白色吉普車代步。

尚未到入學時間，故此天天在街上逛。

一日在大都會美術館東方文物部聚精會神研究一幅八大山人的畫，忽然聽見有人叫她。

「嗇色，嗇色。」

她轉過頭去，心內倒有絲歡喜，他鄉遇故知，不亦樂乎。

可是有一女孩子比她更快快應道：「在這裏。」

原來是同音名，也許叫的是式式。

嗇色復低下頭。

半晌，有人過來笑着用英語問：「你也叫適適？」

嗇色連忙答：「是，我以爲是叫我。」

「多巧。」那女孩圓臉圓眼，十分親切，「東方文物，大英博物館藏品最豐富，老英至懂巧取豪奪。」

嗇色笑。

「雕像頭部與手指最美，都被琢下運返祖國，留待身軀給美人欣賞。」

嗇色一聽，駭笑不已，因活脫脫是事實。

女孩伸出手，「我叫賈適適。」

嗇色寫給她看，「我名甄嗇色。」

「呵，原來這樣寫，」她揚聲，「哥哥，來這邊。」

嗇色抬起頭，看到了剛才叫名字的人。

嗇色何等聰明玲瓏，一看，就知道由他差妹妹過來搭訕，故只笑不語。

「我的孿生兄弟，叫賈祥興，來，我們一起逛。」

可是嗇色不想結交朋友，「我有事要先走一步。」

兄妹倆交換一個眼色，適適說：「改天一起喝杯茶如何？」

「好。」

「這是我們電話地址。」

嗇色只得收下。

溜出大都會，走到街上，看手上地址，才納罕世界那麼細小，他們兄妹竟與她住同一幢公寓大廈，低兩層，保不定會在電梯裏碰上。

回到公寓，她做了一個沙律，捧到小露台，開瓶白酒，坐着慢慢享用。

忽然心底昇起一絲罕有喜悅，呵，昇格做大學生了。

也許什麼都學不到，也許畢了業也等於失業，可是這畢竟是一個值得羨慕的身份。

嗇色對留學已有豐富經驗，可是大學給予他們的自由，卻令她訝異，前後才隔一個暑假，之前什麼都受管制，之後一切憑自主選擇，太奇妙了。

嗇色選讀新聞及政治科學兩項科目，登記當日，已結識了一大幫同學。

回家時嘴角含滿意笑容，進了電梯，按下十字，有人急急跟進來。

「你好。」

嗇色呵一聲，適適。

那人微笑，「我叫賈祥興，我有個妹妹，叫適適。」

嗇色抬起頭細看那人，「我們見過面嗎？」毫無印象。

那人說：「你不記得我了。」

嗇色連忙也說：「你好。」

「你來訪友？」

「不，我住這裏。」

賈祥興不信有如此好運氣，「我住八樓。」

嗇色並無進一步表示，「那多好。」這三個字一點意思也無，可是討人歡喜，不會

犯錯。

181

電梯到了十樓，她輕輕走出，說了聲再見。

為什麼拒人千里之外？

因為嗇色相信，約會的異性，至少要叫她的心大力跳動幾下，或是手心冒汗，不能太舒服，否則，還不如在家看電視。

而這位某君，就是令她太鬆弛，堪稱一點感覺也無。

反而是他的妹妹適適，活潑明朗，嗇色願意再見一次，甚至多次。

說到曹操，曹操即到。

門鈴一響，門外正是賈適適。

她帶來一盆水果。

「原來是芳鄰。」

「歡迎請進，告訴我關於紐約的尋幽探秘之道。」

適適笑，「你喜歡看一個城市的陰暗面？」

嗇色問：「你可是學生？」

「我比你大，早已畢業，我們兄妹開了一爿小小畫廊。」

182

「生意好嗎？」

「過得去，扣除生活費用，所餘無幾，每天叫做有個地方去，那日在大都會參觀他們的禮品部、想佔爲已有。」

嗇色問她要啡啡還是要茶。

適適說：「我兄弟受你英國口音迷惑。」

嗇色笑答：「叫他加強意旨力，否則殆矣。」

「告訴我關於你。」

「乏善足陳。」自身有何可說。

適適看着她，「那麼，告訴我，長得美，是否天下樂事。」

嗇色怔住，「美，我？」

「你不知道？」適適吃驚。

「不不不，我手腳太長，脖子太細，我怎麼算美。」

「那麼。」適適笑，「舉個例，誰是美人。」

「我的繼母。」

183

適適說：「呵，她也在紐約？」

「不，她已去天國。」

「對不起。」

嗇色笑了，「不關你事。」

兩個年輕女子，一直聊到華燈初上。

「由我作東，出去吃飯。」

「我猜想你哥哥也會參加。」

「總得有人付賬呀。」

「我請你好了。」

適適忽然異常堅決，「我們孿生，心意相通，十分相愛，我萬萬不能丟下他，你要是喜歡我，也得接受他。」

嗇色駭笑，「好好好，快去叫他。」

這時電話鈴響了。

嗇色一聲喂，臉色便融解下來，適適在一旁看着，不用問，女人明白女人，對方必

184

是她意中人。

她深愛他，以致眼中胸中已無法容納他人。

適適恐怕她兄弟要失望了。

她去喚他吃飯。

電話另一頭，正是利佳上。

三個年輕人在樓下會合，散步到意大利餐館。

嗇色從早到晚，都是白襯衫藍長褲，看上去更加清逸可人。

一頓飯時間，嗇色沒說什麼話，可是一直很客氣。

——「我不吃肉，繼母病重時許過願，願吃素若干年。」

「不，我不介意一個人住，宿舍條款太嚴格，像做修女。」

「希望學習獨立生活多過吸收學問。」

飯局散後一起散步回家。

看着甄嗇色入屋，賈祥興問妹妹：「有無希望？」

賈適適答：「零。」

「不致於那樣悲觀吧。」

「再拖廿年，她不過永遠把你當作老朋友。」

賈祥興洩氣，「謝謝你。」

「她的心屬於別人，你看不出來？」

「誰？」

「不知道，給她一點時間，她或許會告訴你。」

「在她公寓裏，你有否見到什麼人的照片？」

適適笑，「那是很膚淺世俗的做法，你若真愛一個人，你會記得他的樣子。」

賈祥興低下頭，「又來遲一步。」

「看樣子不止一步。」

「賈半仙，看樣子你真的料事如神。」

「她不防我，單獨與我在一起時，活潑得多。」

「真羨慕你。」

那邊廂嗇色回到室內，放下鎖匙，更衣休息。

186

利佳上在電話上並沒有說什麼，只問聲好。

開學之後一切忙碌起來，不消數週，自有來約會的同學，嗇色對洋人比較輕鬆，他們比較受得起，看得開，而且不大容易被傷害。

這天，一位姓史蔑夫的同學一連提出好幾個要求。

嗇色笑答：「我的答案按次序是不、不、不、可、不。」

史蔑夫問：「應允哪一條，可是出來跳舞？」

「不，是借腳踏車給你。」

「咄！」

「喂，得些好意需回頭。」

「放學我來拿車子。」

傍晚史蔑夫來了，嗇色知道他是半工讀苦學生，平時食用比較差，特地做了牛排請他。

這洋小子感動了，他問：「你這樣守身如玉，爲的是誰？」

嗇色微笑，「你說呢？」

「那幸運的人是誰?」

嗇色感喟,「他不一定覺得幸運。」

「什麼!」

「他天天吃得到牛排。」

史蔑夫溫柔地說::「你收服了我,嗇色,不論幾時,吹聲口哨,我即趕來,你懂得吹口哨吧。」

嗇色笑起來,收了碟子,拿到廚房去。

史蔑夫幫她洗盤碗。

「告訴我關於你自己。」

每個人都那樣要求。

「我是一個學生,有什麼可說?」

這時有人掀鈴,嗇色去開門,門外站着賈祥興,與史蔑夫一照臉,開頭大家都一怔,然後立刻知道對方不是假想敵,立刻鬆懈下來,不過,又覺得多一個人始終討厭,於是採取沉默。

188

賈祥興同嗇色說了幾件事，放下當天中文報紙，看了史蔑夫一眼，告辭而去。

史蔑夫正喝咖啡。

嗇色，「又不見你問他是否那個人。」

史蔑夫不假思索，「當然不是。」那只不過是名跑腿。

嗇色不服，「你怎麼知道？」

「咄，你當我昨天才出生？」

嗇色只得笑了。

那年冬季苦寒，一場雪接着一場，嗇色聽見同學抱怨說：「像他媽的西伯利亞」，靴底沾滿融雪的化學鹽，車子寸步難行，天天遲到不是辦法，嗇色只得加倍早起。

十分辛苦的時候也問：：這些都是為什麼呢，一轉念，想到若非繼母搭救，甄嗇色豈敢妄想有機會到外國來吃這種鹹苦。

講師進課室來，「嗇色，只有你一人準時來聽課。」

嗇色微笑，「我就住在樓上，我無藉口遲到。」

翌日風雪更大，飛機場隨時關閉，上學前，賈祥興來看過她，同她說，晚上一起吃

189

意大利麵可好，嗇色答應，他忽然大力按她的頭。

這個動作令嗇色想起一個叫耳朵的人。

她已經不大記得耳朵的五官，他身段彷彿比較矮小，同賈祥興差不多。

那日，課上到一半講師忽然解散學生，因下午天氣會更加惡劣。

嗇色獨自來到停車場，鵝毛大雪向整個廣場撲過來，睜眼只見白濛濛雪片飛舞。

嗇色居然還有興趣張大嘴迎接雪花，年輕真是好。

就在這個時候，她看到一個高大的身型站在面前。

眼花了。

怎麼可能。

可是那人對她喊：「嗇色，還不快開車走。」

她撥開面前大雪，看得一清二楚，是，是利佳上。

他終於看她來了。

嗇色笑道：「你挑得個好日子。」

「我自多倫多來。」

「到該埠做什麼？」

「我將擔任多大一年客座教授。」

嗇色一怔，多市與紐約只需一小時飛機。

雪下得更急了，利佳上頭上與長大衣肩上很快積有一層薄雪。

嗇色踏前一步。

利佳上已經這樣說：「多市與紐約最近，我可以時來看你。」

嗇色哽咽，可是聲音儘量平靜，「還不快上車。」

忽然之間，她踏前一步，雙臂緊緊摟住利佳上，臉埋在他胸前。

利佳上輕輕說：「多謝溫馨歡迎。」

嗇色說：「我一直納罕，靠在這個胸膛上的感覺如何。」

「可否告訴我？」

「大衣太厚，毫無感覺。」

「笑死我。」

他們終於上車，幸虧吉普是四驅車，雪地行走不成問題。

191

到了公寓，利佳上說：「恐怕我得借宿一宵。」

「你沒訂酒店？」

「有，可是此刻車子難以抵達。」

「沒問題，我有睡袋。」

他脫下大衣，斟一杯酒喝，「有無食物？飢腸轆轆。」

廚房只有隔夜白飯，「臘腸蛋炒飯如何？」

「殺死人，快拿來。」

嗇色馬上走進廚房。

她的手藝認眞有限，可是蛋炒飯並不難做。

捧着碟子出來，看到利佳上正在讀文件。

他取出膝上電腦，「你的打印機可否借給我一用？」

嗇色指給他看，「請便。」

他一邊吃炒飯一邊接駁電腦。

「唔，這是我吃過最好的炒飯。」

「謝謝你。」

嗇色渾忘與鄰家有約。

她泡出一杯龍井茶。

利佳上訝異，「何來這樣好的茶葉？」

這才猛地想起，「是鄰居送我。」

門鈴響了。

嗇色出去開門。

是送茶葉的人。

賈祥興一見她便說：「你怎麼不過來？我以為你叫風雪擋住了。」

嗇色不語。

「別開窗，否則你會以為住在咆哮山莊。」

他伸手去拉嗇色的手。

這時，他聽見室內有人說：「嗇色，我需要更多紙，還有，可以添飯嗎？」

他愣住了。

他怎麼可以那麼笨，他連忙鬆開嗇色的手。

他應當一早自嗇色眉梢眼角看出端倪。

只見嗇色心思有點恍惚，可是有掩不住的複雜神情，既高興又無奈且為難。

那叫她的聲音，是何等沉着與自信。

賈祥興不由得退後一步。

他聽得自己輕輕說：「適適做了一大盤肉醬意粉。」

嗇色點點頭。

「你若不方便過來，我取來給你。」

「麻煩你了。」

賈祥興回家去。

他妹妹看見他笑嘻嘻過去，灰頭灰腦過來，不勝訝異。

「發生什麼事？」

「嗇色的男朋友來了。」

「她向你介紹？」

194

「不，我沒見到他。」

「那你怎知那是他？」

賈祥興枕着雙臂，「我感覺到。」

「我這就過去拜會他。」

「你順便送食物過去吧。」

「喂，別頹喪，不到最後一步，不知誰勝利。」

「你說得我好像有機會下場似。」

「反正是零，不打這場仗白不打。」

適適捧着食物過去。

來開門的是一高大英俊的男子，他需欠身遷就適適的高度，他親切地笑道：「你必是賈小姐了。」

適適凝視他。

他只穿着普通襯衫西褲，可是整個人看上去是那樣瀟灑自然，身體語言可親之至，他立刻接過她手中盤子，並且延她進內。

195

等。

適適後悔叫哥哥打這一仗，她不應對親生同胞花言巧語。

適適也看到了齒色，慢着，她應當心花怒放才是，為何反而臉帶愁容。

噫，她同他的關係可能有點複雜。

適適坐下說及天氣，怎麼樣整天沒有一個人客上門等等，然而扯到下雪實在可怕

他們靜靜聽她發表意見。

適適終於識趣地告辭。

回去同哥哥報告：「他好似比她大頗多。」

「長得怎麼樣？」

「我所見過最富魅力男士。」

「嘩，你的職業便是看男人，見識無比廣闊，所言不虛。」

「謝謝你。」適適啼笑皆非。

「他如約會你，你會出去嗎？」

「你開玩笑，天涯海角，在所不辭。」

196

聽見妹妹如此說，賈祥興怔住了。

適適不會說謊。

「為什麼？」

「那是一個使女人覺得像女人的男人。」

「啐，我使你覺得像什麼？」

「妹妹。」

「因為你真是我的妹妹。」

「不，某些異性從不令我們心跳，他們永遠是兄弟、同事、好友。」

賈祥興悻悻然，「我不幸就是這一類。」

適適不再談這個話題。

賈祥興把窗打開一條縫子，雪片紛紛竄進來，可是一遇暖空氣，立刻融化。

他寂寥地回到自己房間去。

早上，雪停了，市政府剷雪車天未亮就開始操作。

齒色捧着熱茶杯在窗口看街道風景。

197

利佳上在沙發上醒來，問道：「交通如何？」

「步行最快。」

「學校可開放？」

「聽收音機才知道。」嗇色笑嘻嘻，「同幼稚園生一樣聽特別新聞報告。」

「你希望逃學一天？」

嗇色轉過頭來，「我一向是好學生。」

「過來這邊。」

嗇色並沒有走過去，背光靠着窗，身形苗條。

利佳上歎口氣。

半晌，他說：「我該出門去辦事了。」

嗇色緩緩走向前，蹲下坐他身邊，「我一直納罕，靠在這樣的胸膛之上，滋味如何。」

她輕輕把臉靠上去。

她聽到他心跳，體溫泪泪轉到她臉上。

198

利佳上問她：「感覺如何？」

「你仍穿着襯衫。」

他揭開毯子，「多謝你提醒我，我得換件襯衫，行李袋放到何處去了？」

嗇色亦喚醒自己，「我給你做早餐。」

「一塊無牛油麵包與一杯清茶即行。」

「你是我所認識節食最成功的人。」

利佳上笑笑。

他也是少數清晨起床就好看的人。

他淋浴更衣。

嗇色知道他行李裏起碼帶着半打白襯衫。

「百貨公司幾點開門？」

「你要買什麼？」

「女同事托我買件銀色面子羽絨外套給她女兒。」

嗇色駭笑，「銀色，那是一種可以穿在身上的顏色嗎？」

199

利佳上笑了，「有人喜歡。」

「所以這世界多姿多彩。」

他們又開始迴避對方，儘談些不着邊際的話。

剛欲出門，適適過來問：「要不要同一輛車？交通非常擠塞。」

利佳上很客氣，「我要到皇后區探朋友。」

適適只得聳聳肩離去。

利君對甄嗇色說：「朋友對你很好。」

「出外靠朋友。」

上一句是在家靠父母，可是，甄嗇色並無父母。

無論在何處，她靠的都是自己。

怎麼樣說每一句話，怎麼樣走每一步路，都小心翼翼，沒有表示怕人家覺得她冷淡，太過熱情又怕人家嫌棄，無論坐同站，都似多了一隻手或是一條腿，那種感覺，真是卑微傷心。

再沉默、再低調，一個無人縱容的孩子仍是多餘的孩子。

200

即使將來出人頭地，名利雙收、家庭幸福，那烙印是永久的烙印。

她陪他去買禮物，試穿示範，售貨員勸她也買一件，她連忙雙手亂搖。

深藍色對她來講已經很好。

利佳上忽然覺得肚餓，買路邊熱狗來吃。

嗇色坐在路邊等他。

「你要遲到了。」

「不怕，十一點才有課。」

「我送你，放學我來接。」

「小心駕駛。」

她還是遲到了。

講師與同學都以詫異目光看着她。

脫下外套在角落坐下，嗇色發覺白襯衫上有一點黃色芥辣印子。

這一點芥辣分明是陪利佳上剛才吃熱狗時濺上。

她坐得有那麼近嗎，不是有大衣罩着嗎，白衣上的漬子往往來得最神秘不過，而

201

且，芥辣是無論如何洗不掉的漬子。

嗇色比往日更加沉默。

講師不知說了什麼，嗇色沒聽到，她惘然抬起頭，耳朵都燒紅了。

放學時嗇色撥電話給利佳上，他顯然在車上，立刻回答說：「告訴我怎麼走。」

嗇色把地址說清楚。

「給我二十分鐘。」

她到圖書館坐下。

史蔑夫看到她，馬上走到她身邊。

「放學去喝杯熱可可。」

「我有約。」

「你有約？」他假裝大吃一驚，「誰會約你？」

「信不信由你，」嗇色微笑，「自然有人。」

「我得問此君是誰。」

「朋友。」

202

「你初到本地，何來朋友？」

嗇色但笑不語。

史蔑夫無論如何不服氣。

片刻時間到了，嗇色挽起背包。

史蔑夫靜靜跟在她身後。

嗇色已無暇理會是否有誰跟在她身後，走出校門，看到自己的車子便忽忽奔過馬路。

史蔑夫呆呆看着她。

只見一高大男子打開車門讓她上車。

對面馬路並不是那麼遠，史蔑夫可以清楚看見她如花笑靨。

她從來沒有為誰那樣笑過。

車子駛遠良久，這金髮小子仍然呆呆站在馬路上。

在車廂裏嗇色擦着冰冷鼻子，「去何處？」

「週末無事？」

「沒有。」

「去拉斯維加斯。」這當然不是真的。

嗇色笑彎了腰，「好呀。」

「不，去威尼斯。」

那是陳綺羅最鍾愛的城市。

嗇色苦澀地思念繼母。

「到倫敦。」

「一定要到別處去嗎？」

「我知道了，到長島。」

「好的，一言為定。」

「太冷了，我渴望脫掉襯衫。」

「那最容易不過，讓我們到墨西哥。」

利君看她一眼，「我以為你會說家中最暖和。」

嗇色低下頭微笑，「你一直在等我先有表示。」

204

他溫柔地說：「那是不對的，我人已經主動來到你面前。」

嗇色仍然微笑，「我無此勇氣。」

利佳上低聲問：「你另有他人？」

「沒有。」

「那麼，我可以等。」

嗇色落下淚來。

「我不會催你。」

「對不起。」

「誰也沒有做錯，何用道歉。」

他把車停下來，擁抱她。

「你會等我？」

「永遠。」

「永遠是很長的一段日子。」

他微笑，「在我的年齡不是。」

205

那一天，他搬到酒店去住。

嗇色微笑，「你怕人說話。」

他沒有解釋，只是笑笑。

後來才知道他特地來參加的會議便在酒店舉行。

嗇色坐在一角看他發言，他有一股自然的學者風度，他知道他的功課，有備而來，資料充份，言語簡潔幽默，聽眾反應熱烈。

會後嗇色幫他收拾講義，有人問：「這位漂亮的小姐是——」

他順口答：「甄嗇色小姐。」

從前他會說：「我的女兒。」

現在，嗇色失去了原有的身份，可是將來的新身份又未敲定。

她笑笑不語，心中卻有一絲淒惶。

週末過後，利佳上折返多倫多。

「有時間過來看看。」

嗇色頷首話別。

206

寒假頭一個星期她原本打算與賈適適一起到邁亞米度假。

她等他來叫她，可是他讓她自己作決定。

嗇色躊躇得很厲害。

適適勸：「聽從你的心。」

嗇色歎口氣，「我的心從來不予我忠告。」

適適笑，「我的也是，可是它說什麼？」

「它叫我到多倫多去。」

「那麼去好了。」

嗇色意外，「我以為你會反對。」

適適溫和地說：「可能是一個錯誤，你與他只能相處一段短時期，但又怎麼樣呢，你才十九歲，不犯錯又似乎不像年輕人。」

嗇色不住點頭。

「我會給他一個意外。」

適適豎起一隻手指，「千萬不要給任何人意外，詳細把日期時間通知他。」

嗇色很為難，她額角冒出亮晶晶的汗珠。

適適知道，只有一個人在最愛另一人之際，任何一點點小事，才會引起如此大躊躇。

她非常同情嗇色。

適適揚着手，歎着氣，「去吧去吧，給他意外吧。」

嗇色收拾簡單行李，乘飛機到多市。

在飛機場她想撥電話到他宿舍，可是心想不過尚餘二十分鐘車程而已。

她叫了計程車。

到他門口按鈴時是黃昏七時。

這時才認為適適所說十分真確，他要是不在家可怎麼辦呢。

但是他來找她，也從來不預先張揚。

嗇色按鈴。

聽到腳步聲傳來，她十分高興，可是門打開了，嗇色一怔，應門的人竟是一名金髮女。

208

幾乎百份之九十的金髮全是染的，深棕色的髮根露了出來，未及補染，約近三十歲的她臉上有點泛油，粧褪了一半，可是略具風姿。

她看着薔色問：「找誰？」

薔色沉着應付：「利教授。」

「利出外替我買香煙。」

薔色說：「那我進來等他。」

那女子忽然冷笑一聲，「你是他學生？你可有預約？」

薔色忽然很尖銳地答：「我是他的女兒，我同他終身有約。」

那女子退後一步，面露詫異尷尬之色。

薔色進屋，乘勝追擊：「他沒告訴你嗎？」

順手打開所有窗戶，皺着眉頭。

她轉過頭去，「一有人抽煙，整間屋子都臭。」

然後在最好的一張沙發上坐下，雙目炯炯地看着那女子。

那女子適才的自信忽然消逝，她不知如何應付屋主女兒無禮的控訴。

209

嗇色發覺女子身上穿着混合人造纖維料子製的一套紫色衣裙，半跟鞋已踢得十分殘舊，這是北美洲典型白領女打扮，年薪約三萬美元左右。

嗇色忽然吃驚，她掩住了嘴，這等刻薄的目光莫非似她生母。

養母感化了她，可是她身體裏流着生母的血，一到要緊關頭，遺傳因子會得發作，簡直情不自禁。

剛才一連串動作是多麼叫人難堪。

就在這個時候，利佳上推門進來。

他一眼看到了嗇色，愣住。

假金髮女郎連忙上前，「利，她是你的女兒？」

利佳上立刻笑，「你們已經互相介紹過了，嗇色，真是意外的驚喜。」

嗇色冷冰冰地坐着，不為所動。

那女子猶豫一會兒，取過架子上一件大衣，「利，我先走一步，明日在辦公室見。」

可是嗇色的壞因子一發不可收拾。

她伸出手來，「香煙呢，」自利佳上處取過紙袋，塞到女郎懷中，「別忘記你的香煙。」

她伸出手來，「香煙呢，」自利佳上處取過紙袋，塞到女郎懷中，「別忘記你的香煙。」

利佳上錯愕地站在一旁，不知如何應付這個場面。

那女子勉強一笑，「再見。」

利佳上還想說什麼，被嗇色凌厲目光阻住，她在女子身後大力關上門。

她冷笑，「你不是想送她回家吧。」

利佳上駭笑，「你怎麼會忽然出現，而且舉止言行統統像甄嗇色？」

女客一走，嗇色靜了下來，「不，也許這個才是眞嗇色。」

「你好嗎，你沒有事吧。」

「我很好，我無事。」

「那位小姐是我的臨時秘書，好心來幫忙處理文件，慢着，我爲什麼要對你解釋？」

嗇色質問：「你讓她在屋內抽煙，還替她做跑腿去買香煙？這種洋婦一個銅板一打。」

利佳上大吃一驚，「你並不認識她，爲何仇視她？」

「因她有非份之想！她前來啓門之際先仇視我。」

「那不是眞的。」

「我的感覺錯不了。」

利佳上看着她，「你語氣似一個妒意不可收拾的愛侶。」

「我，妒忌那洋婦？」嗇色提高聲線。

利佳上笑出來，「更像了。」

嗇色刹那間恢復了沉靜憂鬱本色。

「你到多市來度假？」

她輕輕答：「不，我來邀請你私奔。」

利佳上顯然仍在介懷，「你倒處處告訴別人你是我女兒，還如何私奔？」

「我以爲你一向不管別人說些什麼。」

「可是我卻十分關心你說些什麼。」

「我這次特地來同你吵架才眞。」

212

嗇色站起來拉開大門。

「慢着，」利佳上搶過來，「你以為你要走到哪裏去。」

他緊緊把她摟在懷中。

嗇色聽得他深深歎息一聲。

「對不起在你同事面前失態。」

「你是第一個管我的人。」

「我遠遠不如綺羅大方可愛。」

「她仍然在生多好，我亦不會有份之想。」

「綺羅叫我永遠懷念。」

這不是眞話，她一直覻覻他的胸膛。

「來，看看這裏的客房。」

嗇色說：「我還算幸運，假使她穿着睡袍來開門，吃不消兜着走的是我。」

利佳上這時已完全原諒了她，「那你要在清晨來。」

「你會嗎？」

213

「不一定，看情形，一個男人是一個男人。」

嗇色笑了。

金髮女子留下一隻粉紅色塑膠打火機。

品味需要龐大的基金支持，可是金錢又未必買到品味。

嗇色把廉價打火機丟進垃圾桶。

她們都喜歡東方男人，因為他們手頭比較寬裕、又願意照顧女性。

洋婦一直以為大多數華人太太都不用工作，家中僱有傭人，而且有能力戴名貴珠寶。

嗇色笑了。

羨慕得十分妒忌，可是又佯裝看不起人。

她也想來挿一腳。

嗇色冷笑一聲：待我死了再說吧。

一抬頭，看到牆上鏡子裏的反映，只見自己睜圓雙眼，吊起眉梢，咬牙切齒的樣子，哎呀，好像一個人，這是誰？

活脫脫是一個較爲年輕的方國寶女士。

嗇色呆呆地看着鏡子，多年來養尊處優的生活並未能抹煞她的本性，一到要緊關頭，原形畢露。

利佳上問：「看牢鏡子幹什麼？」

嗇色轉過頭來，「你說呢？」

利佳上笑，「可憐高堂明鏡悲白髮，朝如青絲暮成雪。」

「那是什麼意思？」

利佳上溫柔地答：「那是說，不要在任何地方掛鏡子。」

嗇色低下頭。

午夜醒來，十分歉意，利教授明朝該如何向女同事解釋呢，那女子一口氣下不去，又會否再上門來同她鬥三百回合？

都叫嗇色難以入寐。

她起來，披上大衣，走到窗前。

貼近玻璃已經覺得冷。

她索性打開窗，哆嗦幾下，反而精神。

215

窗外有什麼在蠕動，是浣熊嗎。

看清楚一點，樹叢下有兩個人。

那對少年男女緊緊擁抱熱吻，因為年輕的緣故，並不覺猥瑣，反而有點像荷利活電影中蓄意安排的性愛場面。

他的手伸到她毛衣底下，這樣零度天氣一點也不覺得冷，什麼時候了，時鐘顯示是凌晨三時，那麼晚還不回家，父母有無掛念他們？

嗇色歎息一聲。

如果她有父母，她才不會叫父母擔心。

那對年輕男女忽然發覺有人在看他們，倒底是人類，忽覺有羞恥之心，摟着低頭離去。

嗇色猶自在窗前站了很久很久。

直到手足冰冷，才回到房間去。

她撥電話到賈祥興家去。

「吵醒了你。」

「不不，已經是早上，該起來了。」

「你那邊天亮沒有？」

「多倫多與紐約並無時差呀。」

無論說什麼，賈祥興都不介意，聲音喜孜孜，她自動找他，那意思是，在她心裏，還有他的位置，只得一點點，也不要緊。

「幾時回來？」

「過兩天。」

「可要我來接飛機？」

「還以為你永遠不會問。」

「我一定來。」

「帶我參觀你的店舖。」

「隨時歡迎。」

嗇色說：「我怪想念你們。」

賈祥興覺得盪氣迴腸，活到八十歲，他都不會忘記這個破曉時分的電話。

217

嗇色輕輕向他道別，掛上電話。

賈祥興用手抹一把臉，看向窗外，天濛濛亮了。

他在博物館第一眼看到這個女孩子就愛上她。

老成持重的他從未見過那麼秀麗沉靜的人兒，鵝蛋臉、短髮、白襯衫、藍長褲、平跟鞋，身段無比纖美，上帝偏心，在製造某些人的時候，特別精工。

她渾身上下一點裝飾品都沒有，樸素得不似真實世界裏的少女。

那少女在同一個早上向利佳上攤牌。

她一邊微笑一邊悲哀的說：「我要走了。」

利佳上靜靜等待下文。

甄嗇色輕輕說：「沒有人會同深愛的人結婚吧。」

利佳上不作聲。

「何等辛苦。」

利佳上輕輕問：「那麼你認為我同綺羅並不相愛？」

「你們是例外。」

218

「你又緣何這樣年輕就考慮婚姻？」

「我與其他家庭幸福的女孩子不同，我很想早點有個自己的窩，生兒育女，得到精神寄托。」

「這是否意味着我將失去你？」

「怎麼會，你在我生命中永遠地位超然。」

「眞沒白在英國受教育，現在說話學會語氣雷霆萬鈞，實則毫無份量。」

「眞了不起是不是。」嗇色笑了。

「我會一直在這裏等你。」

「胡說，不久將來，你便會再婚。」

利佳上不語。

「答應我，求婚之前，查清楚她的金髮是否眞的。」

「能這樣捉狹，可見還是愛我。」

眞的，對賈祥興，她才不會如此計較。

她見到賈祥興兄妹，一直微笑。

219

適適高興得團團轉。

她一直嘰嘰呱呱說話，男女主角反而無言。

「嗇色，趁假期剛開始，到長島我父母家去玩，好不好。」

嗇色說好好好。

她最羨慕人家有娘家，一切都是現成的，在那裏，家長撐着一把大傘，擋風擋雨，還有，付清一切賬單。

現成的床舖被褥食物冷熱水隨時享用，有事大喊「爸爸媽媽」，無他，就因爲運氣好，說不定多吃一碗飯就有大人拍手讚好。

還有，嫁出去十年八載之後，少女時期的房間還照原來式樣佈置，像間紀念館。

老傭人捧出三菜一湯來，一邊抱怨沒有新花樣一邊吃個碗腳朝天。

適適有娘家，而嗇色沒有。

「你會喜歡我爸媽的，他們十分大方。」

接着的一段日子，嗇色每日睡到日上三竿，由賈祥興中午自店舖回來把她叫醒陪她吃早點。

下午她找資料寫功課，然後出去接賈祥興打烊。

賈氏老家接近海堤，風景如畫。

賈先生太太年紀不小，仍然相敬如賓，對世事於子女根本全無要求，自然非常快活。

管家是墨西哥人，已經做了超過十年，似半個自己人，賈家歡迎每一個客人，對甄嗇色更加另眼相看。

嗇色對這樣的家境非常滿意。

這裏可沒有追着女兒要錢的生母。

賈祥興未料嗇色會這樣鬆弛。

她躺在繩網床裏曬太陽可以睡熟。

他憐愛地說：「餐餐吃三碗飯也不見你胖。」

「三十歲時才發肉。」

「我不怕。」

嗇色笑了，「現在你當然這樣說。」

221

賈祥興說：「嗇色，讓我們結婚吧。」

「我還沒有畢業。」

「婚後繼續讀書大不乏人。」

「你對我並無充份瞭解。」

賈祥興笑，「這世上所有的婚姻其實都是盲婚。」

說得也眞確無比。

知人口面不知心，日久才見得到眞面目，吃驚兼傷心，即刻離異。

他同她到鐵芬尼去看指環。

「喜歡哪一隻，告訴我。」

嗇色說：「如果決定結婚，指環不重要。」

賈祥興卻道：「指環是男方對女方的一種尊重，文藝小說中一條草做指環是不切實際虛幻飄渺可笑的承諾，不足以信。」

他說得很好。

「鑽石白金可永久保存。」

222

結果嗇色只挑了一副耳環。

翌日，指環卻送了上來，尺寸剛剛好。

嗇色戴上細細觀賞。

「很漂亮。」

嗇色隨即除下，放回淺藍色小盒子，還給賈祥興。

「好，我暫時保存。」他蠻有信心。

她把這件事告訴利佳上，他說：「如果這是叫我妒忌，你注定失敗，而且，對方無辜，你別太傷害他人，那不公平。」

嗇色在電話中說：「我是真有意結婚。」

「若果賭氣，那是傷害自己。」

嗇色忽然說：「我已長大，我與你無話可說。」

她掛上電話。

她跑到賈家，幫適適做賬。

回到家，已是深夜，電話錄音並無留言。

223

這不是賭氣，這是無話可說。

嗇色沒睡好，做了一個噩夢，進了一間鬼屋，但是她卻沒有驚怖，在樣子古怪的魍魎魍魍中穿插，直至夢醒，雖然不太愉快，但是真正令嗇色害怕的，卻是一直向她要錢的生母。

那清早嗇色去敲門：「我的指環呢。」

好一個賈祥興，睡眼惺忪，立刻打開小型夾萬把指環遞給甄嗇色。

嗇色套上指環自顧自上學去。

賈祥興大聲叫：「YES!」

那日下午，兩兄妹去接嗇色放學。

融雪，一片濕滑泥濘，道路骯髒到極點。

他倆坐在車內等候，一邊看附近公園內一羣年輕人踢泥球，伸腿一踢，整隻球帶着大團泥巴飛出去，樂趣無窮。

適適問：「到什麼地方結婚？」

「當然是風和日麗的地方。」

224

「要早點訂做婚紗禮服。」

「她穿很簡單式樣就像公主一樣。」

適適看着哥哥，「我眞替你高興。」

「你呢，你有打算無？」

「你少理我，儘管自己游上岸是正經。」

兄妹相視而笑。

賈祥興忽然說：「嗇色出來了。」

可不就是她。

嗇色一走進公園範圍，立刻聽見有人叫她。

她抬起頭，看到同學史蔑夫，那洋小子故意濺幾點泥巴到她身上，惹她注意。

本來笑笑走開就無事。

這也一貫是甄嗇色處世作風，可是今日她人卻異常不甘心，她伸手去抓史蔑夫。

衆球友大聲喝采。

史蔑夫如泥鰍一般滑出去，怎會給她逮到，嗇色追上去。

賈祥興大驚失色，立刻下車。

適適在一旁喃喃說：「甄嗇色這一面我們好似還沒看清楚。」

賈祥興聞言怔住。

說時遲那時快，嗇色手一長，已抓住史蒉夫球衫，說怎麼都不放，掙扎間她亦變成泥人。

史蒉夫服輸，嗇色逼他道歉。

只聽得嗇色清脆笑聲在春寒料峭的空氣中如銀鈴般傳出去。

適適又說：「至少她快活。」

賈祥興問：「是因為訂了婚的緣故嗎？」

「希望是。」

賈祥興奔過去。

嗇色看到他，十分不好意思，迅速恢復常態。

「你都看見了？」

賈祥興點點頭。

226

嗇色端詳自己，解嘲說：「幸虧耳環戒指都還在這裏。」

賈祥興語氣十分溫和，「不見了也不要緊。」

適適在一旁歎口氣。

嗇色問她：「他說的是眞的嗎？」

適適頷首：「全眞。」

賈祥興摟着一個泥人回家去。

嗇色淋浴時他在浴室門口問：「那人是你同學？」

「同系同班。」

「眞幼稚。」

「有人還踩花式滑板呢，長人不長腦，眞羨慕。」

賈祥興感慨：「華人的確老得快。」

「是呀，即使在外國出世，到了五六歲，也得到中文班去上課。」

賈祥興笑，「我就是叫這個整得死去活來未老先衰。」

嗇色裏着毛巾浴泡出來，整張臉亮晶晶。

227

賈祥興看得呆了。

他伸手過去握住她的臉。

嗇色掙脫。

他詫異，「我以為我們已經訂婚。」

嗇色坐到一角，「我還沒準備好。」

賈祥興也不是全無脾氣，「你得好好準備。」

嗇色一臉落寞，「我知道。」

賈祥興又自覺言重，不捨得她不開心，但終於不能再說什麼，他開門離去。

整件事是失敗的。

電話錄音上仍然沒有留言。

第二天，史蔑夫追上來，「嗇色，你身手好不敏捷。」

嗇色不去理他。

「喂，我道過歉，你也笑了。」

「回家後越想越氣。」

「我賠你衣裳。」

「算了吧你。」

史蔑夫還想說什麼，嗇色忽然趨過身子在他唇上重重一吻。

史蔑夫呆若木雞，好一會兒才迴過神來，怪叫：「好傢伙，這是怎麼一回事？」

看，毫無困難。

可是，同樣的親熱用不到賈祥興身上。

真是悲哀。

嗇色默默走開。

當日下午，她去找賈祥興。

自玻璃門看進去，見他細心招呼客人。

古時中國人把生意人地位排得相當低，實在有其原因，士農工商，只見賈祥興小心翼翼，稍微欠着身子，佝僂着背脊，賠着笑，無限殷勤地跟着一對洋人夫婦背後走。

一日要服侍多少客人？將來，她是否要出任他的助手？還有，孩子們可得承繼事業？

229

嗇色驚出一身冷汗。

她想轉身走，可是賈祥興已經見到玻璃門外的她。

他過來拉開玻璃門，歡喜地叫：「嗇色。」

嗇色看到他有一絡頭髮疲乏地掛在額角上，招呼客人原來是這樣勞累的一件事。

她輕輕說：「我一會兒再來。」

「不，」他極不捨得她來回回那樣跑，「為什麼不進來呢。」

嗇色只得進店去。

小小畫廊裏擺滿未成名畫家試探之作，十分討好，作品適宜點綴客廳牆壁。

洋夫婦見到嗇色，十分訝異她秀麗外型，指着其中一幅畫裏穿清朝服飾的少女問：

「你是模特兒？」

真有點像，同樣的鵝蛋臉、大眼睛。

嗇色笑了。

以前流行香港水上人家旦家漁女畫像，後來中國開放藝術家們眼光拓大，又畫旗裝，妙哉。

230

他倆終於選購一張少女持荷花像。

賈祥興笑逐顏開。

嗇色瀏覽一下，真沒想到標價如此高，所以說，逢商必奸。

做成那一單生意後，賈祥興恢復平時神態，「請坐，我斟杯茶給你。」

那邊有小小一張茶几，兩張沙發。

嗇色過去坐下。

茶几上有適才客人喝剩的意大利咖啡，將來，斟咖啡的必定是她。

「適適呢？」

賈祥興答：「在第五街逛百貨公司。」

嗇色覺得有口難言，「我去找她。」

賈祥興笑，「你怎知她在哪一家？」

嗇色答：：「我有靈感。」

「緣何精神恍惚？」

「我沒事。」

231

「有什麼話，可直接對我說。」

這是對的，何必先對適適說，然後才叫適適對他講。

嗇色也反對一走了之。

她鼻尖泛着油，取出手帕，細細抹一下。

終於她說：「我尚未準備好。」

「我們有的是時間。」

「我想，我永遠都不會準備好。」

賈祥興詫異了，「你欲悔約？」

嗇色答：「我們彼此不適合。」

賈祥興說：「可是，你這樣反覆，會傷害到無辜。」聲音相當平靜。

「對不起。」

「一句對不起，不足彌補他人終身的創傷。」

嗇色也忿慨了，「終身？哪裏會那麼嚴重。」

至多將來拖兒帶女，路過馬路，看到一個皮膚白晳少女之際，刹那間許會聯想到甄

232

嗇色，一輩子？不要說笑了。

他們總愛把創傷誇大，以便說話。

賈祥興抬起頭來，臉上哀傷之色使嗇色心驚。

他沉默一會兒才說：「你連試也不肯試。」

嗇色伸手去安慰他。

他避開，「別碰我，別拍我的頭拍我肩膀，我不是一條狗。」

嗇色為難地縮回手，脫下指環，放櫃枱上，轉身離去。

她回公寓，開了一瓶白酒，坐在露台上，對着夕陽獨飲。

翌日，醒來，已紅日高照，她梳洗完畢，去拍賈家大門，希望獲得原諒。

可是看到工人在搬傢具。

「喂，」她大聲問：「搬去何處？」

「長島。」

真沒想到賈氏兄妹決定避開她。

嗇色立刻尷尬地走到街上去。

233

她等着適適來話別，可是沒有，她跟着哥哥走了。

她可以找到店裏去，她也知道賈氏老家地址，要找，總找得到，可是嗇色反而鬆口氣。

過兩日，她也忽忽搬走，更換了電話號碼。

現在，每天上學放學，她都十分小心，看看前後左右，有無人尾隨。

她的疑心是多餘的，賈祥興是正當生意人，他不會懷恨於心，也不會做出什麼不合情理的事來。

嗇色又有一絲失望。

叫一個男人放下一切尊嚴爲女性失禮地拉拉扯扯哭哭啼啼究竟是難得的，當時可能可憎可厭可怕，但若干年後想起來，卻是魅力佐證。

搬一次家消耗不少，她打電話到石律師處撥錢。

一日放學回家，甫掏出鎖匙，有一高大人形閃出，嗇色失聲尖叫。

那人受驚，也大叫起來。

234

一看，卻是利佳上。

嗇色忽然淚如泉湧。

利佳上擁抱她，「噓，噓，這是怎麼一回事，搬了家也不告訴我，石志威急得不得了，叫我來看個究竟，這是紐約，魯莽需付出代價。」

嗇色一聲不響，把臉埋在他胸膛之前，一直默默流淚。

「開門讓我看你的新居。」

嗇色仍然沒有動靜。

利佳上歎口氣，「情緒如此不安，如何讀好書？」

半晌，嗇色伸出手顫抖地摸索他的面孔。

利佳上握住她的手，放在唇邊。

他倆緊緊擁抱。

因為在街上，所以可以放肆一點。

新居裏只得一茶一几。

「怎樣寫功課？」

235

「在圖書館做。」

「電視機呢？」

「我不看電視。」

「不可置信。」

薔色此刻眼睛鼻子嘴巴都已紅腫，可是仍然不失是個美少女。

利佳上溫和地說：「原來傷人者自己亦會元氣大傷。」

「你知道什麼！」

「我一切都知道。」

「我不信。」

「人家受了委屈，什麼都告訴了我。」

薔色大吃一驚，「他來找你？」

利佳上說：「不，我去找他。」

薔色怔住。

「是石律師告訴我你想結婚。」

236

四處都佈滿了眼線。

利佳上一踏進畫廊，賈氏兄妹就迎上來，以為是貴客上門。

利佳上挑了兩張不為人注意的小小水彩風景畫，然後自我介紹。

一早畫廊並無其他生意，他坐下來喝一杯香片茶。

賈適適心緒比較澄明，她忽然輕輕問：「利先生可是甄嗇色的繼父？」

利佳上有點尷尬，早知一進門就說明自己的身份。

他連忙欠欠身，「可以這樣說。」

適適沒有放過他，接着略略提高聲音，「聽說，你對她有特殊感情？」語氣有責備成份。

利佳上這時發覺畫廊的空氣調節偏冷。

他答：「嗇色並非拙荊所生。」

賈適適一愣。

利佳上繼續說下去：「她是我妻子前夫的女兒。」

適適沒想到嗇色身世如此複雜，不禁怔住。

利佳上再說得清楚一點：「她親生父母一早離開了她，不過，她在我家，是一位很受尊重的小朋友。」

賈祥興在該剎那完完全全原諒了甄嗇色，也許，一個童年如此不愉快的女孩，成後有權任性一點。

利佳上終於問：「聽說，你們打算結婚？」

賈適適再訝異不過，「她沒告訴你？她悔約了。」

不知怎地，利佳上非常高興，可是面子上不露出來，「那，打擾兩位，我先走一步。」

他拿着兩張畫走出畫廊，臉上泛出一絲笑意，隨即收斂，忽忽往新地址找嗇色。

她的新家是一座鎮屋的二樓，他站在樓下往上看，只見窗戶緊閉。

他一直站在街角等。

直到看見她回來。

嗇色似乎又長高了，仍然穿着深藍色外套，臉色白皙而平靜，情緒看不出異樣。

可是他一叫她，她回過頭來，大聲尖叫，嚇了他一跳，接着，她淚如泉湧。

238

可見是受了委屈。

這時他才想起來，「那兩張水彩畫呢。」

忽忽下樓去，兩張畫仍然扔在樓梯角。

嗇色說：「假使是兩筒麵包，早就被人揀走。」

利佳上只得笑。

嗇色說：「這種畫，自未成名年輕畫家處以一百數十元買來，轉手賺十倍。」

「做生意嘛，有燈油火臘需要兼顧。」

他把畫拆開。

畫中人同嗇色幾乎一模一樣。

穿着深藍外套、白色襯衫，倦慵地看向窗外。

另一張是低頭看書的側面。

嗇色訝異，看署名，右下角只見兩個英文字母，噫，是賈祥興。

嗇色不語。

是充滿愛意的兩幀寫生。

239

嗇色一直不知道他會繪畫，也不發覺他已將她記錄在筆下。

不過生意人畢竟是生意人，畫好了，放在店裏賣，能賺錢千萬不要放過，賠本生意千萬不要做，回報率低的投資需即刻縮手。

所以他立刻搬了家。

嗇色放心了。

他與她，都會沒事。

說真了，都是十分有保留的人。

嗇色坐下來鬆口氣。

她雙目紅腫漸漸褪去，面孔向着窗外的她就是畫中人。

「我勸你把書讀好。」

嗇色凄涼地微微笑，「綺羅去世給我的啟示是，也許凡事不宜拖延，否則就來不及做。」

「所以你覺得要迅速結一次婚。」

「是。」

「爲何又悔婚？」

嗇色不語。

「覺得內疚，對不起人家？」

嗇色嗤一聲笑，「哪裏有這樣偉大，是我發覺無法與他親熱。」

利佳上一怔。

「我心中始終只有一人罷了。」

「那人是誰呢。」

「你又何必問。」

「但說不妨。」

甄嗇色刹那間恢復了佻皮本色，答道：「主耶穌基督。」

利佳上看着她，「那男孩應當慶幸他離開了你。」

「胡說，他會一輩子想念我。」

「因爲你待他壞？」

「不，我待他十分公平。」

241

「所有刻薄的老闆也都那樣說。」

他倆凝視對方。

都知道再也不會找到更愛的人。

「當你廿一歲，不再受石律師監護，又能獨立自主的時候，再決定結婚未遲。」

嗇色低聲說：「多麼浪漫，這是向我求婚嗎？」

利佳上輕輕答：「你我均知那是沒有可能的事。」

嗇色不出聲。

「我們在一起經歷過太多事情，彼此太過熟稔，雖無血緣，也似我真繼女，我嘗試掙脫枷鎖，終不成功。」

嗇色仍然沉默。

「當我看見你之際，你只得十二歲……」

那雙晶瑩的大眼睛已經常常偷窺他，叫他心驚。

他總擔心有事會發生，可是二人相安無事。

是他建議把她送出去留學。

242

綺羅亦即時明白這是一個好主意。

等嗇色大一點，當必定明白三人之間的關係。

「我希望你願意讓我永遠照顧你。」

嗇色微笑，「好呀。」

「語氣中請稍微加些誠意。」

「好——呀。」

「還是不夠。」

嗇色伸手過去，用手臂搭住他的肩膀。

她常常看見綺羅那樣做，好讓利佳上雙臂圈住她的腰身。

嗇色嚮往這個姿勢，它充份顯示了男歡女愛。

可是利佳上並無把手擱在她腰上的意思。

他告訴她，他將轉到新加坡去教一年書。

「抽空來看我。」

「有直航飛機嗎？」

243

「一聽這句話，就知道不打算來。」

嗇色低頭，「避得太遠了。」

「由此可知我對自己的意旨力越來越乏信心。」

「不，你根本毋需控制什麼，太謙虛了。」

利佳上無話可說，便道：「來，吃飯時候到了。」

嗇色忽然吟道：「思君令人老，努力加餐飯。」

利佳上大表詫異，「這古詩你自何處學來？」

「一個人也不能永遠不長進。」

利佳上不由得笑起來。

那一次之後，嗇色便與他疏遠。

一個住在紐約的少女如果要令自己非常繁忙，那還是有辦法的。

她很快找到新的嗜好、新的朋友、新的歇腳處。

畢業那一天，石志威律師來觀禮。

這個老好人感動得眼睛紅紅。

244

穿着學士袍的嗇色伸個懶腰，「早知老得那麼快，就不讀書了。」

「這是什麼話。」

「媽媽泉下有知，必定安慰。」

「這才像話。」

嗇色低下頭。

「為什麼不讓利教授來觀禮？」

「他整天在大學裏改博士論文，哪裏在乎。」

「這是我聽過至壞的推搪。」

嗇色訕笑。

「你不想見他？」

「人家會說話。」

石志威點點頭，「長大了，明白事理了，忌諱一點也是好的，利教授此刻在學術界頗有名聲，外頭一直傳他同繼女曖昧，那是有損害的。」

石律師的想法絕對代表全世界人的意見。

245

嗇色低下頭，「你知道我們一年也見不了幾次面。」

「可是街外人不明白。」

「我何必叫他們明白我。」

石志威笑，「我年輕時也那樣想，可是，人是羣居動物，若想生活愉快，還需爭取大衆瞭解。」

嗇色伸手去替他整理領帶，微笑道：「石律師說的，都是金石良言。」

石志威看見雪白一雙小手伸過來，不禁凝視，世上竟有那麼漂亮的纖指。

他停一停神，咳嗽一聲，「我有點文件給你簽署。」

「有關什麼？」

「有關陳綺羅給你的遺產。」

「我已畢業，我打算找工作，我可以養活自己。」

「這是綺羅心意。」

「我會成為富女？」

「不見得，但你會相當寬裕。」

薔色說：「我真正的母親說不定又會聞風而來要錢。」

「許久沒聽到她的消息，你不必過慮。」

「她此刻在何處？」

石志威一怔，「我不知道，你想見她嗎？」

「不不不。」

「她可能在加拿大，說不定住馬來西亞，也許居荷蘭。」

「去去去，去得越遠越好，永遠不見面。」

「這是利教授托我帶來的賀禮。」

扁長盒子，一看就知道是隻手錶。

薔色打開一看，「太名貴了。」

「可不是，美金六萬多，我同他說，不適合少女。」

薔色把手錶戴上，「可是，我已是年輕婦女。」

他倆到俄國茶室吃午餐。

「有男朋友沒有？」

247

「還在找。」

嗇色笑了，「一點條件也無，希望他像個男人吧。」

「真的，」石律師怪同情，「此刻一輩男生都陰陽怪氣。」

她在文件上簽了名，從此可自由動用陳綺羅的遺產。

回到家中，翻開手錶來看，錶肚上刻着字樣：嗇色畢業誌慶，利，年月日。

承繼了陳綺羅的遺產，也承繼了她的命運。

現在什麼都有了，卻已失去了至寶貴的童年，但願她可以往時間隧道裏鑽，走回頭，同十二歲那個手長腳長的孤女說：「我來照顧你，我必定會對你好，因為你即是我，我即係你。」

可是現在她已經廿一歲了。

已有某參議員聘請她擔任助選團成員，嗇色需遷往首府華盛頓工作。

那真是一個新天地。

甄嗇色開始覺得人生可能有點意義。

248

她非常出鋒頭，人漂亮聰敏年輕，又具專業知識，很快受到注意，電視台向她接頭，希望她參予主持節目。

那樣忙，對前事漸漸淡忘。

五月一個週末，參議員開園遊會，她忙完一陣子，坐在紫藤架下喝香檳，猛一抬頭，看到一個高大的年輕人向她走來，她怔怔地朝他看，他使她想起一個人。

他穿白衣白褲，白色馬球上衣領子只敞開一點點，可是已可看到茸茸的汗毛。

她笑笑，喝一口酒。

那年輕人走過來，笑問：「你可是看着我？我是伊安麥考利。」

她微笑，「你家族對你抱負甚高，你不宜結識有色人種女子。」

嗇色知道這個名字，在華盛頓，人人知道人人。

「多謝操心，可惜我已過廿一歲，你是著名的甄嗇色吧，或許你可給我忠告，我打算學中文……」

他令她想起一個人。

在這個美麗的，櫻花盛放的五月天下午，她心思飛出去老遠。

249

就在那個週末，她偕他到康納的克老家農莊去度假。

麥考利家非常反對。

「華府所有女子中，偏偏要選華裔女友，何解？」

「我想我已愛上她。」

「爲什麼？」

「一切，尤其是她低頭沉思的恍惚神情，總似有點心事，叫我着迷，赴湯蹈火，在所不辭。」

「將來你競選參議員之時，傳媒會把這段情取出做文章。」

「那麼，我就一輩子做律師好了。」

石志威律師來看過嗇色。

他約她晚飯。

吃到一半，嗇色忽然問：「教授結婚沒有？」

「沒有，」石志威搖頭，「眞難得是不是。」

「有無女友呢？」

250

「這就不知道了，」笑，「你何不自己問他。」

嗇色也微笑，「見到他時再說吧。」

「他下月將到華府來領一個學術獎。」

「那多好。」

「你會探訪他嗎？」

「不知上司是否會派我去。」

「真替你高興，嗇色，沒有什麼事比看着年輕人步步高陞更加愉快。」

「別給我壓力。」

老朋友一起笑了。

晚飯結束時一位年輕人朝他們走過來，石志威一怔，怎麼那麼像年輕人笑容滿面，一見嗇色，立刻吻她的臉，接着向石律師自我介紹。

石志威見二人如此親暱，而甄嗇色的確已是成人，也只得接受事實。

只是——

嗇色似知道他在想什麼，輕輕回答：「外國人有外國人的好處。」

石志威笑，「可准我將此事告訴利教授？」

嗇色想一想，「隨便你。」

當下年輕人接走了甄嗇色。

在門口，石律師說：「你自己當心，他家是天主教徒，離婚極之麻煩。」

嗇色微笑點頭，與石志威握手話別。

麥考利看着他背影，「他很關心你。」

「是。」

「誰是利教授？」

「我繼母的丈夫。」

「你繼父？」

「不應那樣說，如果我生母嫁他，那麼，他才稱繼父。」

麥考利又問：「利是一個重要的人物嗎？」

「他是一個好朋友。」

「不可嫁天主教徒嗳？」他都聽懂了。

「沒有人想結婚。」

「本來由女方說這話應當叫男方放心，為什麼我聽了卻一點也不覺開心？」

「誰知道你。」

「你們到今日仍不贊成異族通婚。」

「彼此彼此，令尊令堂不見得為此雀躍。」

「人類始終無法大同。」

「我也希望我子女嫁同文同種華人。」

「什麼，你的子女不即是我的子女嗎？」

嗇色看他一眼。

「我對我倆關係充滿信心。」

嗇色不由得訕笑。

她替他整理領帶，他握住她的手。

麥考利深深歎口氣。

凌晨，電話鈴響，嗇色立刻抓起話筒，兼職電視台的她對任何深夜電話都需注意。

253

對方卻是麥考利。

「我在想，假使我倆有孩子的話，會否美貌？」

「不會。」

「喂！」

「你看所有混血兒都是黃髮黃膚黃眼，十分尷尬。」

「父母說，若我堅持娶華裔女子，他們祝福我。」

「他們會來觀禮？」

「他們說會。」

「那多好，」嗇色揶揄他，「恭喜你。」

麥考利知道說錯了話。

「我想多爭取三數小時睡眠，再見。」

翌日，她跟上司飛到夏威夷做一項民意測驗，忙得走油。

麥考利的電話追上來，她真誠地茫然抬頭問秘書：「誰？」

秘書立刻明白，同對方說：「甄小姐開會，不便聽電話。」

254

晚上，她穿一襲吊帶禮服出席晚會，眾男士的眼珠爲那艷光所吸引幾乎沒掉出來，可是知道即使是讚美，亦得小心謹慎，因爲不知在什麼情況下即構成性騷擾。

那樣簡單的一件深藍色裙子，加一副水晶耳墜，就可以形成如此效果，眞正不可思議。

那一晚，每一位男士都前來邀舞，每人跳幾步，就有另外一人前來拍肩膀搶舞。

嗇色老闆訝異，「這是怎麼一回事？」

嗇色笑，「政治生涯沉悶。」

就在這個時候，有人搭住參議員肩膀，他聳聳肩退下。

嗇色抬起頭，意外地說：「是你麥考利。」

可不就是他。

他諷刺她：「你在這裏伴舞還是怎地。」

她笑答：「每件事都有兩面看法，那邊座位上不知有幾多壁花，想伴舞都無人理睬。」

「呵，有得跳還算慶幸？」

255

「自然，愛過總比一生沒愛過好。」

「你這樣想得開眞值得慶幸。」

「我計較的，一向不是這些。」

「爲什麼不聽我的電話？」

「你打過來嗎？」是眞的意外。

麥考利氣漸消，他把她拉到一角。

「一日不見，如隔三秋。」

嗇色溫柔的看着他。

就在這個時候，兩名保安人員找到他們。

「甄小姐，參議員找你。」

嗇色立刻跟着他們離去。

麥考利蹬足揮手，無可奈何。

那夜要到凌晨，他倆才有單獨相處的機會。

坐在車子裏，自名山鑽石頭往下看海灣景色。

滿目如銀盤，銀白光芒灑滿大地，美如仙景。

麥考利說：「嗇色，我想我們也該論婚嫁了。」

沒有回答。

麥考利輕輕說下去：「不過，婚後你似乎得放棄若干工作量。」

沒有回應。

「我知道你會抗拒，此事可從詳計議──」他一轉過頭，呆住了。

甄嗇色坐在鄰座，一動不動，頭側在一邊，呼吸均勻，天呀，她睡着了。

她倦得連嘴巴都合不攏，微微張開，一如嬰兒，臉容皎潔秀麗，可是不省人事。

麥考利啼笑皆非。

他已知來得不是時候，而時機正是緣份。

他把嗇色送返酒店。

「到了。」他推醒她。

「呵，什麼時候了？」

「你去睡吧，明天還需工作。」

「是，是，那永遠做不完一天二十小時的工作。」

之後，回到華府，他們就疏遠了。

麥考利有段時間十分頹喪。

他父母內疚地問：「不是因為我們吧？」

麥考利相當清醒，「開頭我也以為是，可是事實不。」

「倒底為什麼？」

「後來又以為是工作，可是經過觀察，工作與我一樣只是她的逃避。」

「另外有人？」

「她有心事，但我又沒發現另外有什麼人。」

「算了。」

麥考利知道父母反而放下心頭大石。

可是他時常會想起她。

一日在她辦事處門外靜候，她沒看見他，與同事出去附近買三文治。

不知怎地，嗇色那日居然穿一件紅色大衣，那紅一萬丈以外都看得清楚，映得她如

258

一朵紅雲似，令人覺得只有這樣的人才配穿紅。

麥考利正傷心地凝視，忽然發覺身邊有個人，也在看着同一方向。

那人高大豪邁，穿着長大衣的身型不知有多瀟灑，他也正向嗇色遙望。

只見他似笑非笑，神情專注，無比憐惜地的目光落在嗇色身上。

麥考利怳然吃驚，這是誰？

嗇色在那邊馬路像是覺得有人看她，驀然回首，麥考利挺身而出，以為嗇色發現了他。

嗇色不顧往來車輛疾步奔過馬路來。

麥考利滿面笑容迎上去。

可是不，慢着。

她看到的並不是他。

她與他不過距離數步之遙，可是她卻奔向另一人懷中。

剛才那個穿長大衣的男人緊緊擁抱她。

麥考利要到這個時候，才忽然明白，是什麼令到甄嗇色心不在焉，寄情工作，並且

259

覺得身邊的人可有可無。

剎那間他覺得無比傷害，像是胸口中了一拳，跟蹌的往後退了兩步。

更叫他難堪的是嗇色仍然沒發現他，她已隨那人走遠。

麥考利呆呆站在一棵大樹旁，傷透了心。

日後，他並沒有向嗇色提起這件事，可是，他也沒有忘記這件事，也許，要待孫兒問他什麼叫得不到的愛的時候，他才會悵惘地說起該剎那的感受。

伊人已經遠去。

嗇色說：「你從來都不預告你將在何時出現。」

利佳上笑，「生活沉悶，有點意外之喜也是好事。」

嗇色把雙手插在口袋裏，笑嘻嘻看着他，「什麼風把你吹來。」

「我來領一個獎。」

嗇色頷首，「連你也不能免俗，填表申請參加角逐。」

「為什麼我是知道你會取笑我。」

「如果這世上有什麼人瞭解我，那人就是你了。」

260

「你那未婚夫呢？」

嗇色愕然，「我何來對象？」

「聽說是一金髮藍眼的小夥子。」

「呵，那只是普通朋友。」

利佳上大吃一驚，「這是什麼外交口吻？」

嗇色說：「他家不喜歡黃人，查實他們也不過是蘇格蘭移民，上世紀末馬鈴薯連續十年失收，飢寒交逼，不得不冒險來到新大陸。」

利佳上說：「你不難改變他們觀點。」

「世上要克服的事太多，我無暇去理這一家人。」

他倆找到一間小小餐館坐下。

嗇色看着他，「你還是老樣子。」

「近況如何？」

「不見得。」

「老了許多。」

「參議員已保薦我入籍。」

「那多好，旅遊有正式護照方便得多。」

嗇色微笑，「千萬不要到敵國去，否則持花旗國護照者統統要站出來。」

利佳上微笑，「我想念你。」

「我也是。」

「還記得我們三個人在一起的好時光？」

「你指綺羅在生的時候。」

「是。」

「沒有人會比我們更加相愛。」

頒獎會在華道夫酒店舉行，場面隆重嚴肅。

甄嗇色是觀禮嘉賓之一。

利佳上穿着燕尾服上台領獎，掌聲雷動，嗇色十分替他高興。

利教授致謝辭之際只有三句話，嗇色如釋重負，她最怕領獎人謝祖宗謝爹娘謝三任前妻及子女。

262

慶祝會隨即舉行，嗇色跟着一眾走進宴會廳。

她與利佳上失散。

在走廊中她留意到有一位女士的手袋打開，可以看到錢包。

她好心過去提點：「當心東西掉出來。」

那位女士笑了，「謝謝你。」

嗇色見她是華裔，且端莊可親，便加多一句：「今晚衣香鬢影。」

「可不是，」女士笑說：「我似鄉下人進城。」

一般鄉下人通常不會如此自謙，甄嗇色對她另眼相看。

嗇色剛想自我介紹，已經來到宴會廳門口，每個客人都要經過保安檢查，看身邊有無藏着武器。

經過金屬探測門，已經不見那位女士。

她看到利佳上被一班朋友圍住，知道需在一邊等候，她有點不耐煩，便轉頭向另一角落走去。

是故意的吧。

263

永遠有更要緊的事在同時進行中，他不想與她正面接觸。

正在這個時候，嗇色聽見利教授叫她：「原來你在這裏。」

她欣喜地轉過頭來。

嗇色有點尷尬。

利佳上笑說：「我一早知道你沒有這個耐心。」

嗇色要到這個時候，才發覺他身後跟着一個人。

那個人正是剛才自稱鄉下人的那位女士。

嗇色不動聲色，維持笑容。

只聽得利教授說：「我妻子陳慶璋。」

嗇色若無其事那樣伸出手來相握，「剛才已經見過了。」

陳女士笑說：「原來就是嗇色。」

嗇色問：「什麼時候結的婚？」

「一個星期之前，你是第一個知道。」

264

嗇色說：「真替你們高興。」

陳女士笑，「謝謝祝賀。」

這時有人過來與利佳上說話，他忙着應付，嗇色乘機溜開。

她鎮定地離開宴會廳，走進走廊，忽然覺得胸口悶納，五臟翻騰，靠着牆壁，便嘔吐起來。

她用手帕搗着嘴，滿以為會吐血，可是沒有，空着肚子的她只吐了黃水。

有人問：「你沒事吧？」

熱誠地把她扶到一張椅子上坐下。

然後斟來一杯暖水給她。

嗇色喘息片刻，抬起頭來，「空氣好不混濁。」

「誰說不是。」

那是一個華裔年輕男子，有一雙慧黠的眼睛。

嗇色微笑，「未請教尊姓大名。」

「林世立，你呢？」

「甄嗇色。」

「多麼奇怪的名字。」

「是，很多人都那麼說。」

「你好些沒有，我送你回家休息可好。」

「你是我救星。」

她輕輕歎息。

到了門口，那年輕人忽然醒覺，「當然，我真笨，你便是電視上那位新聞報幕員甄嗇色。」

嗇色疲乏地說：「還不是國家電視，不過是地區性新聞節目。」

他看她走進屋內才走。

嗇色的面孔向床仆下去，她那樣躺着直到天亮。

當然，太陽一旦昇起來又是另外一天另外一個故事。

嗇色聽到鬧鐘摸黑起床更衣沐浴。

倒底年輕，自頂至踵淋一次熱水她也就勉強清醒過來，理想睡眠時間是九個小時，可是她一直只能睡四五個鐘頭。

她將昨夜穿過的晚服丟進垃圾筒。

火速趕到電視台，取到新聞稿，讀幾遍、喝咖啡、化粧、梳頭，坐到鏡頭面前，擠出笑臉，以清晰動人聲線讀出頭條。

一切工作完成後，天尚未亮透。

她不怕熬夜，也不懂得累，她的心已經掏空。

她與她到飯堂喝咖啡。

嗇色走到接待處一看，卻是陳慶璋女士。

「甄，你有訪客。」

嗇色賠笑，「我被朋友接走。」

「教授說昨晚怎麼一轉眼不見了你。」

「教授說，自幼看你長大，像自己女兒一樣。」

嗇色只是微笑。

「切莫疏遠，我們的家即是你的家。」

「我明白。」

「如果你不介意，你可以認我做阿姨。」

嗇色連忙站起欠一欠身，「不敢當。」

「可是高攀了？」

「求之不得呢。」

「那我就放心了。」

嗇色說：「稍後我把結婚賀禮送到華道夫去。」

「中午我們就走了。」

「中午之前一定送到。」

「何必這樣客氣。」

「禮數不可少。」

「教授說你已有好幾年沒回家。」

「可不是，兩年來還是第一次見他。」

「他說，那是你避讒言的緣故。」

嗇色直認不諱，「是，我們有一位行家，因有人說他愛講是非，他亦不分辯，只是與所有人斷絕往來，避不見面。」

「那好似損失太大了，變得似懲罰自己。」

「交友不慎，活該受罰。」嗇色淡然而笑。

陳女士說：「這次回家，我們會計劃生育。」

「是應該這樣，」嗇色的聲音十分溫柔，「孩子越多越好，約四五個最理想。」

「你也有這種主張，請來探訪弟妹。」她十分喜悅。

陳女士終於在十五分鐘後離去。

嗇色到附近珠寶店去挑選禮物，心不在焉地買了一對金錶，囑人十萬火急送去。

完了禮數大功告成。

她忽然想到許多年前，綺羅告訴她，欲再結婚的消息。

她是多麼害怕，怕那男人進來之後，會把弱小的她趕出門去。

現在的感覺也是一樣，她已經被趕走，陳女士特來告訴她這一點。

既然利佳上已把陳綺羅忘記，那麼，甄嗇色也應該把過去收到腦後。

她怔怔坐着，新聞室是何等擾攘煩忙，她一個字一個人也聽不見看不到，沉緬在私人天地。

直到有人叫她：「甄，出發了，西北區有命案」，她才如大夢初醒，跟着大隊跑到街上。

她是一名弱女，總想抓住一些什麼，開頭是生父，接着是繼母，兩個人都不在了，只得把精神寄托在利教授身上。

過了廿一歲，真正一切都得靠自己。

汽車電話響起來，正是利佳上的聲音，「終於找到你。」

「要找總會找得到。」

「謝謝你的禮物。」

「不客氣。」

「有空來看我們。」

「一定。」

「我們並無請客。」

270

「這是你一貫作風。」

「嗇色——」他像是還有話要說。

嗇色把話筒接近耳朵，直至發痛，她淚盈於睫，感慨萬千。

「現場很緊張，是宗什麼新聞？」

「情殺案，男方刺殺前度女友，正與警方對峙。」

「我們保持聯絡。」

「是，一定。」

嗇色聽見攝影組同事大叫：「兇手向警方開鎗！」

利佳上嘆一聲掛上電話。

甄嗇色留在現場五個鐘頭，警方才成功破門而入，將兇手揪出。

嗇色搶過去把麥克風遞到那漢子嘴邊：「先生，你為何行兇？」

那男子嗚咽地說：「我愛她，我不能放她走。」

警察撥開記者的攝影機。

嗇色回到新聞車上，坐下，筋疲力盡。

271

她捧着頭，撥一撥短髮，「天，他愛她。」

有人搭腔，「眞諷刺是不是。」

「給我咖啡。」

那人自暖壺斟出一大杯香噴噴黑咖啡，嗇色骨碌骨碌當瓊漿玉液那樣吞下。

她用手背抹一抹嘴。

抬起頭，呆住。

給她咖啡的人並非同事，乃是昨晚送她回家的林世立。

又救了她一次。

「你如何找到我？」

「我在螢幕看到現場直播，故此趕來探班。」

她笑了。

「一起吃晚飯？」

晚飯？嗇色抬起頭，只見滿天晚霞。

嗇色呼出一口氣，「我哪裏還有力氣。」

272

「先回家休息一下。」

她說：「我還得回公司去打點六點鐘新聞，改天吧。」

林世立說：「我可以等。」

開頭好像都那樣說。

甄嗇色笑了。

她關上新聞車車門。

不久她在車子裏憩着。

做夢，看到自己手小小腿小小，還是個孩子，正在拍一隻彩色斑爛的大皮球，皮球滾出去，她一直追，追到一個大人腳下。

那是綺羅，她俯下身來，拾起皮球，輕輕說：「嗇色，你沒抓緊利佳上。」

小小的嗇色心平氣和：「他永遠屬於我，來日方長。」

亦舒系列 ⊙ 亦舒系列 ⊙ 亦舒系列

*即將出版

亦舒系列 ⊙ 亦舒系列 ⊙ 亦舒系列